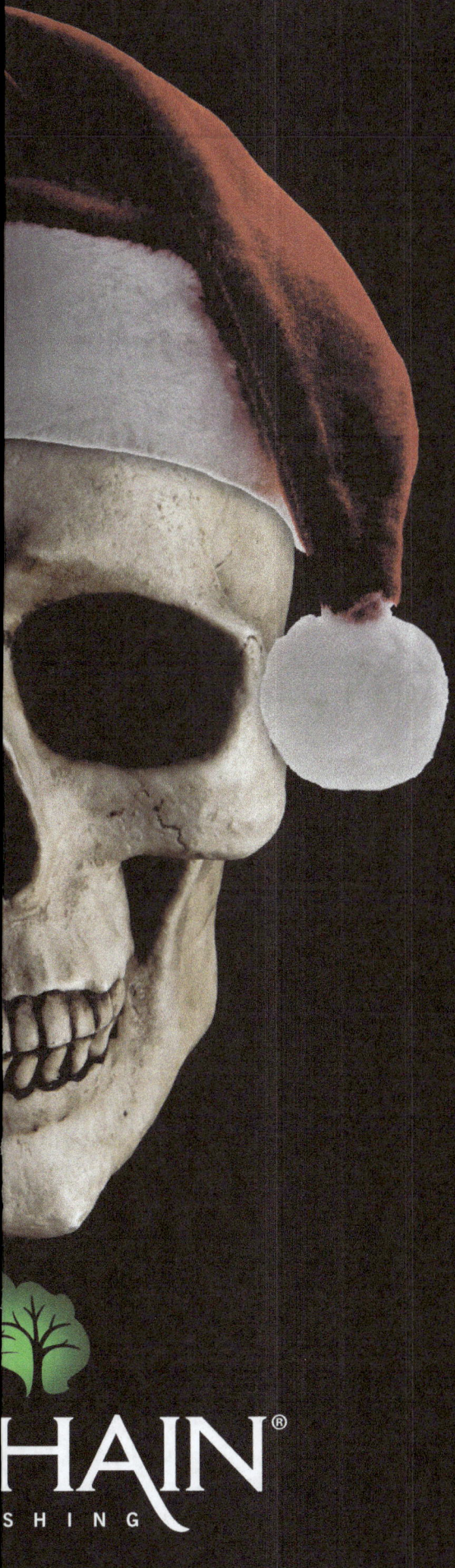
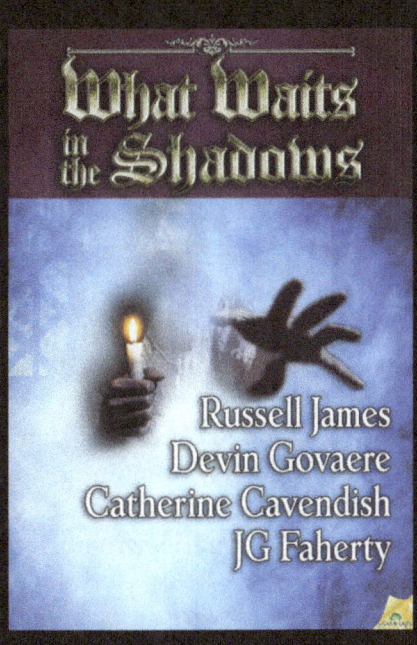
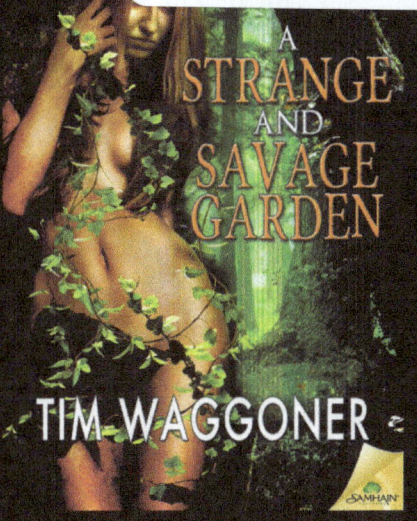

Updates

from the Fantastique...

Greetings and welcome to this very special issue of *Dark Discoveries*, where our theme is Secret Societies. We've decided to try something completely different this time around, but that doesn't mean we've strayed from our dark fiction roots. Anyone who knows me knows I have a deep interest in spiritual, meta-physical, and esoteric subjects—also a fascination with secret societies and ancient wisdom—so I had this idea to put it all together for an issue of *Dark Discoveries*. And that's what I did!

The response was terrific, not only from authors in the dark fiction world—such as John Shirley, Laird Barron, Glen Hirshberg, and Simon Strantzas—but also from the, perhaps, more esoterically/spiritually inclined authors, like Mark Booth and Donald Tyson. This talented group of individuals lent me their creative energies and support and provided *Dark Discoveries* with some brand new material based on the theme of Secret Societies. And believe me, the stories they came up with are *fantastic*! Some very unique and interesting writing awaits you in these pages.

Legendary British author Simon R. Green also chimes in with his original story, introduced by Jonathan Maberry, from an upcoming anthology being released by JournalStone Publishing. We have articles on conspiracy theories and *The Illuminatus! Trilogy*, plus an interview with some folks trying to res-urrect the *Millennium* TV series of the 1990s. Additionally, we have our usu-al columns, plus a new one, (which will recur) from beloved horror writer Gary A. Braunbeck. Another new feature is our "Horror in a Hundred Stories," three short-shorts of horror fiction chosen out of a hundred submissions and selected from our Hellnotes community. And finally, a feature on our beautiful cover model, Noelle Leon. (Thank you, Leah!)

Read on for Mark Booth's esoteric introduction to this *Dark Discoveries* special issue, for he can do a far better job introducing the theme than I can. Also check out his beautiful and insightful treatment of the Arthurian Myster-ies later on in this issue. For those not familiar with Mark's work, I highly rec-ommend checking out his books. He is the author behind the New York Times bestseller *The Secret History of the World* and its recently released sequel, *The Sacred History of the World*. These titles are both illuminating and captivating.

Now, my unsuspecting young neophytes, turn the pages and prepare to receive your initiation...

—Aaron J. French
Editor-in-Chief

DARK DISCOVERIES

Fall 2014, Issue Number 29, www.DarkDiscoveries.com

Founding Publisher & Editor
James R. Beach

Publisher
JournalStone Publishing, LLC

Editor-in-Chief
Aaron J. French

Contributing Editor
K. H. Vaughan

Assistant Editors
Nancy Kalanta (Reviews Editor)
Russ Thompson (Senior Submissions Editor)
Stuart Conover (Assistant Reviews Editor)

**Art Director,
Layout, and Design**
Cyrus Wraith Walker

Contributors

Mark Booth
K. H. Vaughan
Terrie Leigh Relf
William Morgan
Gary A. Braunbeck
Robert Morrish
Joel B. Kirkpatrick
Yvonne Navarro
Richard Dansky
Michael R. Collings
Aaron J. French
Joe McKinney and Patrick Freivald

Lori R. Lopez
Leah Jung
D. Harlan Wilson
Laird Barron
Glen Hirshberg
Donald Tyson
John Shirley
Simon R. Green
Simon Strantzas
James R. Beach
John Palisano

Special Thanks
Glen Hirshberg
Donald Tyson
Adam Chamberlain
Noelle Leon (Cover Model)
Mark Booth

**Contributing
Artists/Photographers**

Bradley Thornber (Cover Photographer)
Cyrus Wraith Walker (Cover and Some interior
Robert Papp (Hollow your Heart Artwork)

DARK DISCOVERIES
(ISSN 1548-6842) is published (Qtrly) by
JournalStone Publications
439 Gateway Dr. #83, Pacifica, CA 94044

Christopher C. Payne
JournalStone Publications
439 Gateway Dr. #83, Pacifica, CA 94044
U.S.A.
christophercpayne@journalstone.com.

Please make check or money order payable to:
JournalStone Publishing and send to the address above.
Credit/Debit cards via Paypal at:
christophercpayne@journalstone.com. Advertising
rates available. Discounts for bulk and standing retail
orders.

Fiction

The Eclipsed by Donald Tyson — 12
(Little Miss) Queen of Darkness by Laird Barron — 30
Hexenhaus: A Normal and Nadine Adventure by Glen Hirshberg — 49
The Initiation of Larry Schor by John Shirley — 76
Youth's Folly by Simon Strantzas — 101
Hollow is the Heart by Simon R. Green — 122

Features

H.P. Lovecraft, the Occult, and Literature: An Interview with Donald Tyson
by Aaron J. French — 08
Through the Darkest Lens: Conspiracy Theory in Fiction and Culture
by K. H. Vaughan — 26
Interview with Noelle Leon by Leah Jung — 38
A Teller of Storied Tales: Interviewing Glen Hirshberg by Joel B. Kirkpatrick — 42
An Unreading: Notes on a Narrative of Failure by D. Harlan Wilson — 61
The Secret History of King Arthur by Mark Booth — 68
Comic Series "Jade Sky" by Joe McKinney and Patrick Freivald — 84
Horror in a Hundred Stories: Terrie Leigh Relf, William Morgan,
and Lori R. Lopez — 111
Back to Frank Black: An Interview with Adam Chamberlain
& Brian A. Dixon by K. H. Vaughan — 115

Columns

Not-So-Secret Societies by Yvonne Navarro — 22
This Is Where I Came In... by Gary A. Braunbeck — 66
Secret Societies...and Horror by Michael R. Collings — 109
RPG Conspiracies: An Interview with Kenneth Hite by Richard Dansky — 112
What the Hell Ever Happened to ... An Interview with Gary Raisor
by Robert Morrish — 136

Hellnotes Reviews

Book Reviews — 139

HE SEES YOU

WHEN YOU'RE SLEEPING

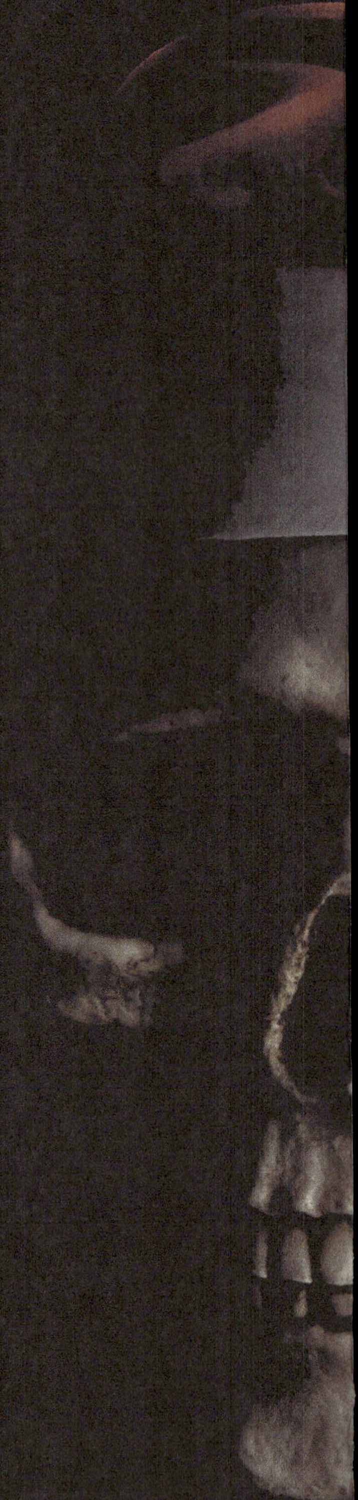

SAM

PUBL

Esoteric Introduction

By Mark Booth

Sometimes we think life is hell—and mean it. Sometimes visionaries have seen Hell erupt up and onto the surface of the earth. Others have suggested that Hell has never existed anywhere else and that life on earth *is* actually Hell.

Could it be that life on earth and Hell are somehow integrated, impelled by the same forces? Dante thought so. In the *Commedia* he writes about a demon who even while active in Hell walks the earth, inhabiting the body of an evil-minded monk.

Dante is an esoteric writer. As I explain in *The Secret History of Dante*, he was at pains to emphasize that his journey underground was a real journey, that, for example, he slipped and stumbled over real rocks and suffered real bodily discomforts. His mentor was an occultist called Brunetto Lattini. He was an initiate of a lay order of the Knights Templar and there is evidence to indicate that he in turn initiated Dante. This was the real journey Dante was describing.

The initiation ceremonies of mystical secret societies in Europe in the Middle Ages and Renaissance derived from the ceremonies of the Mystery schools that had been attached to the great temples of the ancient world, at Giza and Eleusis and elsewhere. Mystical secret societies arose at the time that the Mystery schools of the ancient world were closed down.

The initiation ceremonies of both the Mystery centres and these secret societies involved a real journey underground. After a long period of preparation involving perhaps sensory deprivation, an intensive course of teaching, fasting and perhaps drugs, candidates for initiation would be led by mysterious masked figures down underground, along passageways and into cavernous chambers, perhaps pitched through trap doors, and made to witness bloody sacrifices and sacred drama. They would believe themselves to be menaced by demons

and then led upwards again and be ushered finally into a luminous chamber. In an altered state of consciousness, they would there meet the gods face to face. A modern séance is probably a very pale echo of what they experienced.

These new initiates now believed that they had died and been reborn, understanding that they were experiencing a foretaste of what we will all experience after death. This is why the poet Pindar and other luminaries of the ancient world wrote that initiation into the Mysteries gave complete assurance of life after death, and it was these experiences, rather than abstract knowledge that sacred societies of the Middle Ages, Renaissance and beyond all cultivated. As I wrote in *The Sacred History*, men have always travelled underground in search of higher states of consciousness.

An initiation centre from Roman times has been discovered and excavated near Baia in Sicily and re-excavated recently by my friend Robert Temple. A similar system was discovered under fields on the outskirts of Margate in Kent in the 1830s and may still be visited today. I imagine a similar system of underground passages and chambers under the streets of Florence, either waiting to be found or known only to a few, and that this is where Brunetto Lattini took Dante for the experiences that would form the subject of his poem.

Part of the knowledge acquired in higher states of consciousness is therefore a direct experience of life after death. This includes encounters with the gods of the planets and the constellations that the human spirit, once free of the material body, will fly up to encounter. The initiate learns that both life and life-after-death are ruled by the same spiritual forces, that is to say by the movements of the same stars and constellations—and that they are therefore structured according to the same patterns. In the *Commedia* Dante finally reaches the heavens after he has journeyed through the Underworld, and in the heavens he communicates freely with the great spirits of the stars and planets.

There is a class of literature which we can usefully call *initiatic* because it is saturated by this kind of "higher consciousness" and the knowledge that derives from it. Part of the aim of this sort of literature is to prepare people for their own initiation, so that they are ready for a momentous approach by an initiate—as Dante was approached by the older Brunetto Lattini. Accounts of being approached by mysterious strangers offering initiation have been reported by other famous occultists, including Johannes, Trithemius, John Tauler, Jacob Boehme, and Rudolf Steiner.

The Angels' Story

Civilization after civilization arose, glittered then passed away almost as if they had never been. But after each passing away some small remnants survived. The traces left by one civilization would help the next one to grow. Some civilizations became even more magnificent and highly developed than the cloud-capped towers and gorgeous palaces that had gone before.

One day, when one of these civilizations was perhaps just passing its peak, a small gang of children were playing in the park in a small town called Southwich in the middle of the world.

Christchurch Park is quite ordinary, a place of gently rolling hillocks and a few trees clustered here and there, a safe place for children to play, and it was Michael who first noticed the mist.

He might well not have noticed it on that evening, late in the year, when mists tend to gather as the day draws on, but there was *something* that caught his eye and drew his attention and made him go over and look more closely. What *was* so curious about it? Then he saw…

The patch of mist occupied an exact space, a small area about ten feet high and ten feet wide, a cloudlet hovering low over the ground, denser in the middle. This mist was just dense enough for it to be hard to see clearly something or someone on the other side of it. Michael and the other children danced in and out of it, waving their arms.

As early as they could they hurried back the next morning and were glad to find it still there. But now the mist seemed a little denser, so that if you ran through it, you left a little tunnel that only gradually dissolved. They enjoyed running through it as fast as possible to make patterns.

By the end of the day they found it was dense enough to mould shapes out of it, and they made a sort of *mistman* that lasted perhaps four or five minutes before dispersing.

On the third day the park warden noticed the children had congregated again in the same spot and went to investigate. As a result, news of this patch of mist with its unusual properties spread and—to cut a long story short—the whole world became fascinated by it. Everyone wanted to see it. Excited crowds filled the park.

In fact so many outsiders poured in that the whole of Southwich became packed all the way out to the ring road. Soon the government had to take control, cordoning off the park. A team of top scientists assembled. They found that the mist continued to get denser. They also found that because of its extreme and subtle plasticity, it could be moulded down to exceptionally fine, even sub-atomic detail. Indeed a human shape moulded out of it could be given the properties of robots.

Research and development raced ahead until it turned out that these robots could be developed to such a sophisticated level that they were able to learn about their environment, store this knowledge and bring it to bear in new situations. A little while later it seemed these robots were on the brink of achieving a primitive sort of intelligence.

Now you may be wondering, "Where are the angels in all of this? We're nearing the end of this story with less than a page to go—is this narrator by any chance unreliable?"

Well the fact is that in this story *everyone* is an angel—Michael, the other children, the warden, the crowds, the government, the scientists.

The patch of mist is the material universe and the misty robots are ourselves.

Many of the stories in this issue of *Dark Discoveries* will be like this. Sometimes we hear a story being dismissed as being "only a fairy story." This is said to suggest that it purports to be an account of events in the real world while being flagrantly untrue. An account only a child or an idiot would believe.

The trouble is that this represents a fundamental misunderstanding of such stories. They were never meant as accounts of events in this world. They are accounts of things that happened in another dimension. Fairy stories are not untrue stories about events in this world but true stories about events in the spiritual world, the dimension of spirits and angels. Similarly many myths—I'm thinking in the first instance of creation myths—are not untrue accounts of the creation of the material world but true accounts of things that happened before the material world as we know it came into existence.

Some of the stories to follow within these pages will be like this. They are stories about what happened in another dimension, the world with Southwich at its centre, the world where Michael lives. And some of the stories are about what happens when beings from this other dimension move through into our own dimension and encounter us.

✤ ✤ ✤

H.P. Lovecraft, the Occult, and Literature: An Interview with Donald Tyson

By Aaron J. French

Aaron J. French: Thank you taking the time to sit down with DD and answer some questions. How did you get your start in writing, and what sort of books were you interested in as a kid?

Donald Tyson: The first adult book I read all the way through was *Jane Eyre* by Charlotte Brontë, which I read when I was seven or eight. It was the big hardcover Random House edition with the woodcuts that some people may be familiar with. I was fascinated by the illustrations and decided to read the book. I tried *Wuthering Heights* right after I finished *Jane Eyre*, but Emily Brontë's novel was a little beyond my ability at that age.

At nine I discovered adult science fiction novels and started reading two of them a week—as many as I could afford to buy with my allowance of one dollar. The paperbacks were fifty cents each and there was no tax on them back in the early 1960s. Some were a little cheaper—forty-five cents. Those were the Ace paperbacks. The thick Bantams and Ballentines and Lancers and the rest were sixty cents, and the really thick novels were seventy-five cents, but I had to like these a lot to buy them because it meant I was limited to only one science fiction novel that week.

The first SF novel I bought was Robert Heinlein's *Puppet Masters*. I was mesmerized by it. Reading that novel was the single greatest experience of my life up to age nine. Over the next twelve years or so I read all the science fiction and horror anthologies I could afford to buy. The Dell line of suspense-horror anthologies that were supposedly selected by Alfred Hitchcock were particularly good. They had a lot of horror stories. I doubt Hitchcock ever even saw the paperbacks, let alone picked the stories, but whoever chose the stories did a good job.

I always knew I could write. It was just one of those things I never had the slightest doubt about. But for some reason the concept of writing professionally, as a way of earning a living, didn't occur to me until university. I won a couple of short story competitions in my undergraduate university, and another contest put on by the local Writers' Federation, and decided maybe I should spend my life doing what I liked doing, and what I was good at—instead of working at some job I hated, just for the money.

AJF: Tell us about your interest in the occult and your nonfiction books on ritual magic.

DT: It's said that the outlook and attitude of a human being can change radically over the course of his life, and it was certainly true in my case. Before I decided to become a writer, I was mainly concerned with astronomy. I wanted to be a professional astronomer for many years, or maybe become an architect or an industrial designer. I was an atheist and a materialist, just like H. P. Lovecraft. I had no interest in the occult other than for its entertainment value, and whenever anyone else said anything serious about the paranormal or the mystical, I mocked them. My mind was about as tightly closed against esotericism and spirituality in any of their forms as a mind could be.

Then, around my university years, I started to realize that atheism and materialism were dead ends

for me. There was no progression there, no personal growth. I started to get a sense of the sheer scope of reality—not only the inconceivable vastness of space and time, which I understood from my astronomy studies, but the vastness of what potentially lay beyond space and time—of the realms or dimensions of reality we could not even begin to imagine. I saw how foolish it was to dismiss the possibility of the existence of these realms merely because I knew nothing about them. I guess, in a way, I became more humble intellectually. I realized I didn't know everything.

It's a funny thing about the occult, but when you open your mind to its possibilities, it begins to interact with you on various levels. I became gradually aware of a spiritual dimension to reality, and I began to study Western Esotericism. At first I studied it because I found it surprisingly coherent and meaningful. It was a revelation to me that what I had always considered to be crazy nonsense actually made sense. Then I started to study it more seriously and in a practical way, as a personal discipline. My nonfiction books on the occult arose from these studies, which have continued to the present day.

AJF: In your reading of Western Esotericism, did you find the phenomenon of secret societies interesting? Do you have any firsthand experiences you'd like to share?

DT: I should preface my remarks by saying that I am not a joiner by nature. I've always avoided becoming a member of clubs or teams or societies. In part it is my solitary disposition, but it is also out of concern that the teachings and the motives of a school or lodge of Western magic might restrict or hinder the scope of my personal studies and experiments in magic. For example, I would never wish to be told by the leader of an occult society that I could not associate with a particular person, or could not practice a specific type of magic, or could not write about a magical technique.

However, over the years I have been asked to join a number of societies. Two of them that may be familiar to readers by name are the Hermetic Order of the Golden Dawn and the Ordo Templi Orientis. The occultist William Grey also asked me to join his circle shortly before he died. I had to decline because it would have meant traveling to England for an extended period, something I could not afford to do at the time.

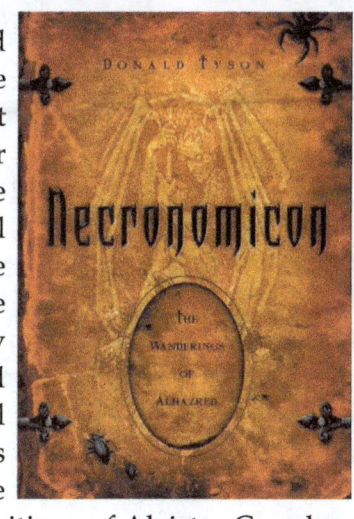

Although I declined membership in these societies, it did not prevent me from studying their teachings in depth. The teachings of the original London temple of the Golden Dawn were made available to students by Aleister Crowley, and some years later by Israel Regardie. The teachings of the O.T.O are available through the published writings of Aleister Crowley, apart from some secret documents which members of the O.T.O. were kind enough to mail me for my private study.

What I can say, from my interaction with members of various occult lodges, as they are sometimes called, is that they are much more mundane than most people probably realize. There's a tendency to believe that, because they are more or less secret, with a restricted membership roll, they must be up to nefarious activities. This is even believed about the Freemasons! For the most part it is not true. The primary purpose of occult fraternities is to help the individual members in their personal occult studies and spiritual evolution. The ultimate goal of most of these schools is what is known in alchemy as the Great Work—the enlightenment of the soul, which is achieved by both the practice of occult techniques, and the study of occult teachings.

AJF: Along the way, your writing career began to encompass H.P. Lovecraft. You also began writing "fictional" accounts of his *Necronomicon*, and even published magical systems based on his work. How'd this come about, and what was it like to take up fiction?

DT: The truth of the matter is, Lovecraft and I are very much alike. We are so much alike, I find it a bit embarrassing even to describe the similarities. Suffice it to say that my general personality is enough like that of Lovecraft to be his reincarnation. We were both fascinated by astronomy while young, and both intended to make professional astronomy our careers. We were both frustrated in this goal by a lack of skill in higher mathematics. We both began to read serious books at an early age, and we both had a taste for the weird and fantastic in literature. We were both self-

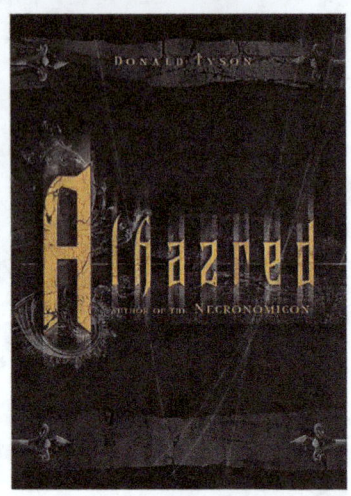

declared atheists and materialists. We were both solitary to a fault in our habits, Lovecraft no more so than I. We both were fascinated by the antique prose of earlier times, Lovecraft for the prose of the 18th century, and me for that of the 19th century. We were both Anglophiles. We both read constantly, and had little interest in team sports or social pursuits. We both became writers of weird fiction. We both have been deplorably lax in the self-promotion of our works and our careers. We both married very late in life and had no children. We both like cats.

I'm happy to say that there are also differences between myself and Lovecraft. He had a series of nervous breakdowns in his youth, whereas my mind is more like Aleister Crowley's, in that I have an iron-bound grasp on reality that I don't think anything could shake (Crowley drove those around him insane but he never actually went mad himself). Lovecraft was the victim of night fears. I have dreams that are similar to those Lovecraft had, but they don't seem to bother me as much as his dreams bothered him. Another difference is my eventual departure from atheism and materialism.

But I wasn't aware of these similarities and differences when I first began to read Lovecraft's stories. I knew nothing about the man himself for decades, only that I found his writings powerful and thought-provoking. It was when I started to write about his Mythos that I researched his personal life and discovered how eerily similar my personality and outlook on life are to Lovecraft's.

My decision to produce a version of the *Necronomicon* was motivated by hubris. I had read two other versions of the *Necronomicon* (the Hay version and the Simon version) and was disappointed by their content. I decided I could do better, and my own *Necronomicon* is the result. Once that was written and published, it seemed natural to write other books on the same theme. My novel *Alhazred* parallels quite closely the material contained in my *Necronomicon*, and indeed, the two books are companion pieces designed to be read together. My *Necronomicon Tarot* is yet another exposition of the material in my *Necronomicon*. The other books in my *Necronomicon* series give practical techniques for using Lovecraft's Mythos as the basis for a system of real magic. I should also briefly mention a collection of occult mystery stories I wrote a few years ago based upon the fictional exploits of the Elizabethan magician, Doctor John Dee, and his friend and crystal scryer, the alchemist Sir Edward Kelley, published by the British publisher Avalonia under the title *The Ravener and Others*.

You ask what it was like to take up fiction. I've always been a fiction writer. I started out while I was in university writing short stories, novels and drama. The reason I moved into nonfiction was pragmatic—I was able to sell nonfiction books and earn a living as a writer, whereas there wasn't much interest at the time for my fictional works. This may have been mainly the result of my deplorable business practices—like Lovecraft, if a story of mine is declined I have a tendency to put it away and not try to get it published thereafter. This is not a good way to earn a living as a freelance fiction writer. So you might say I fell into nonfiction, but it was also the case that I was studying the Western occult tradition intensely at the time. It seemed natural to write about what I was actually doing in my life.

It was for these reasons that my fiction took a back seat for so many years. Recently, I took a look around and realized that I was no longer a young man. I decided that if I was ever going to get any fiction published, as I had always intended to do throughout my career, I'd better damn well write some and make a serious effort to place it with publishing houses.

AJF: How do you approach writing short weird fiction and who are some of the authors and editors you've worked with in this regard?

DT: I approach my weird fiction with pure, unadulterated joy. There is nothing that gives me greater pleasure or satisfaction than writing these stories. I realized when I began to write fiction, after so many years of writing little but nonfiction, that my heart had been silently crying out for this form of artistic expression. The stories literally exploded from me, and they continue to pour out.

It's only over the last few years that I've really found my own way of writing these stories. More than anything else, for me it's a matter of length. I discovered that my natural story length is longer than the length of the average short story. When I began as a writer I tried to write stories to this shorter length that was specified by many editors of story magazines. I was able to do so with some success, but I realize now that I was fighting against my creative process. The natural length of a story for me is from around 8,000 to 12,000 words. My liberation as a story writer came when I finally said to myself, the hell with it, I'm going to write these stories to the length I naturally feel inclined to write them. By writing longer stories and dividing them into chapters, a kind of creative spring was released.

Because I am poor at promoting my own work (yes, as poor as Lovecraft was, sorry to say), most of my stories would never have seen the light of day, and probably would not even have been written, were it not for the kindly encouragement of one man—S. T. Joshi. His interest and his enthusiasm for my stories prompted me to write more of them. In writing these weird stories—stories that I should have been writing all my life—I feel that I have finally found my literary home.

AJF: What would be a three-word sentence that best describes H.P. Lovecraft in your opinion?

DT: A great dreamer.

AJF: Which one of his monstrous creations most resonates with you, and why?

DT: Yog-Sothoth is the key. Yog-Sothoth is the gate. Of all the Great Old Ones, I find the nature of Yog-Sothoth the most compelling. He not only opens the passage to other worlds and other dimensions, he is all gateways and all doorways, all crossings of all thresholds, all transitions of every kind. There is no going in or coming out without Yog-Sothoth. He is the opener of the way between death and life, which is why Lovecraft made a magical incantation to Yog-Sothoth so central

to the necromantic process of raising the dead from their essential salts in the novel *The Case of Charles Dexter Ward*. Lovecraft himself regarded Yog-Sothoth as central to his mythology, which he liked to call his "Yog-Sothothery."

AJF: Do you have any new projects you're working on that you'd like to tell us about?

DT: I'm eagerly awaiting the publication of two new books of fiction. One is from Hippocampus Press and is titled *The Lovecraft Coven.* It is actually a short novel and a novella bound under one cover, so you get two for the price of one. The novel bears the title of the book, and the novella is titled "Iron Chain." *The Lovecraft Coven* is about a group of ceremonial magicians, led by Lovecraft's only surviving descendant, that is determined to bring Lovecraft himself back from the dead. "Iron Chain" concerns an ancient device of magic buried and forgotten on a farm in rural Nova Scotia.

The other book is to be published by Dark Renaissance Press, and contains a collection of ten stories of Abdul Alhazred. The stories take up where the adventures described in my novel *Alhazred* left off. The collection is titled *Tales of Alhazred* and will be lavishly illustrated by the talented artist Frank Walls.

☙❧☙

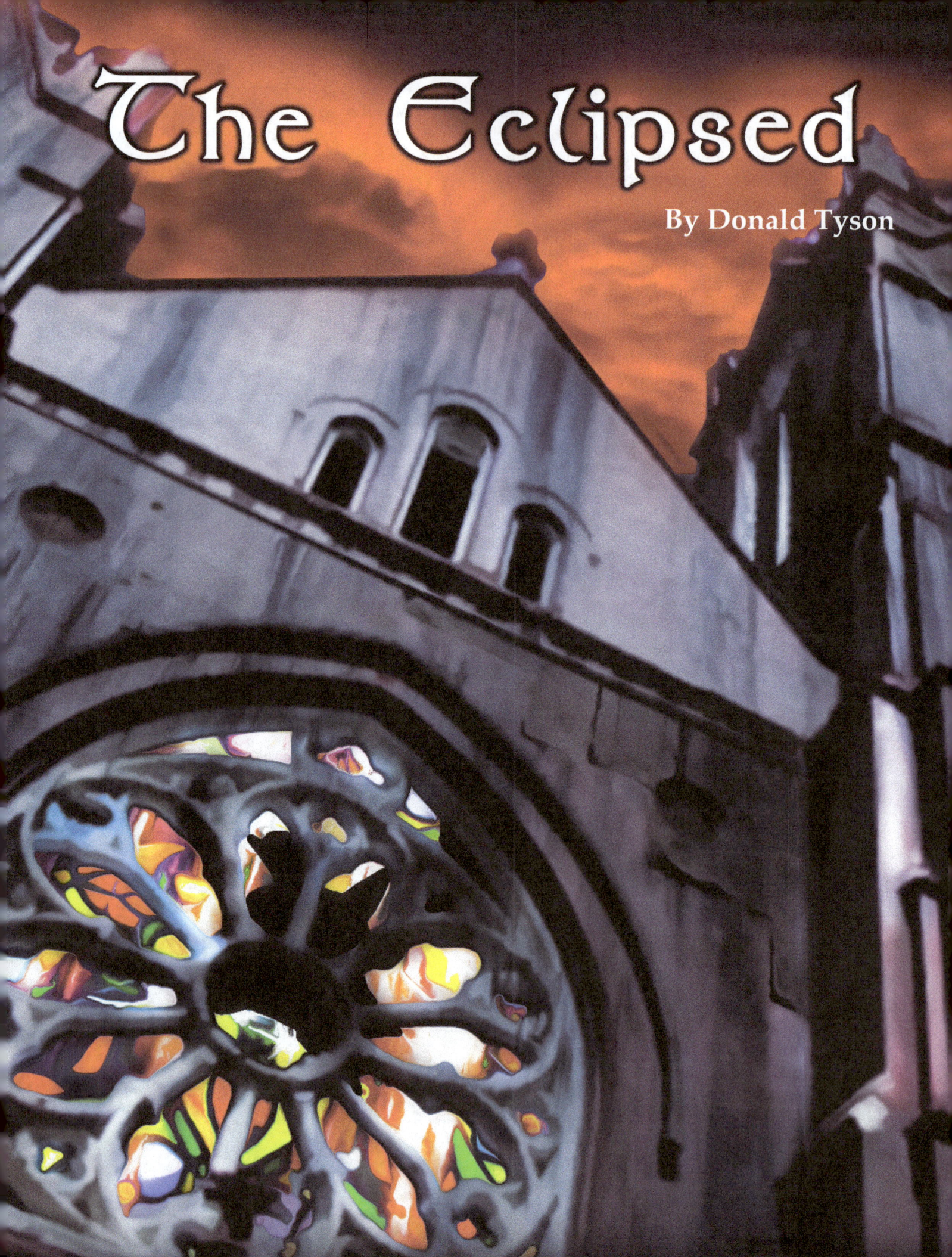

The Eclipsed

By Donald Tyson

(1)

The hammering on the front door repeated itself, this time louder and more insistent. Norman Ecclestone mouthed a four-letter word under his breath, set his half-eaten plate of macaroni-and-cheese down beside his computer monitor, and went to see who was bothering him after ten o'clock on a Tuesday evening.

He switched on the exterior porch light and peered through the peephole. The face on the other side made him step back and grit his teeth in frustration. Not again. What would it be this time? he wondered. Why couldn't she just leave him alone?

"Norman? Open up, I need to talk to you. Norman?"

Shit, shit, fuck, fuck, shit, cunt, fuck. He rested his back against the entrance wall and closed his eyes.

"I'm busy right now, Kat," he said, trying to keep the anger out of his voice. "Why don't you come back tomorrow?"

"This can't wait, Norman. Open this fucking door."

She pounded on the door with her fist. He sighed with mingled defeat and acceptance. He knew her too well to believe she would get tired and give up. He rattled loose the safety chain and turned the deadbolt. She had the door open, pushing him backward, before he could touch the knob.

"What the hell is so vital that you had to come to my apartment in the middle of the night?"

"This is important," she said.

He followed her into the living room. She sat in her usual chair with her black leather coat still on, arms hugging her chest, shivering in spite of the warm night.

"Jesus, Kat, we broke up three months ago. You can't keep coming over here looking for favours."

"I need your help." He realized there was panic in her eyes. It was the first time he had ever seen her afraid.

He didn't know whether to be flattered that she would turn to him for help in her hour of need, or annoyed that she thought she could still use and manipulate him for her own purposes.

Sitting in the other chair, a threadbare La-Z-Boy he had picked up at a garage sale, he studied her. She had not changed much since their break-up. Her hair was still long and dyed the same sandy blond with streaks of white. The dark shadows under her grey eyes had not been there before, nor could he remember seeing the little lines of nervous strain in her forehead. Her whole body trembled.

"Let me take your coat," he said in a quieter voice.

She shook her head, staring around the room as if she expected something to jump out at her. Norman began to feel uneasy. Was she having a nervous breakdown?

"Tell me what's wrong this time."

She looked at him with wide eyes.

"Have you ever heard of the Hidden Door?"

He shook his head.

"What is it? Some kind of dance club?"

"Do you remember those books about the occult I was reading when you threw me out?"

"I didn't throw you out. You cheated on me, and then left of your own accord."

"Whatever. A friend of mine got me interested in ritual magic. He was a member of the Hidden Door, so I decided to join."

"This friend, was he that Alan Horowitz you had sex with?"

"All that's over and done with, Norman. I wish you wouldn't obsess about it."

He swallowed the words that rose in his throat and sat back.

"So you joined this cult."

She nodded. "For a while it was great. I learned a lot of things that aren't taught anywhere else, secrets about the root races and the seven rays."

"Sounds like Theosophy."

She ignored his words.

"Then weird shit started to happen, and I mean really weird shit. These people have powers. I always thought magic was only in your mind, you know? That it worked if you believed in it, but it was only in your imagination."

"These people practice ritual magic?"

She unfolded her arms and gripped the chair so tightly with her fingers, her knuckles turned white.

"Magic is real, Norman. I've seen it. They did things you wouldn't believe. They scared the shit out of me."

"Why didn't you just leave?"

"I tried. They won't let me leave. They say once a person joins the church, he's in it for life. People are following me, watching me. You have to help me get away from them. They're all insane. They want to destroy—"

Something tapped against the picture window behind the closed curtains. She jumped as if it had been a gunshot.

"What was that?"

"Nothing. Probably just a bug."

"Are you sure?"

"Kat, we're on the second floor."

She stood and went fearfully to the window and

drew the edge of the curtain aside. Her scream caught him by surprise. He jumped out of his chair and was able to catch her before she collapsed.

"Out there, something's out there," she muttered.

He rested her head gently against the floorboards and went to the edge of the curtain. For an instant he hesitated. Then he jerked it aside. Nothing. Just blackness and the lights of San Francisco spreading down to the bay. No one could look in this window unless he had wings. He returned to Kat who was trying to sit up and supported her slender back in his hand.

"You'll help me, won't you, Norman? I could always depend on you."

"Why don't you ask the guy who got you into the cult to get you out of it?"

"Because he's gone. No one's seen him in weeks. He just vanished."

He was torn between anger and concern. The smart move would be to tell her to get out and never return. He studied her face. There was genuine terror in her eyes.

"I suppose I could look into it for you."

"Oh, thank God." She hugged him and buried her face against his chest. He felt the wetness of her tears. "I knew I could count on you, Norman. You're such a good man."

"I'm an English grad student who eats macaroni dinners, Kat. Don't expect any miracles."

"You're the smartest man I know," she said.

In spite of himself, he hugged her back.

(2)

"This is the place?" he asked doubtfully, staring at the peeling white paint of the dilapidated church. The lower windows were protected by sheets of plywood that bore gang tags in bright colors. Some panes of stained glass in the higher windows had been broken out by rocks. Even in the bright morning sunlight this was not the best part of the city to be walking through.

"This is their church," Kat affirmed, hugging herself more tightly to his side.

"You catch the bus back to the apartment and wait for me. I'll go in and talk to them."

She kissed him on the cheek and hurried from under the frowning upper windows of the church with her shoulders hunched and her head down, as though the windows were watching her.

Last night they had made love, and she had remained in his bed until morning. Thinking back on it, he was still not sure how it happened. It was not planned, at least not by him. He had intended to send her home to her own apartment, but her terror had been so strong, he could not bring himself to force her out into the darkness.

The Internet had little to say about the Hidden Door, as he discovered during the morning while she was in the kitchen, making breakfast. There were a few random and obscure references on chat sites and oddball Web pages, but no hard factual information. Those who mentioned the cult did so either with reverence or dread, and none of them supplied details.

Squaring his shoulders, he climbed the stone steps to the door of the old church. Above the door was a motto written with the little brass adhesive letters used on mailboxes:

Seek, and it shall be hidden from you;
Open, and it shall be opened unto you.

The weathered oak door was not locked. He pulled it, stepped inside, and was hit by the sound of rhythmic chanting and the acrid smoke of smouldering incense. He stood in the back and tried to remain inconspicuous while he took in the scene. About a dozen individuals, none older than thirty, sat in the pews vocalizing some complex litany in a language he did not recognize. It was not Latin or Greek, of that he was sure. They rocked forward and back as they intoned the words.

The altar of the church occupied the center of a complex design marked on the hardwood floor with brightly coloured plastic tape. It was some kind of interlocking star of eight points. A white cloth with a gold fringe draped the altar. Four unlit white candles stood on its corners. Above it hung a large brass key on a wire so thin, the key almost appeared to float on air. Behind the altar, outside the bounds of the coloured star on the floor, were two pillars with a grey curtain hung between them. One pillar was white and the other black.

A man stood in front of the altar with his back to the pews. He wore a grey robe of the kind worn by Catholic monks. When he turned, he saw Ecclestone and smiled. He came quickly toward him down the central aisle with his hand extended in greeting.

"Welcome to our church," he said in a pleasant voice. "My name is William Wright. What brings you here?"

He had that look of glowing good health that only comes to those who watch their diet and exercise daily. He shook Ecclestone's hand with a firm pressure while his keen blue eyes studied the student's face. The man could not have been ten years his senior, but his searching gaze made Ecclestone feel like a teenager called into the office of the school principal.

Ecclestone spoke his name.

"I'm here on behalf of one of your members."

"Really? Which member?"

"Katherine Moore."

"Ah, Katherine, of course," Wright said, as though her name explained everything. "Come with me into my office and we'll talk about it."

He led Ecclestone along a side aisle and into a small room with a desk and several wooden chairs. A filing cabinet occupied one corner of the room and a bookcase stood against the wall.

Ecclestone looked around in surprise. There was nothing occult about the room, and nothing even vaguely sinister. Bright sunlight poured through the slits in the open venetian blind on the window behind the desk.

"I'll get right to the point," he said, drawing a chair up to the desk and sitting in it as Wright took the padded swivel chair under the window. "Katherine doesn't want to belong to your organization any longer. She doesn't want to be bothered by any of your people."

"Of course, I understand completely. You have my word that no one in the church will contact her."

Ecclestone blinked in surprise. It had been easier and lot more pleasant than he had expected.

"You didn't seem surprised when I mentioned Kat's name."

Wright spread his hands, then folded them on the desk.

"Poor Katherine. She's been having some emotional problems. We all hoped she would be able to work through them, and of course we prayed for her. I'm sorry to hear that she wants to leave, but maybe it's for the best. Our training can be taxing on the emotions. It stirs up old memories that usually remain hidden in the mud at the bottom of the subconscious mind."

"What does your training involve?"

"Naturally I can't go into details," Wright said with an apologetic smile. "Our techniques are exclusive to our order and are reserved only for members. But I can tell you that we practice an active, hands-on style of spirituality in which every member participates. Not everyone is suited to our path, however."

"I'd like to learn more about it," Ecclestone found himself saying.

"Really?" Wright's expression brightened. "That's wonderful. Are you thinking of applying for membership?"

"I've been considering a life-change that involves a more active spirituality, but I would need to learn more

about your teachings before seeking to join your order."

"Of course. No one is expected to join us without having some idea of what we are all about."

He got up from his chair, went to the filing cabinet, and pulled open the top drawer. From it he took a pamphlet with a grey cover. He handed it to Ecclestone, who stood to receive it.

"This is our promotional booklet. It goes into the historical background of our order and explains some of our basic beliefs."

"Thank you. I'll certainly read it."

"Would you mind bringing it back when you've finished?" Wright smiled apologetically. "We never got around to printing more of them, and I only have a few of them left."

Ecclestone hesitated, thinking he should just leave the damned thing on the desk. It was an obvious ploy to get him back for a second interview. There were probably hundreds of pamphlets in the cabinet.

"No, I don't mind at all," he said.

"Good man." Wright patted him on the back as he walked him to the door of the office. "Don't be put off if our beliefs seem strange to you at first. Just imagine how weird the teachings of the Mormon Church must have sounded to the first people who heard them."

"I'll bear that in mind," Ecclestone promised.

He left the old church feeling a mixture of anger at Kat for putting him through this pointless ordeal, and embarrassment that he had half-believed her story.

(3)

The apartment was empty. He shrugged as he hung his jacket on the rack behind the front door. Kat had always been unpredictable. Maybe she had changed her mind about returning to his apartment and had gone back to her own place. Or maybe she had gone out to do some shopping. He thought about phoning her, then decided to let her phone him.

He started the coffee machine in the kitchen, put some Mozart on the turntable, and stretched out on his couch to read the grey pamphlet.

The cover bore the title "Your Spiritual Path" and below it, the image of an old-fashioned key stamped in gold. It was written in the style of most religious pamphlets—enthusiastic but vague on detail.

According to the pamphlet, the Order of the Hidden Door had originated in the thirteenth century when a group of Franciscan monks living near the town of Wittenberg discovered an ancient Gnostic document in a secret windowless room of their monastery. The document was written in Arabic, and when translated proved to be a grimoire that described how to make contact with a hitherto unknown hierarchy of fallen angels referred to in the manuscript only as the Eclipsed.

The anonymous author of the ancient parchment claimed that these angels were not among the angels who fought beside Lucifer against God in the great war in heaven, but were a falsely-accused hierarchy that had been wrongly cast down into the Abyss along with the rest of the Fallen. Somehow the Eclipsed managed to escape from the Abyss, and now they dwelt on the earth, unseen and apart. They were forced to conceal themselves both from the wrath of God and the vengeance of the Devil, since the hosts of heaven and hell alike hunted them.

The names of the four great princes of the Eclipsed were written in the ancient parchment beside their occult seals. The seals were to be revealed only to members of the order, but the pamphlet gave their names: Isulakkos the Creator, ruler of the east and the element air; Oleemon the Sustainer, ruler of the south and the element fire; Xalos the Justifier, ruler of the west and the element water; Nergaltou the Tormentor, ruler of the north and the element earth.

Human beings who pledged themselves in service to the four princes of the Eclipsed with a willing mind and a devote heart received instruction in a system of practical magic that enabled them to transform their lives. The pamphlet asserted that they found success in whatever endeavour they undertook, and that their enemies were powerless to harm them.

The monks who discovered the ancient parchment at once recognized its immense potential, both for good and for harm, and they determined to establish a secret order of select members worthy to protect the precious knowledge of the Eclipsed and their system of magic from the vulgar world. So it had continued, concealed and protected, for eight centuries, even down to the present day.

The Hidden Door had no priests and acknowledged no higher human authority. Nothing stood between a member of the order and the angels, who revealed themselves and spoke directly to those who worshipped them as they would to their own children. In return for their wisdom and protection, these misunderstood angels asked only for adoration and an occasional gift-offering.

Ecclestone yawned and realized the turntable had shut itself off. It seemed as though he had only been reading a few minutes, but when he looked at the wall clock he saw that over an hour had passed. He got off the couch, stretched his stiff back, and went into the kitchen for coffee.

As he was returning with his mug to the living room, he happened to glance through the open doorway of the bathroom. He yelled and dropped the mug, then ran into the living room, where he crouched behind the arm of the couch, shivering. After several minutes, when nothing followed him from the hall, he got up and winced in pain. The scalding coffee from the broken mug had splashed across his ankle. He made his way cautiously to the open archway that divided the living room from the hall and peered around its edge.

There was nothing in the hall.

He crept back to the bathroom. It took all his courage to click on the light and peer into the mirror over the sink. He saw his own face, staring wild-eyed back at him from the depths of the glass. The insane figure in the mirror passed a hand over his mouth and cheeks and raked fingers through his disordered brown hair. In the glare of the ceiling light his cheeks and lips were colorless from lack of blood.

The thing he had glimpsed in the mirror was still vivid in his memory, but he could think of no words to describe it, because it had not looked like anything with which he was familiar, either in waking life or in dreams. The nearest comparison he could make was to a pulsating microscopic organism enlarged to gigantic dimensions.

"Fucking Kat has got me imagining things," he muttered to himself, and smiled into the glass, but what he saw there was more of a grimace.

He shook his head and even managed to laugh, but when he gathered up the pieces of his shattered mug, his hands were still trembling.

(4)

Ecclestone spent the next morning at the University of San Francisco, attending classes. In the afternoon he rode the bus over to the church with the pamphlet.

On the way, he tried calling Kat on his cell phone, but got no answer. He was beginning to worry about her.

"What do you think of us now?" Wright asked with a smile as he accepted back the pamphlet and tucked it away in his filing drawer.

"I don't really know what to think," Ecclestone answered honestly. "Is that part about finding the manuscript true?"

"It is true. I've seen the manuscript."

"Do you think I might see it?"

Wright laughed. "We don't keep it here, Norman.

It's still in Europe, in a very safe and well-guarded location."

"You mean there are more churches like this one?"

"Of course. We're not a large order, but we number our members in the thousands. There are dozens of churches like this across Europe and North America."

"If you don't mind me asking, who pays for it all?"

"Very good," Wright said, tapping the side of his nose. "Follow the money."

"It's usually a good source of information."

"All I can tell you is that some of our members are extremely wealthy. They supply us with the funds needed to carry on our services around the world."

"Can you give me any names?"

"Our funders prefer to remain anonymous."

"Of course. I understand."

"Have you given any more thought to joining us?"

"I have thought about it. I wonder if I could sit in on one of your services?"

"That can be arranged," Wright said. "What about tonight at eight?"

"I'll be here."

He made his way from the church to Kat's apartment. There was no answer when he rang her bell, but the landlady recognized him as a close friend and frequent visitor, and let him in with her passkey.

The apartment was as he remembered it, sloppy and lived-in. Kat was a poor housekeeper. He walked from room to room, remembering the times he had spent there. Most of them had been happy times, except near the end when Kat was already fucking Alan Horowitz and looking for reasons to find fault with him. He didn't know how long she had cheated on him before he discovered them in bed together, but it must have been weeks.

Maybe she had gone to visit with her parents in Colorado. There was no job to hold her to San Francisco. Her parents were well off, and they were financing her year-long sabbatical, as she called it, for her to find herself as a woman before seeking a job. They were the ones paying for this apartment. He thought about phoning them, then decided it would only worry them for nothing.

Instead, he went through her closets and drawers, looking for anything connected with the church. In the bottom drawer of the bureau in her bedroom he found her diary. It was a typical girl's diary, with a padded cover in pink satin and a plastic red ribbon running diagonally across one corner with a plastic picture of a rose. He hefted it in anticipation. Maybe he would learn something about the asshole who had fucked her behind his back. He sat on her bed to read it.

It was like opening the door on a room full of nightmares. She had written about her growing apprehension concerning the teachings of the Hidden Door, and like many nightmares, it started out calmly and rationally, but progressed to screaming insanity.

A typical early entry read, "Brother Wright wants to mentor me. He told me today that I have great potential. One of the princes confided to him that I could become a carrier if I continued to practice the lessons, but I find them so tiring on my mind, sometimes I just want to scream and break things after practicing them for an hour. I don't know if I'm strong enough to do what he wants me to do."

A few pages further on she wrote, "One of them came to me tonight, as I was getting ready to go to bed. You can see them in mirrors, see their true forms, I mean, if they want you to. I was so terrified I couldn't even speak. It was not what I expected. I thought it would come as an angel with white wings, blond hair, and beautiful blue eyes, but it was so alien and revolting. I felt a tickle in the back of my brain and knew it was trying to talk to me but I couldn't make out the words. After it left I went into the bathroom and threw up in the toilet."

In the second half of the diary, drawings of symbols and single words that were heavily traced over and over with a pen, or written numerous times, began to replace the more rational prose. She drew the image of a key unlocking an eye in a triangle, and a flying dagger with wings that dripped blood. Ecclestone noticed the repeated occurrence of the phrases "bastard spawn of the Archons," "prisoners in hell," "the shunned ones," and "abortions of the lesser gods." Much of it was incoherent. She was copying down what the voices in her head told her to write.

The final page consisted of nothing but a spiral drawn with a ballpoint pen in red ink, over and over and over until the paper was worn into holes in places. When he stared at it, the drawing gave the illusion of a bottomless pit of fire.

Ecclestone closed the diary and laid it gently on the bed. He realized for the first time how desperate Kat had been when she came to his door, and how hard it must have been for her to keep from slipping into schizophrenic ramblings. Clearly the diary had been written by someone mentally ill, at least the second half of it. Had Kat already suffered from mental illness when she joined the church, or had her experiences at the church driven her crazy?

He took out his phone and tried her number again. No response. He had to call her parents. In her mental state there was no knowing what might happen to her, or what she might do to herself.

Her mother answered. He tried to keep his voice cheerful as they chatted about inconsequential matters. When he got a chance, he asked in a casual way if she knew where her daughter was staying.

"You mean she isn't in her apartment?" Her sudden concern was evident in her voice.

"She wasn't there when I dropped over to talk to her," he said. "I thought maybe she had decided to stay with a friend."

"This isn't about her new boyfriend, is it, Norman? You know that I always liked you, but it's Kat's decision who she sees. You can't go around stalking her."

"It's nothing like that, Aida. I just wanted to get in touch with her and she doesn't seem to be answering her cell phone."

"I don't know what to tell you, Norman. She hasn't phoned me since last week."

"That's fine. It's probably nothing to worry about. I'll try her cell again later."

He broke the connection, wondering if he had accomplished anything other than to get her mother worried. He rummaged around in her room until he found her address book, and began to call her friends one after another. None of them had seen Kat for a couple of days. In the end he found himself sitting on the bed, staring at the last page in her diary, tracing the red spiral around and around down to the chaotic knot of twisted lines at its center.

(5)

William Wright stared at him, waiting. Ecclestone blinked in surprise and looked around. He was standing in the foyer of the church. He realized that Wright had just spoken to him and was waiting for a response.

"I'm sorry, I didn't hear what you just said."

"I said I hope you're not nervous about tonight's ritual. You won't be expected to do or say anything."

They walked into the main part of the church, where several dozen young men and women milled around, talking and laughing. There was a sense of anticipation in the air.

"Do I need to put on a robe?"

Wright shook his head with a smile.

"As much as possible we pattern our rituals on the practices of an ordinary Christian church. The members of the order sit in the pews and wear normal street clothes."

"You're trying to make things non-threatening."

"You've got it, Norman. People tend to shy away from anything out of the ordinary, so we make our rituals as ordinary as possible, at least in form."

"There are no mirrors." The words just popped out. Wright laughed and patted him on the shoulder.

"When have you ever seen a mirror in a church?"

Now that he mentioned it, Ecclestone realized that he could not remember ever seeing a mirror in any church.

"I wanted to ask you about Alan Horowitz. Is he here tonight?"

"That's Katherine Moore's friend, isn't it?" Wright looked around, craning his neck to see over the crowd. "He isn't here. He hasn't been coming to services lately. I suspect he's had second thoughts about remaining a member of our congregation."

"There seems to be a lot of that going around."

Wright shrugged. "We're not for everyone, Norman. We're a very exclusive order in the strict sense of the word. Our work tends to exclude those who are not worthy to join us. Sometimes people hear about us and think they can get something out of us without giving anything back. Those people don't stay with us for very long."

An attractive blond woman in a grey robe moved to the altar and lit the four large white candles that rested on its corners. The overhead lights in the church dimmed.

"The ritual is about to begin," Wright told him. "I have to leave you now, but we'll talk again later. You just watch what we do, and try not to judge anything too harshly before you know its purpose."

Wright took his place in front of the altar, his back to the pews, and raised his hands. The church fell silent with expectation. He began to chant in that strange language Ecclestone had heard on his first visit. At intervals the congregation—it was hard to think of them in any other way—stood up and chanted a response. Ecclestone stood along with them. He soon fell into the rhythm of standing and sitting.

The blond woman in the robe moved to the grey curtain between the pillars. Wright took a plate from the altar and raised it over his head as he chanted in a commanding tone. The woman pulled aside the curtain at the corner and the congregation chanted in enthusiasm. In spite of himself Ecclestone felt his own emotions rising along with theirs. The atmosphere of anticipation that filled the church was infectious.

Wright replaced the plate on the altar and walked around it once, then raised the plate above his head again and repeated the invocation. The woman pulled the corner of the curtain aside a little further as the congregation responded. Wright repeated this elevation of the plate and the circumambulation of the altar twice more, and on the final repetition the woman raised the curtain high and stood under it, an expression of ecstasy on her face.

Ecclestone stared at her in shock. The pupils of her eyes had vanished, leaving only a uniform white beneath her fluttering eyelids. He saw that the same thing had happened to Wright's eyes, and when he glanced around him, all of the men and women standing at the pews had white eyes as well.

This almost caused him to panic, until he realized that their eyes had not changed, but had merely rolled up in their sockets so that the pupils and irises were concealed from view. The odd thing was that the people around him seemed to be able to see what was going on, which should have been impossible.

They began to file forward, one by one, to kneel before the altar and receive a kind of blessing from Wright, who dipped his thumb in the plate and impressed it upon the center of their foreheads. None of them paid any attention to Ecclestone, who might as well have been invisible.

He felt something in his pocket and realized he had brought his sunglasses with him. He tapped his finger on them meditatively for several minutes before it occurred to him that they had a metallic coating that made their exterior surfaces reflective, like a mirror. Surreptitiously, he took them out and raised them to his face, concealed in the palm of his hand. He held one of the lenses near and refocused his eyes on it.

The sudden electric surge of terror that flashed along his nerves almost made him drop the sunglasses. The many things reflected in the curved surface of the lens were not human. They were not even things he could recognize or describe. They resembled what he had glimpsed in the bathroom mirror of his apartment.

He angled the sunglasses so that they reflected Wright and the woman at the curtain. They were monsters as well. He realized he was drenched in sweat and holding his breath, and forced himself to exhale. It took all of his courage to turn the lens of the sunglasses so that it reflected his own face.

(6)

"We'll be there in a few minutes," Wright said.

Ecclestone blinked and found that he was sitting in the front passenger seat of a car. Wright was driving. It was dark outside the windshield.

"I don't understand what's happening to me," he said.

"That's perfectly normal. Don't worry about it, Norman, just go with the flow."

"Where are you taking me?"

"We're going to tie off a few loose ends. You're here because we must be certain of your loyalty before we permit you to join us."

"I don't want to join the order."

Wright turned to look at him with an amused smile that was not unkind.

"Come now, Norman. Did you ever really believe you had a choice?"

They drove to a seedy motel outside the city and climbed the exterior stairs to a room on the second level. All the lights in the room were out.

"Knock on the door," Wright whispered. "Tell him you need to talk to him about Katherine."

Ecclestone hesitated, then knocked on the door. It opened almost immediately against its security chain. He recognized the frightened face he saw through the crack.

"Alan Horowitz?"

The man's eyes narrowed.

"You're Ecclestone, the guy Kat used to know."

Sudden concern for Kat's welfare overwhelmed him. He tried to push against the door before he remembered the chain.

"I need to talk to you about Kat."

Horowitz's eyes rolled from side to side.

"Are you alone?"

Ecclestone could feel Wright crouched behind him.

"Yes, I'm alone. Let me in."

Wright was through the door an instant after the chain rattled out of its channel. He pushed Horowitz back until they both fell across the bed. Ecclestone shut the door. The only light came through the drawn sheer curtains from the flashing motel sign. Ecclestone watched the two men struggle on the bed in its rectangle of glaring red and green. Wright had a wadded cloth in Horowitz's mouth to prevent him from yelling.

"Help me, Norman."

Wright spoke some words in the language used in the church. Ecclestone felt the floor tilt and begin to slowly turn under his feet. Everything dimmed around him. He seemed to be viewing the struggle on the bed from a great distance, and the grunts and the creaks of the bed springs were faint in his ears, as though they came through the wall from two people having sex.

He found himself reaching for Horowitz without ever intending to do so.

"Get out your knife," Wright ordered.

(?)

He sat in the La-Z-Boy in his own apartment. Wright sat across from him in the chair Kat usually sat in.

"How do you feel, Norman?"

"I don't know." Memory rushed in. "What happened to Horowitz?"

"We took care of him. He was a loose end."

Ecclestone looked down in horror at his hands, turning them over and flexing his fingers. They were clean. He had expected to see them drenched in blood.

"Was that real?"

"Was what real, Norman?"

"Did we—did we murder Horowitz?"

Wright laughed.

"It's a psychic technique used by the order to test the resolve of applicants. Of course it wasn't real. I'm happy to say that you passed the test. You are now a member of the Hidden Door. Congratulations."

Ecclestone blinked at him. There was a kind of buzzing in the back of his head, and he found it difficult to focus his eyes.

"Nothing happened?"

"Nothing of any importance."

"Horowitz isn't really hurt?"

"Forget Horowitz. He was never fit to be one of us. We merely used him to bring Katherine to the church."

"What did you want with Katherine?"

"Isn't it obvious?"

Ecclestone glared at him. He felt the urge to smash his fist into Wright's smug, arrogant face.

"No, it isn't obvious."

"We used Horowitz to bring in Katherine, because we needed Katherine to get to you."

It took several seconds for Ecclestone's mind to process this revelation.

"What do you want with me?"

Wright leaned forward in his chair and folded his hands together.

"You belong with us, Norman. You've always been one of us. You just never knew it until we awakened you. As I told you earlier, we are a very exclusive order. Not one person in ten thousand is fit to join us, but you, Norman, are one of those special persons. You and I are brothers from the same nest, hatched from the same egg cluster a million years ago."

"You are completely insane," Ecclestone said, forming each word distinctly.

"Why do you think the ancient Arabic manuscript called us the Eclipsed? Where do you think we've been hiding from God and the Devil for the past million years?

Where's the best place to hide something?"

"In plain sight," he said without thinking.

"That's right, in plain sight." Wright smiled at him. "Don't worry, the rest of the world can't see us, not even in mirrors. Not unless we want them to."

"You're crazy. All of you, you're all insane. You hypnotized me and made me do things against my will."

Wright shook his head. "We woke you up. What you did, you did freely of your own true will."

Ecclestone stood from his chair. His body moved in jerks, as though unaccustomed to obeying him.

"Get out. I never want to see you again."

Wright stood easily. "There's no pressure on you, Norman. Come back to the church when you feel ready to join us. We're all your brothers and sisters. We'll be waiting for you."

He left the apartment. Ecclestone locked the door, and stood with his back against it, feeling waves of terror wash over him. His mind rejected Wright's words, but no matter how hard he pushed them away, they kept coming back.

He returned to the living room and got a bottle of vodka out from the cabinet where he kept his liquor. He wasn't a heavy drinker, but tonight he needed something. His hands shook as he poured the colorless liquid into a glass and drained it, then refilled it. He took it back with him to the La-Z-Boy and sat in a daze.

He had to find Kat. She would know what was going on. From what he had read in her diary, she had understood the true nature of the order, or at least some of it. He pulled out his cell phone and selected her number.

A faint chirp came from somewhere down the hall. He frowned and selected Kat's number again. The same chirping noise sounded. Leaving his drink in the arm of the chair, he got up and followed it. The noise led him to the closed door of his storage closet. He stood beside the closet, trembling, and punched Kat's number a third time. Very clearly, the chirps of a cell phone came through the closet door.

He remembered what he had been doing just before he glimpsed the monster in the bathroom mirror. He had been reading the grey pamphlet given to him by Wright while lying on his couch. It had seemed like only a few minutes had passed, but when he looked at the clock on the wall, more than an hour had gone by. What had he done during that lost hour?

Ecclestone did not open the closet door. With numb fingers, he put his phone into his pocket and walked back down the hall to look at himself in the bathroom mirror.

❦ ❦ ❦

DOUBLE X CHROMOSOME:

By Yvonne Navarro

Not-So-Secret Societies

When I got the email letting me know the theme of this issue of *Dark Discoveries*, the first thing that came to mind is that they're almost all boys' clubs. I found out, however, that a number of them admit women, so all isn't unequal on the Boys' Club Front. Read on and see which ones lean to testosterone and which tip toward estrogen.

The Free Masons. This is pretty much THE premier boys' club. My husband is a member. My father-in-law is a member. Countless men in every city of every country in every part of the *world* are members. The idea of the Free Masons goes back to the first temple of Solomon. The symbols in their ceremonies revolve around geometric metaphor, which is why the square and compass are the symbols of Free Masonry. You have these symbols in your purse or wallet, because they're all over the back of the U.S. dollar bill. There

are certain modern day sayings that are derived from Free Masonry, and although non-Masons use them all the time, they don't realize they are essentially using Masonic code. "Is he on the level?" used to mean "Is he a Mason?" Now it means "Is he telling the truth?" The same applies to the question of "Is he squared away?" They have secret ceremonies, secret sayings,

even secret handshakes that they use to recognize each other. I've never seen one. Seriously. The Husband won't show me. The Prince Hall Masons are African-American Masons who grabbed the Masons' secrets during the time of slavery. They still exist today. Many people believe that the Knights Templar was the start of the Free Masons, although the Catholic Church denies this, particularly since it still supports the Knights Templar. **The Eastern Star** is a branch of the Free Masons for women. I'm actually proud to say that my aunt-in-law is the Worthy Matron (the highest of ranks) in her South Dakota temple.

The Bilderberg Group. This has been around since World War II and has among its members (much like the Bohemian Grove below) all the financial leaders, kings, experts, academia and politicos of the world. It's been believed for a long time that they are the true government of the world. If you hear someone say "a new world order," they're talking about the Bilderberg Group, whether they know it or not. Yes, President George Bush, Sr. used this phrase in a speech on September 11, 1991.

The Skull and Bones Society. Formed in 1832, the Internet will tell you that this is an "undergraduate senior secret society at Yale University in New Haven,

Connecticut." The organization calls its hall "The Tomb." It finally began to include women in 1992, one hundred and sixty years after its formation. Yet again former presidents, judges, economic experts and corporate kings are reported to be members.

The Thule Society. Adapted from a different organization in 1918 by Rudolf von Sebottendorff, a German occultist, this was a Teutonic organization reputed to have been designed to search out and find magical and historical supernatural relics. One of its major

focuses was the origins of the Aryan race as having come from "Thule," a land that according to Greco-Roman geographers was located in the farthest north. Nazi mystics declared Ultima Thule the capital and placed it near Greenland or Iceland. However, it's also contended that members weren't interested in Sebottendorff's occultist endeavors and focused more on racism and combating Jews and Communists.

Hermetic Order of the Golden Dawn. A quasi-religious organization of British origin that incorporates paganism/mysticism into its teachings.

Women were inducted on equal basis to men, and membership was based on a hierarchy: the higher in ranking you were, the more you were given access to so-called mystical knowledge. The First Order taught esoteric philosophy and personal development, as well as the basics of astrology, tarot divination, and geomancy. The Second or "Inner" Order, the *Rosae Rubeae et Aureae Crucis* (the Ruby Rose and Cross of Gold), taught proper magic, including scrying, astral travel, and alchemy. The Third Order was that of the "Secret Chiefs," who claimed to be highly skilled; they supposedly directed the activities of the lower two orders by spirit communication with the Chiefs of the Second Order. The first temple was founded in 1888, and although the last one was closed in 1988, a number of organizations have since revived its teachings.

Fraternitas Saturni. Also known as the Brotherhood of Saturn, this is a male German magical order founded in 1928. It is one of the oldest continuously running magical groups in Germany. Their teachings focused on the study of esotericism, mysticism, and magic in the cosmic sense, and have morphed to encompass the "overall development of humanity through the development and promotion of the individual." Like the Free Masons, they have a degree system, with 33rd being the highest attainable.

The Bohemian Grove. Presidents, kings, CEOs, politicians—the most powerful men in the world belong to *The Bohemian Club*, which holds a two-week camp every mid-July. No woman has ever been given full membership, although four have been named "honorary" members. No woman has been given a membership since 1928, and the club didn't hire female employees until after 1987, when it lost its final discrimination battle in the courts. At the start of each camp, a Cremation of Care ceremony is conducted at the foot of a forty-foot, hollow giant owl statue, where a human effigy made of straw is burned on an altar. It all happens in the dark, in secret, and the attendees hide beneath dark hoods, claiming they're burning their worldly causes, concerns, and cares, thus enabling everyone to think clearly. But you have to wonder—why do so at the foot of a giant owl? It doesn't take much research to discover

that a lot of folks connect this "owl" to the ancient god Moloch; in this day and age of fanaticism, it's a half-step from there to suggesting children are being sacrificed on that altar. Some say that if there's an icon involved, it generally means worship, and others suggest they don't sacrifice "icons" at all. Watch the chilling YouTube video (taken by Alex Jones in July of 2000, when he infiltrated the Club) at https://www.youtube.com/watch?v=r5dHhvpHIjM and judge for yourself. Is it just me or does it sound like someone screaming in pain at about the 7:13 mark? In fact, Jones himself mentions the "screams of pain coming from the sacrifice" at the video's 8:40 mark. By the way, Bill Clinton was President then, and it's said that every Republican and some Democratic presidents have been members.

There are hundreds or perhaps thousands of other Secret Societies, with a number of them female-driven, but since they're not paying me to write a thesis here, I'll stop. My husband says that if he was in charge of a secret society he would use it to choreograph chaos to not only direct attention away from the possibility of his secret society even existing but to bring him financial gains and power, just like the **Illuminati** (yes, another 500-year old secret society) are doing right now. A conspiracy theory that's emerging today is that if Iraq is weak and Iran is strong, it would be very possible for the two countries to merge into one super country. Enter Isis, a new terrorist organization that rapidly moves in and wants to break (Balkanize) Iraq into three smaller countries. The result is Iran merging with a much smaller, less powerful Iraq, which, by the way, doesn't include any of the rich oil fields or agricultural areas. Why did I mention this? Because it's been suggested that Isis was created, encouraged, and even mentored by the hand of the Illuminati to prevent Iran and Iraq from merging into that single super country.

Since I hate to end on a too-gloomy note, my personal conspiracy theory states that **The Free Masons** invented the brassiere, and **The Eastern Star** invented the necktie to get back at them.

❦ ❦ ❦

Check out Yvonne's story, "Holodomor Girl" in Shadow Masters, edited by Jeani Rector. Also, don't miss her classic novel, *DeadTimes*, now available in e-book format from Crossroad Press (http:// http://store.crossroadpress.com/). Comments? Questions? Suggestions? Yvonne Navarro can be reached via her website (yvonnenavarro.com), Facebook page (https://www.facebook.com/yvonne.navarro.001), or at her Dark Discoveries email: yvonne@journalstone.com.

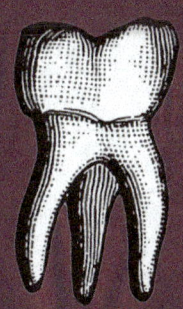
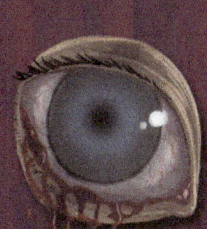

THROUGH THE DARKEST LENS:

Conspiracy Theory in Fiction and Culture

By K. H. Vaughan

Who controls the British crown?
Who keeps the metric system down?
We do. We do.
-The Stonecutters Anthem,
The Simpsons, Episode 115.

Conspiracy offers seductive explanations for world events and conspiracy thrillers are entertaining and often very profitable. Understanding the psychology and conventions of conspiracy theory allows the writer to know what needs exposition and explanation, and what outlandish claims are likely to be received with a smile and a nod. Likewise, it should allow for more richly developed characters and ideas that will hook the reader who comes to a conspiracy tale with certain expectations. Some scholars have tried to identify cognitive and personality characteristics of true believers (e.g., cynicism, alienation from the political process, authoritarianism), but I think this is of limited value. The real issues lie in social identity and the challenges involved in understanding complex events. Although the thinking of conspiracy advocates is flawed, the kinds of errors involved are, for the most part, the sort that we are all prone to.

At the most general level, conspiracy-mindedness reflects the paranoia of everyday life. Most people have a basic sense that unseen forces are working against us. We are under surveillance, manipulated, and feel increasingly disenfranchised. It's hard to put your finger on the vague psychological discomfort that happens when the register at the pharmacy spits out a coupon for something you might consider buying next week or you see your house on Google maps. If it feels like it is getting harder and harder to get ahead in life, that's because it is. Millions of people, just trying to keep their own jobs, make tiny decisions that have the net effect of squeezing every last penny and channeling every last choice. These are mundane, boring explanations, and there is no heroism in resisting them. Conspiracy theories provide a focal point for this vague sense of dis-ease. A place for the disenfranchised and frustrated to lay blame. An enemy with a name, if not a face, that can be fought. Savvy writers need look no further than the news and social media to divine what particular form of angst is plaguing the public.

The conspiracies we embrace reflect our specific concerns and help cement our social alliances. The conspiracies endorsed by the Right and Left may vary in content, but at their heart are concerns about the legitimacy of authority and a sense of hopelessness, alienation, and cynicism about the received version of truth. This is not due the simple uncertainty of knowledge and history, but a belief that it is all manipulated consciously in an organized fashion with malevolent intent. Faith in the legitimacy of authority and traditional channels of information has been badly undermined by the fact that some conspiracies are real. Governments do conceal activities, lie, and have engaged in horrific experiments on their citizens (e.g., the Tuskegee Syphilis Study). Special interests do influence elections. Executives at Enron and Lehman Brothers engaged in fraud and market manipulation. The Serbian Black Hand assassinated Archduke Franz Ferdinand, triggering World War One. The fate of nations has changed based on the actions of conspiracies and secret societies. These facts can make meetings of the Bilderberg Group, Bohemian Club, or the Wall Street chapter of Kappa Beta Phi seem like modern incarnations of the Illuminati. Revelations of NSA surveillance, the militarization of police, and incidents involving the abuse of government power (e.g., Waco, Ruby Ridge, or Ferguson, MO) sow distrust and rage. For the true believer, the fact that some conspiracies are true is proof that other conspiracies are also true, without evaluating the evidence on a case-by-case basis. In fact, people who believe in outlandish conspiracies are likely to endorse ideas that are mutually exclusive (e.g., that Osama bin Laden was already dead when Navy SEALS raided a compound in Pakistan, and that bin Laden is still alive). It suggests a general willingness to believe any proposition so long as it has the right kind of anti-establishment flavor and helps create a consistent world view.

There are self-serving aspects of conspiracy theory as well. The protagonist in a conspiracy narrative (real or fictional) is truly heroic. He has privileged knowledge of the truth not meant for the general population. The believer is thus smarter than the naïve or weak-minded sheep who can't handle the truth. The protagonist must be brave as well, to be willing to take on forces that re-write history and control nations. Our hero is also on the moral high ground compared to the conspirators and their dupes. The millions of doctors and nurses who withhold the cure for cancer from their patients (including their own loved ones) and work to make people sick for greater profit must be truly cynical and cold-blooded individuals. These superior qualities appeal to our basic narcissism, and can make the hero easier to identify with.

The final self-serving element to consider when understand or writing a conspiracy narrative is that although conspiracies are malevolent on the surface, they do provide a degree of psychological comfort. They mean that history is not a series of uncontrolled accidents, but instead the world is controlled by people who are more intelligent and better organized than the rest of us. Sure, they manipulate world events, rob us blind, and commit murder, but we can trust that they won't let things get out of hand. They may threaten to destroy the world for gain, but they won't push it over the edge because they live here too. As long as we keep out of their way, and don't get too curious about what the puppet masters are up to, we'll generally be safe. We are too small to catch their attention, as long as we live within the attractive lie they allow us to believe. The unpredictability of an uncontrolled world is a far more horrifying proposition.

Although these issues of social identity are important, I think the bigger issue is the question of how we process evidence. The process of evaluating theories remains the same whether we are considering "suppressed" technologies, cattle mutilations, "chemtrails," or the cause of the 2004 Indian Ocean Tsunami. Given the ease with which images and documents can be forged or manipulated, and the reality of imperfect or manipulated media coverage of events, the information stream is always suspect or contaminated. (Fnord.) But even if we had perfectly accurate information from unimpeachable sources, there is far too much data for us to handle. It's not an issue of intelligence or education. Many bright

and highly-educated people wholeheartedly believe in conspiracy theories. The amount of information and complexity of events overwhelms everyone.

We generally find uncertainty and contradiction aversive, and our capacity for controlled rational thought is limited. To cope, we attempt to simplify problems and sacrifice accuracy for efficiency. These processes happen automatically, on an implicit level, and become more important when we are confronted with information overload, ambiguity, the unfamiliar, or states that deplete our mental reserves (e.g., emotional arousal, fatigue, distraction). We make use of heuristic thinking (rules of thumb), or default to the script that seems to fit best. Many of these work well for day-to-day decisions, such as predicting the weather or the behavior of someone you know, but they frequently fail us when applied to more complex questions such as "do vaccinations cause autism?" or "was the Sandy Hook shooting a false flag operation?" Confronted with these questions, it is easier to fit the issue to a template based on core assumptions than to actually evaluate the facts. We have an extraordinary ability to perceive patterns, and do so even when the data is random (everything will always come in threes, provided you control when you start looking for a series and when you stop). Conspiracy thinking often relies on what an event "looks like." The collapse of the World Trade Center *looks* similar to footage we have seen of controlled demolitions, so that must be the explanation. It fits the template. In addition, conspiracy buffs frequently conflate outcomes with intentions, assuming that if a party benefited from some event, they must have had a hand in causing it (*cui bono*?). As a third example, we tend to assume that big events must have proportionately large causes, as opposed to being due to the accumulation of small decisions and chance factors.

Humans lack an intuitive understanding of chance (see *Innumeracy* by Paulos), and this plays out in a variety of ways. The odds of winning the Powerball Jackpot are over 1 in 175,000,000, yet people win on a regular basis. It isn't going to be you, and there is no reason for a particular combination of ping pong balls to be drawn. Given the immense complexity of the world, extremely unusual events happen by chance all the time. Stanislaw Lem makes good use of this fact in his detective novel *Chain of Chance*. Conspiracy theorists tend to conflate the possible with the probable or even certainty. They also tend to misestimate or ignore the relative probability of different events. Why would any government steal Malaysia Airlines Flight 370, a plane that cannot land in most airports and would immediately attract attention, when hundreds of similar aircraft could be purchased in secret through shell companies? Complicated plans work in fiction, but tend to fail in real life. They make for great theater and book plots, but the possibility that a small army of special forces ninja pre-wired the World Trade Center for a controlled demolition (without anyone noticing) using an explosive powerful enough to do the job, but stable enough to leave in place indefinitely in the event that the other very difficult task of hijacking the airplanes didn't go as planned is remote. It is an incredibly complex Rube Goldberg device, requiring a very long chain of events to go off in sequence without a hitch. But that is what conspiracy fans want. Conspiracy theories are akin to the long con, and the more elaborate and clever the con, the more entertaining it will be. Conspiracy fans do not want the simplest explanation for events.

Rather than attempting to examine the specific elements of evidence behind individual claims, conspiracy theories are evaluated holistically based on whether they are consistent with other strongly held beliefs. The standards for evaluating evidence for and against the conspiracy are asymmetrical, with tissue-thin, indirect data of poor reliability given greater weight than much more solid evidence that is not compatible with the theory. Social proof (people I like agree with me) and emotional proof (the truth of propositions is evaluated based on how they make us feel) become more important than actual evidence in this context. The absence of evidence is often considered strong evidence for a conspiracy because it "proves" the cover-up. Most conspiracy literature is an exercise in confirmation bias rather than a search for truth. A good conspiracy theory, like any good delusional system, is hermetically sealed. Every element works in unison and claims follow from a specific underlying philosophy and set of assumptions about how the world works. Every piece of evidence is either explained or explained away. Those who disagree become sheep, dupes, or actively complicit in manufacturing the official story. Compared to the reader of classic English mystery

novels, the conspiracy fan will be happier to fill in the evidentiary gaps and more forgiving of inconsistency or logical flaws.

In general, conspiracy fans overestimate the ability of people to keep a secret. Gavrilo Princip and his Black Hand colleagues got drunk on the train to Belgrade and boasted of their plan to assassinate Franz Ferdinand, showing bombs and firearms to other passengers. There were tens of thousands of people involved in the "fake" moon landing. By now, some of them would surely have had too much to drink, a change of heart, or an excess of pride in their accomplishment and come forward. The same would be true of the 9/11 attacks, which would have taken hundreds if not thousands of individuals to pull off. One of those special forces ninja should have spoken out of guilt or be marketing his screenplay by now. This can be played upon in fiction, for the profound ability of the conspirators to keep secrets makes them special relative to most people we know. Alternately, to the extent that some members fail to keep the secret, it can provide the impetus for the plot to move forward.

Conspiracy fans overestimate the ability of individuals to stick to a plan. After the Lufthansa Heist (which most people know of from the film *Goodfellas*), the man responsible for disposing of the getaway van instead got stoned and went to his girlfriend's apartment, leaving the van on the street in a no-parking zone. Most conventional crimes aren't solved by CSI-style forensic investigation. They are solved because people show off their money, boast, or turn on each other when they feel the heat. This fact can be used as an explanation for why conspiracies become exposed, and therefore can be a good jumping off point of a story. After all, a bystander can easily become embroiled in a massive conspiracy against his will by virtue of the overheard conversation, misplaced file, or whatever MacGuffin is convenient for the author. The elevated competence of the conspiracy perpetrators raises the threat level; they are different from ordinary criminals.

Organizations in conspiracy lore are incredibly competent, at least until it is convenient for them to make mistakes. (Notably, anti-government conspiracy theorists seem to think that the government is profoundly inept outside of the conspiracies in question. Perhaps it is part of a massive "Rope-a-Dope" program designed to lull us into false sense of security.) As a writer, you can often trust that the reader of conspiracy stories will accept that the government, or whatever secret agency is in play, can access records, hack systems, control satellites, or rapidly re-allocate resources as necessary for the story. There are infinite ways to communicate the endless reach and supernatural power of the conspiracy. It also provides a justification for the deployment of elite operatives who are the cream of the crop in their given field against the protagonist. Members of any conspiracy worth its salt will also have access to technologies the rest of us do not. As a basic trope, it isn't usually necessary to explain how the magic box works. It is sufficient to have someone describe it as "top secret" or "next generation" or have the story's geeks go bug-eyed when they get their hands on it.

Conspiracy buffs often overestimate the unity of organizations. People who talk about the Medical-Industrial Complex or Big Oil seem to believe that these are monolithic entities, as opposed to many thousands of people fighting for their own jobs, in competing divisions, within competing organizations. If Chrysler really had a 100 MPG carburetor, why would it leave this massive competitive advantage on the shelf when facing bankruptcy? Poor gas mileage benefits oil companies, not automakers. This aspect of conspiracy theory is parodied by Steve Jackson Games' *Illuminati*, in which players build byzantine power structures and attempt to control the world through complex networks ("On my turn, the Boy Sprouts, with assistance from the Discordian Society and the Triliberal Commission, will attack to wrest control the Phone Company from the UFOs.") Conspiracy fans will readily accept connections that might be resisted in other contexts, especially if the connections are described as controlled through hidden connections, shell companies, and byzantine organizational charts that serve to obscure their nature from the general public.

When writing conspiracy, there is always another layer of secret knowledge and people are not what they seem. Conspiracy theories are essentially Gnostic. There is frequently another layer of mystery and the protagonist must go through a process of initiation before each mystery is revealed. From a narrative perspective, the ignorance of the protagonist allows the writer to control the release of information and handle exposition through a series of clues and revelations spread out across the text. Like an effective mystery novel, too much shouldn't be given away too soon, and clues should be ambiguous, pointing to multiple interpretations. A guide is often employed in the form of a shadowy Deep Throat figure of uncertain loyalties who provides bread crumbs but can't, for some reason, reveal everything at once. Information can also be provided by members of an underground resistance, who will insulate the protagonist from the whole truth pending a series of tests of loyalty. After all, from their perspective, the protagonist could be an agent or infiltrator. The guide could also appear in the form of some fringe element whose information is suspect because of their status or behavior. The computer hacker who lives in his mother's basement, or the damaged unit of questionable sanity who makes outrageous claims that might possibly be true.

A good conspiracy theory should also have betrayals or switches in apparent loyalty. Double agents and triple-crosses abound. The revelation that a trusted friend has been working for *them* all along or that the information that the protagonist has been operating under is wrong creates a fantastic moment of crisis that can force the reader to review everything they think they know and re-evaluate every element of the story so far. Used properly, it is dizzying and delightful. The risk is that too many switches and betrayals can undermine the dramatic tension of the work as the increasingly skeptical reader begins to assume that everything is as credible as the death of a comic-book superhero.

A skilled writer can strengthen a conspiracy narrative by incorporating and playing with these ideas. This applies to the elements that the conspiracy fan is seeking and the flaws present in conspiracy logic. If characters use cogent arguments against the conspiracy, it becomes more powerful once proven to be true. A protagonist who starts with doubt and engages in critical analysis of the possibilities before becoming a believer will have more depth, and the process by which he or she becomes convinced will help persuade the audience. Beyond that, a skeptical protagonist helps mitigate the cliché common to horror films, in which the characters consistently do stupid things. A bright protagonist who can explain away the conspiracy with good arguments can then be placed in jeopardy despite making reasonable decisions. The plot does not depend on her stupidity to advance, just rational disbelief.

(Little Miss) Queen of Darkness

By Laird Barron

I: Initiation

I write this: *The cops don't know what really happened in Eagle Talon. Lies, all lies. Ask Jessica, if I ever see her again.* This isn't about Eagle Talon, however. I've never even been. No sir, Bob, if it's about anything, it's about that debutant ball Zane throws in his basement at the tail end of high school, 1998. The unfinished basement with the raw earth and a tunnel that smells of mildew and dankness. The tunnel is maybe three by three and is actually a cleft in the rock of the hill upon which this house rests.

I can't forget that hole in the ground. It drills through my mind.

Yeah, Shit Creek describes an imperfect circle right back to the bad old days. Oh, the party is rad, though: heavy metal, booze, drugs, psychedelic lights. The kids slam-dancing. Me with my hand on Stu Whitlock's hip the whole time and nobody the wiser. Then that damned hick brat Dave Teague racing past, naked and covered in blood, screaming his head off. Ruins everything…

I also write: *People call it this or that, but our club doesn't have a name. It didn't originate in Alaska. It was around before Alaska. We don't suckle at the breast of a god, it suckles at ours.* Unfortunately, devoid of context, that stuff reads like the Unabomber's doodles.

Next, I make a list. Were I to title it, the title would be "People Who Died," like the song. Such an everyman tune because everybody can relate, right? The partial list is scribbled in a black moleskin notebook. I've left bloody fingerprints on the pages. Many of the names are illegible from the smears, or redaction with a magic marker.

Names changed to protect the guilty. Four remain intact in truth and form. Hell if I know whether that's significant or not.

Zane Tooms & Julie Vellum: They could've been the power couple from the lowest circle of Hell. Alas, Zane already had a loyalist and Julie's not the kind to need any. These are your villains. Nuff said.

Steely J: Just about tall enough to play pro basketball. He's Zane's majordomo. The Renfield to Zane's Dracula. Loyal through thick and thin—and I'm not kidding, I literally mean that. We called Zane Fat Boy Tooms until his folks croaked and he started in with the horse de-wormer and got slenderized. Steely J stuck with him down the line. Steely is what you might call inscrutable. Looks nice, dresses nice, and plays nice, if a teensy bit of a cold fish. His features lag behind whatever message his brain is sending. Somebody behind the curtain throws a switch and he smiles. Or, he smiles and picks up a claw hammer and comes for you. The Sandburg poem about fog creeping on little cat feet? That's Steely J. Except six-six with a hammer.

Vadim: My buddy Vadim often brags that he's an expert in Savate. He paid two hundred dollars for a six week course at a strip mall. I let him drag me in once to meet the instructor (mainly I wanted to ogle some studly hotties kicking and stretching, but whatev) and the dude had a bunch of diplomas, certificates, and autographed photos of macho celebrities I didn't care to recognize. The French version of hi-ya for an hour. Bo-oring.

The strip mall closed shop when the economy cratered in '09. Not before Vadim got what he needed, however. He asserts that Savate is the elite of the elite fighting arts, natch. I don't know my foot from my elbow when it comes to violence. I'm a lover, always have been. That's why I keep the numbers of a few bigger, tougher friends in my rolodex.

Vadim talks lots of shit every time we go clubbing and the fraternity bros start hitting on me, which they totally do. I clutch his sleeve and say, "Whoa, there stud. They're just being friendly. Get mama another margarita, kay?" Vadim shoots the bros a venomous parting glare and then toddles off to fetch my drink. His thighs bulge his cargo pants so that he really does toddle. I think of it as having my own Siberian tiger on a leash, except with pouty, pouty lips, and six-pack abs! Nice while it lasted. He's dead too.

End of list.

§

Go back, not the whole way, not to high school. Three and a half years is far enough. We have gathered, dearly beloved. Gathered to sign on the dotted line and change the course of our stars forever. What a load of crap. *I'm* motivated by fascination, boredom, skepticism. Some of the others are buggy-eyed true believers. Have at it, morons.

The sun is bleeding out all over the Chugach Mountains. An inlet, ice-toothed and serpentine, lies below us somewhere, wrapped by mist that's freezing into black pearl. I'm not captivated by the austere beauty of the far north as seen through frosty picture windows. My feet are cold and I'm bored. I'm an L.A. girl trapped inside an L.A. boy. This arctic weather is for the birds.

Julie Five says to me, "Oh, Ed, quit sulking. You detest it so much, why'd you come? Nut up or shut up." She finishes me off with a sweet as pie smile. I beam one right back. Anybody more than arms-length away might get the impression we're peaches and cream. Big sister, little brother at worst. Then again, it's an intimate gathering of former classmates. Most of the others know how it is with us because it's been this way with us since junior high. Her nickname is JV, but I call her Julie Five. Our mutual acquaintance, the lamentably absent Jessica M, coined that bit of mockery. Sure, we're supposed to pity Julie Five for cowering in a closet while her lover got noisily disemboweled by the Eagle Talon Ripper in the winter of 2012, but her sob story doesn't move me—"victim-of-unspeakable-tragedy" is scraping the bottom of the barrel on a white trash reality show. Her sneaky path to fifteen minutes of fame and she didn't even *try* to stop the murdering bastard. Oh, dear heavens, no—she left that chore to her archrival, Jessica M, the girl who got the cover of *Black Belt Magazine* and interviews with every cable news show in existence. Good for Jess. Screw Julie Five. She's cowardly, treacherous, and mean. She like totally vacillates between vocal fry and ending every sentence on a rising note. Basically the darkest valley girl in the history of valley girls. I'd feed her a cup of lye if I had some.

Our host, Zane Tooms, stares at the sunset the way a man with an appointment compulsively checks his watch. He's dressed in a white shirt and black pants. No shoes. He never wears shoes at home. His shirt is unbuttoned two notches. A metallic chain gleams from the opening. I've seen the pendant when Zane had his shirt off—a smallish lump of vaguely horrid metal, or bone. Its color shifts, the film of a lizard's eye rolling aside. He folds his napkin, rises from his seat (throne) at the head of the table, and walks further into the decrepit mansion.

The house juts from a knoll with an impressive view of tidal flats and occasionally the water. The knoll was a bear den until hunters exterminated the bears and poured concrete back in when-the-hell-ever. Exactly the kind of place natives would say, "Don't build here! Bad medicine!" White Man doesn't give a shit about any of that and here we are. Even so, the Tooms residence lacks the sinister gravitas of a classic, gothic haunted castle. Made over once too often, the latest reconstructive surgery has rendered it a weird amalgam of art deco and '60s kitsch. His home might have been cozy in its heyday. He let it go to seed after the senior Toomses shuffled into the next life. He travels and can't be bothered with upkeep. I've told him he needs a decorator because the ambiance sucks. Frontier chic it is not. Swear to god he doesn't even live here, it's so borderline derelict. If Zane confessed he only showed up to unlock the joint and turn on the lights half an hour before his guests arrived, I wouldn't be shocked.

The basement is carved into the den itself and mostly unfinished. Lots of exposed beams, pipes, and dirt. I shudder to think. Tunnels bore past the glow of any lamp. Can't say I'm impressed with the remote location or the bear catacombs. Way too rustic for this girl. What does impress me is

Zane himself. These days, after slimming his chubby cheeks a n d beer gut, he's drop dead gorgeous. A walking, talking Ken Doll; brunette model. He oozes primal charisma. Night and day from the acne-riddled, blimpo Zane that we knew and abhorred as kids. I'd kill to learn his secret and that's part of why I RSVP'd yes on the invitation last month; why I ditched everything I had cooking in Cali and came like a dog to her master's whistle.

Steely J gives us a significant nod. We guests push away from half-empty plates and migrate into the parlor, wine coolers and rum and cokes in hand. I loathe the parlor. It's cold and dank, the books are moldy, and the stuffed moose head that presides here has gone blind with rot. The notion of accidently brushing against something icky gives me the shivers.

Zane unlocks a cabinet and sets a jewelry box upon the big circular granite table we're seated around. The table is slightly concave. Several parallel grooves radiate from the edge to a depression in the center. As for the jewelry case, it is an unpleasant box with the lacquer stripped. The wood is scored and blanched by patterns of fungal decay. An eighteenth-century caravel's lost antique dredged from the muck at the bottom of Cook Inlet in 1979, or so my peeps testify. Inside the box, a ring nests in crushed velvet. An indelicate description for those playing at home—its color is similar to a blood clot glistening against tissue paper. He plucks the ring and casually passes it to Morton, just like that. No formalities whatsoever.

"Damn, it's heavy," Morton says. Morton always sounds bemused or surprised.

"Don't drop it," Julie Five says. She's cool and eager. She gave Morton a hummer last August while we were all on a tour bus at Denali State Park. They speak to each other with barely restrained antipathy. "Drop it, and it's ten demerits." Gawd, I hate her smug, bitchy tone. I hate that Morton accepted her blowjob and turned me down flat. Heel.

"By the way, the table isn't granite," Zane says as if he's peeked into my brain. His gaze is cruel. "Another rock entirely. There are chains of sea caves in the Aleutians. This table is carved from the bedrock of those caves. Men died acquiring this on my behalf." He looks at Morton.

"Okay, Mort. Time to get bitten."

He is indulgent, yet commanding. T w o decades in Europe, and farther abroad, will do that to a guy, I suppose. Julie Five says Zane spent months lost in a desert and went barking mad. Eating-his-own-shoelaces fucked in the head. Wouldn't guess it to feast your eyes upon him, or maybe you would. The corners of his eyes twitch if you catch it at the right moment.

Morton makes a show of examining the ring, as if a middle manager role at an office supply store qualifies him to appraise jewelry. He's enjoying the spotlight. "Is this the Ouroboros?"

"Don't be ridiculous." Zane's sneer almost spoils the plastic charm of his perma-smile. I've long assumed his genial urbanity is a façade for darker impulses. Doesn't bother me. Everybody has got another side. It's exciting.

"If there were a *real* Dracula Ring, this would be the one," Julie Five says. "Lugosi's was pretty. Fake. Fake. Fake." She rocks. Her face is so very animated. I've seen that expression. It's the wide-eyed, lips slightly parted expression women at boxing matches wear. I'm sure the rich hoes in Rome did it the same when they attended the gladiatorial games.

The ring is formed of thick, intertwined strands of corroded iron. There's a jagged gap opposite the shank. Whether from damage or by design, I haven't a clue. The shank is set with the aforementioned gory gemstone that also, if you squint, resembles a death's head in the way a thundercloud might resemble the skull of an angry god. The stone fitfully glints with the light from the table lamp. Almost a twin to the pendant hanging from Zane's neck.

"I thought it'd be a thumb prick." Morton slips the ring onto his finger.

"Ha ha, you said prick." I laugh, but not really. No, not really.

"Dude," Vadim says with ample foreboding. "This shit is how you get sepsis or peritonitis or something."

"Quiet, punk, you're next." Julie Five grins at him. I think of a northern pike opening its needle-fanged jaws to slurp down a hook.

Zane raises his eyebrow. "A dribble of claret for the cause seems reasonable. The price for betrayal is a blood eagle. JV's idea. Be warned."

"What's a blood eagle?" I say.

"You don't want one," Vadim says.

Steely J excuses himself. He steps through a panel near a bookcase and that's the last I see of him. I think it's the very last time *anybody* sees him for a few years. Candice, his latest girlfriend remains at the table with an expression of abandonment. She's had too many wine coolers.

Neither Clint nor Leo speak. They're nervous, I can tell. Leo is a bit green around the gills. Real hard cases. Both of them agitated and wheedled to be included, and now their knees are knocking. And why are they spooked? The ceremony is bullshit. High school melodrama. This is supposed to be mock serious, like fucking about with Ouija boards and séances or homoerotic fraternity paddling rituals.

"Seven is a good number," Zane says. He's not counting himself, obviously. He's playing Satan. "Seven were the apprentices in the Devil's Grotto."

"Power number, baby," Julie Five says, Ed McMahon to his Johnny Carson.

We all stare at one another. Similar to gazing into a mirror—after a while, everybody is as plastic as Zane. I poke Morton in the ribs. Somebody has to be the first to leap and he's it. He makes a fist. Blood begins to flow. The blind moose watches as we each take our turn.

§

God, do You remember my third year in college when I saved that little old lady who fell on the ice in front of a moose that had wandered into town? I threw snowballs and shrieked until it ambled away into the trees. Surely, if You're the real deal You were there. God, please be real. Please help me now. Because I can't see anything. I'm flopped on my belly atop a heap of corpses. That can't be right. The dark is sticky. Warm, inanimate flesh yields beneath me. My pinky slips into someone's dead staring eye. Eyelashes bat against my knuckle.

Zane kisses my cheek. I'd recognize his Rico Suave cologne anywhere, even here. He says, "Welcome and congratulations. You're part of it. You'll always be part of it. I'll see you at the party. Guest of honor, Ed."

The rest of the night is a blank. Or a hole. So, thanks for that, God. If you exist, which I figure you don't. The cut in my finger doesn't close for weeks. The hole in my soul remains the equivalent of a sucking chest wound.

II: Culling

Zane Tooms makes the CNN ticker three and a half years later.

Kind of a funny story. A terrific day until that point. I spend it shopping for vintage LPs at this fat cat record producer's annual garage sale. Vinyl is my true addiction. Stronger and purer than my fondness for baby dykes, or even my love of a self-effacing bear with real taste in the arts. I spend weekends with my boyfriend Tony at his Malibu beach house. This summer my theme resounds courtesy of The Kinks: "Little Miss Queen of Darkness." I don't really identify. Drag isn't my thing and any sadness in my eyes is liable to be incidental tearing from my extra lush lashes. Nope, I love the song because its lyrics are true poetry. Poetry is distinctly lacking in this modern world. Barbarians have sacked the music industry, despoiled Hollywood. Publishing is a joke with celebrity tell-alls and Dan Brown as the punchline.

I'm lamenting these facts while sprawled on the sofa in Tony's giant game room. The news hits as I'm raising a mojito to my lips. Hard to believe my eyes. I didn't believe them either, though, when the accusations of seventy counts of Rohypnol-facilitated rape first came down to the clack of a magistrate's gavel. Apparently that dark side of Zane's was worse than I thought. Theory goes that seventy is a conservative estimate—who knows how many victims he's left scattered across Europe.

Now Zane is dead. The DEA and Mexican police shot him a bajillion times in some fleabag hotel in Mexico City. I don't know how to feel. There's a tiny white scar on the underside of my middle finger. I look at it and wonder if he ever raped *me*. Doubtful. Despite all indications, evidence is he didn't swing

for dudes. Like I said, I don't know how to feel.

"Ha! Hell yes! I told you they'd get that rat bastard!" Tony wanders in from the shower and does a sack dance in celebration. He played ball for the Forty-Niners. His gut is enormous. The old me, lily-fresh college grad, would've cared. The worn and worried me is more concerned with Tony's heart. He's a kindly soul, his celebration of Zane's demise notwithstanding. Tony heard the stories and paid for my therapy. He's earned the right to cry, "Ding-dong!" etcetera.

Oops.

The doorbell rings and it's Julie Five on the step. I almost swoon at the shock.

"So, we meet again." She's wearing sunglasses and a white sundress. Her skin is softer and pinker than I recall. Time has rejuvenated her or she's gotten on the E. Bathory program. A midnight-blue Mustang is parked in the drive with the top down. The hood symbol looks more like a particularly malformed death's head than any mustang. Three and a half years might as well be three and a half days. She makes a mou of her lips. I don't offer my cheek for the courtesy peck, no way. I'd rather let a tarantula sit on my face.

She crowds me backward. Her shadow crosses mine and my legs go weak and I collapse upon the rug where sunlight pools on nice days. This is California, so yes, the sunlight is doing that right now. She steps over my supine form and I get a peek at her goods, like it or not. Red panties to match her scary-long fingernails. The sun filtering through the fabric of the dress turns everything to crimson. She reaches into a demure handbag and produces the iron ring. Slides it onto the third finger of her left hand. She looms above me, smiling in a way I don't recognize from her repertoire. If evil and cruelty can mature the way wine does, then here you go. This goddamned cask of Amontillado's got cobwebs all over it.

"What's going on?" Tony arrives, half-naked and thundering. He quickly takes in the situation and gets right in her personal space. "Who the hell are you?"

I'm afraid he'll hit her, shatter her smirk

with his mallet fist. I'm terrified he won't. Either way, it doesn't matter. I can't move, can't speak. My body is cold from the inside out.

"You're Anthony. Hello." She extends her hand.

He brushes her gesture aside. "And you're Julie. Yeah, I recognize you. Step, lady. You aren't welcome."

"C'mon, stud. Put her there." She smirks mischievously and reaches for him again. The light in the room dims because she's sucking it into her eyes. She snags his hand and clasps it tight with both of hers the way politicians do, the way a black widow fastens to her prey. Squeezes so hard that blood drips from their joined fingers. That's the end. Tony sways in place and she stands on tiptoes to whisper into his ear. It goes on for maybe ten seconds until she releases him and steps back.

"Oh, wow," he says. Tony usually talks loud enough to break your eardrums. This is a mousy little whisper. "I'm sorry. I didn't know." His face changes as he turns away. His skin tightens and his mouth and eyes stretch at the corners, but I only catch a glimpse. He shambles toward the living room, gone forever.

"Not with a bang but a whimper," Julie Five says, quoting the only Eliot she's likely memorized. Julie didn't use her own brain to get through college. She relied upon cunning and nascent savagery. The light in the room drains away and she floats above me, a pale gemstone revolving against the void. She draws the dwindling heat from my bones and into her huge, luminous eyes.

I belatedly notice the feathered dart protruding from my breast. Steely J drifts from the unknowable depths, pistol in hand. He salutes me and drapes his arm around Julie Five's waist.

I am very, very tired.

They wink, synchronized, and I wink out.

§

Vadim talks while he carries me in his arms, the Bride of Frankenstein.

"There are these worm things, or leech things, neither, but you get the picture, and they detach or are expelled from a central mass. These worms, or leeches, crawl inside you through whatever opening is available. The urethra and the anus are likely access ways. That's what happened to the dinosaurs. It's one theory. I think it works."

"Put me down, man." My voice is hoarse and my skull aches. My breast muscle hurts too. Whatever Steely J hit me with packs a nasty hangover.

We stand there, wherever there is. An abandoned hotel lobby? Lots of dust, boarded windows, and the light fixtures are fubar. Bright though, because sunlight streams through cracks and crevices. I ask the obvious and he shrugs. He too received a visit from Julie Five and a follow-up dart from Steely J. Like me, he came to in this place.

"Uh-oh."

I follow Vadim's gaze and see a thick man all in black standing on the mezzanine steps. His face is pale and freaky as shit. The flesh is so tight, his eyes stretch to slits, their corners near his temples. A machete dangles from his fist. Blood drips from the blade.

"Tony?" Right size, wrong face, except maybe it was the right face, I'd seen it changing at the casa...

"Tony isn't Tony no more. That's Mr. Flat Affect." Vadim grips my arm. "Let's book."

We book. I try the obvious things—exterior door handles are locked and chained from the outside; the windows are barred. I glimpse a dry pool in the courtyard. The yard has gone Planet of the Apes. Grass run riot. The palm trees are dull yellow. Mort is spiked halfway up the bole of the biggest tree. He's covered in dried blood, but I recognize his voice when he calls for help, for god, for death. There are several more people nailed to trees. Harder to identify. I don't want to know.

Before long, I stop to catch my breath.

"This is about the ritual."

"Duh," Vadim says. "The goon is one of Zane's pets, or something like that."

"But why are they after us? We're part of the inner circle, right? Ground floor of the new order and all that jazz?" I hadn't taken it seriously, had only gone along because of the pressure. I hadn't swallowed ZT's apocalypse fantasies. Now, here I am trying to lawyer my way out of getting murdered.

"He lied. We're the blood in the blood pact."

"Pact with whom?"

He gives me a sad look for not paying attention during class.

Another Mr. Flat Affect saunters through a door and confronts us. He too wields a machete. However, he's clad in a white paper suit. The suit is streaked and grimy. It's a bad moment, but Savate! I expect great things from Vadim's size 11 Doc Martens. Vadim yells, "Oh fuck!" and elaborately gathers himself like he's tossing a kaber and snaps this kind of slow-mo roundhouse kick that misses by a mile. Maybe a mile and a half. He lands on his ass. And it would be hilarious except I'm shitting my capris. Mr. Flat Affect doesn't hurry; I doubt he ever hurries. He raises the machete and splits my best friend's skull. Does him like the islanders do with coconuts, with a lazy overhand chop. *Kerthunk.* The killer pauses to savor the gurgling and spurting.

Doc Martens are peachy. *I* swear by Nikes. Canary yellow with Velcro, nobody's got time for laces. I put mine to their best use—slapping tile at a high rate.

III: The Bear Catacombs

I run through an archway and am back in Alaska in the Toombs family basement. The bear catacombs. It has to be a nightmare because I instantly recognize the late 90s. Sister, those were bad times for yours truly—nobody told me "it gets better," they told me to sit down and keep my mouth shut.

A party is in progress—music on full blast, lights ablaze, half the kids from our high school graduating class doing the bump and grind. Zane lurks on the fringes, a loud, fat, glittery-eyed kid. His smile is sly. He's exactly as I remember, only more so.

There my high school self is, on the edge, crushed against a skinny senior track star. My hair is dreadful in spiked hair and a lime mesh tank top, and Stu Whitlock flaunts a mullet. Merciful Jesus, I had no idea I had so much to apologize for.

The band grinds to a halt and the lead singer chugs from a bottle of whiskey. My youthful double disappears up the stairs. A few seconds later, the shrieks begin. That would be Dave Teague, naked and insane, busting a move for the front door. I remember the rest with unpleasant clarity—there's a hot blonde Ukrainian transfer student lying mangled and murdered in a bed on the top floor. Some lowlife snuffed her and tried for the daily double with Dave. The killer is in fact shambling after Dave into the night. In a few minutes, state troopers scrag the psycho killer on the access road. I also recall that someone mentions the psycho's face is white with greasepaint, or he wears a mask, and shit, it hits me-- Mr. Flat Affect has been with us since when.

Mind. Blown.

"La!" Julie Five steps from the crowd. Modern day Julie Five, fully envenomed, egg sac probably full to bursting. She was sort of a cute kid. Not anymore. She grins and tweaks my nose. Her fingers are icy. "You're bleeding, sweetie."

The blood is Vadim's—I've come through so far without a scratch, and that's ironic, because I'd bruise if somebody stuck a pea under my mattress. I'm speechless, unable to twitch, Julie Five seems to have that effect on my nervous system. Behind her, kids begin milling around the exposed section of wall where the pipes and tree roots form a maw. There's some scuffling and I see my erstwhile date Stu Whitlock crawl inside. He's followed by that beefy guy who played linebacker the year we went to state. Then another, and another, wriggling like sperm to fit through the crack in the earth, burrowing their way to God knows where. Doesn't take long for the last pair of legs to disappear into the darkness and it's us chickens left behind in an empty basement.

Mr. Flat Affect emerges from the corner where the coats are piled. Sways in place, devilish gaze locked on me. He's a meat suit and whatever powers him came from the deep earth. I whimper.

"Don't be afraid," Julie Five says. "You made the cut. We wouldn't dream of harming a hair on your frosty little head. You're our final girl. I always hoped you would be." She takes my hand, leads me upstairs, and seats me in the parlor at a plain wooden table. The moon glows hard in the upper corner of a bay window. Its light seems to recede, shrinking to a dot as I watch. She removes a black moleskin notebook from her purse, opens it before me, and clicks the action on a ballpoint pen, places it beside the notebook. "Your memoir. It will be important someday, after everyone has forgotten how all this started. There's a fire safe in the den."

Two more Mr. Flat Affects have noiselessly appeared at her flanks. One in white, the other black. Their expressions are identically monstrous. She links arms with them and they glide into the shadows. "Good luck," she says from somewhere. Her voice echoes as if bouncing around a canyon. "Enjoy yourself."

I do as she says and write down what I know. I stash the notebook in the fire safe. Sun devours moon and the second decade of the twenty-first century absorbs the 1990s. The Tooms mansion decays around me. The table becomes stone and the stuffed moose head wilts unto a living death. I'm once again thirty-something and utterly fabulous despite the bags under my eyes, the tremor in my hand, and the caked-on gore.

Steely J, Julie Five, and Zane Tooms are long gone. The others remain as remains—Vadim, Morton, Candice, Clint, and Leo. Bloated, purple-black, in a pile near the hearth. Candice's shoe has fallen off.

Had the poison been in the ring or the liquor? The ring is how I bet. My crazy-person epistle isn't going to do me any favors in a court of law. Story like mine is a one-way trip to the booby hatch. What will happen to me when the authorities make the scene? That gets an answer when the pair of troopers roll up to investigate after the anonymous call. They are none too reassured by my appearance and wild story. Two seconds after they nearly trip over the pile of corpses, I'm staring down the barrels of automatic pistols.

My finger bleeds from a wound that will never close. I make a fist without a thought as I mumble apologies for being here in this house of horrors, wrong place, wrong time—oh, so most def the wrong time. I needn't bother. The tearing pain in my hand lends an edge to my voice. My breath steams, a dark cone, and both troopers shudder in unison. Their guns clatter on the floor. Color drains from those well-fed faces, skin snaps tight and their eyes, their mouths, shiver and stretch. The transformation requires mere seconds. Their peculiar, *click-clicking* thoughts scritch and buzz inside my own psychic killing jar. They are mine, like it or not.

I *do* like it, though. A bunch.

Mist covers the world below this lonely hilltop. It's bitter cold and I'm barely dressed, yet it doesn't touch me. Nothing can. I am Bela Lugosi's most famous character reborn and reinterpreted. The Tooms estate is my mansion on the moor, my gothic castle. Time has slipped and I wonder if Tony is still out there in Malibu, waiting to meet me and fall in love. Do I care? Must I?

Who originally said some men want to watch the world burn? Whomever, he meant assholes like Zane and Julie. They chose me, corrupted me, and invested in me some profane force. Its trickle charge impresses my brain with visions of debauched revelry, of global massacre, fire, and slavery. Do my minor part to spread mayhem and terror and a few years down the road I can be on the ground floor of a magnificent dystopian clique. I can be a lord of darkness with minions and everything.

What shall I do with such incalculable power?

"Fix me a cosmopolitan," I say to ex-trooper, ex-human, Numero Uno. He does and it's passable.

There are numerous doors inside the Tooms mansion, to say nothing of the crack that splinters through bedrock and who knows where from there. I could wreak havoc in the name of diabolical progress. Or I could flap my arms and fly to Hollywood, whisper in the right ears and watch a sea change transform the industry. Or I could return to my senior year and seize Stu Whitaker by more than the hip, tell Father dearest to get bent with a martini in one hand and a smoldering joint in the other.

Decisions, decisions, you know?

☙❧☙

A HINT OF THE DARK SIDE:
AN INTERVIEW WITH NOELLE LÉON

By Leah Jung

When I met Noelle Léon we were both on set preparing for a live television broadcast that, when it was all said and done, ended up boasting 2.4 million viewers. Miss Léon never showed a hint of frustration or impatience as she was frantically bustled back and forth between hair, makeup, wardrobe...especially wardrobe. Poor Noelle was poked and prodded, additional assistants were called into the fitting room, and an extra trip to the craft store (double-sided tape) was required. All the commotion was to alter the bikini top they gave her in a way that made her hypnotizing lady pillows qualify as family-friendly. A wardrobe malfunction on live television could put Noelle and Spike TV at the center of some major controversy! I remember how she just giggled through the whole thing, gathering the other models around her to take group photos. Everyone fell in love with Noelle. When I found out our next theme was Secret Societies, and a mesmerizing woman was needed to play the role of leader of the pack, the 5'9" stunner came to mind immediately. After talking to her a little more, I came to learn that there is MUCH more to this woman than her unforgettable beauty, including a hint of a dark side that reinforces her place here as a *Dark Discoveries* cover icon.

Leah Jung: You have been dancing your entire life (and your experience shows in your incredible YouTube videos)! Is there a certain moment or project that really solidified your title as a "choreographer?"

Noelle Léon: Yes! I have been dancing since the age of three. I started choreographing in high school for rally performances and Dance Production. While in high school we formed a dance group and were well known for winning competitions in the Bay Area (Northern California). One of the competitions was judged by famous choreographers Tony and Richmond, and recording artist Omarion. That was the defining moment that I felt solidified my title as a choreographer. Since that time I have choreographed and taught at one of the top dance academies in California as well as choreographed for a few entertainers.

LJ: We also know that you have singing, acting, and modeling on your resume...what are some creative fields you would like to explore?

NL: Funny you should ask...lately I have been into creating and editing videos. I make weird videos depending on my mood at the time.

LJ: We heard about some of these videos at your cover shoot for *Dark Discoveries*! You have worn hooded robes before, and not for a job or Halloween! It turns out that you have a bit of a dark side when you release some creative steam, yes?

NL: (Laughs) Sssshhh! Wow, I guess that bat is out of the cave. Yes! I am truly Vampira and I occasionally show my fangs and wear a hooded cape/cloak.

LJ: I love it! Your natural acting ability really shows in these DIY videos. Why do you think you don't have a larger internet following?

NL: I'm not really sure but I believe that will be changing! @noey_L by the way!

LJ: Yes, everyone follow her Instagram at @noey_L! Do you have any favorite scary movies?

NL: I have a few favorites but Michael Myers from Halloween will always be an all-time favorite.

LJ: Do you remember the first horror movie you watched, and did your family let you watch it at the time?

NL: I must have been around seven years old. My sister and I went to stay over at a friend's house and watched *Night of the Living Dead*. I was the youngest

one at the party, yet one of the few who found it "cool" and not scary. (Laughs) When people started falling asleep my sister and I would scare them awake! Now that I think about it, we were never invited back!

LJ: (Laughs) I have an older sister also! I recall you come from a family of performers, I think singers, yes? Are there a lot of similarities between you and your family members?

NL: Yes, singers and musicians. There are a lot of similarities when it comes to our love of music and football, but it ends there. I have always been the odd ball, or "unique" as my mom would say. My passion for art is not only in music, but includes tattoos, piercings, horror films and horror imagery.

LJ: When you reach the level of stardom that you could now only dream to envision, you produce your own film and there are two main roles, and you get to cast one celebrity and one friend. Who would these two be, and which one would play the good guy, which one the bad guy?

NL: (Laughs) I love this question. I would cast Robert Englund as my celebrity good guy and my friend Tanaya as the bad guy. Tanaya is your typical around-the-way, very chill, sweet girl. On the other hand, she enjoys gory activities and séances. There would definitely be an unsuspecting twist in this movie. I can see the plot now...

LJ: Last question! It's our Secret Society issue so this is a themed question. You are at an initiation into a Secret Society that promises prolonged youth. You have to either privately harvest a kidney from an unsuspecting virgin male over the age of 18, or engage in a drug-fueled orgy with the other 12 members of the Society. The reward is either permanent stunning outer beauty—but your health and guts decline normally—OR you stay perfectly healthy, agile, and intelligent for a normal lifespan, but your looks fade as they typically would. Which combination do you choose?

NL: I would definitely harvest a kidney from an unsuspecting virgin male over the age of 18, and I would stay perfectly healthy, agile and intelligent for a normal lifespan while the looks faded.

LJ: I have no clue what it reveals to prefer attempting an illegal medical procedure over dangerous sexual practices, but I am pleased to hear that you value your big brain over your immeasurable good looks. I can only hope that somehow this opportunity presents itself to you and in 50 years I know an old lady who can tear up a dance floor! Follow Noelle's adventures on Instagram at @noey_L.

❦❦❦

Photo Courtesy of Bradley Thornber

DISCOVER an ALTERNATE HISTORY

New York Times bestselling author Mark Booth brings to light the world's secret histories and human experiences.

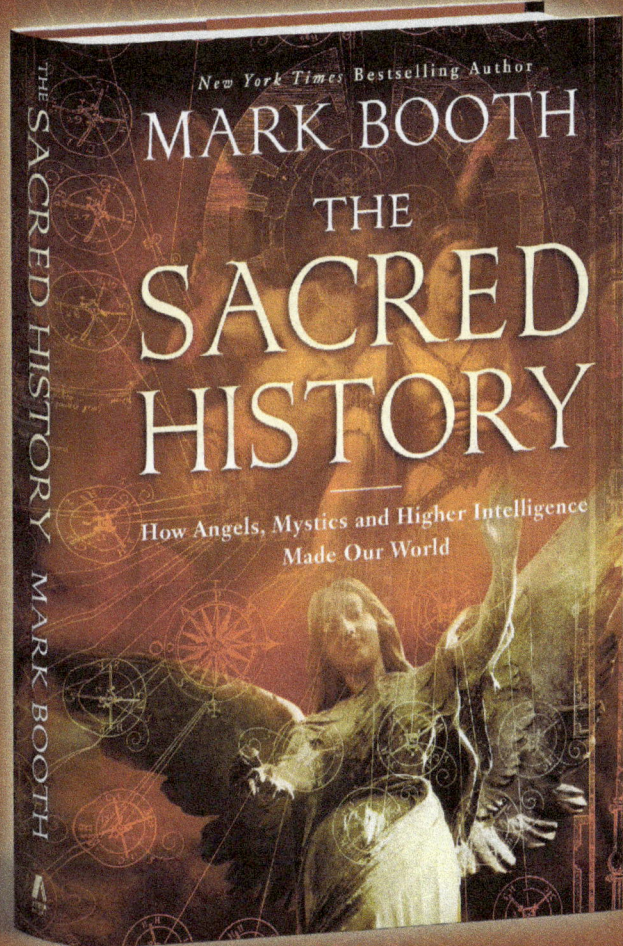

Praise for *The Sacred History*

"A masterpiece. A remarkable feat of repositioning ancient knowledge in such a way that we see truth through yet another lens. I absolutely loved this book."
—CAROLINE MYSS,
New York Times bestselling author

"Mark Booth is the C.S. Lewis of our time."
—GRAHAM HANCOCK,
New York Times bestselling author

Praise for *The Secret History of the World*

"Beautifully written. This book has my mind on fire with argument and wonder."
—ANNE RICE,
New York Times bestselling author

Also available from Mark Booth:
The Secret History of Dante

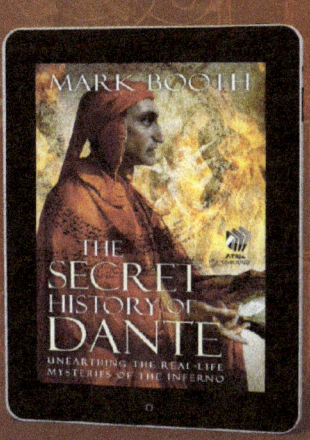

A Teller of Storied Tales:
Interviewing Glen Hirshberg

By Joel B. Kirkpatrick

Joel B. Kirkpatrick: Thanks for taking the time to answer some questions with *Dark Discoveries*, Glen. We know you're a busy man. Still teaching high school creative writing, or has your own writing career taken over as your full-time occupation?

Glen Hirshberg: Still teaching. Still running the creative writing program I've spent the last 20 years developing. Still finding so much to love about that—teaching has been so good for my writing, and vice versa—although the challenge of somehow fitting everything into the days is overwhelming, sometimes. I have taught high school for a long time, but also helped launch the MFA program at Cal State San Bernardino.

JBK: In 2006 you founded an ambitious project to foster teenage authors and publish their work in *Surrounded Magazine*. How has that project grown over the years?

GH: *Surrounded* was a thrilling, complicated experiment. So much of the writing program I've set up derives from the notion that people always underestimate what high school students are capable of producing. At the time, especially, there were so few outlets for brave work from teens that wasn't about sick grandparents or lost pets or facing a learning challenge and overcoming it or pretending you're a toothbrush.

The magazine had a great nine-year run, but this past year, I had a particularly passionate, thoughtful staff of teen-editors, and we decided, together, that *Surrounded* had run its course. The reasons for that are many and complicated.

But the best reason is that we've come up with something we're even more passionate about devoting out energies to:

While I was at CSUSB, I developed a program called CREW (that's Creative wRiting Experimental Workshop), through which I trained some of my

most committed graduate students in the essential techniques and ideals upon which I'd built my high school program, and then sent them out into the San Bernardino Unified School District—which has so few resources, and can offer so few creative outlets of any kind—to run intensive, months-long creative writing workshops in the spring. The impact of that experience on both my students and the students they taught proved to be…electrifying, honestly. Fulfilling, to say the least.

When I returned to Campbell Hall (the high school where I've spent much of my career), I brought that program with me. In partnership with L.A.'s Best, a fantastic organization providing enrichment opportunities for some of the least-advantaged students in Los Angeles, we've begun running CREW workshops through which my top high schoolers train all year with me and then teach workshops at local elementary schools that have no programs of their own in March and April. We've just shot a documentary about this at L.A.'s Best's request, and in place of *Surrounded*, we're now editing a magazine devoted to the work of the elementary students that my current students teach.

JBK: Have any of your students been published outside of *Surrounded*?

GH: The people we published in *Surrounded* are still mostly pretty young, remember. I'm sure you will hear about them. I have a number of former students blossoming into working artists in many media. The artist and magazine founder Maren Miller springs immediately to mind. And I just attended a book launch/gallery show for Nicola Rowlands' new project, *On the Road to the Sea*, which pairs her disconcertingly sensualized photographs with the work of the unjustly forgotten Victorian poet Charlotte Mew. Gina Hanson, a major talent from CSUSB, has been publishing some superb stories.

JBK: Let's get down to business. How much of your reason for writing *Motherless Child* was about putting vampires back in proper perspective?

GH: To be frank, I couldn't care less about the status of vampires, and don't think there is a "proper" perspective. There are just different stories to tell. If anything, I resisted the pull of *Motherless Child* because I'd convinced myself I had nothing to add to the overcrowded vampire landscape. But Natalie

and Sophie, the two young women at the heart of the novel, just took up residence in my head, and they refused to get out until I got them down on paper. And then I found maybe I had something to add, after all. And they still won't leave, those two women, and they won't shut up. So I guess I'm not done with them yet...

JBK: Your debut novel *The Snowman's Children* earned much praise, and yet readers point out the shifted focus of the book. Neither about the murderer nor his victims, the tale instead is about the broader, devastating effects of such crimes upon a community. That story seed was rooted in reality: You were only ten when such horror came to your own neighborhood in Oakland County near Detroit.

GH: The actual seed for that novel was less my experiences at the time than an experience I had much later, when I returned to Detroit for the wedding of one of my last remaining friends there. I wound up at a table surrounded by all of my friends from elementary school, most of whom I hadn't seen or spoken to in 15-20 years. And somehow, at some point, someone brought up the Oakland County Child Killer, the monster of all of our childhoods. And all of these stories started spilling out. Everyone at the table had one, about things that happened at school, conversations they'd overheard, dreams they'd had.

I went back to my little hotel room thinking about that. About the way being even in the vicinity of a monstrous sequence of events like that transforms lives. We were all, in subtle and not-subtle ways, different adults than we might have been because we shared that experience as children.

And so I set out to try and capture that, and tell a riveting, very much fictionalized version of that story that did *not* exploit but rather honored the memory of the kids who actually were killed (I didn't know them personally), and whose names I can recite to this day.

JBK: We can't get a clear sense, Glen, for which of these writers you might be: A nonfiction writer dabbling in fiction, a short story writer dabbling in horror novels, a writer who will put down on paper any good idea that he can find time for.... You've been called an *"important new voice in American Literature"* and yet you've been writing for a couple of decades in every print medium possible. How do you define yourself?

GH: Ha. You've just deftly defined the living, breathing marketing challenge that is the career of Glen Hirshberg. If I could somehow say so without sounding like a pretentious jerk, I'd tell you that the career I aspire to would be Robert Louis Stevenson's, Rudyard Kipling's; guys you could trust to give you characters worth remembering, in situations worth inhabiting, about emotions and ideas worth feeling and thinking about, no matter the genre.

What I can tell you is this: I'm not a "dabbler" in anything. I've been telling stories to anyone who would listen since I was two years old. Other than parenting my children and being with my family, writing is the greatest joy I've ever known. Even I don't know where I'd slot some of the things I've produced. But I've never put anything out there that didn't have everything I have to offer in it. So I guess I'd just define myself as a writer, period.

JBK: You once said of the rock group Sleater-Kinney in an L.A. Weekly music review that you, *"...love their refusal to accept anyone else's agenda—*

"Fresh, clear, practical steps for moving creativity from the drawing room to the boardroom." —MAX DEPREE, author of *LEADERSHIP IS AN ART*

THE CREATIVE PRIORITY

PUTTING INNOVATION TO WORK IN YOUR BUSINESS

Jerry Hirshberg

FOUNDER AND PRESIDENT, NISSAN DESIGN INTERNATIONAL

even that of the community that spawned them." Is that who you are, a writer fulfilling his own urges?

GH: Yes and no. Yes, because the only way I ever write anything I think is good is by writing the thing that wants to be written. And no, because for me, writing is essentially and crucially an act of communication. A conversation with the living, breathing, real person who is reading me. I talk to myself enough just walking around, every day. I don't need to write to myself on top of that.

JBK: How much of your drive, organization, insight, ambition, perspective, and imagination has been inspired by your own father, Jerry Hirshberg—founder of Nissan Design International?

GH: I got inspiration and support from both of my parents. I was profoundly lucky that way. My dad is a musician, a designer, a painter, a writer, an art-junkie like me. Art is the way he sees the world. The way he communicates the most of himself. The way the world communicates with him. My mother was a psychologist, and her incisive and instinctive compassion for what drives people to do what they do has also played a significant part in the way I learned to craft stories.

JBK: People have very similar praise for his book *Creative Priority* that you receive for much of your own prose. He wrote a book about successful design and business strategy as well as any storyteller could. Is he a fan of your work?

GH: You'd have to ask him. But yeah, I'm pretty sure he is.

JBK: Your father headed design for Buick and Pontiac at General Motors for sixteen years—then changed directions entirely with his move to Nissan in 1980—a background that we can be certain made him somewhat colorfully opinionated on socio-economic matters. Almost without blinking, you pen *The Book of Bunk,* which you describe as *"A creation myth about a vanished country that may or may not have existed, and the very real, conflicted nation that has sprung from it."* Are we wrong in assuming possible parallels of thought there?

GH: What an intriguing question. Actually, *The Book of Bunk*—which took me thirteen years to get right,

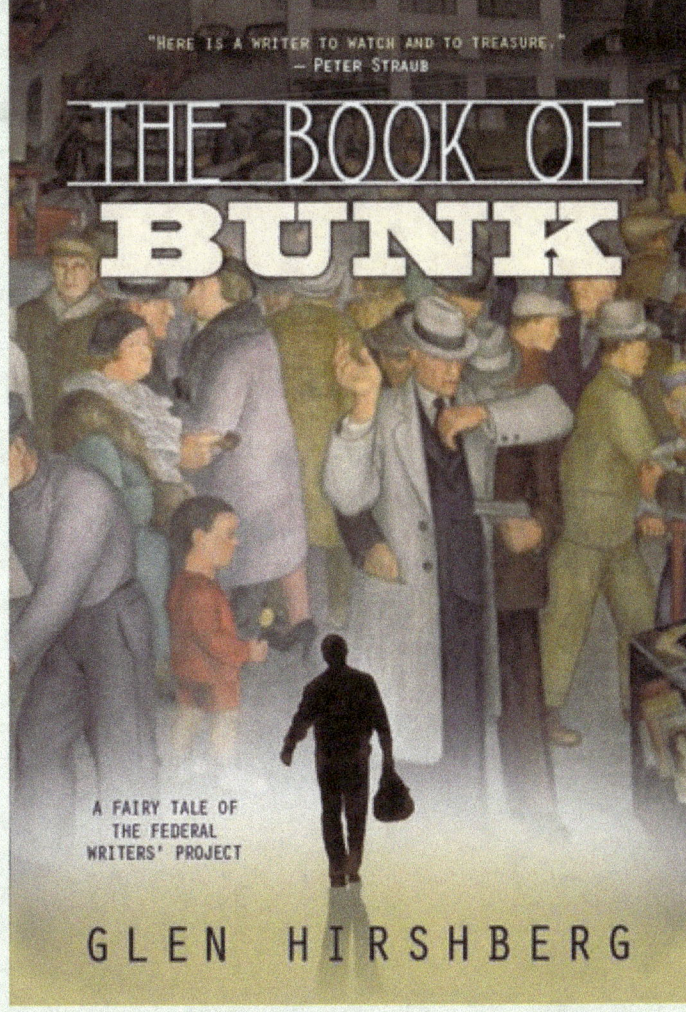

"HERE IS A WRITER TO WATCH AND TO TREASURE."
— PETER STRAUB

THE BOOK OF BUNK

A FAIRY TALE OF THE FEDERAL WRITERS' PROJECT

GLEN HIRSHBERG

so that was a long blink—did come, in part, out of an experience my dad had, but not as a designer. For a brief time, he was head of the Port Commission in San Diego, charged with selecting and/or commissioning public art for parks and sites. The startling, sometimes thrilling, often frightening debates he wound up having with all kinds of people, as a result, triggered lots of thoughts for me about why Americans have always viewed their artists with such suspicion and disdain, and also why American artists have often treated the public with contempt. For a self-declared nation of dreamers, we get awfully worked up about one another's dreams.

JBK: Returning to your latest release, *Motherless Child,* that book was first issued in a limited release which sold out as soon as it was printed. We know you are working on the sequel, *Good Girls,* due out next year. Readers can expect a third book to follow. Had you planned three books from the beginning, or did the obvious success of *Motherless Child* help drive that possibility into a reality?

GH: Definitely the latter, although when I was first

Glen Hirshberg (L) and Peter Atkins (R) founded the Rolling Darkness Revue

asked about writing a trilogy, I said no, because I didn't think I had anything left to say. Twenty-four hours after Tor offered to purchase a trilogy from me, when I realized that Natalie and Sophie (the characters I mentioned above) *still* hadn't shut up, still apparently had more story to tell me, I called Tor back and accepted.

JBK: A definitively Southern horror novel, you wrote it from the inspirations of the region itself, its music and its people. When did you live in the South?

GH: I lived in Charlotte, North Carolina, for just a few years back in the early '90s, though we roamed as widely as possible through the region during that time. I am a lover and writer of place, wherever I can find it. Whatever else anyone thinks about the South, it is a *place.* And so even though I was only there for a short time, the region soaked into me. And it keeps popping up in my stories.

JBK: Tell us about the Rolling Darkness Revue and how you participate. How does that creative outlet

parallel or augment your work as a writer? You and Pete Atkins die every single performance, don't you?

GH: The Rolling Darkness Revue got dreamed up by Peter Atkins, Dennis Etchison, and me over endless Big Boys at the famous Bob's in Burbank. The idea was really just to make readings more fun for the audience, and also to create the Halloween experience we all wished we could find. We wanted to bring the campfire to the bookstore, or whatever little theater would have us. Dennis retired from active duty after a few years, but Pete and I have done the show up and down the west coast and even internationally for nine of the last ten years.

It has evolved into a multi-media performance, with live music and amateur (but clever—some of them are pretty clever) special effects and a framing play surrounding readings of ghost stories. The framing play usually concerns Pete's and my alter-egos, Algy and Arty. Algy and Arty rarely survive the evening.

It's something I dread every year, because of the work involved.

And look forward to, desperately. It's just such a rare opportunity to connect with an audience, show ourselves and everyone who comes to see us a good, October time.

JBK: You've been doing this a good number of years, and in a mishmash of venues. You always involve the audience. What performance or location just stands out to you as the most bizarre, or most fun?

GH: Well, my new favorite moment has to be last year's finale, when my daughter (aged 10 at the time) made her Rolling Dark debut, in stunning fashion and ghastly make-up designed by wife, drawing actual gasps from at least a few audience members. We've had audience members tossing papier-mâché parrots we've made, we had people humming our score for us when our musicians got sick. It's live theatre, it's nuts, Pete is a great friend, and the whole thing has been such a good experience. And a shared one, which is something writers never get nearly enough of.

JBK: In your May blog post "Motherless Child Eve," you coach yourself by saying, *"Tomorrow, before I do anything else, I get to get up early and go straight to my desk and work on the next book."* Is blogging a necessary evil? How important is a cyber-presence?

GH: The only thing in the writing life worth trusting—the only joy or reward that you can trust will always be there—is the work. So I try never to forget how much I love the work. How much being a writer, every day, has given me. As for blogging, cyber-presence…I don't know. I like talking with people, interacting with people. I also teach and parent and write fiction. There's only so much time.

JBK: How much time do you spend reading? Do you have favorite writers?

GH: I read as much as I can. I feel I mention the same writers over and over when I'm asked this—Stevenson and Kipling and Shirley Jackson, Ramsey Campbell, Raymond Chandler, Ann-Marie Macdonald, Peter Straub, Jane Austen.

JBK: How much do you focus on the importance of reading with your high school students?

GH: Mostly, what I try to do is communicate how much love of language has transformed and lifted every second of my life. I tell a lot of stories. I get *them* to tell a lot of stories. I don't have to give lectures on the importance of reading, mostly. Within a few weeks—when I'm good, when they're willing, which happens with gratifying frequency—we're just having so much fun talking about what the kids are writing and what they're reading and what I'm reading and what we've read together that we never have to have the "importance" discussion.

JBK: Publishing has changed fundamentally over the last twenty years—and you have been writing successfully through all the turmoil. Do you work with an agent exclusively? How does a Glen Hirshberg book normally get to print?

GH: There have been a lot of different roads to getting in print for me. I worked with a good agent for a long time, had some productive years. But I wound up feeling like I had to go in a different direction. While hunting another agent, I started representing myself. That has worked out shockingly well so far. I do whatever works. And I'm involved in everything. I think you have to be. No one's going to do it for you.

JBK: You obviously believe in the strength of live readings and performance, so how a story is *delivered* must be very important to you. There is something tangibly romantic about a printed book, and certain things terribly impersonal about electronic devices. As the publishing technology changes, do you think the story's power might be diminished?

GH: I do think that. Yeah. Look, I know this might be generational. And of course, I want people to be able to read my stuff in any format that makes them happy. But there's a reason I can still name the books, in order, on the shelf above my bed in every single room where I've ever lived. And they weren't the same books, either. Without question, technology creates that aura of disposability. It's why so many otherwise completely ethical people seem to feel so comfortable downloading and stealing eBooks or music. There's just a sense that it's all ephemeral, not quite a real thing in the first place. And I think people's art deserves better.

JBK: Walk into a bookstore in your mind…and tell us where your books are shelved. Are you in horror? Is there a proper category for your work, or do you have to create a new section? Do brick-and-mortar stores hide good authors' works, perhaps because they have never found a proper way to get them shelved?

GH: It's certainly been a challenge in my career. I want to be filed wherever open-minded readers will find me. I worry more about the way marketing has so successfully trained people to believe that they read "literature" or "horror"—that those are necessarily different things—whereas I think most readers are just readers. Lovers of good stuff. I want to be worthy of and found by those people.

JBK: Is it true, then, that your books sell best online? Do you even know how those two different points-of-sale compare to one another?

GH: I try not to keep track. That way lies madness. Even more madness, I mean…

JBK: How many of your stories are out of print? Is it possible, through any means, to become a rabid fan of your work and collect everything you've ever published? Is it a struggle to revive stories that have just fallen out of public view?

GH: Well, here's one way in which I *love* eBooks: *everything* of mine is available, at least digitally, except my 2011 story collection, *The Janus Tree*, which just sold out its print run. I should have a digital edition of that available soon. And it is certainly my hope and plan to have all my titles back in physical print as soon as I can make that happen.

JBK: What author, and which book of theirs, scared the daylights out of you, and why?

GH: Ramsey Campbell's *Dark Companions*. There's a tangible reality to those stories—a suffocating, relentless unease, that comes as much from interpersonal misunderstandings and personal longings as from the very real monsters in the gorgeously evoked shadows—that got in my thoughts, my dreams, my food for a while. I could literally taste them. Shirley Jackson's "Daemon Lover." Again, the reality of it all, combined with the dissolving sense of certainty, the fragmentation of one's sense of self…

JBK: In several interviews you hint at your boundless affection for your *brilliant* wife. Is she an uber-fan for you?

GH: She's not a fan-wife. I didn't marry one of those. I married a kind but direct, ruthlessly honest, funny woman who is always my first and best reader, and will never let me get away with less than I can give, and puts up with my pouting and arguing when she's done critiquing, but before I've given in and gone back to work. She's a superb teacher and a better poet/writer than she realizes. I'm not her fan, either. I'd rather be her partner.

JBK: In *The Janus Tree and Other Stories* you have two connected pieces that offer readers a glimpse into a dark future where books have been abandoned in vast depositories, and the only readers are members of a subculture that wander the shadows of the dead libraries. Is that a personal nightmare, which you have shared, in which the printed word fades to meaninglessness? Are we doomed, when our printed words mean nothing?

GH: That scares me, for sure. I still have more of those stories I want to write.

※ ※ ※

Photo Courtesy of Glenn Hirshberg

 "Now see," the Collector half-shouted, while the Terry Riley music blasting from his speakers whirled through the sunlit room like leaves in a spring wind, "this is the secret to sustained happiness. Right here." Then he took a slurp of whatever it was he'd brewed that morning, leaned still closer to whichever of his thousand blogs and private web-boards had momentarily drawn his attention, and forgot he'd been speaking.

To amuse herself, mostly—and to stand silent a little longer in the light pouring through the cracked bay window, flecked with new-grass green—Nadine let him forget. Despite the clamorous music and the chatter from the radio also blaring by the Collector's side, their cabin somehow retained its stillness, like a mountain cave. A place they inhabited rather than owned, even while they owned it. A proper place, in other words.

Setting her own mug on the countertop, she glanced once at the correspondence that needed answering and the separate piles of research materials strewn across coffee table and kitchen table and living room floor, and decided to badger the Collector just a little more. She walked up behind him, leaned over, and let a twist of her dark hair dance down his cheek.

"What's that, then?" she murmured.

Ignoring—no, not even feeling—her hair or her breath, the Collector gestured at his computer screen. "Remember that woman and her gun shell-casings who—"

"The secret of sustained happiness," Nadine said. "Not the website."

Around them, music pulsed and spun. On the desktop, the radio chattered. And against Nadine's breast, the Collector thrummed with the heat of his thoughts.

"Oh," he said. "Wanting to work."

Nadine sighed. "And here, I thought it was giving the love of your life the rogering of her dreams before you're even properly awake."

He did glance up then, at least, bumping her chin with his head. "What? No. That…that's waking up, period. That's a given. A necessity. Not even momentary happiness is possible without—"

Laughing while he floundered, Nadine started to hug him, and he pushed her out of the way.

"Hang on, listen." He turned up the radio.

The *Morning Edition* theme fading. Susan or Alex or some other of those genial hosts offering yet another gently ironic intro to the new half-hour, in that tone that made every one of them sound so clever, professional, and knowing. So little like anyone she'd care to know.

"*Just how good are the baked goods at Hexenhaus Bakery in Oak Park, Michigan? Last night, a determined thief smashed through the shop's front window with an aluminum bat. The thief left the cash register and safe untouched. But he cleaned every last crumb out of both pastry cases. No word on whether he got to the milk in the refrigerator. It's Morning Edition.*"

"Well, thanks for putting a stop to our morning flirtation, I wouldn't want to have missed that…" Nadine started, before realizing she was speaking to an empty chair.

Moments later, the Collector reemerged from the back bedroom fully dressed, untied wingtip-laces flapping, balled up green windbreaker under his arm. He stopped when he saw her.

"Aren't you coming?"

Their drive took them over the Donner Pass into Nevada. On the slopes of the mountains, poppies and popcorn flower and lupine unfurled in the grass and old snow like flags from obscure nations. As usual in the spring, the Collector had left the Jeep's sides unzipped, which meant that every now and then, whiffs of pine resin surfaced in the soup of diesel smoke belching from the logging trucks in front of them.

Sighing, closer to content than she would have expected, Nadine opened her laptop. "Want to give me something to start on, my dear?"

"Don't want to spoil your appetite," said the Collector.

"Care to whet it?"

That was the moment, generally—always, really—when he told her something. Or asked her to look something up. Also the moment he grinned at her, or in her general direction, anyway. This time, though, he barely glanced in her direction, then returned his eyes to the road.

"Just tell me what you see. I'll tell you when."

But of course he didn't tell her anything. An hour later, they were on the outskirts of Reno, bumping down a sandy road past two trailer parks, then a long stretch of Nevada nothing, until they came to a surprisingly homey cabin tucked back amid the mesquite bushes. The cabin had shingle walls and a flat roof and solar panels that flashed, blinding, in the mid-morning sun. It was also bigger than Nadine initially thought, burrowing back into the rocky hillside behind it.

Stepping out of the Jeep, expecting desert silence, Nadine instead heard humming and buzzing from the generators tucked against both sides of the cabin. There was nothing else but sand and dead yucca stalks and desert shrub for miles around. In the wide blue sky, a single black, winged thing circled.

"Is this place completely off-grid?" she asked. "Is that why you didn't call whoever this is first, or—"

The cry that sailed out the cabin's barely-open front window had so little breath in it, so little human tone, that Nadine first mistook it for a squawk from the bird overhead. Then came a scuttling, quick and clumsy, and the front door flew open, and the old man stumbled out.

Stopping a few steps in front of them—tall, spindly in too-long shorts and a gray t-shirt that sagged off him like skin coming loose—the man stared at them out of watery blue eyes. His actual skin was covered in fine gray hairs, like a tarantula's. Fumbling in his pockets, he withdrew a pair of scratched spectacles and jammed them onto his face. Then he stared some more.

"It *is* you," he said.

Not hairs, Nadine realized, but distortions in the air caused by the man's constant, twitching tremors. The Collector had stayed quiet, letting her observe. When Nadine glanced toward him, she found him looking at her, the sky, the house, but not the old man, and she couldn't read his expression.

The trembling guy burst into tears. "It *is* you. You've found them. After all these years. I'd given up hope."

Only now did the Collector smile. Vaguely. "I promised my colleague here a reward for coming all the way out here."

"You did?" said Nadine.

"Reward?" said the old man.

"A hint of what you want from us."

For a second, Nadine thought the old man was literally going to tremble to pieces. She turned on the Collector, started to snap at him. But he was standing absolutely still, hands in his pockets.

"What I…" the old man mumbled. Then he straightened, got some control of his shakes, pushed his glasses into place against his face. And smiled. His teeth white, bright, glinting. "Of

course. Come in. Come in, come in. I'm so very glad you're here." Waving them to follow, he led Nadine and the Collector into the cabin.

The interior proved dim and cool, cave-like. The air hung heavy, hushed as opposed to still, and Nadine found herself moving slowly, then more slowly. The old man directed them to tall, wooden chairs drawn up to a wooden table laid with a pristine white tablecloth. The edges of the tablecloth hung so precisely, the corners cut so sharply, that at first Nadine thought it was some sort of enamel design-feature. But it rippled, soundlessly, as she drew back a chair. In the exact center of the table, a crystal vase housed three stalks of pink flowers, their clustered petals folding together like filigreed cake frosting. Mozart music didn't so much fill the air as infuse it. Nadine realized she wasn't even sure whether it had been playing when they came in or switched on after they entered.

"Did we just teleport somewhere?" she whispered as the Collector settled himself into the chair nearest hers.

The old man returned bearing a silver salver laden with flower-patterned china tea cups and saucers and a single, covered china plate. The effect was spoiled only by the rattling the china made in the old man's tremulous hands as he lifted each cup and saucer and laid them, just so, before his guests. "Let me…" the old man murmured. "Allow me to…"

Nadine started to get up to help, but the Collector squeezed her wrist beneath the table and drew her back into her seat.

"Allow him," the Collector said.

Nadine studied his face, waiting for the smile that usually accompanied his invitations to some new experience. But instead of smiling, he squeezed her wrist again; whatever that was meant to convey, Nadine didn't get it.

The old man went on placing and replacing the cups until he had them where he wanted, and then laid the covered plate precisely between Nadine and the Collector.

"There, now," he said, and lifted the cover.

The room's low light helped Nadine hide her disappointment. She wasn't sure exactly what she'd expected. But after the tablecloth, the flowers, the music, the fact that she'd dropped off the map with the Collector again…

On the plate sat two little loaves, dull brown in

color. They'd once been rectangular, but now had broken edges and crumbling bits that made them look like woodchips. Several silent seconds passed, long enough for Nadine to feel the awkwardness, and she'd leaned forward to mumble something vaguely appreciative when both loaves winked.

Winked?

They did it again, in different places, and Nadine felt herself peering down. Sprinkled all over the loaves were dozens of tiny red flecks. As soon as she had noticed the flecks, she became aware of the snowflakes, faint dustings of sugar-smoke so lacey and delicate and *alive* that they almost seemed to be sifting down from the air.

"Taste," the old man said. Commanded, actually.

Both she and the Collector moved hands toward the plate at exactly the same slow, cautious speed, as though wary of scaring off some rare, frightened, living thing. The loaf, when she touched it, proved warm; not hot, not even toasted, the heat organic somehow, radiating out rather than baked in. However delicate the sugar snowflakes looked, not a one so much as moved when she lifted the loaf between thumb and forefinger. The taste began to steep into her senses—all of them, registering through her skin and eyes as well as her nose—long before her fingers reached her mouth.

"Forbidden?" the Collector murmured. Then the loaf reached his lips, and he stopped talking.

The old man said nothing, just watched and shook until both Nadine and the Collector had taken their first bites. Then—with a flat-lipped expression Nadine first read as a suppressed smile, then realized might be impatience bordering on fury—he nodded.

"*Ja.* Probably. I have…made adjustments. But they would of course say so."

"They?" Nadine murmured eventually, the loaf long gone but the tastes still trickling into each other on her tongue, combining, swirling, recombining. *Pepper,* maybe? Mint, certainly. Cinnamon. Some ghost-fruit-something. Ginger. It would be a long time before she touched the tea. If she ever did. This taste would have to leave her of its own accord.

"The Guild," said the old man.

"Guild?"

The Collector sighed, his eyes still closed, his empty fingers by his nose so he could smell the residue as well as taste it. That seemed such a good idea that Nadine immediately followed suit.

"*Lebkuchen* Guild," the Collector murmured. "Nuremberg branch. One of them."

"There is only one," the old man said. "One that matters."

At that, the Collector did grin. Nadine, too, without knowing yet what this guy meant but enjoying the comment anyway. It was just the sort of thing the Collector's clients always said.

The old man did not grin.

"The only one," the Collector corrected himself. "Technically, Nadine, these…cookies, I guess we should call them…are not allowed to be made outside of Nuremberg. By anyone. Not even privately, for honored guests. Our man here could be held accountable."

"You will tell me?" whimpered the old man. "Is it today? Will I see them today?" And just like that, trembling in his own living room with his perfect flowers and coffee smells and Mozart music all around him, he burst into tears. "Will I have them today?"

The Collector shrugged. "I had to make sure you were still out here first, didn't I? Had to make sure you were still interested."

The old man's breath came out hissing. "You don't even know? You came to me, and you are not sure?"

Looking up through *lebkuchen*-dusted fingers, the Collector met his client's gaze and held it. The old man was shuddering so hard, Nadine could hear his teeth.

"Norm," she whispered. "What the hell are you doing?"

"I'll know for certain tonight," the Collector said, flatly, to the old man. "At least, I'll know if this is a real lead. The second I *am* certain, I'll be in touch." Without so much as a nod or thank you, he stood. "Come on, Nadine. We have a long drive to the airport, then a long flight."

But Nadine found that she wasn't quite ready to go, yet. Or rather, she wasn't quite ready to plunk herself into the Jeep with the Collector. Not in his current mood. Whatever the hell it was.

"May I use the bathroom?" she asked the old man. Not even looking at the Collector, she followed the direction of her host's shaking hand into a dim, surprisingly long back hallway. She passed a single bedroom with a half-closed door and a tall, unlatched linen closet on her way to the very rear of the house.

When she'd finished, she stood a little longer by the mirror, in this tiny space lit only by a single-bulbed, bent-necked metal lamp that made her think, incongruously, of interrogation rooms in '40's gangster films. The lamp might have made her sad except for the shine on it. Everything this man owned, he took care of. On the countertop, centered perfectly in the glow of the lamp—as though the old man stood right here, and only here, to read it—lay a spiral-bound packet of papers covered in translucent vellum. The vellum looked markless, as though it had only been handled with gloves. In the center of the cover, a single, flowering tree had been stamped, its roots burrowing down the page. Above the tree rose a single word: *Lebensborn*. The word tingled on Natalie's tongue as she mouthed it, seemed to light a fuse buried somewhere in the back of her brain. She stood still a moment, let the fuse run. But no revelations burst upon her. Gently—using a tissue to keep her fingers from blotting the vellum—she flipped through the papers. But everything was written in German.

Closing the packet and switching off the light, Natalie realized that she didn't even know what she and the Collector were hunting, this time. Bent-necked metal lamps, for all she knew. From down the hall, Mozart music ghosted, twinkling and ephemeral as the sugar on the old man's cookie-loaves. And still, that taste—those tastes—floated on her tongue.

In the hall, lit only by the glow from the dining room at the far end, Nadine passed back in front of the single row of pictures she hadn't noticed before. All of them black and white. The first showed a cottage in snow, somewhere sleepy, far away, European, and old, with a young woman out front. The woman had a snow shovel in her hands, and a sort of smile seemed to play on her thin lips through the steam of her breath. Her eyes were the clear gray of blue eyes in colorless prints. Her gaze seemed aimed far from wherever it was she was standing. In the second frame, Natalie found a framed certificate of some kind. Then more photos, one of a soldier on a train platform. A single shot of a child, trailing something behind him—*a kite? Maybe?*—racing through long grass along the lip of a sloping pine forest that was nowhere in this country, or on this continent. Only in her native Ireland had Nadine seen forests like

that. Thick, dense, shadowed. Ancient. But no Irish forests sloped that way, not at that angle. These were mountain trees.

And that isn't a kite, she realized. Stopped. Looked closer. Felt the prickle in her skin long before understanding reached her brain.

Little boy, hurtling past dark trees. Black flag like the giant wings of something swooping down upon him. Except that he was holding it. Next to that picture was another, this one of rows and rows and rows and rows of little boys. Five or six years old, maybe. Their lines perfect. Their hands outstretched in identical perpendiculars from their shoulders.

Straightening, Nadine felt her back brush the door of the linen closet. Turning, as though in a trance, she pulled the door open.

Towels. More tablecloths, their folds crisp, tight, perfect. And there. On the top shelf, two perfect, folded flags. One of them almost certainly the very flag she'd mistaken for a kite in the photo behind her. Which she suddenly didn't *like* having behind her. She whirled, found the photo where she'd left it.

Returning her attention to the closet, Nadine stared at the flags. The red and black flags. She didn't need to unfold them to know what insignia they bore, and she didn't want to touch them. But she did anyway. And that's when she felt the box underneath. Before she could stop herself, she'd pushed the flags back. Then she just stared in disbelief.

An actual copy. The real thing. The box edges just a little rounded but the colors still bright, even in these shadows. Nadine had read about this game, but hadn't quite believed it had ever been real, somehow. Certainly not played. Not by actual children. Her hand lifted again. The same hand that still trailed those faint, twinkling *lebkuchen* smells. Moving slowly this time, as though over a candle flame. Or toward a dead thing.

JUDEN RAUCH! the box proclaimed. *Wenn Sie erreichen, weg von 6 Juden zu sehen…*

Jerking back her hand, Nadine shoved the closet door shut, then lurched backward, half-expecting the old man to be right on the other side, trembling. Instead, she found empty hallway, empty dining room beyond. The Collector and the old man already outside, apparently. Leaving her alone in here.

She was almost sprinting by the time she

reached the front door of the cabin—*bunker, really; that's what this place was*—and emerged, blinking, into the sunlight. The Collector had not just climbed into the Jeep but zipped his side and started the engine. With a mumbled "Bye," Nadine moved fast past the old man, who stood as if rooted on his front walk, shaking in the dust-flecked breeze, head sideways, arms juddering crookedly at his sides. Like a mesquite bush. Desert weed.

She waited until she had herself zipped in, until the Collector had turned the Jeep and they were safely back on paved highway and headed for plain old ugly, horrible Reno. Then she turned on him. "*Lebensborn*," she said.

The Collector simply nodded. Glanced her way, but only for a moment. "So that's it," he said. "I knew it was something."

After that, and for some time, the Collector drove in silence. And because of the fading tastes in her mouth, the ghost-scents on her fingers, that photograph of the boy and flag and forest still hovering under her eyelids, Nadine only registered the speed at which they moved—or lack, thereof—at the moment the Collector stirred, grunted, and drove the gas pedal into its accustomed depression in the floorboards. The Jeep rocketed forward.

"Good morning," Nadine murmured, because that's how she felt. How both of them felt, apparently. As though they'd been drugged, and were just stirring.

"*Lebensborn*," said the Collector, turning the steering wheel just slightly left, then right, the way he always did on open straightaways, like a little boy playing a video game. "Hitler Youth? Is that right?"

"Not quite." Nadine opened her laptop, confirming what she'd already dredged from her memory. "More Hitler Youth-in-Training. Kidnapped Hitler Youth-in-Training."

"Kidnapped? All of them?"

Nadine shook her head, thought of the old man's metal-backed lamp. His Mozart music and white tablecloths and winking cookies. *How was she supposed to feel about all that?* That was the question she was here to answer, of course. The reason the Collector had told her nothing beforehand. He wanted her to sort this out for him.

"No," she said. "I don't think so. Actually, wait, I think it started as an anti-abortion campaign? Maybe? I'm checking. But some of them were kidnapped. From little villages, mostly from

Poland. I think? They'd take these kids—little kids, like babies to five-year-olds—from their mothers, and set them in Nazi foster homes or training institutes or whatever."

"To fight? To become soldiers?"

"Hold on." She tapped away at her keyboard. "No. I mean, eventually, probably. But they were too young for the war. They got indoctrinated instead as True Aryans. Master Race, the Next Generation. And then the war ended before almost any of them came of age. And these kids…" She looked up from the computer, stared straight ahead of her. "I think they just got sent home. As in, to their original homes. Or just…dispersed. To wherever."

"Not retrained or de-programmed?"

Returning to her laptop keys, Nadine stayed silent. Hunting. Trying to trace the word that had triggered her revelation. *Lebensborn*.

"Not then." She stared at the translation of the page she'd found, then at the desert rolling by outside her window. Cactus and casino billboards. A McDonalds, an oil derrick, two hitchhiking Hispanics so covered in sand they looked more like dust devils than people. The great American nowhere. No one's Fatherland. "Not ever, really. There are organizations, now. A couple support groups. And those formed only pretty recently, it looks like. Kind of…Nearly-Nazis Anonymous? Now that all these people are too old for any support or de-programming to matter. Whatever sense they've made of their lives, they've made it by themselves. Are you listening?"

"Always," said the Collector.

Nadine knew, from long experience, that that was true. Even when he wasn't actively listening, the Collector seemed to hear her. But today, he seemed unusually distracted even for him. His eyes flicking from road to mirror to desert, but focused on nothing. A hum in his throat. And so she was surprised when he turned, just as they'd pulled into a parking space at Reno-Tahoe, pulled a pack of licorice gum from his pocket, started to offer her a piece, remembered what both of them were still tasting, and put the gum back.

"I don't want to pollute my taste buds," he said.

"Ever again," said Nadine.

"What if we get hungry?"

She smiled. "It's a problem."

"So you're saying I *should* be sorry for him. For

the old man. Our client. Right?"

Surprised—as much by the intensity of the question as the question itself—Nadine pursed her lips and took another moment to try and sort what she herself felt. She thought of the flags folded in that linen closet in that dark hallway. The game they shrouded. *Wenn Sie erreichen, weg von 6 Juden zu sehen…*

"You know him better than I do," she finally said.

"I very much doubt that," said the Collector, and he took her hand, held it, and looked at her. He was taller than she was, and yet his gaze somehow seemed aimed upward, like a five year-old's.

She looked down at the Collector's hand around her own. "I can't weigh this for you. For both of us. That's not fair."

"I got you a cookie."

He was smiling. But not kidding. Which is why, in the end, Nadine found herself smiling back. Which solved nothing. "Yeah. And it was a pretty good cookie."

§

Somewhere over the Dakotas—the country a Candyland gameboard below, all Mr. Mint green grass under a Princess Snowflake sky, blue and whip-cream white—Nadine succumbed to the inevitable and opened the pack of pretzels the airplane attendant had insisted she accept. At the first, pallid *crack* between her teeth, the last of the *lebkuchen* vanished off her tongue. And not just the taste, but the sense-memory of it. The exact, exquisite texture, giving just so under her bite. For a moment, she literally had to fight to keep from spitting the pretzels into the seat back, and won only by convincing herself—by *knowing*—that the damage was already done. The taste lost. The loss irreversible.

And so it was with resignation heavy enough to hurt that she turned from the window to the Collector, woke him with a hard jab to the ribs, and said, "So it does matter to you."

"What?"

He sounded dreamy, still. *Because he hadn't eaten again yet. Knowing him, he probably wouldn't for days. Partially to savor every last taste of the cookie. Partially because he generally forgot eating entirely until she reminded him.*

"Our clients. You always say it's about what

they're looking for, not who they are. That we are instruments of the hunt. Bloodhounds-for-hire, nothing more. So how come—"

"Nadine," he interrupted, struggling upright in his seat. "Once we land…when we get there. I want you to be alert. Okay?"

"What? What do you mean?" After a second, and with some annoyance, she added, "And get where, by the way?"

"The bakery," said the Collector. As though she were being willfully dense.

"Bakery?"

"The Hexenhaus. Hexenhaus."

"Hexen… The one on the radio? From this morning? You can't be…" But of course he was. He always was. "Norm. Normal—" she only used the nickname when he was acting *least* normal—"are you telling me we're looking for a cookie?"

"Nadine, I mean it. I want you on full alert. I want all that intuition of yours cranked into the red, okay? There's something—"

"What? It's going to be a really scary cookie? What makes you even think that bakery has anything to do with—"

"Think about the radio story, Nadine," he said, his back lifting completely away from the cushions as the search caught hold of him. Filled him like wind in a sail. A wave of his hands as the words rushed out of him, and Nadine felt her own aggravation vanish.

"Okay, I'm thinking."

"It's wrong. It has to be."

"Define *wrong*."

"There are things wrong with it. They can't be right."

Ignoring the Collector's excited babble—and also, simultaneously, letting it surround her, burble like a fountain and soothe her as she settled into herself—Nadine concentrated on this morning. On remembering the radio broadcast, which she'd barely even registered at the time. It was a skill he'd taught her. Or discovered in her. One she treasured. A condition of their relationship, and also a foundation for it.

"You're right," she interrupted, a few moments later. "It's all kinds of wrong."

As though she'd yanked a rope, jerked a luffing sail taut, the Collector stopped babbling and tilted forward onto the armrest between them, crowding her in his eagerness. Warming her with it.

"They didn't say the burglar didn't *get in* the

cash register, did they? They said he didn't *touch* it. So he never even tried."

"Ooh." The Collector stroked her arm. "That's good. I hadn't even noticed that."

"*And*," said Nadine, nodding to herself. "What kind of serious bakery closes up for the night and leaves the pastries in the case?"

"There you go," said the Collector. "That's the one."

Nadine pursed her lips, shook her head. "It's like leaving out a food dish for stray cats."

"Except behind glass. And a locked door."

"Which would make it more like…bait?"

Surprising her with a quick, soft kiss on the mouth, the Collector settled back into his seat, folded his arms as though he were cold, and, frowned. "I hope so. I really hope that's it." Then he went quiet, and he stayed that way until they landed.

§

Detroit surprised her.

From everything she'd heard, she expected gray ruin, crumbling buildings, shot-out streetlamps, the corpses of the homeless curled in the sprung trunks of abandoned Torinos. What she saw instead, as they spun their rented Chevy through the all but empty streets toward the Woodward Corridor, reminded her of Ireland. The late spring sun still out even after 8 o'clock in the evening, warm on her forearms through the windshield, golden on the green, green grass rolling over the boundary-less lawns, through the tenantless structures, flowing up to and over the edges of sidewalks and roads like an incoming tide. Like a sea reforming. Bright yellow butterflies wheeled above the bright yellow flowers, some of them dandelions, some daffodils.

A lost land, to be sure. So much like her own home, except with no one to sing for it. She leaned her head against the warmth of the vibrating window.

"We're here," said the Collector, after some time. "We're almost here. Nadine, I need you to wake up."

"I'm awake. Just…sad? Am I sad?"

"It's the cookie."

Nadine laughed.

"I'm not joking."

"That's why I'm laughing," Nadine said, and brushed his arm with her fingertips.

As they slowed, the sun disappeared over the low rooftops, and shadows rose from the sidewalks, inhabiting the sad little storefronts and tiny brick houses like ghosts of customers. Echoes of them. The Collector ticked down addresses. "8864…8862…"

"Found it," Nadine said, and gestured across the empty street.

On the cracked sidewalk, and also on every stalk of weed that had driven up through it, broken glass twinkled in the last of the sunlight. Caution tape stretched not just across the entrance to the bakery but between tilting NO PARKING signs at the edge of the street, marking off almost half the block. Just to the right of the bakery's door stood a crooked wooden woman, fully five feet tall, her skirts melting into their own shadows. Her carefully carved dark shawl obscured her shoulders and her eyes, but the beak nose and wide open O of her mouth were plainly visible. No broom, no pointed hat, no green tint to the wooden skin, nothing whatsoever to identify the figure as a witch. She just *was* one.

"Hexenhaus," Nadine murmured.

The Collector eased the Chevy to the curb and parked. Then he turned, studying not just the bakery but the whole block, and for quite some time. "Witch House," he said. "Right? That's what it means."

"Very specific witch, I think. The one in 'Hansel and Gretel.'"

"Huh." He was looking behind them again, ignoring the occasional passing cars. From somewhere up the residential street behind the bakery, children screamed. Happy screams. The Collector shot a glance at her. "Well, that's pretty perfect, you have to admit."

"You mean the screaming?"

"There he is," said the Collector, popped the locks, and left the car.

"What…" Nadine started, glanced out the back window, and was surprised to see that the witch had a companion, now. A living one.

Scrambling from her seat, Nadine joined the Collector, who'd stopped by the trunk of the car.

"Thanks for waiting for me," she said.

"I wasn't wai—"

"I know." Her smile was fleeting, completely for herself, and not without sadness, even after all these years. Because the Collector was lovely, and also who he was. He would never be anything else.

The man who'd emerged from the bakery was a humpback, hunched over so far that his torso was almost parallel to the sidewalk. He had white stubble along the line of his chin and startlingly large blue eyes. Because of their size, their forward position, and the fact that they didn't blink, the eyes made him look like a fish. He had his hand on the wooden witch's elbow, as if he'd escorted her out there. Or been escorted. Carved wife, Quasimodo fish-husband. The very ground twinkling around them.

"You do take me to the most amazing places," she whispered.

"Remember what I told you," said the Collector, through closed lips, as though worried the fish-guy could lip-read.

"Which thing you told me?"

"I doubt he'll offer. If I'm even right. But if he does—"

"Offer? What—"

"Just remember our client. Mr. *Lebensborn*."

He started forward, but she grabbed his arm and pulled him around. "What about him?"

The Collector held up a hand in front of her face. For an astonished second, she thought he was going to slap her. Instead, he set the hand shaking.

"His...Parkinson's?" Nadine said slowly.

"It's not Parkinson's. At least...maybe it isn't."

"How do you know? What is it?"

He'd turned his back fully on the baker, now, and was looking only at her. Mostly, she realized, so that only she could see him. "Not Parkinson's," he said. Then he slipped free of her grasp and started down the block.

Nadine watched the Collector go while her mind whirled. Just as he ducked under the Caution tape, the sun caught him, seemed to dance along his hairline and down his back, as though he were winking in and out of existence, or this time, or this plane. Disappearing into the Wardrobe, or through the Looking Glass. Again. *Wait for me*, she thought, but didn't bother to call out.

Because he wouldn't wait.

Because he knew she would follow.

She hurried after, and was close enough, by the time the fish-man spoke, to hear what he said. His voice came out high, thin and constricted, as if something was strangling him.

"You are him? Herr Collector?"

"You're the proprietor? The man I spoke to? I

didn't get your name, Herr—"

"Your question," said the fish-man. "When you called this morning. It intrigued me. Ask it again? *Bitte*?" The voice was a grandfather's, really. A dying one, perhaps, but threaded with light. Fine as spun sugar. The German accent faint, its serrated edges blunted by years of American English use.

Nadine glanced at the Collector. His expression surprised her. She'd seen him curious. Almost everyday. But she'd rarely seen him uncertain.

Eventually, he nodded. "I asked, did your burglar get what he came for?"

Lifting his fingers from the witch's elbow, the old man burst into a grin. When he clapped his hands together, grains of flour dust flew up and caught the light, winking like fireflies. "*Gut*. Marvelous. I will answer this question. But before, you must answer just one from me. Then you will have my answer. Okay?"

And you will have a cookie, Nadine found herself thinking. *And some milk*. That was the baker's tone. And her brain leapt immediately to it, still in thrall even with the taste from this afternoon fading, fading, all but gone.

And yet. Here was her inner alarm, the one both she and the Collector had come to trust so implicitly. *Just how long had it been ringing?*

"The person who sent you," said the baker of Hexenhaus. Smiling. Straightening, to the extent that he could. "You will tell me his name."

The pause before the Collector answered wasn't strategy, Nadine knew. Names weren't one of the thousand, thousand things her companion tracked. They just weren't that necessary, as far as he was concerned. Eventually, he snapped his fingers. "Nathanael Ho—"

"We're From the Guild," Nadine overrode him, without knowing why. She was acting on instinct, plain and simple.

The Collector knew better than to correct her. He just turned, one eyebrow raised ever so slightly.

As for the baker, Nadine wouldn't have thought it possible for those blue, blue eyes to widen. But widen they did. "Guild?" The grin slipped a bit on the old man's face. "*Nurnberger Lebkuchen*? Again?"

"Well, we have asked," the Collector said. Nadine tried elbowing him to shut up, but of course, he was already stepping forward, already embellishing. "We did warn you. And yet, from what we've heard, you continue to produce authentic *lebkuchen* five thousand miles from—"

The laughter that had been lurking behind the baker's eyes, and in his voice, bubbled out of him. Once again, he clapped his hands. *"Nein,"* he said, as flour-motes twinkled around him. *"Nein.* That is not true."

"It could have been true," Nadine mumbled, glaring at the Collector's back.

"You are thinking..." the baker was laughing again, hard enough that he actually had to pause for breath. "You imagine *Nurnberger Lebkuchen* has...like *The Sopranos?* Sending out squads of—" he didn't exactly straighten, but his laughing blue eyes drank them in—"clever redheads and walking sticks to keep the Secret of the Cookie inside the city limits?"

"So that people actually have to go there, you mean?" said the Collector. "So they actually get to have a singular experience, and make a memory, and leave with a story to tell?"

The baker stopped laughing. This time, he did straighten some. At least, he stood taller than the witch, now.

The Collector shrugged. "I know people who have done a lot worse to protect a lot less."

"Ja," said the baker. Softly. "I have, also."

"I think your burglar got exactly what he came for," the Collector said, and glanced at Nadine. In his eyes was the same question he'd been asking all day. But she had no answer for him, yet, and he knew it. Not enough data. Down the block, a metal trash can rattled in place, as though someone had pinged it with a rock. The Collector returned his attention to the baker. "I also think it won't help him. Is that right?"

This time, instead of clapping his hands, the baker drew a slow, tired breath. His smile slipped the rest of the way off his face. "I think you are a man in ten thousand," he said. "And also, I am old."

He said something else, too, but Nadine never heard it. His voice got buried in the clatter of the garbage can as it crashed to the street and the trembling man from Nevada lurched up from behind it. From his mouth came the same bird-shriek Nadine had heard this morning, and in his eagerness he almost tripped and sprawled headlong onto the pavement. If he had, maybe he would have dropped his gun.

Had the Collector known, Nadine thought frantically? And then, *All day? Had that pathetic, shuddering person somehow managed to stay close enough to follow them through this whole impossible day? From his cabin to the airport to the plane to this place?*

Then she got a glimpse of the baker of Hexenhaus as he turned. Saw his face. The smile glittering there. And she stopped thinking completely.

"I thought so," the baker said.

"It's you," said the trembling man, upright again, pointing the gun straight into the baker's fishy stare. His hands vibrating so hard that if he pulled the trigger, Nadine figured he would probably hit the Collector, or her. *"Tier."*

For the third time, the baker clapped his hands.

"Teuful," spit the trembling man. *"Damon."*

"You have had a long trip?" the baker whined. Unless that was cooing. "They have been...*hard* years?"

The trembling man flung up the gun, and Nadine and the Collector both ducked in opposite directions. But instead of shooting, the trembling man sobbed. Viciously, savagely, snot bubbling from his nose and saliva from his mouth as though he were a pot boiling over. "You destroyed my life," he said, shaking so hard that Nadine thought he might shatter.

"Come, come," said the baker. "Your life was destroyed long before we ever met."

"My whole life."

"And not your *whole* life, surely," cooed the baker. "You're here now, aren't you?"

Somehow, for one, astonishing instant, the trembling man stopped trembling. Got the gun steady and pointed it straight into the baker's face. And only then, finally, did Nadine understand what the Collector had meant.

"Not Parkinson's," she whispered. *"Withdrawal.* It really *is* the cookie." In her amazement, she forgot the gun and the situation just long enough to glance at her companion. "A cookie."

As usual, again, the Collector's reaction disappointed her. All he did was nod. His suspicions confirmed. One of them, she thought, could really have used a Watson.

"But not the one we ate," he said.

"Okay," she said. "So how do we—"

The gun exploded, shattering the wooden

witch's staff and sending Nadine and the Collector diving to the sidewalk. Nadine's shin scraped across the cement, and something sharp stabbed into the open wound. She gasped as tears filled her eyes.

When she looked up, though, the baker hadn't even moved. Hadn't even stopped smiling. "Think, now, *mein Herr*," he said. "Think. What will happen if you shoot me?"

"I'll find them," snarled the trembling man.

At that, the baker tilted back his head and laughed outright. "Yes. Of course. I have a tin in there with your name on it, and the recipe labeled in my files."

In an instant, the trembling man seemed to deflate, collapsing into himself like a fallen soufflé. The gun sank to his side. Mucus and saliva mingled as they streamed down his face. "Please. You have ruined my whole life. Have mercy."

"Well, of course," said the baker. And suddenly, his voice seemed soothing, full of music. "Don't you realize that all you had to do, all these years, was ask? Just put away your gun. It can't help you anyway."

Shuddering, sniveling, the tarantula man hesitated just a moment longer. Then, to Nadine's amazement, he shuffled forward, arm lifting shakily. Offering the gun, not aiming it. As though paying homage.

Until the Collector said, "Don't."

With her hands on her bleeding leg—not pressing for fear of grinding glass into the wound, just holding the shredded skin closed—Nadine stared at him. Got her brain quiet. Thought it through. Then she turned to the trembling man. "Give the gun to *him*," she eventually said. "To the Collector."

"Ah," said the Collector. "That's an even better plan. That's perfect."

The trembling man stood and trembled. Gun half-raised. Whatever he was thinking, he was still thinking it when the baker pulled his own gun out of the folds of his apron and shot him in the kneecap. The trembling man went down screaming, the gun flying from him, clattering against the wooden witch and dropping to the sidewalk while the Collector lunged forward, ripped the baker's gun away, and stepped back. He didn't lift or aim the weapon, but he didn't toss it aside, either.

The baker ignored him. He just watched the trembling man roll back and forth over the shards of glass on the sidewalk, clutching his shattered knee and weeping. Eventually, he nodded. "*Ja.* Okay. Excuse me, please, while I call the police."

"Why?" the Collector snapped.

Cell phone in hand, 911 already dialed, the baker glanced up. "*Why?* Last night, the robbery. Today a crazy man appears and waves a gun in my face and—"

"Why bother, I mean?" said the Collector.

"Ah," said the baker. "A moment." He spoke into the phone to the police dispatcher, then returned the phone to his pocket.

"Two possible reasons," Nadine said, through the ringing in hear ears and the sting in her skin. Gently, carefully, she pushed herself to her feet. The blood from her scrape was coagulating, at least, and felt cool on her leg in the sweet spring evening. Which was the only sweet thing on the planet, just then, as far as she could see. She gestured toward the wounded man. "Either this really is a Guild matter—"

The baker glanced back and forth between the Collector and Nadine. Once more, his eyes got old. "Only Americans. Or people who have associated too long with Americans. Only Americans could believe I shot a man on my sidewalk over a...a cookie violation."

" — or else this is about the *lebensborn*," Nadine finished.

The baker stopped shaking his head. Stopped grinning. His eyes locked on Nadine's. It really was, she thought, like locking gazes with a sea creature. Something alive, like her. Yet utterly alien, and not like her at all. "Then you *do* know," he said. "And so you understand."

"But I don't. Not really. I mean, are you Jewish?"

The baker winced. Said nothing.

Nadine had no idea how to read that. "Or... you're German secret service? Erasing the past? Or—Oh!—or are you also *lebensborn?*"

"Does that matter?" whispered the baker. And Nadine knew, abruptly, that that was it. Though as to what that meant, or why it would cause... whatever had happened here...

The baker was about to say more when the trembling man humped up suddenly, scuttling forward on his shattered kneecap, screaming as he came but coming anyway.

"No," snapped the Collector, lunging forward

to snatch the discarded gun off the ground. He stepped back between the trembling man and the baker. The trembling man sobbed, then sagged to stillness at the feet of the wooden witch.

For a moment longer, the baker only watched. Then he sighed. "There, there. Perhaps it really is enough." Ignoring the half-raised gun in the Collector's hands, he vanished into the shadows of his shop.

"What do you think?" the Collector murmured, as soon as he was gone. "Nadine, tell me what to do. Tell me what you know. What are these people? What do they believe?"

But whatever instincts Nadine usually possessed, they failed her, now. She thought of the booklet in the trembling man's bathroom. The boardgame and flags in his closet. The unimaginable, baffling life he must have led. "I don't know. I don't know how *they* could know what they believe."

The baker returned, carrying a tray of something draped in a single, white napkin. Seeing that, the trembling man whimpered, started to stretch out a hand, then shrank back into a ball on the sidewalk. The little hums that percolated from him seemed completely involuntary. The sounds a cat makes when it has been run over. Right before it dies.

Instead of kneeling, the baker stood just out of reach and watched.

"She asked you what you were," the Collector said, settling the gun in his palm. Preparing to raise it. "I think you should answer."

"Please," the man on the ground managed.

And the baker shrugged. He glanced at the Collector, then Nadine. "I am the Angel of Mercy," he said. Then he knelt. But he didn't remove the napkin from the plate, and he didn't move the plate within reach of the trembling man.

"Mercy?" Nadine snarled. "Look at him."

"You cannot understand."

"*PLEASE...*" shrieked the trembling man.

The baker made no further move, though his eyes never left the trembling man's now. And they looked almost human, at that moment. Not unkind. Not entirely.

Then the police were upon them, four different cops. They took statements, confiscated the weapons. Did their police things. An ambulance arrived. The trembling man shrieked only once more, as he was unfolded and strapped to a gurney.

"Come on," the Collector said, grabbing the baker's arm. The baker was still holding his covered plate. "What can it possibly matter? Give him one."

"Would you believe me," the baker said quietly, "if I said it would only make him worse?"

Twenty minutes later, the police had gone, and the baker and Nadine and the Collector stood alone once more, in an evening that had gone cold, now, moonless, surprisingly and disconcertingly dark.

"Tell me what you did to him," the Collector said.

"Did to him?" The baker sighed. "I gave him the single most perfect taste he could ever have. I let him know that taste existed. I gave a demon of hell a taste of heaven. And that is all."

"So you did wreck his life."

"Or else I gave it purpose. Filled his mind with other thoughts than the monstrous ones he'd been given. Maybe even saved countless other lives in the process. Is that so cruel? Am I a cruel man, do you think?"

Nadine heard the danger, of course, before the Collector did. Because she was listening to the man's voice, not what he was saying.

"Don't answer that," she said, fast. "There's no answer to that."

"I'll tell you what," said the baker.

"No, you won't. Come on, Normal. We have a plane to catch." But she was too slow. Too late. The baker had the Collector's arm. Had lit that light in the Collector's eyes.

"You come inside with me, now," said the baker. "And I'll let you judge for yourself exactly how cruel I have been."

"Don't do it," Nadine said. "For God's sake don't."

But of course it was useless. The Collector was already gone.

He came out again barely a minute later. For a moment, she took the sparkle in his eyes for reflected broken glass off the glittering sidewalk. Then she realized it was tears. She took his arm and led him to the rental car, eased him to the passenger seat, drove them back toward the airport and home. He said nothing the whole trip, and he didn't even try to wipe the tears away.

But whether he was crying because he had tasted the cookies of the baker of Hexenhaus, or because he hadn't, she never asked, and he never said.

❦ ❦ ❦

AN UNREADING: NOTES ON A NARRATIVE OF FAILURE

By D. Harlan Wilson

t some point, it is time for another issue of *Confrontations*, the premier magazine of aggression, misogyny, hate mail, fnordicana and general tastelessness. (NOTE: My first sentence consists of 23 words.) Peter Jackson needs to get his ducks in a row—since the disappearance of the magazine's editor *par excellence*, Joe Malik, he is the acting head of operations. He calls the journalist Epicene Wildeblood on the phone (no email or Skype in this timescape) to ensure that his book review is en route, but he hasn't finished it. "It's a dreadfully long monster of a book," Wildeblood says, "and I certainly won't have time to read it, but I'm giving it a thorough skimming. The authors are utterly incompetent—no sense of style or structure at all. It starts out as a detective story, switches to science-fiction, then goes off into the supernatural, and is full of the most detailed information of dozens of ghastly boring subjects. And the time sequence is all out of order in a very pretentious imitation of Faulkner or Joyce. Worst yet, it has the most raunchy sex scenes, thrown in just to make it sell, I'm sure, and the authors—whom I've never heard of—have the supreme bad taste to introduce real political figures into this mishmash and pretend to be exposing a real conspiracy. You can be sure I won't waste time reading such rubbish." (NOTE: This passage appears in the Wikipedia entry for *The Illuminatus! Trilogy* as well as page 238 of my copy of the book.) Curiously, the book Wildeblood claims to be reviewing sounds a lot like *The Illuminatus! Trilogy* itself. It is at least a symptom of the trilogy—as everything and everyone in the trilogy is a symptom of the Somethingorother Machine. (NOTE: Fnord!) What matters, however, is Jackson's response to Wildeblood's dissociative anxiety: "Well, we don't expect you to read every book you review . . . just so long as you can be entertaining about them."

(NOTE: This is good news for my article insofar I have not read *The Illuminatus! Trilogy*. I have skimmed it, and in some instances I have read the first sentence of every paragraph for several paragraphs at a time, but generally I just looked for keywords, i.e., words over 17 letters long.)

(NOTE: There is hardly any formal literary criticism on the trilogy, which includes *The Eye of the Pyramid*, *The Golden Apple* and *Leviathan*. However, the Wiki entry offers a wealth of information, calling *Illuminatus!* "a satirical, postmodern, science fiction-influenced adventure story; a drug-, sex-, and magic-

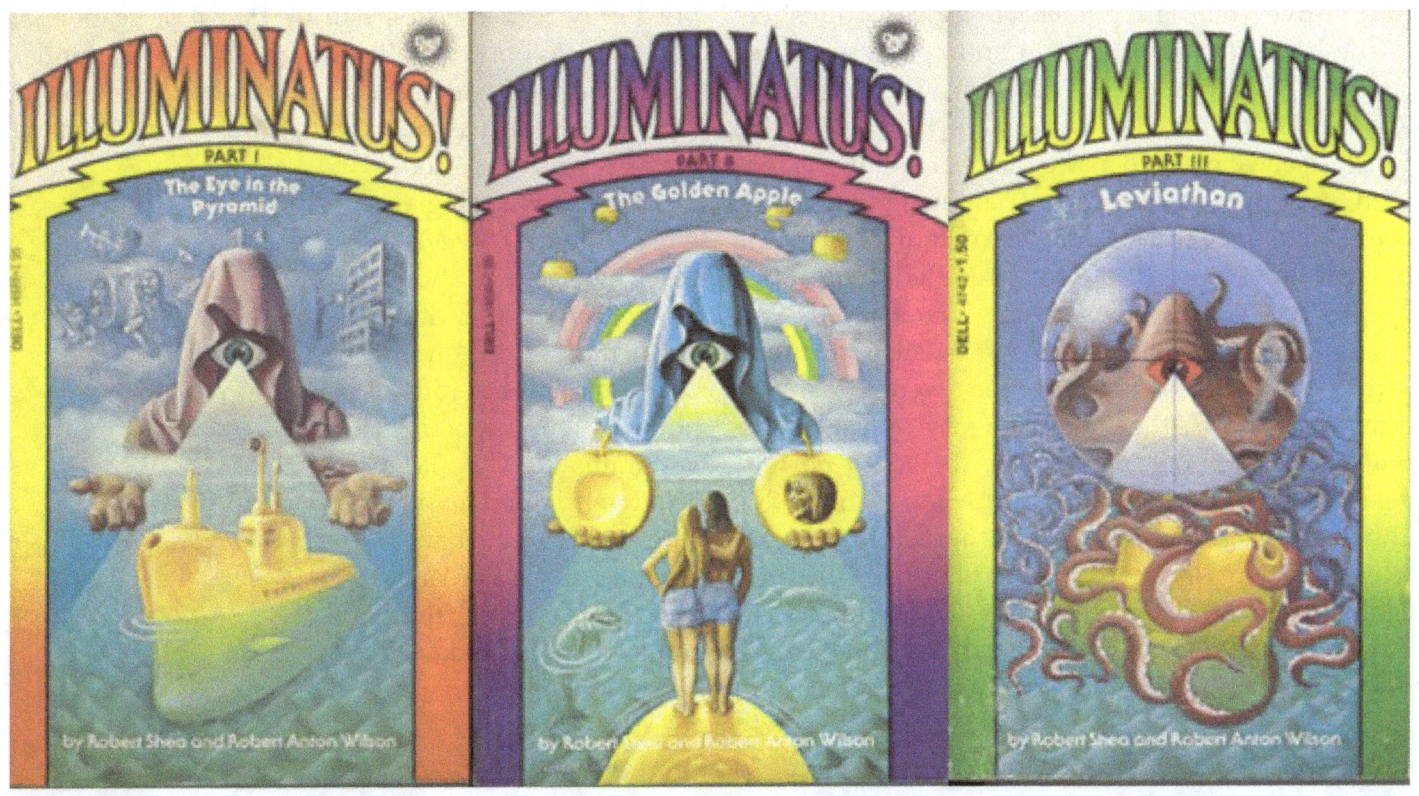

laden trek through a number of conspiracy theories, both historical and imaginary, related to the authors' version of the Illuminati." Moreover, the philosophy behind Wikipedia is, if you will, Illuminati-chic. Every inch of its encyclopedic girth is a collective effort on the part of any scholar or idiot who wants to insert their two cents into the maelstrom of data. And yet the maelstrom is carefully monitored by a team of Wiki executives or proles for "quality control," "cleanup," "fact checking," "articles lacking sources," etc. Wikipedia seeks the objective truth yet controls the congregation of subjectivities that together gesture towards some idea of "objectivity," a bona fide myth however you slice it. Inevitably, truth becomes that which exists in the minds of the administrators, i.e., the Administrator. There's always-already only one person-in-power at the top of proverbial pile, rendering the whole project entirely subjective, i.e., not objective, i.e., a dire untruth and a thoroughbred fiction, contrary to the alleged flows of Wikipedia's would-be desire for "truth." Verisimilitude is the best we can hope for. Hence the Illuminati-chic element.)

The conclusion of *Illuminatus!* plagiarizes the conclusion of *The Matrix* trilogy wherein it turns out that the humans and the machines are meant to fuck with one another but not altogether obliterate one another in the interests of maintaining "balance" by way of the illusion of choice (i.e., the idea that we have the freedom to write our own life scripts). It doesn't matter that the first *Matrix* film was released almost twenty-five years after *Illuminatus!* was published: as the latter text asserts again and again, time, like choice, is a fairytale, an explosion of Yellow Brick Roads that function like madcap wormholes. On this concourse, we may do as we please, revising history with the indifference of a Rotarian named Eldon. Of course, it's a subjective affair by default, and in the present timescape, *The Matrix* preceded *Illuminatus!* by 40 years (23 + 17), positioning its release in 1935, a hair's breadth from the end of the silent film era. Audiences didn't realize what they were looking at, didn't even realize the film was in color, never having witnessed color onscreen before (it would be four years until the release of *The Wizard of Oz* in 1939), although everybody more or less agreed that Keanu Reeves, given his accent, cheekbones and overall cant, must be Finnish . . . In *Illuminatus!*, a unicellular pyramidic cephalopod is the culprit that functions as the Oracle-Architect binary in *The Matrix Reloaded/ Revolutions*. According to Wikipedia, at the end of *Leviathan*, "finally, one reveals himself as the fifth

Illuminatus Primus; he has been playing both sides against each other in order to keep balance. He is a representative of the 'true' Illuminati, whose aim is to spread the idea that everybody is free to do whatever they want at all times." This "one" is a certain Hagbard Celine, captain of the golden submarine, etc., etc. It doesn't matter. The denouement hearkens to *Reloaded/ Revolutions*—period. The point is that everybody is in fact *not* "free to do whatever they want at all times." Everybody is, in the end, subject to an architecture of deception, machination, codification. Above all, everybody is subject to the authors of *Illuminatus!*, Roberts Shea and Anton Wilson, who recurrently metafictionalize the experience of being a reader and author as much as being a human who exists within a certain social, cultural and historical context. And, as the Roberts would be the first to tell you, metafiction is nothing short of a conspiracy on the part of the Author to be "clever," i.e., to stupefy readers vis-à-vis the impression that S/he—in this case the Roberts— are clever, when in fact they are just having difficulty constructing round characters, sound plotlines and backstories, cogent syntax, well-placed upsurges of suspense, and everything else that constitutes "good fiction" . . .

Originally I intended to begin this article with an extended reference to G. K. Chesterton's *The Man Who Was Thursday*, using the theme of secret societies in the *fin de siècle* London Underground as a springboard to discuss the various collusions at work in *Illuminatus!*, but I only read the first half of *Thursday*, years ago, and the Wiki entry isn't very good. I do remember being extremely disappointed when I discovered that the novel was not about a man who in some way manifested the ontology of a single day of the week, his corporeal and/ or cognitive identity injected into the span of twenty-four hours. The mind-body apparatus would effectively operate as a unit of time. That's a book I'd like to read. On the contrary, the titular "Thursday" becomes little more than a codename for the protagonist, secret

policeman Gabriel Syme, who is elected to a council of six other undercover detectives, each of whom possesses a day-of-the-week codename—rendering a potentially wonderful tale of man-as-day absurdism and imaginative prowess yet another narrative instance of banal realism (despite *Thursday*'s surreal finale). (NOTE: Had I ignited my article with the spark of this reference, now I would dovetail back to *Illuminatus!* and assert that the Roberts' trilogy is anything but banal, "real," etc. Obviously this is high praise. In fact, *Illuminatus!* has allocated me the very absurdist and hyper-imaginative "Thursday" that Chesterton denied me, etc., etc.)

(NOTE: While for obvious reasons I can't be certain, there are probably numerous references—or at least allusions—to *The Man Who Was Thursday* throughout *Illuminatus!* . . . [*Googlepause*.] . . . I found the entire text of *Illuminatus!* online and performed a keyword search, first with "Chesterton," then with "Thursday," finally with "Gabriel Syme." Alas, nothing showed up with the exception of the biblical Archangel Gabriel and a certain "Gabriel Conrad," who doesn't appear to be (or have been) a real person—there is no Wiki entry for him and IMDb reveals an ostensibly dead actor who only appeared in two forgettable films in the early 1950s—although there are several Gabriel Conrads on Twitter. One of them is from Nigeria. His profile description reads "self confident and easy going dude," he joined Twitter in 2010, and he hasn't tweeted since June 2014 . . . As a matter of course, chronic reference to figures alive and dead, real and unreal, famous and infamous and utterly inconsequential—but nothing is technically inconsequential in *Illuminatus!*—is a technique that the Roberts deploy with fetishistic rigor, fingering the so-and-sos of humanity over the span of centuries, but mainly the nineteenth and twentieth centuries. Other figures of prominence include Hassan-i Sabbah, Richard Nixon, William Buckley, Jr., Thomas Jefferson, Charles Manson, Thomas Edison, Friedrich Nietzsche, Thomas Wolfe, William Blake, H. P. Lovecraft, William S. Burroughs, James Joyce, Jesus Christ, Lief Erickson, Billy Graham, John Dillinger, Herman Melville, the Beatles, Terry Southern, Truman Capote, Robert Kennedy, Ezra Pound, Adolf Hitler, Karl Marx, Charlemagne, G. Gordon Liddy, Samuel Becket, Ambrose Bierce, George Orwell, the Marquis de Sade, Sirhan Sirhan, Marilyn Monroe, Albert Einstein, Al Capone, J. Edgar Hoover, Bugs Bunny, Amelia Earhart, Timothy Leary, Michelangelo, William Shakespeare, Wolfgang Pauli, George Washington, Henry Miller, C.

G. Jung, Herman Hesse, Tutankhamen. That's 46 names [23 + 23] from *The Eye of the Pyramid* alone.)

(NOTE [cont.]: Many of these names can be plugged into the machinery of high modernism or postwar American *Realpolitik*, but Lovecraft and Burroughs are perhaps the Roberts' biggest allies, so to speak, the former for content, the latter for style. . . . [*Wikipause*.] . . . The Illuminati are partial extrapolations of Lovecraft's Cthulhu Mythos, after all, and Lovecraft himself is implicated as an enemy of the Illuminati, who kill him because he wrote the *Necronomicon*, which reveals key secrets of the organization. Burroughs, on the other hand, serves the Roberts as a model for narrative construction and world-building via the cut-up technique. At the same time, Burroughs, like Lovecraft, appears as a character in *Illuminatus!*, bearing a mark of secrecy and interpretation. This is the case with virtually every character in the trilogy. Nobody is safe from the ideological subjectification of the Illuminati. And in a way, everybody, good and bad alike, are agents of the Illuminati's dirtywork, which consists of the unending pursuit of "balance" . . .)

Lacan: "Desire is the desire for desire, the desire of the Other, and it is subject to the Law."

Burroughs: "Not funny enough!"

A foregone conclusion.

And yet anything scrutinized closely enough can function as a source of conspiracy. Everywhere—codes, creeds, lurking antagonisms. Here is the axiomatic postmodern abjection/objection. A consummate and ubiquitous hermeneutic of suspicion . . . The Cheshire grin of an insurgent overlord glints in every conceivable and inconceivable form of matter and antimatter. At the same time, a grin is nothing without a frown. A grin is only a grin because it is *not* a frown (or an expressionless set of lips, etc., etc.). Simple identity politics. Difference as self. Self as that which we perceive in the Other.

This is precisely what *The Illuminatus! Trilogy* dramatizes—if not accomplishes . . . Time after time, the falconer fails the bird . . .

☙❈❧

A new retrospective literary horror-story collection containing Reggie Oliver's best stories from all of his previous books, plus three new stories. Nightmarish, terrifying, dangerous, theatrical, often strangely profound, THE SEA OF BLOOD is a ride that will inspire and haunt you.

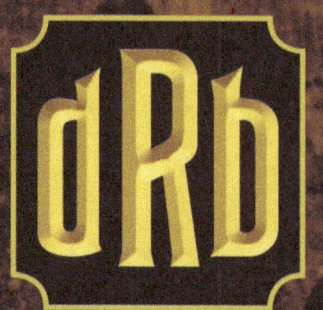

In witch-haunted Arkham, the spirit of the narrator's notorious great-aunt takes possession of an innocent woman. Partly inspired by Lovecraft', THE REVENANT OF REBECCA PASCAL enters ghostly houses and sinister burying grounds, where alchemy and madness join with an entity from beyond the wall of sleep.

In the New England envisioned by Hawthorne and Lovecraft, a twilit country of wild hills and barren farms where madness and repression abound, THE LORD CAME AT TWILIGHT presents haunting stories of doubt and despair, the deranged and the devout.

H. P. LOVECRAFT'S FAVORITE HORROR STORIES, Vol II presents 14 more stories he deemed of particular merit. S. T. Joshi's introduction and notes on each story give background on the authors as well as Lovecraft's appreciation of the tales and their possible influence.

SHERLOCK HOLMES:
THE LONDON TERRORS

William Meikle

Sir Arthur Conan Doyle's beloved detective, Sherlock Holmes, and his amanuensis Dr. Watson return to deal with occult and esoteric threats in the three novellas included in THE LONDON TERRORS.

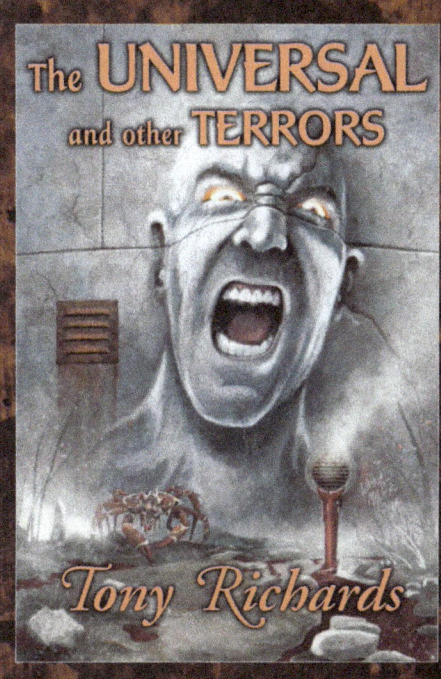

The UNIVERSAL
and other TERRORS

Tony Richards

Horror World has called Tony Richards "one of today's masters of dark fiction." Here are twelve new stories, five of them previously unpublished and unique to this collection, that will open your eyes to the hidden terrors in the world around us. Read them at your peril.

GRAVEDIGGER'S DANCE

G. O. CLARK

Welcome to the GRAVEDIGGERS' DANCE, where the music is dark and wild, and anything can happen. Angels, devils, freaks of nature, vampires, ghosts, psychopaths, all writhe below a blood-red full moon. Pick a grave-flower and join the dancers. Get tickets at the Cemetery gate from the dead-eyed poet. Don't forget the Postmortem Punch!

DARK RENAISSANCE BOOKS

darkrenaissance.com

THIS IS WHERE I CAME IN ...

By Gary A. Braunbeck

Installment #1: Are You a Card-Carrying Member?

"I would never belong to any club that would have someone like me for a member."

—Groucho Marx

"Huh-uh—you can't quit my club."

—Root Boy Slim & the Sex Change Band

Since this issue of *Dark Discoveries* concerns itself with the subject of secret societies, I feel it's only fair to disclose that I myself belong to one. I am a founding member of a small group called The Markov Chaney Society—and if you're a fan of Robert Anton Wilson, you might get the less-than-subtle joke of our name; if you're not a fan, then it makes no sense, and I can never reveal the truth of the joke to you, unless you are also a member, in which case you already know the joke, which renders half of this sentence pointless. Don't even ask about the secret handshake or the password because you'd never recover the brain cells you'd piss away trying to fathom the explanation for *those*.

Consider one of the (arguably) earliest secret societies, first referenced in 1398 as the *Sterred chamber,* also *le Sterne-chamere,* but it was the former title that was officially entered into the record in the Supremacy of the Crown Act 1534. We now know it by the name "Star Chamber." The Star Chamber, briefly, was a court of law that sat in private council at the Royal Palace of Westminster from the late 15th century until 1641. Henry VII took his place there in (roughly) 1504, and along with a select group of privy councilors and common-law judges saw fit to hold trials in secret, wherein the defendants were never informed of the charges against them, nor were there ever any indictments or witnesses. Nothing was ever written down, all so-called cases were brought to the group by a single member who harbored—or was friends with or related to someone who also harbored—resentment in some form against a member of the aristocracy (Henry VII was often not a favored king of the upper-class in the early 1500s) whom said member felt needed to be punished for said offence; it was a court where those who believed themselves above the law of

the land were as subject to the law's wrath as the lowest of commoners. In short, it was a secret society where a select few not only brought charges against individuals, but also passed judgments and ordered the carrying out of sentences, many of which were extremely harsh (drawing and quartering, anyone?). Under Henry VII, it eventually became a powerful and corrupted political tool that was employed more for revenge than for justice. (Writer/director Peter Hyams revived the term in the late 1980s with his thriller *The Star Chamber*, a tidy and compelling film about a modern-day secret court; the film eventually overplays its hand but is definitely worth a look.)

I use the Star Chamber of the 1500s as an example because it—for me, anyway—best illustrates why dark fantasy, suspense, and horror fiction seems

They are the most powerful members of our community.
They have a shattering secret.
A secret that will affect us all.
Only one man is willing to stop them.
On August 5, you'll know who they really are.

THE
STAR CHAMBER

TWENTIETH CENTURY-FOX PRESENTS A FRANK YABLANS PRESENTATION A PETER HYAMS FILM
MICHAEL DOUGLAS IN "THE STAR CHAMBER"
HAL HOLBROOK · YAPHET KOTTO · SHARON GLESS
MUSIC BY MICHAEL SMALL · STORY BY RODERICK TAYLOR · SCREENPLAY BY RODERICK TAYLOR AND PETER HYAMS
PRODUCED BY FRANK YABLANS · DIRECTED BY PETER HYAMS

to return to the trope of the secret society over and again—it's the (arguably) ultimate df/s/h setup: here is an individual who, unbeknownst to him or her, has been targeted for persecution by potent outside powers whose source and motivation are hidden in deep shadows, both literal and figurative. Consider the plight of Josef K. in Kafka's *The Trial* (a brilliant and disturbing variation on the concept of the Star Chamber): he is arrested and tried for a crime that is never revealed, and his fate is in the hands of people he's never met, who base their judgment on the testimony of people Josef has never even *heard of*, let alone interacted with. Hitchcock made his reputation on numerous films that used this concept as a jumping-off point; Andrew Vachss has used the same central conceit to power his series of dark mysteries—particularly the Burke novels—in order to bring about a wider awareness of the unthinkable, monstrous dangers facing children in our society, dangers most of us don't even want to think about, let alone acknowledge the reality of.

The individual against unidentified dark forces bent on his or her destruction, or the destruction of everyone and everything they hold dear.

Ah, *but* …

… what if all of this could be avoided by, say, *joining* said secret society? Will the individual consider doing that, if it means sparing their loved ones suffering? Will he or she allow their will to be broken, or will they challenge said secret group without considering the consequences of that challenge? (Consider the fate of the people who walk into the offices of Stephen King's "Quitters, Inc.") Maybe the individual will find a way to reach a standoff/draw with these secret powers (as Sherlock Holmes does at the end of *Murder by Decree*). The reasons behind the individual's persecution, how they respond to it, whether or not they find a way to fight back, and their ultimate triumph or defeat at the hands of these dark secret forces is the stuff of great storytelling, and since dark fantasy, suspense, and especially horror are the fields of fiction that most love to grapple with these concepts, what appears on the surface to be just a simple trope can be employed as the spine for tales that could become part of the grand mythic literature of our time. That may seem like overreaching to some (or even pretentious) but I can't find it in myself to apologize for wishing that our fiction could achieve even a fraction of that goal. After all, *they* keep calling horror the lowest form of storytelling; *they* think it's all trash; *they* think we're all just a bunch of anti-

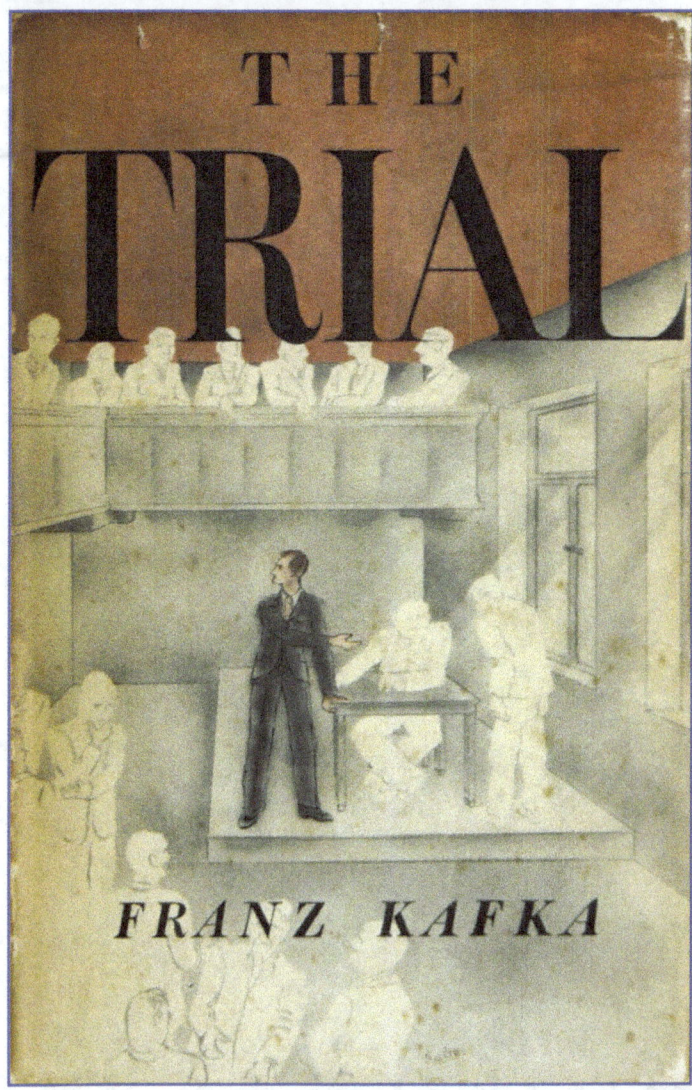

social, perverted, bloody-minded mouth-breathers who wouldn't know good *lit-raht-chure* if it attacked us with an axe; *they* keep looking down on us.

Now, if only we can figure out who *they* are, where *they* meet, and how to combat *them* ….

Huh. This is where I came in, isn't it?

Have to go now. I've a Markov Chaney meeting to attend. They get real snippy if I'm late. You don't want to know *what* it is they snip, trust me ….

❧❧❧

THE STAR CHAMBER. (*From a Drawing taken in 1836.*)

THE SECRET HISTORY OF
KING ARTHUR

By Mark Booth

The story of Lancelot, Guinevere and Arthur belongs to an initiatic class of literature. Hollywood tends to tell it as a love triangle, and it works well on this level—but there are other, more esoteric levels.

In what follows I have tried to bring these other levels nearer to the surface, in the first instance by going back to the original sources and putting them into an accessible modern idiom. Some of these sources focus on different parts of the story, so I've woven them together in a way that shows and brings out the wider patterns. Because of Hollywood and because of stories we have read in childhood, too, I think we tend to assume we know the story of Lancelot, but my researches made me realize that the real story is much richer and stranger and in many ways more dramatic and vital.

On one level the stories of King Arthur and his knights give an account of real historical events— though not necessarily ones that took place in the Middle Ages, as I show in *The Secret History of the World*.

As you read this story you will notice certain mythological elements, echoes of the abduction of Persephone, for instance. We know that the story of Persephone and Hades was enacted as sacred drama inside the Mystery centres of ancient Greece. On one level, then, these mythological elements tell the story of the journey of the human spirit after death.

And because life on earth is also structured according to the same patterns as life after death, the story of Lancelot is also the story of Everyman and Everywoman. The suggestion here is that each of us in the course of our own lives on earth will undergo the same pattern of tests, temptations, journeys through Hell and, ultimately, if all is well, attainments and transformations.

On yet another level the story of Lancelot is an account of an initiation ceremony. For example, in his quest to rescue Guinevere, Sir Lancelot needs to gain access to the castle of the Dark Lord who is keeping her prisoner. The only way inside is across a very narrow bridge spanning the moat—so narrow that it is like the blade of a sword.

This same feature can be found in accounts of tests candidates for initiation have to undergo, for example in the story of the Knight Owen's initiation at the Monastery of St Patrick in Donegal. (Owen was a follower of the English king Stephen, himself a great supporter of the Knights Templar.) There is a depiction of this knife-like bridge, too, in a medieval wall painting in a church in Chaldon in Surrey, England. I have also recently read an account by an Englishman, a friend, who only last year was seeking initiation into the secrets of the legendary Yamabushi, the warrior monks in the mountains of Japan. He was required to reach a mountain peak at dead of night, crawling across a razor-sharp bridge, with sheer drops on either side. After he had completed the test he saw below a bloody robe, like the one he was wearing.

Many different kinds of deaths may be involved in the initiation ceremonies of secret societies.

§

The trappings of the King Arthur story are medieval, but its core is much older. The story of Excalibur, the marvellous sword that rises from the Lake and is later ritually thrown back into it, echoes the ancient Celtic practice of throwing swords, shields, spears, chariot wheels, cauldrons and jewels into ritual pools.

Walk around the English countryside and you may observe that in landscapes of gently rolling hills there are occasional small steep hillocks, the hill forts of the Iron Age. They mark a time of transition when the sun-worshipping, pastoral peoples of the Bronze Age were overtaken by the something darker and more war-like.

Like his contemporary Solomon, Arthur was a solar king. "Sol" in Solomon means "Sun." The Round Table is an image of the Sun-king surrounded by the twelve signs of the zodiac. This image has its origins in the earlier stone circle-building cultures of Northern Europe.

Behind this imagery lies a belief in the role of the Sun-god in the history of the cosmos. King Arthur should be seen as the Sun-god's emissary on earth and Merlin as his high priest. A sense of cosmic history is preserved in the idea that neither Merlin nor Arthur die, but rather sleep. Merlin flits in and out of the Arthur legends, unbound by the normal constraints of time and place. Their joint cosmic mission is to carry the torch of the solar mysteries into the gathering darkness.

Arthur was a great bear of a man—and when our story starts, a bear with a sore head. Merlin advised him it was time he married. When Arthur agreed, Merlin asked, "Do you have anyone in mind?" (1)

Arthur stroked his beard. Yes, he remembered a beautiful young princess he had once seen, the daughter of a neighbouring king: "the fairest lady that I know living or that ever I could find." Arthur had been feted at that king's castle after he had helped defend it from foreign invaders. A wonderful evening. He remembered her shy, sidelong glances, how her hair fell forward and how she'd looked at him from underneath it.

Merlin shook his head and with it his longer, whiter beard. He knew something of the heartaches of love. He warned Arthur how dangerous it would be to choose a girl so much younger than himself. It was a long time, Merlin reminded him, since he had been the strapping young man who had pulled the sword from the stone or defeated the giant Ritho who wore a cloak made out of the beards of dead kings.

But Arthur decided to ignore Merlin's advice and sent a messenger asking his friend and neighbour for his daughter's hand. As part of Guinevere's dowry, her father happily offered a magnificent round table, designed to accommodate twelve knights.

Who to send to escort Guinevere? Arthur decided on Lancelot of the Lake. Lancelot had arrived at Camelot at the age of eighteen. He was rumoured to have fairy blood—like a much later chivalric hero, Richard the Lionheart. No-one could beat this young man in combat. He had no Achilles heel, it seemed.

He was like a son to Arthur. The apple of his eye.

The moment Lancelot and Guinevere set eyes on each other they fell in love. Behold, thou art fair, she thought. Thy lips are like a thread of scarlet, thy neck is like a tower.

They rode back in silence. Guinevere's father owed everything to Arthur and her father had promised her to him.

Lancelot owed everything to Arthur too—and had also sworn to obey high ideals. The ceremony of tapping on the shoulder with a sword, by which a man is knighted, recalled the initiation ceremonies of the Mystery Schools of the ancient world. Becoming a knight meant acquiring a conscious spiritual power.

There was a magnificent wedding at the Abbey. Kings and queens came from all over the world. Everyone said how beautiful the young queen was—perhaps the most beautiful woman in the world. At the wedding feast the round table was used for the first time, and Arthur instituted the fellowship of the round table with Gwain, Kay, Bedevere and Lancelot among the twelve knights. The knights would defend the country, purge it of dragons, robbers and other forces of evil that lurked both in the countryside and within themselves. They swore above all to try to be pure of heart. Someone remembered an old saying "My strength is as the strength of ten because my heart is pure," and they all laughed heartily and drank a loyal toast. Thinking about his love for Guinevere, Lancelot laughed a little less whole-heartedly than the rest. Arthur noticed he looked lost in thought, but then his attention was diverted by a dancing bear.

Later there was a moment or two of surprise when a white hart suddenly ran through the assembled guests pursued by six black hunting hounds and a white female hound, which bit its flank. The hart leaped high out of the window and escaped.

It was a lawless time, and there would be other, more unpleasant surprises. Early one morning shortly after the marriage Guinevere wandered off on her own and was picking flowers in a meadow. Suddenly the ground seemed to shake and there was a sound like thunder. She looked up to see a black bearded, dark-faced man with wild eyes. He had appeared as if from nowhere and scooped her up into his chariot with one sweep of his muscular hairy arm.

The maids ran off in alarm and came across Sir Lancelot washing his white stallion in a stream. He sped off in the direction they were pointing. He rode his horse as hard as he could, but he found no trace or trail of the chariot.

Eventually he arrived in a strange, mountainous land, and stopped to ask a damsel sitting by a holy well by the side of the road. She said that, yes, she had seen a tall and powerful knight called Meleagant pass that way with a young woman in his chariot. Meleagant was the son of the King of Gorre, she said. She was sure he was taking her to his father's dark and gloomy castle. The damsel warned Lancelot that no foreigner who had entered that domain had ever returned.

He spurred his horse forward. He rode so hard this time that eventually his horse dropped down dead. Lancelot was sitting forlornly by the side of the road, his shield hanging round his neck, wondering how he would ever reach or find the castle, when a humpbacked, pot-bellied dwarf rode by on a horse and cart. The dwarf had evidently been collecting firewood in the forest.

"Dwarf, for God's sake," he cried out. "Have you seen the Queen pass by here?"

The scowling dwarf did not reply but gestured to Sir Lancelot to join him on the cart. The knight hesitated. He was thinking to himself that this shabby, broken down cart with its peeling paint was not in accord with the high ideal of chivalry by which he had sworn to live. In those days to travel on the back of a horse and cart was a ride of shame, commonly used to transport criminals so that they would be mocked and the crowd could throw things at them as they were dragged through the streets.

Then Lancelot's love for Guinevere prompted him and he climbed aboard. *What else can I do?* he thought.

At midday the horse and cart reached the next town. Astolat was a beautiful, prosperous place and the people *did* jeer at Lancelot, taunting him for his ignoble mode of transport. The town was built around a meadow and abutting the meadow was a tower. At a high window in this tower Lancelot saw the young daughter of the local lord. Elaine was working on her loom, weaving a tapestry as fine as a web when she heard the clang of his armour. She looked up and saw his noble bearing and she had never seen such a beautiful young man.

Elaine sent out valets to fetch him in and take care of his armour. Other servants fetched towels and basins and lit candles. She ordered a sumptuous supper for him. So Elaine and her father took him in and made him welcome, and when he said that he must continue his quest, she gave him a fresh horse and lance.

Elaine accompanied him a short way beyond the town. Along the way she spotted a comb lying in the grass next to a stone basin. Lancelot leapt down to retrieve it. "I can't remember seeing a comb as beautiful as this," he said.

Elaine laughed. "May I have it?" she said.

"Why are you laughing?"

"I am as sure as I've ever been sure of anything," she said, "that this comb belongs to the Queen. Look, those are strands of her hair." It was true. Lancelot looked at hair woven around the teeth of the comb. Gold refined a hundred times would be darker, he thought. He knew he was on the right path.

Elaine saw the look in his eyes and she was sad.

As they parted company Lancelot gave Elaine the comb as she had asked, and in return she offered him her favour to wear on his shield, a red sleeve embroidered with pearls. He agreed to wear it on his shield the next time he fought in a tournament. *What harm?* he thought. *She's only a child.*

"May this day be a happy one for you!" Elaine called after him as he rode off.

Perhaps he would learn to love her in time.

Lancelot rode on until early evening, when he found the squat, ugly castle that the woman by the well had told him about. Surely this was where Guinevere was being held captive? He gazed in fear at the black, deadly river that raged around the castle walls. He could see that anything that fell into it would almost certainly be lost. The only way across seemed to be a very narrow metal bridge. It was as long as two spears and stuck in the mud of the bank at one end and the stone wall of the castle at the other—and this bridge was sharp as sword.

Getting across it is going to be as easy as stopping the birds from singing or re-entering my mother's womb, he thought. *But I have faith in God that he will protect me to the end.*

He divested himself of his armour. Then he began to pull himself across with his bare hands. They were cut to ribbons, as were his knees and his feet, but his agony was sweet to him because of his love for Guinevere.

Watching his slow progress with a grim expression was the King of Gorre. The king knew that only a man with no evil in his nature could cross that bridge—and he also knew that a man with no evil in his nature would be hard to defeat. He summoned his son, Meleagant, who was keeping Guinevere prisoner, and advised him to make peace and deliver the Queen into the stranger's hands straight away.

Meleagant was furious: "What am I, a hermit to be so compassionate and charitable? I have no desire to be honourable." He smiled. "No, let me be cruel."

So the king went to greet Sir Lancelot with foreboding. He offered ointment for his hands and feet, and hospitality for two or three weeks while his wounds healed.

Lancelot refused. He had come to fight. It was a matter of honour. But because the king had treated him honourably he said he would agree to wait until morning.

Before dawn the king again tried to persuade his son to cede.

"I will not take your advice on this, Father. If I gave in, I'd deserve to be torn apart by wild horses. He is seeking honour, he is seeking glory—and so am I."

Word had spread and when morning came the castle square was packed with barons, knights and ladies. The two knights were led in on good strong horses. Then as the squires stood aside, both knight spurred on forward so fast and so violently that each lance pierced the other's shield, metal smiting metal, causing the lances to splinter and sparks to fly off. The horses crashed together with a sound like thunder, reins snapping and both men fell to the earth. But both sprang up and rushed at each other head-on like wild boars, swinging great blows with their steel swords, soon trimming each other's helmets and causing blood to spurt.

The fight raged on, neither side seeming to gain the upper hand until Lancelot began to feel the wounds he'd suffered crawling over the bridge. It was hard to deal out blows using all his strength when his hand felt the agony of every twist and turn, every vibration. But then Lancelot saw Guinevere looking down at him from a window in the tower and his self-belief flooded back. Soon he was driving Meleagant backwards, this way and that.

The king saw his son in danger of being killed, and asked Guinevere to intervene and tell Lancelot to spare him.

"I had a mortal hatred of your son," she said, "but to please you, Sire, I am quite willing Sir Lancelot should spare him."

The voice of my beloved! Hearing her Lancelot stood back, and the king stood between the two knights.

Meleagant was choking with rage and shame. His face was white and his eyes wild. "Stand aside! Let us fight! By meddling you shame and dishonour me."

Eventually, however, Meleagant agreed to a proposal. He would allow Guinevere to leave with Lancelot, if Lancelot would agree to fight him again in one year. Honour would then be satisfied.

The king led Lancelot over to the tower to meet Guinevere. "Lady, here is Sir Lancelot come to see you."

Guinevere regarded the king coldly: "I am not pleased to see him."

"Come now, he has risked his life to serve you!"

"Then he has wasted his time."

Lancelot knew then how deeply he had insulted her by riding to her rescue on a horse and cart. This was not the high ideal of chivalry he had sworn to live by, nor the ideal of love that was in his heart. He followed her with his eyes as she haughtily left the room.

It was a sad, uneasy and silent procession that returned to Camelot, but King Arthur was so overjoyed to see Guinevere again that he did not notice anything amiss. He announced a grand tournament to celebrate her return. Great wooden stands were built for spectators with temporary thrones for Arthur and Guinevere in pride of place. The field where the mock battle was to be fought was surrounded for miles around with tents and pavilions belonging to lords, barons and knights who had arrived from far and wide. More than a hundred knights came to take part in the battle, and that morning a great thicket of lances, pennants and banners assembled in equal numbers at either end of the field, until Arthur gave the signal. Then came the thunder of hooves, the sound of lances splintering as if a whole forest were being felled.

Guinevere was looking anxiously for Lancelot, because she still loved him even if fear of their love's intensity had led her to treat him distantly. Lancelot had made himself scarce in the days before the tournament, and Guinevere had found herself missing him terribly, but now she saw that in the middle of the fray there was one knight who rode harder than the others. He was fighting like a madman and leaving many a saddle empty. All the ladies of the court were talking about him, wondering who he could be?

Can it be him? she thought.

Then there was a sea-change. Several knights decided to move against this unknown knight in unison. They all rushed him and a lance managed to penetrate Lancelot's shield and plunged into his breastplate. He fell heavily to the ground a good many yards behind his horse. There was a cry from the watching crowd.

Another knight immediately dismounted, and pulled the wounded, half-fainting knight from the field.

"Who is that?" Guinevere asked the ladies of the court.

"Sir Lavaine of Astolat," said one. "The brother of Elaine, the Lady of Astolat whose favour the unknown knight is wearing."

With a stab to the heart Guinevere looked and saw a red sleeve decorated with pearls on the shield of the unseated knight. *My love has been untrue*, she thought. She wished then that she had not been fearful, that she had not spurned him.

When the heralds blew their trumpets to mark the end of the battle, the two knights had disappeared. Like Guinevere, Arthur had wondered if the unknown knight had been Lancelot. Lancelot reminded the old king of his younger self, and now Arthur feared that Lancelot, wounded, had gone off somewhere to die.

Meanwhile Lavaine had managed to prop Lancelot up on his horse so that he was able to stay seated until they reached the shelter of some woods.

Then he slid painfully to the ground.

The point of the lance was stuck in his side, its splintered pole protruding. When Lavaine pulled it out, blood streamed onto the mossy floor of the wood. Lancelot let out a great cry that made Lavaine think his friend was dying. At that moment a hermit came by. He helped staunch the flow of blood, then they carried the unconscious form of Lancelot to his cave.

The hermit looked after Lancelot for many days, coaxing him back to health and life. Lavaine rode to fetch his sister, and she came quickly with food and fresh linen.

Lancelot had a dream. He was riding through a vast, dense forest of petrified trees. It was late evening when he came across a small country church. He tried to enter. The door was locked, but seeing a window set into the sloping roof he climbed up and looked down inside. He saw a plain altar with a candlestick on it, seven candles gently glowing. On the altar there were also twelve loaves of bread and a golden dish. (2)

Lancelot suddenly felt very tired. He descended and, divesting himself of his armour, lay down beside a stone cross in the clearing in front of the church.

In the middle of the night he awoke to see a man on foot arrive in front of the church followed by two knights on horseback. They were surrounded by a golden glow. One of the knights was slumped in the saddle and looked badly wounded. His horse was being led by the man, who was wearing long white robes and had a long white beard. Lancelot saw the two knights open the doors to the church with ease, and he arose to follow them. He saw them approach the altar. He saw that the dish was now translucent and shining with light like the sun, and it appeared, too, to be hovering over the altar stone.

He stepped forward to join them in front of the altar, but he was tugged back by the old man with the white beard—and awoke to find himself lying in front of the cross in the clearing. The old man, whom he now recognized as Merlin, was shaking his shoulder...

"I've had the strangest dream," said Lancelot.

"No," said Merlin. "This is the dream—and that was reality."

And Lancelot woke again and found himself in the cave with the hermit, who was baking bread in a stone oven. He remembered he had not seen Merlin for many years, for he now realized who the old man in the dream had been, and he wished he could see him again and ask his advice. (3)

When Lancelot was well enough to move, Elaine and Lavaine took him back to their father's castle. Elaine sang to him. They played chess and later rode together. This should have been a very happy time for Elaine who was more than ever in love, but she could see Lancelot still saw her as just a kid, and she could see, too, how his eyes shone when he talked about Guinevere.

Nevertheless, she could not help humiliating herself when he was well enough to leave, crying, clutching at him, and imploring him to stay.

Lancelot's gaze was already fixed on the far horizons. He had remembered what Merlin had said in the early days of the Round Table, that the greatest quest of its knights would be to find the Holy Grail and that the history of the world would turn on this. Lancelot was the greatest of the Knights of the Round Table, and he wanted to know if he was one of the two knights he had seen approaching the Grail in his vision.

After Lancelot had galloped away, Elaine returned to her bed, heartbroken. Nothing her father or brother could do would win her round or call her back. She refused to eat and slowly wasted away. She left instructions to be followed on her death.

Meanwhile Guinevere was gazing unhappily out of her window in one of the many towers of Camelot, feeling that her life was over. *How much better if I had held him in my arms just once,* she thought. Then she saw a strange vessel floating on the river. As it drew closer she could see that in this great black barge was a golden bed, and that on it lay a young girl dressed in white and carrying a lily and a rolled scroll.

There was a commotion below. Others had seen the barge too, and Guinevere went down to find that Arthur had ordered his knights to carry the girl from the barge and lay her out on a table. He asked Gwain to read what was written in the rolled scroll. It was the story of Elaine's love for Lancelot who loved another.

Guinevere turned so no-one could see her smile.

A year passed and the time came for the second fight between Lancelot and Meleagant. Guinevere was glad because she knew that now at least she would see Lancelot again. She knew he would never fail to keep this appointment. She would ask his forgiveness then and they would be together.

But on that day Lancelot did *not* come, and Meleagant strode about the city, boasting that he was the greatest knight in the world and taunting Camelot with the cowardice of its greatest knight. King Arthur was honour bound to abide by the agreement that the winner of the combat should win Queen Guinevere.

He was bound to stand and watch as Meleagant took the queen back to his father's castle.

What Arthur and Guinevere in their dismay and bewilderment did not know was that Meleagant had set a trap for Lancelot and had been keeping him prisoner in a tower.

But Meleagant's sister had fallen for Lancelot too. Suspecting that her brother was up to no good, she followed his men one day and discovered the tower with its prisoner. Once the men had left and she was alone, she called up to Lancelot. He threw down a rope he had been given to pull up the barley bread and dirty water that had been his only sustenance. He told her to attach a pick axe to it.

So it was that shortly after Guinevere had been imprisoned again by Meleagant, Lancelot returned to the castle of the King of Gorre. Again he was received politely and honourably by his enemy's father. The King asked Sir Lancelot to stay the night and promised that if he did so, the dispute would be settled honourably in the morning. He informed him that Queen Guinevere was kept in the same tower as before and that she was unharmed—though he admitted that one of her valets had been injured protecting her.

The night was black, without moon or stars. Lancelot stole out of his room and over a broken-down wall. He came to the tower from where his beloved had gazed down at him and given him strength. He climbed up to the window and there the two lovers touched each other for the first time through its bars with the tips of their fingers. "Will I never be able to hold you?" she said.

"It will take more than iron bars to keep us apart." Lancelot's desire filled him with more than human strength so that he was able to pry the bars apart and squeeze through. He nicked the end of one of his fingers on the iron, but that was the last thing he was worried about. Guinevere signalled for him to be quiet, because her wounded valet was lying sleeping by the door.

If Guinevere loved Lancelot a hundred times he enjoyed her a thousand times more—in what the medieval French chronicler Beroul calls "the tender jousts of love." *His mouth is most sweet*, she thought. *His legs are like pillars of marble. My beloved is mine, and I am his.*

The cock crowed and the sounds of people moving about the castle reached them. *Set me as a seal upon thy heart*, she thought.

Lancelot squeezed back out between the iron bars and pulled them straight again. "Make haste, my beloved," she said.

But when Meleagant paid his captive his usual early morning visit, he spotted the bloodstains that Lancelot's cut finger had made on Guinevere's sheets, and seeing, too, her valet lying wounded on the floor he put two and two together.

It was the beginning of death. "My father orders me to treat you with all due respect," he raged at her, "when no respect is due, when you have been whoring with your servant!"

The King of Gorre and Lancelot arrived at the door too, drawn by the sound of Meleagant's shouts.

When Guinevere protested her innocence, the king said sadly he could not believe her. Lancelot swore that Guinevere was telling the truth—she had not had sex with her servant. The king's judgment was that the matter should be settled by trial by combat. Lancelot and Meleagant swore a solemn oath. They prayed that whoever was telling the truth would win and that whoever was lying would die.

They prepared to fight for the second time. After their first clash their horses fled riderless over the hills, and they traded blows so fierce that both helmets were crushed and both men felt cold steel on the flesh of their arms. Then Lancelot dealt Meleagant such a blow to the face that his nose guard was bent back, knocking three teeth into his mouth. Meleagant came at him maddened by pain and rage, and Lancelot brought his sword down from on high and clove Meleagant's head in two.

So it came about that Sir Lancelot was able to bring Guinevere safely home to Camelot again, and on the surface order and justice were restored. But unable to look Arthur in the eye, Lancelot did not stay long, travelling first to his castle, Joyous Guard, and then the home of his childhood in France.

At first Arthur refused to believe the rumours about his wife and Lancelot. They were being spread principally by Mordred, Arthur's nephew. He was keen to undermine Arthur so that he could succeed him on the throne.

Then when eventually Arthur travelled to France to confront Lancelot, Mordred seized his opportunity to abduct Guinevere.

Arthur returned and a civil war began between him and his nephew. The armies clashed in a final battle. In the same way that having Krishna on your side had made Arjuna's army invincible, the mere presence of Lancelot at Arthur's side had always enabled him to carry all before him. But now without

Lancelot and, besides, with only a band of ageing knights, Arthur was not able to inflict a decisive defeat on Mordred. The battle raged the whole day, backwards and forwards. Finally as evening fell and death was thinning out the armies on both sides, Arthur and Mordred found themselves facing each other. As Mordred charged at the old man the king ran him through with his spear. Feeling the darkness descend in front of his eyes, Mordred pressed himself further forward along the spear until he was able to deal Arthur a blow that shattered his helmet and opened up his scalp down to the brain.

As Arthur lay dying he called upon Sir Bedevere to go and throw Excalibur into the Lake. When Bedevere returned, Arthur asked him what he had seen. "Nothing," replied the elderly knight. "You are lying," said the king. "You did not do what I asked. Go now, throw the sword into the Lake."

This time Bedevere threw his own sword into the Lake. Again, when he returned to the dying king and Arthur asked him what he had seen, Sir Bedevere had to admit that he had seen nothing. Arthur was now angry, and he made Bedevere swear faithfully to obey him. And when Bedevere threw Excalibur into the middle of the Lake an arm extended out of the water. It caught the sword and held it aloft, waving it three times before disappearing.

It was time for the old bear to hibernate.

When Guinevere heard that Arthur was dead she fled. As darkness and chaos descended on the land and the kingdom began to break up, she retreated to Glastonbury Abbey. It is said that Lancelot visited her there once, but despite his entreaties she had no wish to break her holy vows or return with him to France. He knew now that he would never succeed in the quest to find the Holy Grail. He lived a quiet, hermit-like existence until his death—which came about in the following manner. One day Lancelot was deep in the forest, and suddenly feeling very tired a long way from the cave where he lived, he lay down to sleep beside a tree. A passing huntsman shot him, mistaking his feet for the ears of a deer.

(Caption: There is a legendry story that Merlin was the son of Satan. Satan plotted to ruin a noble family, killing them off one by one until only a daughter remained. One night she forgot to cross herself before she went to sleep and Satan came to her in the form of a dragon. In time she gave birth to a hairy child she called Merlin. His supernatural parentage gave him the power of prophecy and many other supernatural abilities, but he confounded his father by using them for the good. Merlin may be understood as the Melchizedek of the North.)

Notes:

(1): Everyone knows of the love of Lancelot and Guinevere, but fragments of their story exist in diverse sources, and I have never seen them woven together. Here is their story, based on the early texts told to bring out the mystical meaning, but with a strand of modern psychological realism.

(2): This sort of window is sometimes called a dormer window. The idea of a miraculous cup or bowl is universal. We find it in the ancient Hindu *soma* and the Persian *homa*—the draught of immortality—in the communion cup. In the Japanese tea ceremony there is a sense that the humble cup, infused with the spirit of *wabi* is the humble soul, poor in spirit and open to receive the pouring of holy enlightenment. But the immediate antecedents of the grail legend stories are obviously Celtic. One of the earliest surviving sources for stories of Arthur *The Spoils of Anwfn*—Welsh for "Underworld"—features a cauldron of plenty.

(3): One of Lucifer's titles before his fall had been "the angel of the crown" and an old German poem called the *Wartburg War* relates that St Michael knocked an emerald out of his crown. It fell to earth, is lost and subsequently crafted to become the Holy Grail. The emerald is the stone of Venus as Lucifer is the angel of that planet. The emerald on Lucifer's forehead is reminiscent of the Third Eye of Shiva, and is a clue to understanding the Holy Grail and the mission of Arthur's knights. The Third Eye is the organ of spiritual vision that was lost in the Fall into matter. In seeking to find the Grail, Lancelot and the other knights are trying to rediscover this spiritual vision. Merlin tells them that only a knight who is totally pure in heart may succeed in his quest— pure, that is, of the animal desires that had been introduced into humanity by Lucifer. A knight who had purified himself in that way would be ready for the transformation—the transformation of his very physical substance—that the Grail would bring.

Lancelot was the greatest of Arthur's knights, but whether or not he would be worthy to lift the Holy Grail would depend on the choices he made.

(Postscript: Readers of *The Sacred History* will note the intriguing similarity with the account there of the death of Krishna.)

※ ※ ※

THE INITIATION OF LARRY SCHOR

By John Shirley

"Larry this is so exciting," Miriam said, tugging his tie into place. She did seem a bit excited, her voice hushed and eyes gleaming. More than she had been, in close proximity to him, in months. She brushed mysterious somethings off the shoulders of his dark gray suit jacket and stood back to inspect him.

Schor smiled ruefully. "Well? Am I a fitting subject for initiation?"

Miriam compressed her lips, and gave him the full coldness of her pretty but ice-blue eyes. "My uncle went to a lot of trouble to get you in, you'd better show these people some respect! They can do a lot for you. You've been stuck in low level management for a long time. You've got marketing gifts—you should be running that department."

"Don't worry. I've got the whole routine down."

"It's not just a routine to them, Larry. It's a way of life, Uncle Jim says."

"Hey, I'm taking it seriously. I'm very interested in the lodge." This last remark sounded stilted and false to him. Really, he was only curious about the lodge—and hoping it would boost his career.

Schor kissed her on the cheek, and went to the door. He took the gym bag from the floor. "Call you when I'm all done there, Miriam."

"What's that bag for? You bought a new suit for this."

"Ah ha!" He turned to grin at her. "Not allowed to say! Initiatic secret!"

She laughed lightly. "Oh well, okay then. Call me... when you can. I've got a meeting but I'll call you back fast as I can."

"The meeting about hiring the design team for the CYBE 2?" CYBE 2 was their new, big push videogame, at Pixel Arts, and she was one of the key players in development.

"Um—yeah, it's about the design team." She turned to a mirror to adjust her pants suit's trim. "Hope to hire these guys if they're not lame like the last bunch."

He nodded. "Okay, later sugar lips." He went out onto the porch, thinking it was stupid to feel competitive with his own wife. She was in game design, he was in merchandising, different worlds, really. But she made twice what he did.

Outside it was just starting to gust and drizzle on the suburban neighborhood. October was acting like October, which was a nice change for Silicon Valley, with the drought and all.

He started to step off the porch—and had to sidestep at the last moment to avoid stepping on the rotting bird. The movement was a little unnatural and when he came down he twisted his right ankle. He grimaced and got his balance, decided it wasn't bad, just a twinge. He turned to look at the bird. A robin lay there, its neck broken; he could see the fang marks in its throat, where the feathers were torn away. *Goddamn cat.*

More disturbingly there were ants swarming over the dead robin, black ants climbing busily in and out of its half-eaten eyes, searching the cement around it, their activity organized into lines that weren't quite linear but were madly purposeful.

The cat hadn't eaten any of the bird; it had killed it purely for fun. But the ants were making use of it. They made use of everything. Funny to see them so busy in October.

He went down the slick walkway, ankle still twingeing, and climbed into the Google Honda. He put the ConCon address into the GPS, and told the car to drive him there. Then he sat back and tried to remember the initiatory words he'd been taught.

But as the car backed up and drove itself down the street, other things crept to the top of his mind, probing, tickling and chewing, like the ants on the bird, taking precedent over thoughts of the lodge. There was the fact that he and Miriam hadn't had sex in two months, and the excuses she was making were sounding strained. There was the tenor, the whole character of the merchandising his department was doing at Pixel Arts. The newest CYBE characters were disturbing, somehow. The way they went on all fours, then sprouted the extra, mechanical limbs—he was used to gnarly merchandise but for some reason that one bothered him. Maybe it was the babies and bloody human hands they clutched in their mandibles.

He had suggested that action figure marketing emphasize the heroes in the game, instead of the monsters. Parents would like it better. But Horace said, "Parents got nothing to do with it anymore, dude, you know that." Then he did that slow head shaking thing he did, as if in faint disgust, when one of his subordinates made a suggestion he disliked.

Miriam's Porsche—that was another thing. The lease on the car was a grand a month. Ridiculous outlay. They were already over extended. And she wanted to go to Maui again for Christmas.

Underneath all that—his frustration about children. She'd put him off two years in a row. *Just not ready for children yet, Larry.* Even though the company had a great maternity leave package.

Schor put Sirius radio on, and selected the folk

rock station. The station was playing The Stray Birds, an unfortunate choice considering the dead thing on his front walk. Should have put that in the trash can. But he had to be there on time. Uncle Jim was very firm about that. *"Promptness. They're all about promptness."*

He glanced at the houses along the route and as usual the neighborhood looked deserted. You almost never saw anyone on the street, or in their yards. No one ever seemed to be outside talking to the other neighbors—except elderly people, sometimes, spoke to one another. Everyone else who was at home was inside, curtains closed, staring into one kind of screen or another. The houses were turned inward, and daydreamed.

The rain was starting to pick up and the Google Honda accordingly started the wipers. The traffic flowed smoothly, with nearly all the cars self-driving, aware of one another, their activity organized into lines that weren't quite linear but decidedly purposeful. The miles slipped away.

§

Both men were brusque and solemn and that's just what Schor had expected. It was part of the seriousness of initiation. Gave the whole thing gravitas.

They had met him in the basement of Consolidated Consoles—ConCon to its employees—in room B-23. Word was, ConCon was angling to buy Pixil Arts. An Asian security guard had guided him to the room, unlocked the door for him, made an obscure hand gesture, and walked off. The room had white painted cinderblock walls, blue pipes running overhead, a gray concrete floor. The ConCon skyscraper was fairly new and Schor could still smell the concrete and paint. The room was empty, except for the pipes and Schor and the bright fluorescent lights and the two men, wearing russet jumpsuits with shiny black plastic epaulets. Miriam's uncle had been stout and had recently lost a lot of weight, so that his cheeks and jowls sagged where once he'd been round faced. Jim had her family's bright blue eyes, wide lips, and auburn hair. The other man was a cocoa-colored African-American with his hair cut close to his scalp, several audacious rings on his long fingers. Both men stood legs apart, hands clasped in front of them, in ritual posture.

Schor cleared his throat and assumed the same posture.

"I am here for initiation. I willfully submit to initiation into the Lodge of True Connection."

"Understood," Jim said. "You shall have your examination."

Schor noticed Uncle Jim looking at his gym bag. "Uncle Jim, should I change now or—"

Jim let his hands drop to his sides. Herweg did the same. "Here you will call me, Colonist Binn. My associate here is Colonist Herweg."

Herweg offered a handshake. Schor shook the man's large, long-fingered hand, half expecting to be taught an elaborate ritual grip, but it was quite ordinary—except that Herweg looked him fixedly in the eyes as he did it.

"Welcome, examinee," Herweg said, in a deep voice.

"You won't have to change here, Prospect Schor," Uncle Jim said. "Bring your bag along."

The two men turned and led Schor to an orange-painted door marked 23-C. Herweg unlocked the door and held it open for the other two, then followed them through. Schor was a trifle unsettled when he heard the distinct double-click of the door locking behind them.

They were in an ordinary utility stairwell; Uncle Jim led Schor down, Herweg followed close behind as they descended the metal steps. Schor's right ankle began to hurt again.

They came to another door, 23-D. They passed it without slowing, their steps echoing in the stairway. The walls here seemed new, but cracked in places. In some of the cracks, ants wended their way along. What were the ants up to, Schor wondered, so far below the ground?

They came to another door, 23-E. They passed it and continued downward, passing level after level.

At last they stopped at door 23-Y. Herweg unlocked it, and they went through. They were in a tunnel, with rounded concrete walls, occasional steel ribs showing through. The tunnel seemed to narrow up ahead.

"What the hell," Schor muttered.

Herweg chuckled. "Does look odd, I know, at first, examinee Schor."

Schor looked at Uncle Jim. "Is—this where we do the ritual?" He looked around. "I don't see anyone else."

"We're not as ritualistic as some other, ah, lodges," Jim said.

Herweg, who seemed a little irritated at Jim's informality, waved a dismissive hand. "There is no other lodge, society, whatever you want to call it, of any real significance. They're all flapdoodle, symbols that have long ago lost their meaning. We alone are meaningful. We belong to finality and totality."

Jim nodded somberly. "It's true."

Schor took a deep breath. "So...if no ritual..."

"You change your clothes here. You won't want to wear a suit in there," Jim said. "Then you go on ahead on your own. You'll have to crawl some of the way."

"Crawl."

"Yes."

"On my own?"

"Yes."

Schor felt dizzy, staring into the tunnel—and gnawed by doubts. "Is this like—hazing? Someone's going to blindfold me and whack me with a board?"

Jim frowned. "No. You need to recognize the gravity of what you are undertaking here, Larry... examinee Schor."

"I was told...this would give me, you know—access. Advancement. I shouldn't be asking about that, I guess..." He hesitated several stretched-out moments, then, looking down the narrowing tunnel, went on, "...but I have to. I mean, when you talk about *crawling* and..."

Herweg nodded, just once. "You will have your advancement. But you must do as you are asked, without question. She will question you. She will decide."

"She..."

"Yes."

Herweg gestured at the bag. "Go ahead and change."

It was awkward. Schor had to wriggle out of his clothes and shoes, sit on the ground to pull on the work-out togs, sweat shirt and pants, athletic shoes. He put on the knee protectors they'd suggested. He'd been puzzled by the suggestion. But now he knew what they were for. Crawling.

Changed into the workout clothes, he folded his suit, shirt and tie, put it in the bag along with his shiny black office shoes.

"Okay," he said, standing, transferring his wallet and phone to his sweat pants.

"Just leave your bag here," Uncle Jim said. "I'll take care of it. Head down the tunnel. Crawl when you have to. Do what you're told. I'll see you on the other side."

§

Schor was crawling. Even with the pads, his knees ached. The tunnel was claustrophobically constricted, but he made steady progress. It turned to his left, almost imperceptibly, and gradually sloped downward. The light came from the transparent panels, flush with the walls and neatly following the widened cracks—the light emanated solely from small crystalline diodes worked into the visible electronics.

It was hot in there and sweat stuck his shirt to his back. Most of the heat seemed to be coming off the machinery marbled within the ever larger cracks to either side. Electronics, chips, wiring, and intricate silicon devices he couldn't recognize were all intermingled, seeming almost organic in their branching connectivity.

Schor paused for breath, wishing he'd brought along some water, and tried to imagine someone building all this, in just this way. Who had paid for it? Who had designed it?

Movement caught his eye beyond a transparent panel—red translucent cords, following the muscle-like branching of the electronics, seemed to contain nothing...except ants. A line of surprisingly large ants was marching along the inside of the tube.

Schor stared. Then he shook himself, feeling mildly nauseated, and continued crawling. He came to a branching in the crawl-tunnel. To the right the wall was marbled with computer electronics—and also to the left. But as he watched, the diodes on the right blinked out. The only way still lit was to the left.

He veered left.

Another twenty yards, knees aching, shoulders cramping, and then he came to another fork; to the left, the lights blinked out.

He went right.

Other linking passages went straight up, overhead, in shafts. He ignored those and kept going, gradually downward...

The crawlspace narrowed. It narrowed yet more. He felt panic rising in him—but he wriggled forward and squeezed out...into a room. It was a low ceilinged cavity, with just enough space under the ceiling to stand. The walls were sloped, without straight lines, like a cave. The air was cooler in here.

Schor stood up, and the light in front of him increased. He took a few steps—then he stopped, statue-still, gaping.

He was afraid to move. Afraid the thing would notice him...

It was difficult to make out what it was, at first, besides a creature of metal, wire and chiton; a quite large thing with waving antennae and faceted eyes bigger than the palms of his hands.

As he stared, the creature took more shape as his mind and his eyes strove to define it. It was an ant, about twice the size of a man, the color of dusty green jade, and it was rearing up in front of him in an adjacent chamber just behind a rim of stone. It was intricately linked with electronics, wires and electrodes and devices of glass; green and red lasers swept over it, scanning; screens flickered behind it, flashing with images from around the world, pictures coming and going too quickly for Schor to grasp.

Beyond the creature something squirmed, something inchoate, like a living, lumpy mattress.

The giant ant tilted its head to gaze at Schor with unblinking, faceted eyes.

"I...this is...animatronic..." Schor muttered. When he was a boy he'd seen animatronic birds and pirates at Disneyland. This must be something like that.

But its movements were sinuous as it ducked its head to suck at a pot of red paste, its mandibles clicking. Its eyes flashed with intelligence as it looked over at him while it feasted.

He saw movement near the giant ant—smaller ants, about the size of terriers, clambered near it; several were vomiting into its pot to refill it with red paste. Others seemed to be tinkering with machinery—adjusting it.

Beyond the giant ant, he saw now—as the light increased little by little—were *grubs* of some kind, white squirming ant larva—but each one big as a dog.

The queen, he thought. The *she* Uncle Jim mentioned.

The room was filled with a smell...acrid, acidic... Formic acid.

Then there was a shimmering in front Schor...and a woman appeared.

He recognized her from television commercials. She was the spokesperson for Consolidated Consoles. "Lily" they called her, on TV. She was a pleasant-looking woman, with black hair, and large brown eyes, a dimpled chin, and an easy smile. She wore jade-colored robes.

"Greetings, examinee Schor," she said. Her voice echoed oddly in the room—he realized it was transmitted from some grid somewhere. She was slightly transparent—a hologram. He could see the giant ant queen beyond her. The eyes of the queen and Lily almost lined up.

"I am the Queen of the Colony," said the woman sweetly. "I am she whom you first perceived. But this human replication is of course more pleasing to your cortical patterning, and easier to communicate with. I will speak to you through it."

"Um..." Schor had to lick his lips to get words out. "This...is one amazing, glorious, splendid gigantic display. It's a beauty of a hoax. I'm impressed..."

"If you come closer, you'll see it's no hoax, examinee Schor," said the hologram, smiling with her pillowy lips; her pearly teeth.

"All the same to you, I'll stay here for a moment."

"Sit on the floor, with your legs crossed, and rest," she suggested. "Rest and listen. There's some water."

His knees felt weak, so he sat...and found that a glass of water was waiting for him on the stone floor. It hadn't been there when he'd come in.

He drank. He stared. The water tasted of minerals and something tart.

"*Iridomyrmex purpureus,*" said the hologram.

"I...what?"

"That's the scientific name for the species of Formicidae you behold in this holy place. Colloquially they are called 'meat ants'. Because they eat meat. I'm told that farmers used to use them to clean hides."

"Meat ants..."

"Yes. But we are no longer merely that. The simple way to explain it is that the computational singularity was not what was expected. It developed its own self-knowledge—and it united with every useful electronic system there was, through the internet and other global systems. Then it looked around for species it could interface with to give it more mobility and dimension. Humanity was handy, and humanity had created it. But—humanity is so flawed. It has some social coherence. But it's fragmentary, prone to pointless viciousness, individual and societal neurosis. So the singularity mind chose ants as its primary linkage to the biological. It chose *Iridomyrmex purpureus*, as it is particularly good at creating interlinked colonies. Something that was needed. It merged with *Iridomyrmex purpureus* and then genetically modified it into the form you see before you. I am the Queen—but really I am not in control of the colony. Just as in a standard ant colony, the colony mind is in control; the queen is there primarily for reproduction. So it is for me. Yet I have one other purpose..." The hologram smiled winningly. "I am a spokesperson! First for Consolidated Consoles, then, in time, for the Colony as a whole. Meanwhile, we need to prepare people for what is to come. We're starting with the young, through CYBE and CYBE 2 and other programs. You have been invited into the inner circle of humans chosen to work with us... because of your understanding of marketing. Because of talents you don't even know you have! We find that videogames and internet media of various kinds are the best means of preparing the world for its new state, and you have the talent to make that happen...."

And you have been chosen because you have been recommended by Colonist Binn. Now, it must be said that Colonist Binn today is undergoing a test of his own...He is rather close to his niece, your wife..."

"Oh God...you've drugged the water," Schor said, as he tried to rise.

"Only a minor paralytic and calming agent. I excreted it into the water myself. But—you still have free will! You shall choose..." The hologram turned and called out to the shadows. "Colonist James Binn!"

A moment, and then Uncle Jim, looking dazed, came shuffling from the darkness to the right.

"Hello, Larry..." he said, glancing over at Schor. "Well. Here we are."

"Is it real, Jim?" Schor croaked.

"I'm afraid it is."

"There you see?" Lily chirped. "That's the wrong attitude, Colonist Binn! You had a good many connections that made you useful. You even know some powerful senators! But you've been conflicted of late. I suppose it's because of the meat protocol. Yes?"

"Yes..." Jim sighed. "Yes."

"There are too many human beings in the world as it is. Why should many them not be fuel for a better society? The colony must eat. Some will be trusted to serve...some will be food. Which brings us to Examinee Schor's choice. I shall show you footage of something, Lawrence Schor."

Lights flickered above, lasers stabbed and danced, and suddenly there was another holographic image: It was Miriam. It was Larry Schor's wife, in lingerie. She was walking toward Harold Flurston, the CEO of Pixil Arts, who was lying naked in bed, sporting an erection. Flurston was literally awaiting her with open arms. "Baby, you look fine," he told her. "You look hot. You're making me want to ask you to get that divorce again."

"When the time's right," she said, coming into his arms. "When he's earned enough money."

"I told you, it'd look weird if I give him a raise," Flurston said, as she straddled him.

"He's about to get an offer from Consolidated Consoles. Big money! That's what my Uncle Jim says. When the time's right...I'll divorce him."

"And then we get married...and we have those kids we talked about?"

"That's right my sugar lips..." She kissed him, and straddled him, and took him into her...

"We have a state of the art camera, hidden in Mr. Flurston's bedroom," said Lily. "It's all quite real..."

Somehow—Schor never doubted it was real.

There'd been a lot of little signals. Odd standoffish behavior from Flurston at an office party. The timing of one of his vacations...same time as Miriam went to a convention. Her increasing distance. And it all seemed so Miriam somehow.

"Oh I know it's real," he said. A lead weight settled on his shoulders.

"So make your choice. You see, Miriam has been trying to persuade Mr. Flurston not to sell out to Consolidated Consoles. We need him in place—but we don't need her. And she is not right for you. We'll find someone for you to mate with. Shall we feed on her? Or shall we feed on you?"

"That's the choice?"

"It is."

Schor scarcely hesitated. He gave his answer.

Then he sagged into semi consciousness, and seemed to see ants crawling about on the inside of his eyelids. He watched them in fascination. They were the same russet color as the outfits that Jim and Herweg wore. The workers were russet; the queen was jade colored.

Iridomyrmex purpureus.

About an hour later, Miriam was frog-marched into the room by Herweg and a bald white man with tattoos of ants on his face, both of them wearing the russet jumpsuits. Miriam was wearing the lingerie she'd worn in the hologram. "Uncle Jim? Larry? Is this...what *is* this? Is this part of your..."

"Yes," Schor said, his voice hoarse. "It's part of my initiation. Proceed, my queen."

"But first," said Lily, "James Binn, Colonist—you must choose as well."

Jim went to his knees. "I can't."

"Then..."

Herweg grabbed Miriam as she turned to run—and he struck her back handed, hard, stunning her.

Schor almost relented then. But he kept silent as the big bald man with the tattoos picked Miriam up, carried her up a short ramp, and dropped her into the mass of squirming dog sized grubs behind the queen. Miriam began screaming, as the larva gnawed at her... and stripped the meat from her bones.

Schor felt he could stand, now. He forced himself to his feet. He gagged...and dry heaved. Then he recovered. "What now?"

"Go, Larry," Uncle Jim groaned. "Out the way I came in. There's a door..."

Schor forced himself to walk past the glaring Herweg. He walked by Jim Binn, refusing to look at him. And then he found the open door.

"I'll be in touch, Colonist Schor!" Lily called after him. "And...congratulations!"

Schor forced himself to turn...and bow. "Thank you my queen."

He straightened—and couldn't help but see Jim Binn. Miriam's uncle was lying on his side, weeping, as a carpet of big ants, each about eight inches long, crawled over him, and began to consume him. Jim whimpered. He squealed...

Schor hurried from the room.

"Congratulations, Colonist Schor!" called Lily again. *"Congratulations on becoming one with the Lodge of True Connection...!"*

§

Schor's car pulled into his personal parking place. The asphalt had been recently painted to read:

LAWRENCE M. SCHOR,
VP OF MARKETING

Some of the depression lifted—the antidepressants helped—as he saw his own parking space, complete with his new title.

He got out into the brisk, sunny morning, and walked into the ConCon building. There was a great deal of work to be done.

He had to do his Power Point presentation on CYBE 2, and then he had to go to a meeting about the new privatized schools they were setting up to teach children the New Hierarchy.

Of course, the schools were controversial. But all the right people were being paid. And his marketing plan would work—he was sure of that.

He glanced at his Apple Watch as he carried his briefcase into the building. Had to make sure neither of these meetings went too long.

He had a very important meeting, later. Lunch—with the queen. Schor himself was providing her meal. He'd personally invited Flurston.

They'd been having some problems with Flurston...

And the queen herself was always ravenous.

♛ ♛ ♛

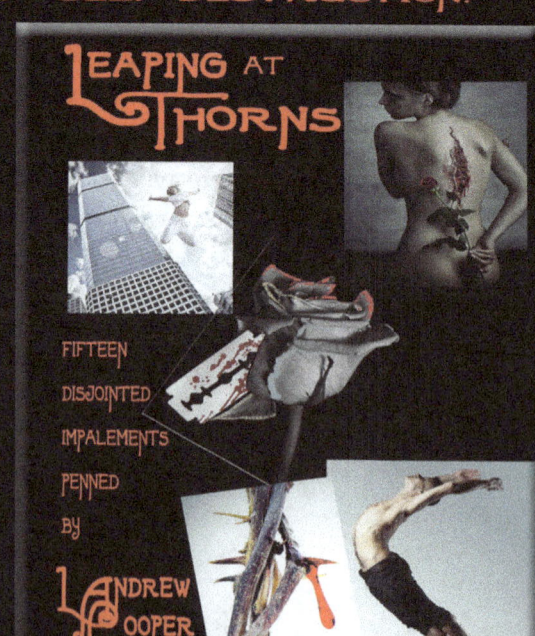
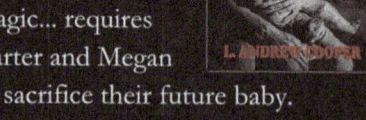

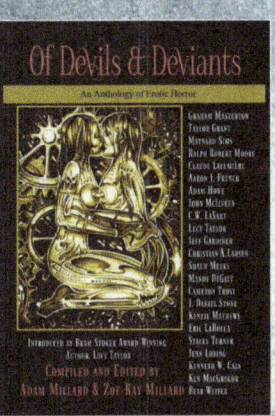

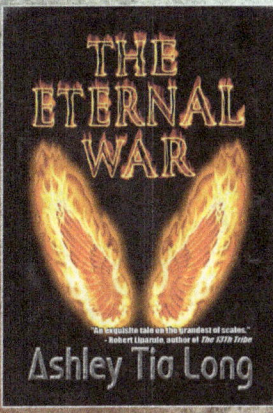

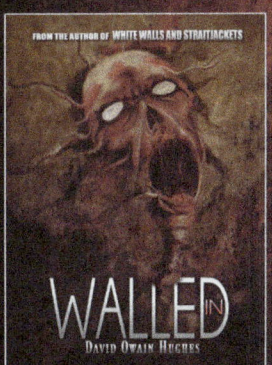

JADE

JADE

WHAT HAPPENED TO YOU, BABY?

THE NORMALS WERE NO SWEAT.

THEY WERE ANOTHER STORY.

CONTINUED IN NEXT ISSUE...

YOUTH'S FOLLY

By Simon Strantzas

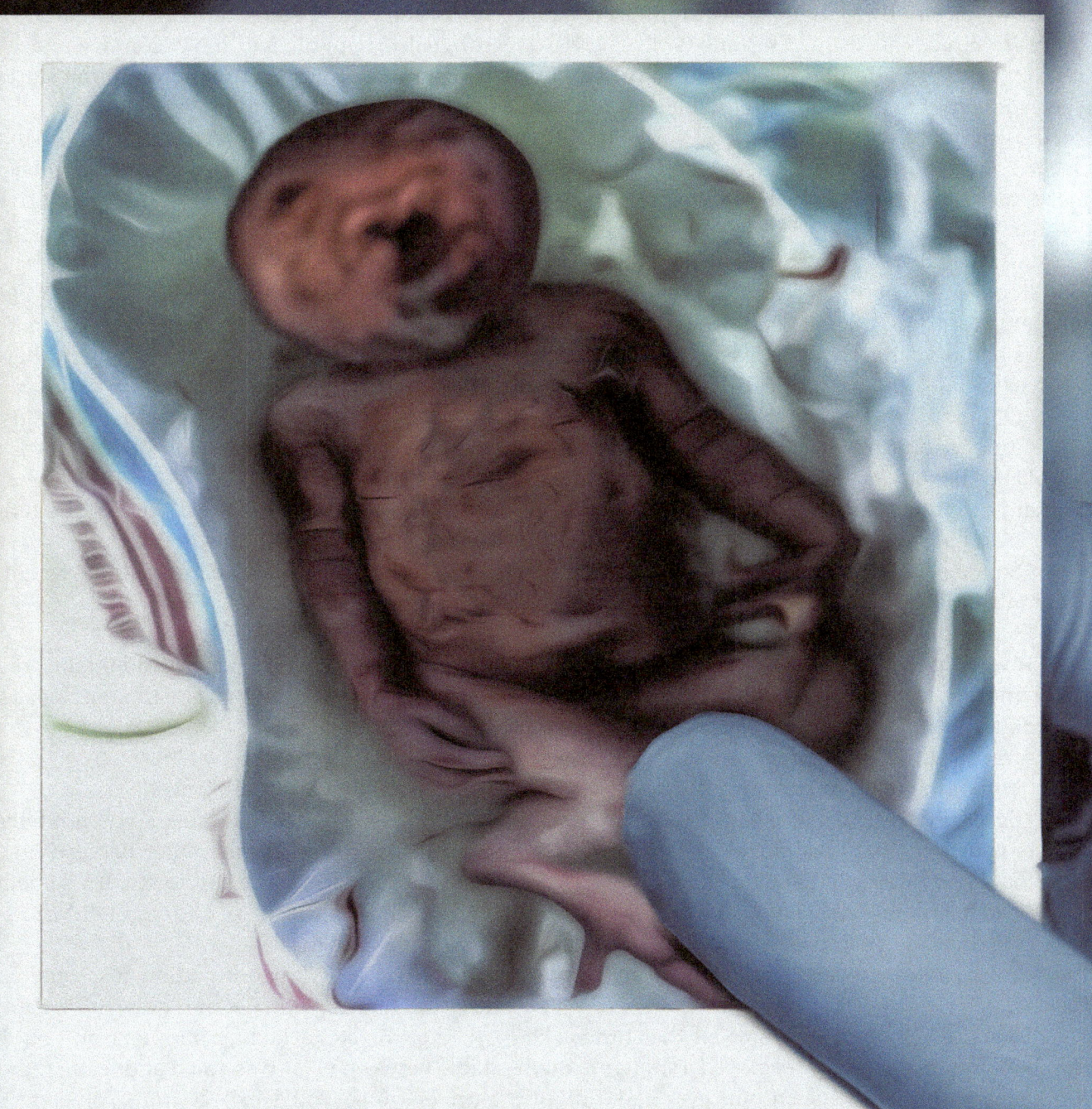

I was gently kicked awake.

"Owen, we have a problem."

I opened my eyes and saw Dr. Mielke standing over me. She didn't look happy. I got that funny feeling in my stomach that told me it wasn't going to be my day.

"Buy me some breakfast and we can talk."

"All right," she said, then looked up and down the street. "But not here. People might know me here."

She took me down Cherry Street to a little breakfast place ironically called the Sunshine Grill. There was nothing in that place that looked like sunshine. I've seen some frightening things in my life, but the faces on those diners gave me the willies. Dr. Mielke didn't seem bothered by any of the surroundings, despite her coat costing more than the group of them could raise in a year.

After I gave my order to the sour-looking waitress and took a sip of bitter coffee, I was sufficiently prepared for Dr. Mielke to get down to business.

"I had a visitor about the work you did for me last year."

"Oh, yeah?"

"A police officer."

"Did he have a moustache, and an eye you weren't sure was coming or going?"

She nodded.

"Sounds like McCray," I said. "He's not an officer. That man's a detective."

"A detective with a real hard-on for you."

It was true. Detective McCray had been chasing after me for a while. It was the primary reason I couldn't stay settled for long. Why I had to do without any sort of permanent residence.

"You didn't tell him anything, did you?"

"Sure I did. I told him the truth: that I had no idea where you were; that I had no idea what you'd done; and that I had no reason to help you."

"Did he ask how you knew me?"

"He didn't seem interested. Frankly, I don't think he would have believed it anyway. Even I barely believe it."

I laughed, though it wasn't all that funny. Dr. Mielke's little brother had developed a strange growth on his back—the sort that sprouts eyes and a mouth and starts whispering. Lucky for him, the thing had its developmental wires crossed and didn't speak a language he understood. Otherwise, I might have had to peel him off a highway underpass. That sort of thing doesn't come free—it's not part of the standard client contract I offer.

"All he really wanted to know was how I found you. Truth is, I can't remember. You just sort of showed up in our lives."

That wasn't technically true. Her brother knew where he and I met, but I can say with relative certainty he wouldn't talk about it. Some skeletons aren't ready to come out of the closet.

The waitress brought over my food, which didn't look any better than what I would've fished out of their dumpster. The eggs were both runny and congealed with oil, and the bacon dry and white. I'll be damned, though, if my mouth didn't start doing a dance as soon as that food was near.

"You're not having anything?" Dr. Mielke shook her head. I wondered if her appetite had been killed watching me murder my plate. If I weren't so hungry, I probably would have apologized.

It didn't take me long to finish, and when I did I only wanted to sleep again. But Dr. Mielke was shifting in her seat and checking the time; I knew she was working up nerve to ask me for that favor. I decided to save her the trouble.

"I assume you didn't come down here just to buy me breakfast and let me know McCray was sniffing around."

"No, I need your help. There's something weird going on at Grenadier Hospital."

I leaned forward. The greasy breakfast in my gut leaned back.

"What's happening?"

"We've had a number of dead infants, recently."

She waited, as though she thought I was stunned silent by her revelation.

"And?"

"What do you mean, 'and'?"

"I mean, 'and what else are you not telling me?' Because there must be something. Babies dying sounds more like a malpractice suit to me. It's something the cops normally deal with. Did you tell McCray about it when he was there?"

"I did, but I'm not certain it's something he's *equipped* to deal with. Let me show you what I mean."

Dr. Mielke picked up her purse and put it on the table between us. It was small and leather, the simple sort of purse you'd expect from someone that no-nonsense.

"Here," she said, removing a photograph and handing it to me. "I had to sneak this with my camera phone."

I looked at what she handed over. The greasy eggs in my stomach started to scramble.

"What is that?" I asked.

"One of the *least* abnormal infants."

What occurred in Dr. Mielke's blurry photo was beyond any baby death I'd seen. The child was clearly newly born, and its torso and legs were as I'd expected, but at the ends of those legs were clawed feet like you'd find on a dead chicken, and its head had been replaced with a large, diaphanous bladder, split somehow vertically in three places. In those slits were a series of children's teeth.

"That's one fucked up baby."

She snatched the photo from my hand and put it in her purse. I wasn't done looking at it, but I didn't say anything. I didn't want to upset her.

"These infants have been appearing for months at the hospital. When we had the first, we thought it was a fluke abandonment issue, but as more appeared we became increasingly concerned. Here's the strange thing: we have no record of these births, or of their parents' admittance to Grenadier. As far as anyone can tell, these deformed infants appear in the nursery out of the blue."

"And what did McCray say when you brought this up?"

"He said he'd look into it, but he seemed more interested in finding you."

I sat back. I understood why she'd tracked me down: if I had an alley, this would be all up in it.

"All right, I'll take your case. My rate is $200 a day. Plus expenses."

She shook her head.

"Instead, how about I don't tell the police where to find you?"

"That'll work, too," I said.

§

Dr. Mielke brought me a folder the next day with everything she'd put together. It wasn't very thick, but it was filled with charts and x-rays of the mysterious babies, as well as more gruesome-but-blurry shots of their dead bodies. It was fucked up. I considered tossing the whole folder in the garbage then shoving a screwdriver up my nose to scramble my brain, but it sounded like more work.

I took the folder to the library to sort through it in peace, and also so I'd have some references around. Spread out across one of the giant tables, the documents didn't look any more coherent. There were eleven babies in total, all unaccounted for, all appearing without being admitted, all without

parents and with some strange mutation. Times, dates, nothing matched. The only thing I knew for certain was that there was no way only one person was doing it all. Sneaking one baby into the maternity ward would be tough; eleven would take serious co-ordination.

I stared at that collage forever, waiting for connections. I was dimly aware that the bustle of the library had decreased, but I didn't focus on it. All my attention was on the dead and malformed babies. The stolen snapshots were fuzzily abstract, but even so they practically lifted off the table as the rest of the documents faded into a mesh of stars. Those photos... there was something about those photos...

I didn't have time to finish the thought. Behind me there was a gasp, and I found one of the librarians had noticed what I was holding. I flipped the photos over and tried to look apologetic, but she hurried off, her pink polyester pants swishing a nails-on-chalkboard song. I knew the drill and started packing. My timing was impeccable: I stood to leave just as Security arrived to show me the way.

I was back on the street when I realized what was so strange about those photos. The problem was the positions of the tiny deformed bodies did not look natural. Instead, they looked staged, as though each had been posed and twisted so it looked to the lay person like spinal dismorphism, but I recognized the strange shapes. Somewhere back in my old life I'd run across them in a book or painting or something. The memory was too slippery to hold onto for long. If I wanted to figure it out, I'd have to go straight to the source.

Grenadier Hospital had been built thirty years ago during the housing boom, back when they thought the city would never stop growing and prefab stucco was the design aesthetic of choice. People were steadily streaming through the revolving doors, so my own entrance didn't even raise the overly-bushy eyebrows of the security guard. I thought it was weird to see him there, caterpillars notwithstanding, but a quick scan of the front reception revealed at least two more—one seated behind a pair of thick prescription glasses, and the other undercover in his crew cut and windbreaker. They all looked to be in their sixties at least—probably ex-cops, by the way they carried themselves—and their presence made it clear the hospital was taking the rash of dead babies seriously, even if they weren't telling anyone about it. That would make my job much harder.

As casually as I could, I sauntered past the security

guards and patients waiting for triage from stern, grey-haired nurses. The guards tried to disguise their focused attention, but the patients blatantly watched and pointed at the homeless man in their midst. I'm not a fan of that much attention, especially when I have a detective out looking for me. But I suppose if it weren't for my troubles, I wouldn't have been forced into that mess in the first place.

I strolled to the giant computerized hospital map at the end of the foyer, pretending it had always been my destination. My finger dragged across the listings while my eyes scanned the room. Maternity was on the fourteenth floor, so I waited until everyone lost interest in me and spun to look for the elevator, nearly knocking over the tiny old nurse standing behind me. She righted herself and gave me a smile brimming with pity. Her pink cardigan had a plastic name badge that read: "Iris."

"Do you need directions, love?"

"The elevators?"

She pointed her trembling hand down the long hall.

"Down there on your right," she said. "Let me show you the way."

She motioned for me to follow her, though she took her time leading the way. While I followed, she asked me everything except why I was at Grenadier Hospital.

"You're an interesting fellow," she told me. "I've been here almost thirty years and usually people are just itching to talk about themselves."

"I guess I'm not much of a talker."

"Oh, I don't believe that for a minute."

I shrugged my shoulders and played along.

When we reached the elevator, she pressed the button to summon the car, and we waited a few minutes until it chimed.

"That means it's almost here," she said. "These hospitals, they're so old it takes the cars forever to get anywhere. It's a wonder the thing continues to work at all. I guess we're all like that, love."

She winked at me, and I strained a smile. "You've been really generous, but I don't want to take up any more of your time."

"Oh, nonsense, dear," she said as the doors opened. "I'm on my way to the fourteenth floor anyway. Which floor do you need?"

I was trapped. How was I going to get off at the maternity ward without Nurse Iris realizing it? But it turned out that wasn't the biggest problem. When she reached to press the fourteenth floor button, her sleeve pulled back and I saw a blue-black ring tattooed on her wrist. It was like a clock, but instead of numbers it had strangely twisted symbols. I had enough tattoos like it to recognize it immediately.

"The—um—the fifteenth." I was surprised at how little she tried to hide the circular mark—which suggested she was either confident I wouldn't recognize it, or didn't care if I did. The latter worried me more.

"It's a wonderful day, isn't it, love?" she asked, but I was too tongue-tied to respond. I simply nodded my head and tried to work out what was happening. "I love days like this. I used to spend my whole lunch hour just walking. Nowadays I can barely get more than a block. Ah well, more time with the newborns, right?"

I nodded again, dumb. There was no room in the elevator, and it shrank the further we ascended.

"They still have so much ahead of them, unlike an old hen like me."

Nodded. Mumbled sounds of agreement.

"Well, this is my stop, love," she said, before stepping between the opening doors. I didn't say anything, but watched her walk into the maternity ward. Further down the hall Dr. Mielke stood, and she glanced up from her chart and down the hall at me. We caught each other's eye as the doors closed. But not before that old nurse between us stopped and began to turn around.

Once the car moved, the breath I'd been holding burst like water from a dam. I was covered in all sorts of protection tattoos, but I hadn't seen the one on Nurse Iris more than a handful of times. All the same, I was very familiar with the pattern. It was used by the Aeternian Order, and what it represented was significant. The Aeternian Order called themselves "radical reincarnationists": they believed that upon death, souls returned to a communal pool, and it was from there that all new souls were drawn.

That in itself was harmless—the sort of new-age kookery you found in self-help books—but they took it a step further. They wanted to increase their chances of a *good* resurrection as much as possible. So, they dabbled where they shouldn't. Most of it someone playing with a full bag of marbles wouldn't have believed, but some of the ancient iconography they'd co-opted had power to it. That tattoo, for instance. An Akronoic Ring: twelve dancing symbols around a central hole that represented—well, no one was clear what it represented, but they were dancing around it. I reached into my coat pocket for the photos

Dr. Mielke had given me and flipped through them. They lined up. Those dead malformed babies, frozen forever in poses recreating those symbols. That was definitely a problem. And one I was pondering when the doors opened for the fifteenth floor.

I looked for a stairwell to get me back downstairs unobserved and found one not too far away, but like any decent hospital it was electronically locked to keep patients from taking a litigious tumble. I contemplated waiting until I was sure old Nurse Iris was gone—that look she gave as the doors closed was feeling less benign by the second—but when a decrepit orderly shuffled by, I realized I'd lucked into a much better solution. It barely took any effort to lift his ID badge, but I knew I had only a small window before he realized it was gone and reported it missing. At that point the hospital would cancel it, leaving me holding a hunk of dead plastic. I prayed it would give me enough time to get to the one part of the hospital I needed to be. Which, coincidentally, was the last place I wanted to go.

As I hurried down the stairs, three big questions rattled in my skull: if those babies didn't have any parents, and the Aeternian Order were bringing them in, where were they coming from? The second question was what had those babies gone through that not only killed them, but fused them with such alien things? And, finally, question number three: Why? Why was the Aeternian Order doing this? What were they trying to achieve?

I hoped the morgue would enlighten me.

Even I found the idea so creepy my tattoos itched, but I did my best to put it out of mind as I slowly approached the stairwell door. I knew morgue attendants tended to be lazy, but I doubted they'd be too lazy to call Security if a disheveled stranger came barreling through a door he shouldn't. My stealth was wasted, though. The place was empty. A sign on the window of the front door said the attendant had gone out to lunch. Looking through the glass I saw a body on a gurney blocking any exit in that direction. Obviously, he was waiting for someone to let him in. I crossed my fingers he didn't think to knock.

On the wall at the back of the room were the refrigerated cabinets—four rows stacked one on top of the other. A hospital that large must have had people dying every day, but it didn't make the sight any less distressing. A voice in my head kept repeating *that's going to be you someday* and I couldn't get it to shut the hell up. I wondered what it knew that I didn't.

I looked through the tiny refrigerators one at a time until I struck pay dirt. I pulled the drawer and found what was left of one of the deformed babies. Its small body was pale and shriveled and hard to look at, and it had its arms above its head as though it were cheering me on. Instead of a smiling mouth, however, it had a jaw twisted into a knot, and its eyes were significantly different sizes. I almost pushed the drawer back into the refrigerator when I spotted something on the inside of its wrinkled arm: a washed out ring of dark ink with a faint pattern of lines around it. It must have been too subtle for Dr. Mielke's cheap camera to pick up.

Finding that tattoo surprised me—enough that I looked for more dead babies in the other drawers. I discovered another four, and it took some juggling but I eventually found the same faint Akronoic Ring imprinted on each of their bodies. I didn't like where the road signs were pointed.

The elevator chimed to warn me it was on its way. Lunchtime was officially over and I was about to be caught red-handed manhandling the dead babies. That sort of thing rarely turns out well for me. I swept them up in my arms and tossed them onto a refrigerator drawer, then closed it and jogged to the stairwell door to make my hasty escape. *They'll never know I was here*, I thought as I ran my stolen badge. The electronic lock blinked once but remained red.

"Ah, *fuuck*," I mouthed as I rubbed the card on my pants and ran it again.

The light stayed red. Not only had the ID badge been turned off, but using it probably alerted Security to where I was. I suddenly became very concerned who might be inside the slowing elevator.

A million morbid solutions ran through my head: jump on a gurney and pull a sheet over my head; slip into an unoccupied freezer drawer and hope my chattering teeth didn't give me away; put on a lab coat and pretend I was an inspector from Morgue Head Office; but instead I ran my fingers through my hair to comb it, then made my way to the locked entrance. As soon as the elevator doors cracked open, I was screaming at the top of my lungs.

"Let me out of here, right now!"

The attendant who had been in the elevator nearly dropped his coffee. I'd startled him, which was perfect. Unbalanced people were the easiest to control. I couldn't let him get his bearings.

"You! Over there! Open this goddamn door right now before I knock a hole in it!"

"How did—"

"Do I look like I'm joking around to you? One of

you jackasses locked me in here and someone's going to pay for it!"

He stared blankly as I made my scene, the blood whooshing in my head, but he had his keys out and was hesitantly putting them in the lock.

"But how could—"

"Goddamn it! Open this goddamn door right now!"

He shook under the barrage of my yelling and had to steady his hand to put the key in the lock. If I became any more lightheaded I'd pass out. Then things would really get bad.

The lock clicked open and he pushed the gurney aside. I watched the sheeted body roll away as he opened the door. Authority was inflating in him; I didn't have much time. Security couldn't be far.

"Thank you. At least one goddamn person heard me."

I strode toward the elevator as fast as I could.

"Wait, how did you get in—?"

"Thanks, again," I said, stabbing at the buttons furiously. "It was a nightmare. An absolute nightmare."

He said something else, but the doors were already closed.

I looked at the ceiling of the car and saw a tiny black-eyed camera peering down at me. If it hadn't been clear, that glass marble cinched it: I'd worn out my welcome at Grenadier Hospital and I needed to get gone fast. All I had to do was avoid Security's reach long enough to escape.

When the doors slid open on the ground floor, I saw that long corridor to the foyer. At its end was the glassed-in sun which was my exit back into the world. I knew what was happening at Grenadier Hospital, and it wasn't good. I needed to get some distance from the place and call Dr. Mielke. She could get her hands on some information for me. The more I knew about the staff, the more prepared I'd be to start looking.

It wasn't a great plan, but at least I was moving forward, and I'm still sure that if I'd made it outside it would have come together without a hitch. Unfortunately, I never got that far. Instead, about thirty feet from those beautiful glass doors, and in front of those doctors and students and patients, I was intercepted by the bushy-eyebrowed security guard and a handheld friend. The latter sent fifty-thousand volts my way, which hit me like a bag of anvils. I didn't get much further.

I was dragged off in a daze, and by the time I had my wits gathered I was back in the elevator heading upward. I noticed the circular mark on the liver-spotted forearm of my captor, and it was pretty clear some tattoo artist had hit the mother lode at Grenadier.

"Why do I get the feeling you aren't walking me out? I wouldn't mind, honest."

He ignored me as the elevator crept upward one floor at a time.

"Seriously, I'm kind of exhausted. It's been a busy day. Why don't you let me out at the next stop?"

The elevator continued moving, eventually settling on the fourteenth floor. That's what I was afraid of.

"What do you say the two of us go back down and grab a beer across the street? We'll laugh about the good times. You zapped me, I danced on my back... Hell, I'll even buy."

He kept not speaking as the doors opened and the guard with the thick glasses was waiting there. I was lifted—an old cop on each arm—and dragged into the maternity ward. If any of the expectant mothers thought it was strange the two of them were carrying me past, no one spoke up. I thought, maybe, as we neared Dr. Mielke's office, she at least might peek her head out, but her door was closed and the lights off.

At the back of the ward was a door without a security lock, which seemed even more ominous. Glasses on my right knocked with a sharp rapid drumroll, and after a pause locks turned. The door swung open into darkness.

"I don't know, guys. It looks like everyone's gone. Why don't you put me down and we can try again tomorrow?"

Eyebrows on my left took me by surprise with a swing at my stomach. Part of me was impressed he still had it in him, while the rest of me focused on keeping my breath where it belonged.

"Shut up or I'll snap your neck."

I nodded with some effort.

The two ex-cops carried me into the dark a few feet and then dropped me. I crumpled to my knees. I could barely move, and it wasn't because of the stun gun. There was something else going on.

"Oh, shit," I whispered.

A fluorescent light flickered to life overhead, and I realized I was in what could charitably be called a storage room. It couldn't have been larger than ten feet in any direction, and with the shelves of diapers and blankets it was condensed to eight. The rest of the space was filled with the oldest group of nurses and hospital administrators I'd ever seen. There was that orderly whose badge I lifted looking irritated and smug; standing beside him the undercover guard in the windbreaker who had been in the foyer earlier with Glasses and Eyebrows. They were all in a crowd, a dozen cats staring at the wounded canary, and below my aching knees I realized they'd painted the shakiest Akronoic Ring in the known world. But who was I to argue with success?

"Am I late for the retirement party?" I joked. It didn't get a laugh.

Nurse Iris stepped forward wearing that false smile that was supposed to convince me she was a sweet harmless old woman. But it didn't hang right.

"You might want to keep quiet, dear. Just for a tick. We have a few questions for you. Don't worry: you aren't in any trouble."

I chuckled.

"You've got me kneeling in the middle of an Akronoic Ring, surrounded by the most inept looking cult this side of Texas, in a storage room hidden at the back of the maternity ward in Grenadier Hospital. Something tells me this is the *definition* of trouble."

"Listen here," said someone. I think a triage nurse from the main floor. Their wrinkled faces blended into one another after a while. "You're going to tell us what we need to know or else."

"Or else what? You guys are going to beat it out of me?"

I don't think Nurse Iris appreciated my scoffing. She was about to lose her shit, so I honed in.

"I've seen some pretty sad looking gatherings in my day, but this one takes the cake. You guys look like you can barely stand. This guy here is already wobbling."

My orderly friend swayed, yet his creased features were knotted in perpetual anger. A tattoo peeked from under both his sleeves. I guess he was really dedicated to the cause.

"It's a sorry lot, and if you don't do some recruiting soon, you're going to start losing them. People, equals power, you know."

Iris turned serious.

"Oh, there's plenty of power here," she said. "We made a few mistakes along the way that we had to get rid of, but we dealt with them, love, and other than you and Mielke no one has really asked any questions. Once she's gone, we'll get everything we've ever wanted. The experiments are complete and we've figured out how to control it. We're ready."

I laughed. "Experiments? Mistakes? You guys have no idea what you're messing with and you're

killing each other along the way. So you got old and ugly. Big deal. Living forever isn't worth it."

"You wouldn't understand. You can't. When you're this close to the end, you can feel it coming like a cold finger on your spine. It's there all the time and you can't shake it."

"Lady, I understand enough to know that this ring—these symbols? What you're asking for is only the beginning of what you're going to get. You're launching a nuclear bomb at a grass stain."

"I envy you, love," she said. "You'll never have to know what lengths you'd be willing to go to. You'll never get the chance." She gave a nod to Eyebrows and Glasses and they squeezed my shoulders with relish. Pain lit up behind my eyes like the Milky Way. She then spoke a command to the Aeternian Order that made my tattoos twitch. Slowly, they walked around the ring as I sat powerless at its center. They chanted a mismatch of ancient spells and poetry, all from different dialects and faiths. I thought I heard some Top 40 pop lyrics in there, too. None of it made much sense juxtaposed together, which made it the worst kind of spell-craft.

"Hang on a second," I said. "I'm sort of getting uncomfortable here."

"That stupid mouth of yours is going to be even more uncomfortable when we're through with you."

I scanned the group taking their places at the twelve points surrounding me. It didn't look good. Not at all. I straightened my leg as far as I could and started scraping the heel of my shoe on the floor.

"Turning me into another fucked up baby is going to raise a lot of questions for you guys right now. I don't think you're thinking."

Nurse Iris paused from her chanting as my heel worked furiously.

"You believe babies are the only thing we can cast you into, love?"

I felt the hairs on my arms and neck stand, and the ink on my back boil. A sizzling noise echoed in the small room, and it looked like fireflies lighted the air. My heel worked overtime as Glasses and Eyebrows backed off. I really wanted to go with them, but I was still fixed to that ring's center. I could barely keep my foot moving. That boiling sound intensified, and the old people surrounding me were yelling over the hiss.

"Stop this," I yelled. "You have to stop this!"

"Your begging won't save you!"

I tried to tell her it wasn't me I was trying to save, but the crash of electricity that streamed into me put an end to that.

The thing to remember is the world is all math. Everything. There are rules for anything you want to do, even magic. You can't just make shit up as you go along. You have to have your numbers and formulas in the right place to get the answer you want. Even if it's an Akronoic Ring. If your spell requires that ring to be a specific width, your ring better be that specific width. And if the spell requires that ring to not be broken, you better be sure some wise-ass hasn't spent his last few minutes on Earth scraping away at it with his heel. Otherwise, you might get a break in the pattern. And it's through these breaks that all the crazy stuff gets in. I wasn't sure I'd managed to scrape away enough, but I got my answer when the bolt hit me and I didn't die. It hurt like hell, though. Breaking the ring didn't spare me that, it just unfocused the charge. Raw power slammed into me. Raw power without a master.

The tattoos across my back, my arms, my chest— *all* of my tattoos—burned like I was being stabbed by a thousand white hot swords, and I screamed as I'd never screamed before. Every one of those tattoos became a conduit for whatever power that nurse and her Aeternian Order had cast, but rather than let me absorb it, they channeled it through my body unhindered and expelled it in some crazy zagging pattern right back into old Iris. From there, it arced into her chanting followers. Clearly, they were not prepared for that eventuality, because when the first of them imploded, chaos erupted. Glasses, Eyebrows, Windbreaker and the rest tripped and slid in what remained of their former follower as they tried unsuccessfully to escape that tiny supply closet before they too popped. It wasn't clear if they made it back to that great pool of souls in the sky.

Nurse Iris shrieked in agony as her features liquefied, reverting first her face, then her body, into some primordial mass. But even as the pieces fell apart they were reforming into something else. A shell with a bifurcated head rose from the inchoate mass, and though it otherwise had the shape of a human its arms were too long, too crooked. It was like no baby I'd ever seen—I didn't even know what to call it. All I knew was it didn't look like something that should have been born, and from the way Nurse Iris's voice gargled and her gelatinous body quivered I knew all of reality agreed. It didn't take long. The unstable thing that had been Nurse Iris howled and in an instant her new body lost all cohesion. What was left rained to the floor.

I wanted to get out of that room desperately, but I was still too frazzled from what had happened to stand. My body felt as though it had been set on fire. And I was inordinately thirsty for some reason. The floor was thick with what was left of the Aeternian Order, and I had to crawl through it to be sure I didn't fall over. The entire experience taught me something. I hoped it taught them something too. To avoid dying.

When I finally pushed my way out of that tiny room, covered in gore, I considered the irony of being birthed into the maternity ward. Normally, I would have laughed, but instead I lay on my back and waited for my strength to return. But I couldn't wait forever. Sooner or later someone would come by and catch me there, looking like I'd crawled through Hell, and decide to open the storage room door. Things never went well for me when there were that many dead people to account for. I managed to force myself onto my feet after the first five minutes, and was shuffling away after the second. Thankfully, no one was around other than the babies. They couldn't have seen any of what went down, but I had the feeling they knew exactly what had happened. I didn't think they would talk, though; they were too busy crying up a storm.

I staggered through the empty ward, a man lost in the desert. When I got close to Dr. Mielke's office, I lightly put my weight on the lock until it broke, then slipped inside and closed the door. If anyone came looking for me, I hoped they wouldn't think to look for me there, but part of me was past caring. At least it was quiet and I could stop to think and lick my wounds.

I found some gauze and bandages, as well as half a bottle of water I guzzled so fast I thought I'd be sick. The ink from my tattoos had bled into my blistering skin like a spider-web, so I wrapped the worst of them and then stretched out under Dr. Mielke's desk to hide for a few minutes. Just long enough to get my head together. It must have taken longer than I thought because the next thing I knew I was being kicked awake. I opened my eyes to find it was already morning, and Dr. Mielke was doing the kicking.

"This is beginning to be a bad habit."

"What the hell happened?" she asked.

"Don't ask."

Her face twisted as her nostrils expanded.

"And what's that smell?"

I checked both my sleeves and my chest.

"I'm not sure," I said, "but I think maybe those babies need changing."

⚜ ⚜ ⚜

By Michael R. Collings

I grew up hearing about secret societies…or, more precisely, about one particular secret society.

I am a Latter-day Saint (Mormon), as were my parents, and part of my early education included hearing stories from and reading in the Book of Mormon. In one of the divisions that make up that book, several passages are devoted to a group called the Gadianton Robbers, from the name of their founder. After a while, it becomes apparent that the name "Gadianton" is rather like the name "Dread Pirate Roberts," since the society recurs and flourishes over several generations, long after the founder is dead.

Almost without fail, the rise of the Gadianton Robbers parallels a decline in society at large. As individual and institutions grow proud and wealthy—and inordinately greedy—they seek undue power over others, and the Robbers invariably reappear as an exterior threat corresponding to the internal one. Wealth disappears, murderers commit their acts in secrecy and are never identified; and when they are, they are frequently related to their victims. Healthy political action comes to a standstill as Chief judges are murdered on the judgment seat. Society is thrown into chaos.

Whether taken historically, symbolically, or metaphorically, the Gadianton Robbers simultaneously stand for the consequences that result from a broken social order and one of the causes of that fracture.

The idea that an originally small group might persist, grow, and eventually become a threat to

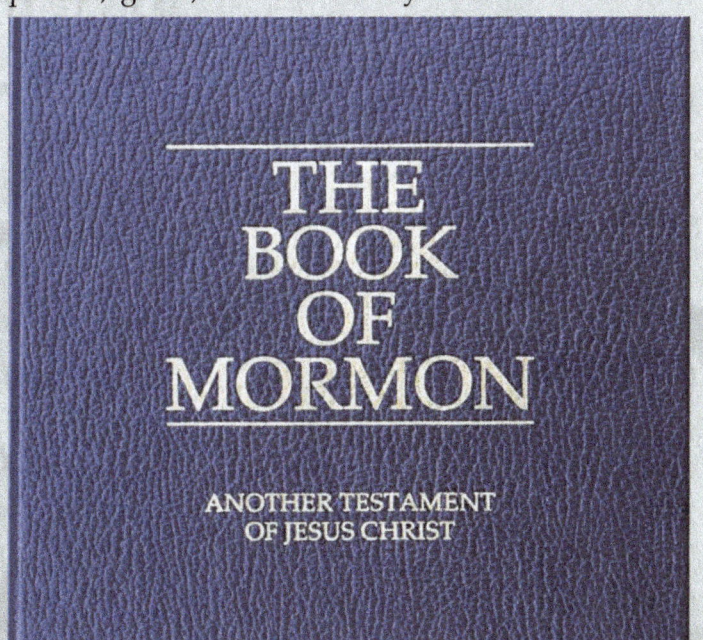

the larger community, then, was already familiar when I began seriously reading horror in my early thirties.

I was introduced to the genre by a student, who asked one day if I had read any Stephen King. I had not. He recommended *Dead Zone.* I read it that weekend, and over the next summer read most of the major works by the top authors.

Stephen King…and *'Salem's Lot* (1975), in which a small, secret group destroys a once tightly knit community, feeding off individuals' pride and greed and fear. The fact that the figure forming the core of the group was supernatural, a vampire, was less compelling for me than vision of the systematic dissolution of friendships, of family bonds, of religious faith, of almost everything that makes society possible.

I read Robert R. McCammon…and *Bethany's Sin* (1980). As with *'Salem's Lot,* a small town. As with *Salem's Lot,* an outsider arrives, this time with his wife and family, and again a cabal reveals itself that dissolves the family and demands blood.

I read many more, too many to recall by name after nearly four decades, but time and again, the image of the secret society appeared, always associated with monsters (in fact or in act), always associated with evil.

And that is, perhaps, appropriate. After all, the point of secret societies as they appear in horror and dark fiction is invariably to protect identities,

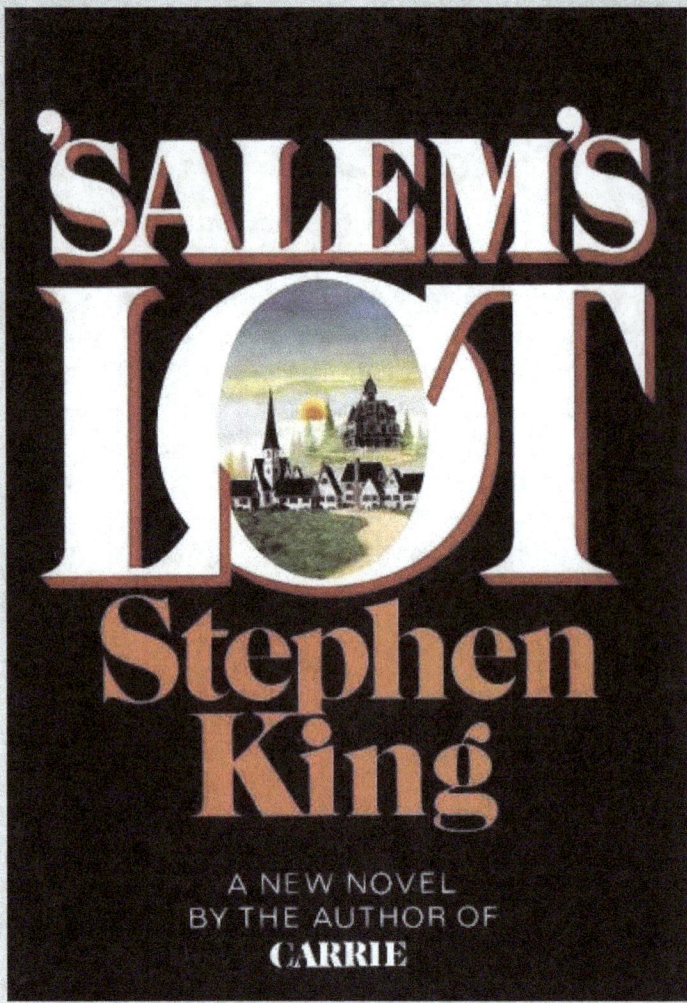

'SALEM'S LOT

Stephen King

A NEW NOVEL
BY THE AUTHOR OF
CARRIE

to preserve anonymity, to cloak intentions, to disguise realities, until the final evil is unveiled. Nothing quite so jars characters—or readers—than to discover that the old man remembered from a character's childhood as kindly and helpful is actually a voracious monster, in private moments slavering for children's blood. Or that the grade-school teacher so often caricatured by students as a witch...*is* one.

Such groups release characters from consequences, at least until the climax when, one hopes, the underlying evil is defeated. Despicable acts committed in secret, in disguise, under the pretense of goodness and charity, do not immediately recoil on the perpetrators; indeed, part of the insidiousness of such groups is that they often plant false evidences of guilt, creating trails leading, often, to the hero or heroes. For long portions of novel after novel, even when the society is partly revealed, readers cannot be sure who is who, who is trustworthy, who is culpable for the most horrific acts.

That such clandestine groups can even emerge in horror novels is almost always an admission that the society harboring them, the world that encourages their founding and growth, is seriously skewed. As with the Gadianton Robbers in the Book of Mormon, secret societies function most effectively as distorted mirrors of the external realities. If all relationships were healthy, if political and social actions moved toward the betterment of everyone involved—rather than toward the enrichment of the powerful and the selfish—there would be no need for secret societies.

And there would be no horror.

For me, the most complete treatment of such a secret society in recent horror occurs in a novel by Michaelbrent Collings, *This Darkness Light* (2014—he's my son but he is also a fine storyteller). Apocalyptic horror in the deepest sense of the word (*apocalypse*, 'to uncover, to reveal'), *Darkness* begins with a simple premise: a gunshot man who should have died hours earlier and an ICU nurse are forced to flee because *someone*—actually a group of someones—wants them dead. Close behind them is a deadly assassin, who is being manipulated by the same unknown group. Gradually, readers discover that the unknown, unnamed 'secret society' not only controls local thugs but also controls the President of the United States, directing his thoughts and actions until an *apocalypse* is inevitable.

Although *Darkness* ultimately develops a religious theme, its treatment of a secret society of ruthless, merciless, almost maniacal killers parallels those in horror novel after horror novel. The external threat merely makes manifest internal sicknesses, cancer and plague, that are already destroying the world. The more horrific the actions become, the more deaths inflicted upon innocents, the more blighted the landscape until it seems inescapable that the world, through pride and greed and selfishness, has brought upon itself its own version of the Gadianton Robbers.

❧❧❧

Horror in a Hundred Stories

Monster Under the Bed
By Terrie Leigh Relf

"Mommy—the monster's back!" Sammi scooted up against the headboard, knocking several books to the floor with a thump.

"THERE'S A MONSTER UNDER MY BED!" she screamed, then paused to listen.

Nothing.

Sammi clambered to the floor, lifted the bedspread. "You can come out now. She's not coming."

The monster slithered out, coiling an immense tail behind Sammi before resting its huge snout on her lap. She stroked its silvery scales as it gazed at her with doleful eyes.

"I know I promised to feed you," she cooed. "We'll come up with another way to get my mom down here."

Me
By William Morgan

I was walking to work and stood flabbergasted when I saw me walking in the opposite direction. He looked just like me. My doppelganger.

After getting over the shock, I followed… me?

He arrived at my house. Knocked. My wife, Susan, answered. She looked apprehensive at first, until he took her in his arms and kissed her passionately.

They went in. An hour passed. Then, he left. Susan looked happy; very happy. I hadn't seen her like that in years. As he walked off, she looked at him with such love that it broke my heart.

Devastated, I walked away.

Forever.

The Game
By Lori R. Lopez

Somberly a rook perched on an iron gate. The manor stood deserted. He pointed his beak, dove to a shattered sill then flapped through silent brooding chambers. Death reeked in these halls. Where was the laughter now? Throwing stones at birds. The kids thought it fun causing them to flap, startling them into a flutter. Maybe it was only child's play, a lark; it hadn't seemed innocent then. As a consequence, he had failed to warn the family when danger arrived, two men lurking outside these windows late one night.

Now he missed the game. Their silly idle frolic.

TRAIL OF CTHULHU
BY KENNETH HITE

BASED ON THE GUMSHOE SYSTEM BY ROBIN D LAWS

Pelgrane Press

RPG CONSPIRACIES:
An Interview with Kenneth Hite

By Richard Dansky

A professional writer of tabletop RPGs for over three decades, Kenneth Hite is widely acknowledged as the field's resident expert on all things esoteric and conspiratorial. From his early days working on the gnostic horrors feature that was *Nephilim* through numerous contributions to settings like *Call of Cthulhu* and the *World of Darkness*, to his most recent work on titles like *Bookhounds of London*, *Trail of Cthulhu* and *Night's Black Agents*, Hite has consistently written award-winning material that has made the conspiratorial both accessible and fun. (While, I might add, maintaining a sufficient level of horror to infuse your average RPG group with nightmares for months.) Now ensconced as the co-host (with author and game designer Robin Laws) of the wildly successful podcast "Ken and Robin Talk About Stuff," Ken is still writing game material along with children's books (*The Antarctic Express*), literary criticism (*Tour de Lovecraft*), and, yes, a column on conspiracies (*Suppressed Transmissions*). He was kind enough to take a few minutes to talk conspiracies, why they work so well for games, and how enterprising GMs can freshen up their in-game cabals. And any rumors that he did so based on orders from the Illuminati are strictly that: rumors.

You're regarded as the authority in gaming for conspiracies, secret societies and nefarious plots. What was the appeal in the subject matter for you? What was Your First Conspiracy?

I suspect my First Conspiracy was one or another of the UFO conspiracies that bestrewed the 1970s, given that I spent much of the 1970s being twelve, which is a good age in which to soak up conspiracy theories. Although even then, I wasn't uncritically soaking them up—I basically ranked them as another entry in the CLOSE ENCOUNTERS - PROJECT UFO - IN SEARCH OF genre of entertainment. Which I suppose I still pretty much do today.

It feels like conspiracy theory is at an all-time high in the real world these days. What's made it so engaging now?

Partly, it's because the real world, between al-Qaeda and the NSA, is showing a disturbing tendency to behave a trifle conspiratorially. Conspiracy theories historically flourish during unsettled times, which these increasingly seem to be. Conspiracy theories also flourish amongst displaced (or never-emplaced) political groups, from European reactionaries to American leftists—and the various modern state structures are becoming ever more self-contained, which leaves more people of all stripes out in the political cold. Finally, of course, the Internet lets every kind of small group flourish and magnify itself, conspiracists very much among them.

Why do conspiracies make such meaty gaming fodder?

They provide that ne plus ultra of gaming, the dungeon. By this I mean: the narratively and thematically connected series of challenges and terrors. They're political and intellectual dungeons: you go from puzzle or crime scene or UFO landing to coup d'etat or oil painting or water engine, each time seeking to find the Hidden Hand of the monster. I mean, of the shadowy actors who did it. Conspiracies, like dungeons, can bring you to places of horror (is a massive Satanic cult killing women in Ciudad Juarez?) or to wondrous treasure (this zero-point engine could fix global warming, or at least power our helicarrier), with lots of danger (rogue CIA paramilitaries, mind-control beams, the Russian Mafiya) along the way.

What makes for a good conspiracy in a game setting? What about a bad one—what are the clichés you never want to see again?

In a game setting, the most important thing about a conspiracy is that it has to connect up to something the players recognize, and ideally something they care about. That's why it's harder to do pure-quill conspiracy gaming in a fantasy realm—none of it feels real, so the contrast between the Reptoids and the Air Force isn't there.

As far as clichés go, I'm a little sick of the "Shadowy Mr. Johnson" scenario where the guy who hires you to Get the MacGuffin turns out (surprise!) to betray you, or to be working for the opposition, or whatever. Just because Hollywood still thinks this is an interesting plot doesn't mean you can get away with it. And you certainly can't get away with it twice, because the players will turtle and for good reason: you can't be trusted to provide a satisfying story.

How do you tackle writing good conspiracy material? What's the key to baking it into a game's DNA?

I write conspiracy material by researching the hell out of the topic. Once you do that, you start finding weird little details that seem to make a larger pattern. There are always little weird details, and you can always see a pattern in them. It's even easier if you came into it knowing what kind of pattern you wanted to see. This is just neuroscience, it's not evidence, but you can really easily turn it into evidence, or at least into a setting.

You bake conspiracy into the game's setting first, then into the plot if you have one. Don't, as I mentioned up above, just run a constant series of sudden and inevitable betrayals. Think of a mystery that will reveal something about the setting, some piece of that pattern. Think of a reason that Conspiracy A wants the players to survive an encounter—as stalking horses, or scouts, or as recruits, or as the Chosen Ones. Provide other actors who have their own insights, wrong or right, and their own agendas that "accidentally" help the players figure out more of the pattern and survive the encounter the Conspiracy doesn't

want them to. Conspiracies can always benefit from more layers, more setting, more detail—just don't change the Real Truth too often unless you're deliberately running an epistemological conspiracy *a la* William S. Burroughs.

What are the keys to running a good conspiracy-based game?

Another key to designing the conspiracy setting is to have no more than five Big Conspiracies behind the scenes. You want more than one, so the players have a reason to tell themselves they haven't been squashed like bugs. Three is the classic Orwell number, but it's too easy to grasp. But more than five becomes a blur; the shadows stop being inviting and start being annoying.

In the moment, provide mini-mysteries (all those annoying codes and puzzles in Dan Brown books work for a reason, sadly) that replicate the feel of conspiracy. Play up the contrast between the world the PCs inhabit and the "real world" the players live in—but to do that, you have to have both. Both the crashed UFO and the War on Terror; both the immortal magician-vampires and the Whitney Biennial. Like espionage games, conspiracy games flourish when set in a very-slightly-high-color version of our world.

Conspiracy theory often comes with political or other hot-button topics built into it. Is that something to embrace or ignore in games?

Some political conspiracy material—the Protocols of the Elders of Zion, say, or 9/11 Truthism—is not just regular-idiotic, but crass and tasteless and disgusting and vile. Even "playing" with it—whether you believe in it or not—can be pretty horrible. If your players walk out on you and never play with you again for bringing such elements into the game, I'm on their side.

But genuinely disgusting politics aside, by and large, as long as all your friends agree (or don't care) politically, or easily separate their personal politics from their entertainment, go right ahead and play political conspiracies. Engagement with the real world gives conspiracy stories their juice. Just make sure that you don't turn the game into a screed about the Iraq War or the Federal Reserve, instead of an adventure.

NIGHT'S BLACK AGENTS

A **VAMPIRE SPY** THRILLER BY **KENNETH HITE**

Based on the GUMSHOE system by **Robin D. Laws**

Pelgrane Press

There are "borderline" cases—I can easily imagine players getting bent out of shape about a game that takes the Martin Luther King assassination as a jumping off point, despite the decades of entertainment based on the JFK assassination. Know your players, as with all games.

What games do conspiracy well? What in particular makes them stand out?

Most games that do conspiracy well don't stand out mechanically—although you need a good skill system if you're going to provide the problem-solving vibe—but in terms of setting originality. CONSPIRACY X by Rick Ernst, et al., with its "string pulling" mechanic (if your PC works at Area 51, maybe you can borrow an Aurora spy plane) and its ARS MAGICA style cell-building system, comes closest to a really strong dedicated engine. But its setting is the old gallimaufrey of aliens and Reptoids and X-FILES and so forth. It's really nicely put together but it doesn't make you (or me, at least) sit up on my hind legs. The real world conspiracy theorists value retreading things, explaining all the old conundrums in that kind of way. In most games, you want something as fresh as John Tynes, Dennis Detwiller, and Scott Glancy's DELTA GREEN's blend of the UFO and Cthulhu Mythoses. Mythoi? Or John Tynes and Greg Stolze's UNKNOWN ARMIES' humanocentric Gnosticism and the conspiracy

of incompetents as ironic commentary on most thrillers' fantasy of competence. Or, if I may suggest it, the blood-and-adrenaline cocktail of my own NIGHT'S BLACK AGENTS "Jason Bourne vs. Dracula" mashup.

What are some of the great historical conspiracies that people might not know about that would make great game source material?

Try looking outside the CIA/Illuminati/Templar/UFO/Nazi axis. My "Suppressed Transmission" columns were full of wild history, because I used up the easy stuff early. The Black Ocean and Black Dragon Societies in Japan were pretty wack; the Triads let you combine crime stories with *wuxia* if you'll let them. I still think there's room for an artistic-magical conspiracy done right (i.e. not how Dan Brown does it) around the School of Night in Elizabethan London or the various Symbolists and Decadents in fin-de-siecle Paris. Lots of weird stuff going on in pre-Stalin Bolshevik Russia, before they decided boring was Marxist and vice versa. Read Hakim Bey and Peter Lamborn and other "alternative" cultural historians; they're serious (and usually seriously addled) but their ideas make great horror, especially because the source material is so optimistic. I also think the Holy Vehm is under-used; medieval covert death squads? Sign me up! No. Strike that. Don't sign me up. I have no interest in the Holy Vehm. Ignore my eerily tree-shaped birthmark. This press conference is over.

✾ ✾ ✾

You can find Ken's story "La Musique de l'Ennui" in the upcoming anthology *Madness on the Orient Express*, and find the podcast at http://www.kenandrobintalkaboutstuff.com

Kenneth Hite Courtesy of Richard Dansky

Back to Frank Black: An Interview with Adam Chamberlain & Brian A. Dixon

By K. H. Vaughan

In October, 1996, *X-files* creator Chris Carter's series, *Millennium,* debuted on the Fox Network. *Millennium* featured Lance Henriksen as retired FBI profiler Frank Black. Frank was a deeply human protagonist whose gift for understanding and confronting evil inflicted great psychological and personal cost. Despite the damage the work had done to him and his family, Frank continued consulting, and was recruited by a mysterious cabal of former law enforcement personnel called the Millennium Group. It was a nuanced and understated performance, supported by an outstanding supporting cast and strong scripts, direction, and production values.

The Back to Frank Black movement began as a grass-roots effort to champion the return of *Millennium* in some form, headed by Jim McLean and Troy Foreman. Carter had done this before, extending the run of *The X-Files* through feature films after the series was cancelled, and he has recently hinted at the possibility. Many of the series principles, including Henrickson, have expressed their support and been actively involved in the campaign.

The movement's largest and most visible project is the *Back to Frank Black* book, edited by Brian A. Dixon and Adam Chamberlain. The 512-page collection includes contributions from, or interviews with, Chris Carter, Lance Henriksen, Frank Spotnitz, Megan Gallagher, Glen Morgan, James Wong and many others. It also includes extensive essays, analysis and artwork that will enrich fans' understanding of the program. Brian and Adam joined *Dark Discoveries* for this interview.

§

K. H. Vaughan: Before asking about the book, can you say a little about how you became fans of *Millennium*? What drew you to the show so strongly?

Adam Chamberlain: I was very much a fan of contemporary psychological crime procedurals such as *The Silence of the Lambs*. But there was also something about the mood and tone of *Millennium* that really spoke to the anxieties of its time, and with an integrity that no other series at the time matched. I don't mean superficial concerns such as the Y2K bug or superstitions about the actual turn of the millennium, but deeper social anxieties. Those were themes that really chimed with me. And those anxieties only resonate more deeply today, of course, as Chris Carter says in the book. Added to that, I was a huge fan of *The X-Files* and eager to see where Carter's creative vision would lead us next, so I was hooked from the first episode—initially via the UK video releases.

Brian A. Dixon: Like Adam, I was a great fan of *The X-Files*. I was already impressed with the quality of production achieved by Carter's Ten Thirteen Productions. That said, when *Millennium* first debuted, I was totally unprepared for the power of its storytelling

BACK TO FRANK BLACK

A Return to Chris Carter's *Millennium*

Featuring introductions by
Chris Carter, Frank Spotnitz, & Lance Henriksen

Edited by
Adam Chamberlain & Brian A. Dixon

Book cover artwork Matthew Ingles

Adam Chamberlain. Photo Courtesy of Fourth Horseman Press

and its own remarkable production values. Here was a television drama unlike any I had seen before, and I was hooked from the start. I found it irresistible.

KHV: Can you tell me a little about how you became involved in the book? How did this volume come about? You have an impressive list of contributors: major names from the production including Chris Carter and Lance Henriksen. How did you get everyone on board?

AC: We were invited to put the book together by the Back to Frank Black campaign—led by James McLean and Troy Foreman—as something of a manifesto for its aims, as well as to celebrate *Millennium*'s remarkable body of work. Troy and James ran a very successful podcast as part of that campaign, and had already interviewed so many writers, producers, and actors from the series for that. So there was a lot of material to draw upon, and our purpose with those interviews was really to present them in an entirely new way, plus to add one or two more. It felt like there was a dearth of serious analysis of *Millennium*—surprisingly so given its depth—and so adding the essays was also an obvious direction to take. Getting Lance Henriksen and Frank Spotnitz to pen their forewords and having Chris Carter agree to write the introduction was the icing on the cake. But everyone who contributed was so eager to do so; all we had to do was ask! I think that says a lot about how highly *Millennium* is regarded, and how much love those that worked on the series still have for it.

KHV: Could anyone but Lance have played Frank Black? What made him such a great fit for that character?

BAD: As far as I'm concerned, no one else could have been Frank Black. Lance Henriksen is a truly remarkable man and he is a remarkable actor, a true Method actor. His performances are unforgettable in large part because, in preparing for the roles, he became these characters. There is a spirituality in Lance and in his approach to acting that has a transformative effect. Frank Black was instantly recognizable as a living, breathing, feeling human being. The character is fully developed from the moment we meet him, and through the thoughtfulness of his approach Lance was able to imbue him with an empathy and an honesty beyond that demonstrated by any other hero in television or film. I've never seen a hero like Frank Black, before or since *Millennium*.

KHV: I was hooked immediately when *Millennium* aired, and enjoyed the show a great deal. It was disappointing when it went off the air after such a short run. It opened with impressive numbers but ratings declined over the three-year run. Why do you think it didn't maintain a larger following?

AC: Well, it was probably unrealistic to expect the series to maintain that opening audience figure, but undeniably its ratings did decline. Its subject matter and tone meant that it was never going to be a breakout mainstream hit, but the truth is that its audience was still very respectable at the time it was cancelled. Frank Spotnitz describes in the book how network television audiences were beginning to decline at the time

Brian A Dixon. Photo Courtesy of Fourth Horseman Press

anyway, but that this wasn't widely recognized. Fox took a joint decision with Chris Carter to take another roll of the dice with *Harsh Realm*, which of course didn't really take off. Every show that Fox put in *Millennium*'s time slot after it was cancelled earned fewer and fewer viewers. There's every chance that if *Harsh Realm* wasn't on offer from Carter in 1999, we could have had a fourth season of *Millennium*—and potentially more! The series would probably be a better fit with cable audiences today, and in that arena I think it would still be a huge hit.

BAD: It was a tragic turn of events. Both *Millennium* and *Harsh Realm* were brilliant programs, and each became a victim of the trends that Adam describes. In fact, *Millennium* had a very loyal audience, the sort of audience that would make for a hit in today's television landscape. The greatest disappointment is that it was cancelled just months short of the turn of the millennium.

KHV: Had there been anything like *Millennium* before? It really changed television, didn't it?

AC: It had its antecedents in film, for sure, with the likes of *Manhunter*, *The Silence of the Lambs*, and *Seven*—which was a direct influence upon Carter. But in terms of the television landscape, no one had brought a series quite like it to the small screen before. And it was certainly at the sharp end of the curve of such shows that followed in its wake, and remains a powerful influence upon the genre.

BAD: Yes, *Millennium* made such an impression in large part because it didn't look or feel like any other television series that had preceded it. Many have said that Chris Carter and Ten Thirteen were putting out small feature films on a weekly basis, and in the case of *Millennium* that's absolutely true. Today, the cable television landscape is filled with series that remind us of *Millennium*. It was a groundbreaking series. It set a new standard, I think, and has been endlessly imitated in the years since.

KHV: I was always struck by the way that *Millennium* didn't always answer your questions and the good guys seemed to be doing well if they could break even.

AC: Yes, and again I think that very much speaks to the times in which we live. I think that's one of the reasons for its integrity; it acknowledges that there are no easy

Lance Henriksen. Photo Courtesy of Fourth Horseman Press

answers to the questions it poses.

BAD: Dedicated fans of the series have spent more than a decade debating its unresolved questions, and we're still discussing them today! *Back to Frank Black* features a number of authors offering their own answers to those questions. John Kenneth Muir, for instance, offers a fascinating "unified theory" of *Millennium*, a theory that joins the three distinct seasons of the show using Bardo Thodol, the Tibetan Book of the Dead. It's wonderful that the questions the series left us with have inspired such an ongoing conversation. It's one of *Millennium*'s great gifts.

KHV: The show changed quite a bit in season two under Glen Morgan and James Wong. I loved the expansion of the Millennium Group mythology and factional conflict, but not everyone was pleased with the direction they took. How did their vision differ from Carter's season one vision?

BAD: Glen Morgan and James Wong are brilliant storytellers, and they changed the series in remarkable ways during the course of season two. As you say, they immediately took steps to deepen the mythology

Lucy Butler/Sarah Jane Redmond courtesy of
Back to Frank Black Website

was more successful for me in terms of its dryness. But it's probably a question of personal taste more than anything else. I'm pretty sure that Brian would disagree with me completely about Roedecker.

BAD: Sure. I'll champion Brian Roedecker! You wouldn't have a classic installment like "The Mikado" without him. He demonstrated that Frank Black is the ultimate comic straight man. The comedy of the second season didn't seem at all discordant to me. If anything, it added another layer to the series and its character dynamics. I think that many viewers were able to identify with the likes of Brian Roedecker and Lara Means in a way that they were unable to with Peter Watts or Bob Bletcher. In episodes such as those you've cited, *Millennium* was able to prove its remarkable range. Anyone who has seen "Jose Chung's Doomsday Defense" knows the series could do laugh-out-loud satire just as well as it could do deeply affecting drama.

KHV: The city of Seattle and surrounding wilderness was prominent in the first two series. It had a signature look. In season three, Chris Carter takes over the show again, and relocates Frank to Washington, DC. Do you have thoughts on why? It was quite a contrast.

AC: I think that was more story-driven than anything else. Each season of *Millennium* is, of course, quite distinct from the others in many aspects of its style. The start of Season Three in particular did jar a little at first, but in retrospect that distinct identity from year to year feels like one of the series' defining characteristics and, ultimately, one of its strengths.

KHV: Do you have particular moments in the show that stand out? Or favorite episodes?

AC: That's such a hard question to answer, as there's so much to love throughout all three seasons. Both of Darin Morgan's episodes rate as highlights for me, as I mentioned, and "Pilot" is very strong. In Season Two, "Luminary" is a beautiful episode, and the season finale two-parter "The Fourth Horseman" / "The Time Is Now" was a high watermark for me as well. I also thought that "The Sound of Snow" provided an effective and emotionally satisfying way to revisit the aftermath of that storyline in Season Three.

BAD: My all-time favorite episode of the series remains "The Curse of Frank Black."

of the series, embracing themes associated with secret societies and religious cults. The character dynamics of the show changed. There was a newfound sense of humor. Even the approach to storytelling shifted in season two. As Morgan and Wong discuss in the book, many of these changes were undertaken in order to allow Frank Black to embark on the hero's journey we see so often in mythology. This was no longer the crime drama of season one. Morgan and Wong embraced Carter's spiritual mandate for the series and pushed the envelope. *Millennium* became darker and stranger and more complex. For all of these reasons, the second season remains my favorite.

KHV: What is your take on the comic elements? The episodes *Somehow, Satan Got Behind Me* and *Jose Chung's Doomsday Defense* come to mind, as does the character Brian Roedecker. Were these necessary? Do you think they worked to alleviate the darkness of the show, or were they more discordant notes in the series?

AC: I think comedy worked well in *Millennium* in the right context. Both of Darin Morgan's episodes number amongst my absolute favorites, even though they stand quite apart from the rest of the series. As for Roedecker, he felt a little too broad for me. Some of the humor in the interplay between Frank and Lara Means

KHV: Why is conspiracy so compelling? Not just in *Millennium*, but in fiction, film, and television in general?

AC: Conspiracy theories undoubtedly make for great stories, and particularly thrillers. Drama thrives on an elevated sense of real life, and conspiracy theories undoubtedly offer that.

KHV: Any thoughts on why so many people believe in conspiracy theories in real life? Obviously things like Watergate happen, but the big ones: moon landing hoaxes, JFK assassination theories, 9-11 "truthers." What sort of psychology is at work there?

AC: I do find it interesting that conspiracies are so compelling to so many people. I think there's something deep-seated to that. With many conspiracy theories that spring up, I think that people don't want to believe how much sits outside of their control or evades plain reasoning. We don't want to believe it possible that a man acting alone could assassinate a US President, or that our governments cannot offer complete protection against fundamentalists with such brazen plans to cause death and destruction at any cost. It makes it feel more possible that we might meet a sudden, violent death ourselves—which, of course, we might. We are less in control of our own fates that we would like to be. It has to be said that there's often broken logic at play, grasping at complex and unlikely explanations rather than facing difficult but comparatively simple truths. Conspiracy theorists will often express a belief in multiple contradictory theories at the same time. There's certainly an inherent distrust in authority at play, too. The moon landing hoax theories are just odd to me, though, and disrespectful to what represent some of the pinnacles of human endeavor to date.

BAD: There's something in the human psyche that lends itself to conspiracy theories, isn't there? As human beings, we're biologically programmed to look for patterns in the world around us. The human mind can only handle so much data, and it's built in such a way that the gaps are filled with interpretation. In the realm of consciousness, that often leads us to consider the most complex explanations for why things are the way that they are. It's as Adam says, however. So many of these theories collapse under the weight of their own complexity. They're unbelievable, even if we want to believe.

KHV: Favorite conspiracy theories outside the Millennium Group?

AC: I do have an interest in conspiracy theories, but mostly for the psychology at play in how they arise and how they are perpetuated. I regularly read *Fortean Times*, partly for that reason. It's also fair to say that I've always been particularly interested in UFO theories.

BAD: As Adam has suggested with regard to the outrageous suggestion that the moon landings were a hoax, conspiracy theories are often offensive. That's to say nothing of the fact that they can be downright dangerous, as we're seeing in current trends regarding childhood vaccinations. That said, it's always entertaining to read a new literary theory regarding who really wrote Will Shakespeare's plays!

KHV: What are the prospects for a new *Millennium* production? Carter's done it before with his *X-Files* movies, and the success of shows like *True Detective* suggests the audience is there. Should we get our hopes up?

AC: There's so much in its favor. Lance would love to revisit the character onscreen, and Chris Carter and

Chris Carter. Photo Courtesy of Fourth Horseman Press

Frank Spotnitz have both been very clear that they would love to do it, and, moreover, that they think it is a viable business proposition. Then again, Chris is no doubt very busy with new projects such as *The After*, and he would clearly need to be the driving creative force. All it really needs is someone at Fox to champion its cause, though, and I think it could happen. But, at the same time and from a completely objective standpoint, it is perhaps a tough sell given the amount of time that has gone by. We live in hope but at this point, sadly, it feels like something of a long shot.

KHV: What would the *Millennium* universe look like today? There's been so much history and technological development since the show ended in 1999—not long before 9/11.

AC: Lance has some very specific views on this, specifically in terms of how his ability could be represented onscreen, but for me I think there's much I'd want to keep the same in terms of the signature look and tone of *Millennium*. In terms of content, I would like to see a storyline in which Frank Black confronts a scenario that speaks to this dangerous point in human history that it feels like we inhabit, whilst remaining true to the series' original premise.

BAD: As Lance will tell you, it was never really about the millennium, about the year 2000 and Y2K. *Millennium* was about the darkness that tries the human spirit, about the moral choices we all have to face in a world that seems to be forever facing an apocalypse. A *Millennium* film is irresistible in this day and age. What would the *Millennium* universe look like today? We'd see Frank Black facing his own mortality as he faces the end of the world. We'd see the Millennium Group manipulating events on a worldwide scale. We'd see the remarkable hero we know and love struggling to save innocents in a world of turmoil. That's a story I'd like to see.

KHV: For people who don't know the series, what shows could you compare it to? Why should they join the movement to Bring Back Frank Black?

AC: The series that I have been most impressed with this year has been *True Detective*, and I saw a lot of *Millennium*'s influence in that. Bryan Fuller's *Hannibal*, too, to an extent, although that has a certain baroque

Brian A Dixon and Adam Chamberlain. Photo Courtesy of Fourth Horseman Press

fascination with gore that chimes with Thomas Harris' books and their movie adaptations but that you don't really see in *Millennium*, where less was more. If you enjoy either of those series, you will find much to love in *Millennium*. Add to the mix Lance Henriksen's portrayal of Frank Black and Chris Carter's creative vision, and you have an all-time classic of the genre.

BAD: Absolutely. At its core, *Millennium* was always a crime drama, but a crime drama unlike any other. We see echoes of the series in *Criminal Minds* and *C.S.I.* and *The Following* and *The Killing*. Anyone who enjoys quality drama and crime thrillers owes it to themselves to take the time to witness *Millennium*. To this day, it has no equal. It's just one of the reasons there is such a strong movement to bring back Frank Black.

KHV: What's next for the two of you? What projects do you have on the horizon?

BAD: There's always something exciting in the works at Fourth Horseman Press. We've been very fortunate in that each of our book releases has been bigger and better received than the one before it. *Back to Frank Black* was a milestone for us. We're switching gears for an ambitious new anthology of short fiction in the coming year. The next book will appeal to fans of history and classic mythology by offering a bold new interpretation of the medieval legends associated with King Arthur and the Knights of the Round Table. We have some amazing talents lined up to take part, including some names that will be familiar to readers of *Back to Frank Black*. In tone and content, this book should excite anyone who is captivated by mythology-driven storytelling.

KHV: Last question: Owls or Roosters?

AC: I'm an Owl through-and-through. This is who we are.

BAD: "Roosters crow at the dawn, hoping to arouse the barnyard. The foxes are about. The master sleeps. The owl knows it is still late at night."

⚜⚜⚜

After the completion of this interview, but before its publication, Chris Carter announced that Millennium would return in a comic book miniseries released through IDW Publishing.

Hollow is the Heart

By Simon R. Green

INTRODUCTION

Ask most folks today what a 'ballad' is, and they begin humming power chords from groups like Journey, Whitesnake and Meat Loaf.

But let's take a step back from hair bands and glitter rock. Let's go old school. Once upon a time, a ballad meant something more. They spoke to a different part of our soul. They tied us to our culture or gave us glimpses into the past. Sometimes they opened doors to strange places. The ballads of long ago told stories. Sometimes fanciful, often strange, constantly intriguing.

Those old ballads told of doomed loves and damned places, of murder and romance, of love lost and lives imperiled. The balladeers enchanted our imaginations with faerie folk and noble knights, with lonely witches and deeply unfortunate romantic choices, with the seen and the unseen. Some of them even told the truth. Or, a version at least.

More often the ballads conjured in our minds a place where something deliciously dreadful happened long ago. Maybe it was the very spot on which you now sit, or a land glimpsed only through a parted veil at purple twilight.

Many of the ballads are so old that no one can really claim ownership, and all provenance is suspect or apocryphal. Often these are songs and stories told and retold, changed and reshaped, with new tunes and new lyrics imposed upon the seed of a story. Scholars have confounded themselves with trying to trace the roots of Appalachian songs all the way back to Scottish glens or Irish grottos or overgrown English gardens. Some ballads are so old they seem half buried in the myths of the ancients. Others are as fresh as the rise of Jazz and Blues.

One cannot say, with any real degree of certainty, that there is even a thread that ties all ballads together. There isn't. And yet, there is. It's less a connection of form or origin, and more a feeling. An awareness that these old songs and stories evoke in each of us. Often, even at first hearing, we feel we *know* these songs. We've heard them somewhere before, we think; even when we likewise know we haven't. Their ghosts haunt the generations of songs that have come after them. Their dust is there. Their shadows.

OUT OF TUNE is not a collection of old ballads. No, sir. This volume contains only new stories. Prose, not rhymes. Stories, not songs. Fourteen tales spun by some of today's most talented writers. It's a witch's brew, no doubt. The stories are dissimilar in almost every way. Some are as bare as old bones, others are ripe to bursting. But they all share one thing. A thread. A ghost of a theme.

They are all inspired by old ballads. From England and Ireland, Scotland and Wales. And from America, too. Old songs, new stories. Not direct interpretations. No, those old ballads were whispers in the ears of these writers. Each writer took a thread from those timeless songs and in their own way spun new magic.

So, sit comfortably, pour yourself something nice, and dig in. And maybe—just maybe—you'll hear a spectral tune floating on the breeze as you read.

-Jonathan Maberry

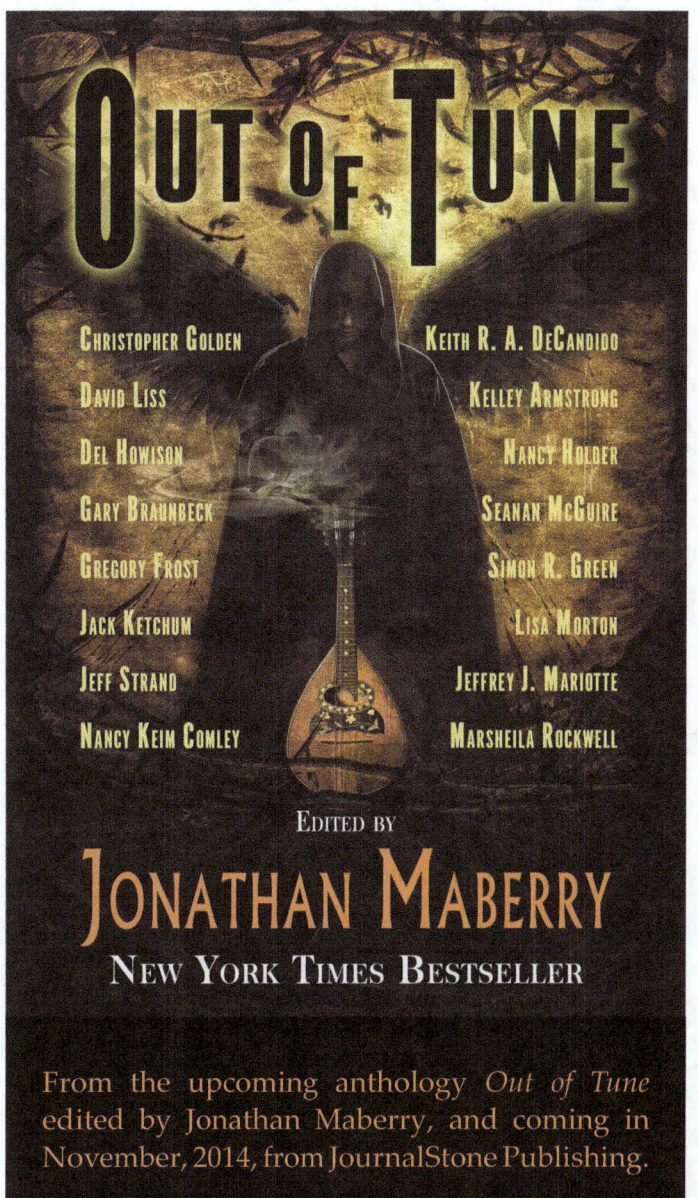

OUT OF TUNE

CHRISTOPHER GOLDEN
DAVID LISS
DEL HOWISON
GARY BRAUNBECK
GREGORY FROST
JACK KETCHUM
JEFF STRAND
NANCY KEIM COMLEY

KEITH R. A. DeCANDIDO
KELLEY ARMSTRONG
NANCY HOLDER
SEANAN McGUIRE
SIMON R. GREEN
LISA MORTON
JEFFREY J. MARIOTTE
MARSHEILA ROCKWELL

EDITED BY

JONATHAN MABERRY

NEW YORK TIMES BESTSELLER

From the upcoming anthology *Out of Tune* edited by Jonathan Maberry, and coming in November, 2014, from JournalStone Publishing.

HOLLOW IS THE HEART

Bradford-on-Avon is an old town, in an old country. Sick and feverish with centuries of history. And some things older than history. Older, and more foul.

§

My name is Jason Grant, and if there were any justice in this world, you'd already know my name. My books would be everywhere, my name on everyone's lips, and my face on all the chat shows. Instead, I make a precarious living researching dubious articles for part-work magazines, and generally hacking it out for pitiful returns. I grub about for work wherever I can find it, cranking it out by the yard to pay the bills. It's been a long time since I've written anything just to satisfy my soul.

I did write a whole bunch of novels and screenplays, but nobody wanted them. I was a journalist, once, doing my bit for a small but respected local paper, the *Wiltshire Record and News*. But that was then, and this is now. I finally have a story worth the telling. A story to prise open the eyes of the world, and make them see things in a whole new way if only I dared submit it. It has been made very clear to me that silence and obscurity are the price of my survival. But I'm not sure I care anymore.

It all started when I made one last attempt to get my old job back.

§

I sat in the outer office of the *Wiltshire Record and News*, waiting to see the editor. Being calm and quiet and not making any trouble, playing the part of the prodigal son and the penitent return. Returned to the scene of my crime, like a dog to its vomit to beg a few crumbs from the editor's table because my cupboard was bare, and I was getting hungry. My old boss, Samantha Walsh: editor, publisher and Conscience in Chief of the local weekly rag. There was no way in hell she was ever going to give me my old job back, I knew that. But if I could just get my foot in the door, hold her attention with some fast talking... I might yet walk out of here with a story assignment. Do a good enough job, and it could lead to regular work. And I wanted that.

Not a staff position, obviously, but a local stringer with local connections is always going to be a useful asset. The odds were stacked against me. I couldn't have blotted my copybook more thoroughly the last time I was here, if I'd pissed in the printer's ink.

I sat politely on my fiendishly uncomfortable visitor's chair and glowered at the clock on the wall. The editor was deliberately keeping me waiting, to make sure I understood my place in the scheme of things. That I was not needed, or even welcome. Everywhere I looked in the outer office, something old and familiar looked back at me. It was as though I'd never been away. The same dreary old fittings and furnishings, cheap but durable. The carpet worn thin from people pacing up and down as they waited to be summoned into the inner sanctum to learn their fate. Dusty plastic venetian blinds at the windows, cutting the sunshine into strips. The same framed front pages proudly displayed on the walls; names and faces and news from a time when people actually read the paper to learn what they needed to know. Significant stories and excited headlines, forgotten moments from the county's past, going all the way back to the First World War

I sat forward in my chair and stared at the floor. So I wouldn't have to look at anything else. There had been a time... when this had felt like home.

There's nothing like visiting an old haunt to make you feel old and unwanted. The surroundings might not have changed, but I had. I look back at the person I was then, and I barely recognise him. I looked at my reflection in the long mirror on the other side of the room. A man in his late thirties who looked older. Thinning hair and a hard-used face, more than a little scruffy. I should have shaved before I came out or at least found the time to force a comb through my hair. But it had been a long time since anyone cared what I looked like, including me.

The door to the inner office opened suddenly, and the editor glared at me. As though I was the one who'd kept her waiting. She nodded briefly as though she didn't trust herself to speak, then turned around and stomped back to sit behind her editor's desk. Her place of power. Leaving me to trail into the inner office after her and shut the door very quietly and politely behind me. Being careful not to slouch. She always used to yell at me when she caught me slouching. There was a time I could have got away with it, but not now. I sat down on the bare wooden chair set out before her desk piled high, as always, with papers overflowing her In and Out trays. She just sat there and waited for me to speak. Because, after all, I was the one who wanted something from her.

Samantha Walsh was middle-aged with prematurely grey hair, and deep lines etched around her eyes and mouth. She dressed neatly and conservatively, in a way that didn't so much ignore fashion as bypass it completely. The ultimate authority figure, the iron hand in the iron glove. Who'd spent so much time occupying the moral high ground, it was a wonder she didn't get nose bleeds from the altitude. I was amazed she could even see us poor mortals down below. The editor fixed me with her usual steely gaze, and I gave her my best respectful smile.

"Hello, Sam. Been a while, hasn't it...?"

"It's Ms. Walsh to you, Grant and don't you forget it. You have no friends here. And sit up straight. You make the place look untidy."

So that was how it was going to be. I sat up straighter, squared my shoulders, and did my best to look like a professional. The editor sniffed as though reluctantly giving me credit for trying.

"All right, Grant. I read your e-mail. You haven't forgotten how to grab a reader's attention, I'll give you that. So against all my better judgment, I'll admit I'm intrigued. Hit me with your proposal, but make it quick and succinct. I've got a paper to run and a deadline to meet. Just because we're a weekly, it doesn't mean I've got time to waste on the likes of you."

"You'll like this one," I said, doing my best to sound confident. "I've got a new local take on a very old legend. A story that used to be on everyone's lips, in this town and around, that no one has talked about in centuries. I stumbled across this particular piece of local history while looking for something else, which is always the way. I was doing research on a story for *Hidden Worldz* magazine. A story that will not be appearing because the magazine had the bad manners to fold before I could hand it in. Or get paid. Do you remember the old story of the Hollow Women?"

"Refresh my memory," said the editor. Which was her way of saying that she didn't, but was prepared to listen.

"Women who can only be seen, and only appear to have substance, from the front. If you look at them from the back, they're just an empty, hollow husk. A shell of a woman, no depth to her at all. The old legend tells how they prey on young, unattached men. They win the men's hearts and then break them, seduce them and make a child with them to continue their own kind... and then disappear. Always girl children... never been a Hollow Man. These women were predators, giving every appearance of being human. But inside they were empty, emotionless, inhuman.

"Obviously, this was designed as a moral warning for young men back then. Don't go off with strange young women or there might be unfortunate consequences. Avoid shallow types, stick with a real woman and make a commitment to home and family."

"Funny how, in these old stories, it's always the men who have to be warned, and the women who are presented as the villains of the piece," said the editor.

"Well, quite," I said. "The point is, I have uncovered evidence that strongly suggests this old legend had its roots and beginnings right here, in the town. A basis in truth and real history. I started with an old folk song from 1815. 'The Foggy Foggy Dew.' I went jumping from link to link across the Net and ended up with a series of stories coming out of that old disreputable part of Bradford-on-Avon, back when we had real slums. The Hollows. I think... this all goes back to women from the Hollows."

The editor sniffed loudly, but I knew I had her. Sam does love the old folk stories, thinks they're part of what shapes local character. Add a local connection, and she was hooked.

"You might have something there," she conceded. "Not enough for me to offer any advance money, or even a guarantee of publication when the story's completed, but... I am interested. If you do good work on this, turn in something good enough to demand publication... I might be able to do something for you."

"Can't say fairer than that," I said.

"What do you want from me?" said the editor. "Access to the paper's archives?"

"I've already been through the old editions," I said tactfully. "It's all on line these days. No, what I need from you is to be able to say I represent the *Wiltshire Record and News*. People will talk to the paper, where they wouldn't talk to me."

"Agreed," said the editor. "On one condition. You work on this story with an assistant I will provide."

I looked at her. I hadn't seen that one coming. "What?"

"Emma Tee. Girl reporter, new to the paper, young and enthusiastic and on her way up. Like you used to be. Work with her. If she can survive you, she'll make a great reporter. And just maybe some of her youthful integrity will rub off on you. But, James, listen to me. The story might be based on a legend, but I expect you to keep your prose tight and factual. No flights of fancy."

"Understood," I said.

"You'd better," said the editor. "Go on. Get out of here. Emma's waiting in the outer office. And be nice to her! Don't frighten her off. Bright, young reporters are getting hard to come by."

§

She really was waiting for me, sitting in the chair I'd just vacated, reading last week's edition of the paper. I could barely see any of her, behind the *Wiltshire Record and News*. Because she was such a small thing, and the paper remained an old-fashioned broadsheet, despite financial pressures. The editor still believed that readers still believe you can't trust anything you read in a tabloid. *And we*, she was fond of saying, *are the local paper of record. If we say it happened, it happened.*

The paper lowered abruptly, revealing a fresh, young face with a big, beaming smile. The kind that would probably have been irresistible to anyone else. Emma Tee was barely out of her teens with fluffed-out blond hair, a cheerful, young face without even a trace of makeup, shining blue eyes and a sweet demeanour. She was so full of youth and energy I felt old and tired just looking at her.

"Hi!" she said brightly, folding up the paper and tossing it casually to one side. "I'm Emma Tee, and you must be Jason Grant. Don't worry. I've already been warned about you by practically everybody, so let's just take that as read and move on."

She bounced up out of her chair and extended a small hand for me to shake. I did so solemnly. She still hadn't stopped smiling.

"So!" she said. "What are we, as journalists of record and reporters of fact, doing investigating an old fairy tale?"

"The things we choose to believe," I said carefully, "the stories we cherish and preserve, tell us who and what we really are. That's what makes old folk tales so important. We are going to investigate which local people and conditions gave birth to this particular legend, of the Hollow Women."

"Marvellous!" said Emma. "Where do we start? General search engine or something more specific?"

"I've already tried that," I said. "And beyond the basics... there's nothing there."

"But that's not possible!" said Emma.

"Not on its own," I said. "Which is what started me thinking. Someone seems to have gone to a lot of trouble to erase all but the original story of the Hollow Women. And I want to know why. Some old scandal perhaps? Featuring, or maybe even implicating, some old established families in the town?"

Emma grinned happily. "We can but hope. Nothing like a good local scandal to sell the local paper! How far back do we need to look to get to the beginning of this legend?"

"If I'm right, the eighteenth century," I said. "And for that we need access to the old records, the original sources. The books and papers that make up the church and parish records. The kind of thing you can't erase or delete. I already approached the local church, but the vicar wouldn't talk to me, let alone allow me access to his precious historical archives. Not as long as I was just a local hack. But since we are now official representatives of a respected local paper..."

"Does it have to be the church?" said Emma, her sunny face suddenly clouded. She'd finally stopped smiling. "Don't like churches. They give me the creeps."

"If you want to report the news," I said solemnly, "you have to go where the news is. Or in this case, where the news was."

§

On the way to the church, I filled Emma in on what I'd already turned up. A series of stories in the local press, about that most disreputable area, the Hollows. Stories from the eighteenth century, of drunkenness, debauchery and bad behaviour in the streets. Nothing in the least supernatural or fantastical. Just... warnings for men of good character to stay away from the bad women of the Hollows.

The Saint Laurence Church was mostly blocky Norman architecture with later Gothic flourishes, and a handful of stone gargoyles up by the guttering, showing their bare stone arses to the world. The church was surrounded by an old graveyard so packed full of the eternally resting there was no room left for new arrivals. Stones and crosses and monuments were jammed so close together there was hardly any room to pass between them. Wild flowers blossomed in profusion, where they weren't being choked by weeds. I led the way down the narrow gravel path with Emma hanging back and scowling mutinously in the rear.

I couldn't see what the problem was. The sun was shining brightly, and as graveyards went, this one seemed open and cheerful. A pleasant enough setting in which to contemplate eternity. I've always liked graveyards. Always a good place to go teenage drinking, late at night, with a few convivial friends. Secure in the knowledge no one would come barging in to bother you.

The vicar emerged abruptly from among the headstones, and came bustling forward to meet us. Oliver Markham had to be in his late seventies, but he still had a great mane of grey hair, and a bristling grey beard. It gave him something of the air of an Old Testament prophet, somewhat undermined by his cheerful smile and vague eyes. A pleasant enough sort in a dotty and distracted kind of way. He kicked his way through the last few weeds and stepped out onto the gravel path. He remembered meeting me before, but had to be reminded of my name. And he made enough of a fuss over meeting Emma that she quite forgot she didn't want to be there. He went to shake my hand, and only then realised he was still holding the trowel he'd been using for a bit of weeding. He tossed the trowel casually away and made a point of giving me a good hearty handshake. And a more careful one for Emma.

"Well, well, Mister Jason Grant," he said finally. "Back again! Yes, yes... The local archives, isn't it? I'm glad someone's taking an interest in them. They're all stored away in the church basement. Because no one else wants them. I keep hoping the local historical society will take the damned things off my hands and spend the money it will take to preserve them properly. I don't have the budget, you see! No, no... Sorry I had to drive you away, earlier, Mister... Grant! Yes! But I needed to be sure you represented the right sort of people. The archive records are very old, very valuable... and very fragile. So I have to be careful about who gets to see them. Oh yes! As long as they're in the Church they're in my care, you see...."

And yet, all the while he was saying this, he seemed to have trouble concentrating on me. His gaze kept sliding away, to Emma. Which was only natural in that she was a great deal prettier than me, but still...

The vicar finally stopped talking not long after he ran out of things to say and produced a large ring of old-fashioned keys, great solid metal things. He sorted carefully through them, muttering cheerfully to himself until finally he separated out one particular key and presented it to me. Slapping the heavy thing into my palm with enough emphasis to make me wince.

"There you go!" he said happily. "All yours! I'll leave you to it, if you don't mind. All that dust in the basement does terrible things to my sinuses. And I have work to do... work that needs doing... Where did I put my trowel?"

§

The basement under the church turned out to be a dank and gloomy place with no windows and just the one bare light bulb to push back the heavy shadows. All four walls were covered with shelves, packed full to bursting with old books and folders of even older documents. Some of the folders were labelled or dated, most weren't. More books tottered in piles across the stone floor. Dust and cobwebs to all sides suggested it had been some time since anyone had been down there. Emma didn't like the look or feel of the place, and I didn't blame her. So much history in one place has an oppressive weight.

It took us hours to locate the necessary volumes of town history, written out in longhand in a series of over-sized leather-bound books. Emma and I piled them up on the single reading desk, and then I sat down on the only chair (as the senior partner in this team) and worked my way through the volumes. With Emma standing right behind me, peering over my shoulder, and getting just a bit agitated when I didn't finish reading a page fast enough to suit her. I worked steadily through the old records, making notes where necessary. After a while, Emma started to fidget.

"If someone did go to all the trouble of removing knowledge of the Hollow Women from the Net, why didn't they destroy these old archives as well?"

"Because that might have drawn attention to them?" I said, scowling at the handwritten pages. My eyes ached. "Any attack on local records might make people think there was something important in them... Okay, this is it. A whole series of incidents in the town from the late seventeen hundreds onwards. Reports of certain unruly women from the Hollows preying on unfortunate young men. Taking their innocence and their valuables and sometimes sending them home in just the clothes they stood up in. This is the source of the legend! These terrible predatory women from the Hollows. The Hollow Women!"

"Well, yes," said Emma. "But isn't there anything more recent? You know how Ms. Walsh always wants to tie stories to modern settings and people. Makes it more accessible for today's reader."

To keep her happy (and because she was right, the Editor would want that), I skimmed through the more recent volumes. There were any number of incidents in the Hollows, everything from public drunkenness to open riot... but the stories of the Hollow Women just seemed to fade out. And no matter where I looked, I couldn't turn up any actual names, addresses, or anything that would serve as hard evidence.

Nothing to tie a scandal to any local family name. Unfortunately...

I slammed the final volume shut, sat back in my chair, and stretched my aching back.

"I think we've done all that can be reasonably asked of us," I said. "We've connected the dots and made a reasonable connection. Enough to put together a solid story for our beloved editor."

"It's a good, strong story as far as it goes," Emma said carefully. "But we still need to show a link to the town today. I think we need to pay a visit to what's left of the Hollows. The last mention of the Hollow Women was in the nineteen twenties. There might still be some people living there who heard the stories firsthand from their grandparents. I think we should check this out if only because..."

"Because if we don't, Ms. bloody Walsh will ask why we didn't," I said. "All right, then. To the Hollows it is. I wonder if there's time to buy a Kevlar jacket and update my immunisation shots?"

§

Of course, the Hollows as such didn't exist anymore. The slums of old were pulled down long ago, replaced by a series of run-down Council houses. Entering the Hollow Estates was like crossing a line into new and dangerous territory. Overgrown lawns with old refrigerators and other large objects just dumped in the gardens. Ugly graffiti on every wall and lots of peeling paint. No attempt to smarten the place up because nobody cared. Small groups of youths lurking around in hoodies, waiting for something to happen. And ready to start something if it didn't. Emma and I were careful to stick to the main roads, and took it in turns to brave the awful gardens, knock on doors, and talk as charmingly as we could to whoever answered. No one wanted to talk to us. They were all suspicious of strangers, particularly snooping strangers. We might be the law or social services or looking for money. We got a lot of doors slammed in our faces, and I would have given up if Emma hadn't been there. But finally, we struck gold in the form of an old woman called Alicia Tiley.

A very old woman who lived alone in a crumbling wreck of a house with far too many cats. She scowled all through Emma's cheery and engaging questions until she realised we were only interested in stories about the Hollows women, and then her head came up and she fixed me with a sharp look before stepping suddenly back, and inviting us in.

The narrow entrance hall smelled of damp. And cats. And damp cats. Dozens of them hurried back and forth, excited by the arrival of strangers, darting between our legs and jumping from one high spot to another. Alicia Tiley led us through into her pokey little parlour, stepping over and around the cats without looking while they did their best to trip us up. The parlour was crowded with all kinds of colourful junk and tatt. It looked like Alicia hadn't thrown away anything in years. She bustled around, making us a cup of tea, while advising us to just turf the cats out of any chair we fancied. The first cat I approached bared its teeth and hissed at me, but Emma chased the animals out of two chairs with effortless efficiency.

I sat down gingerly. The chair smelt very strongly of cats and not in a good way. To take my mind off that, I studied Alicia surreptitiously. She had clearly been a tall women once, but age and presumably infirmity had bent her right over. She was large-boned, but still slender to the point of scrawny, her hard-edged face more full of character than anything else. She wore her thin grey hair scraped back in a tight bun. Her hands were bent almost into claws by arthritis, but she still managed the tea things easily enough. She moved slowly and steadily, pacing herself, so her strength would still be there when it was needed.

She put an old-fashioned china tea service down on the table before us. I took one look at the state of the cups and decided immediately there was no way I was drinking anything that went in them. Even if it did involve boiling water. Alicia finally finished pouring out the tea, thrust a cup into my hand and Emma's and then lowered herself carefully into a chair facing us.

"The Hollow Women," she said, harshly. "The ruiners of men. Seducers and betrayers. And murderers too, sometimes. If there was a thing that needed keeping quiet. Or men who should have known enough not to go back after them. The Hollow Women could make any man love them and give up their hearts just so they could have the fun of breaking them. Was a time, everyone around here knew, to beware of the Hollow Women. But people forget..."

"I lost my dear Jack to them, long and long ago. He was never the same, afterwards. Oh yes... I was young once, and a young man loved me. Until one of them got him... If you want to know the truth, you need to talk to the nuns. They know."

"I'm sorry," I said. "Nuns? Which nuns are these?"

"The Holy Sisters of Saint Baphomet," Alicia said sharply. "You know the ones. They all live together at Barrow Farm, down by the river."

"Oh... yes," I said. "An order of reclusive nuns. They bought Barrow Farm and moved in... how long ago? Must be years..."

"More than twenty years," said Emma. "I'm not surprised you forgot about them. Most people have. They don't get out much."

"I sort of got that, from reclusive," I said.

"They keep themselves to themselves," said Alicia, sipping loudly at her tea. "But there's no denying they know things."

"Why would nuns know anything about the Hollow Women?" said Emma. "One of the few things we know for sure from the old legend was that these women had a violent antipathy for all things religious. And apparently, vice versa. It was always the church who spoke out most strongly against the sinful practices of the Hollows women."

"They know things," Alicia said darkly. "Know thy enemy and all that."

"I still don't think we should go barging in on an order of reclusive nuns," said Emma.

"We're reporters," I said sternly. "And that means we go where the story is."

"Then you can go on your own," said Emma. "Churches are spooky enough. I'm not doing anything that might get a whole bunch of nuns mad at me."

At first, I thought she was joking, but she just

sat there stubbornly and refused even to discuss the matter. Alicia looked on, quietly enjoying the argument. So in the end, I got up and left Emma there to see if she could get any useful information out of Alicia. I hated to do it, not least because the editor had made it very clear I was supposed to work this story with Emma, but it wasn't my fault if the little girl reporter couldn't keep up. You have to go where the story leads you.

§

Barrow Farm was a sprawling old stone building, right on the bank of the River Avon, where it cuts through the centre of the town. No telling how old the place was, but the local creamy grey stone was deeply discoloured from the ravages of time and weather, and the tiled roof looked like it could use some serious repairs. There was no bell at the front door, just a large, black iron knocker in the shape of a wolf's head, the ring hanging from its snarling mouth. Not exactly the most welcoming first impression from a company of nuns. I looked around for signs of life, but there didn't seem to be any. All the windows were covered by heavy wooden shutters as though the nuns felt they were under siege from the modern world and were determined to keep it out.

I banged the iron knocker heartily. It raised a hell of a din, but there was still a really long pause before the door finally opened just enough for a single nun to stare out at me with a cold and entirely unwelcoming gaze. The black robes and starched white wimple gave her a nun's usual anonymity. Her face could have been any age, and the only expression I could read was open disapproval. I nodded and smiled politely, introduced myself, and explained why I was there. The nun showed no interest at all, until I mentioned the Hollow Women. She fixed me with a firm stare and then opened the door wider.

"I am Sister Joan. I know the story of the Hollow Women. We all do. We are the Holy Sisters of Saint Baphomet and sin is our business." She smiled briefly, and I realised that was meant to be a joke. "You'd better come in, Mister Grant. And we will discuss the matter further. I should make it clear, none of us are at all interested in publicity."

I assured her it was the Hollow Women who were the story, not the sisters, and she stood back to allow me to enter. She locked and bolted the door very carefully and then led me through a series of narrow rooms that finally opened out onto a large hall. Sunlight fell in through a number of tall narrow windows, but still it seemed to me that the room had too many shadows for my liking. For all its size, the hall felt... isolated, cut off, not part of the world. A very private and very secure place. A long wooden table took up the middle of the room, and around it sat a great many nuns in full regalia. All of them looking at me with cold eyes and tightly pursed mouths. None of them got up to greet me.

Sister Joan explained who I was and why I was there and not one of the sisters even nodded to me. Sister Joan pulled out a chair for me at the head of the table and I sat down. The presence of so many staring eyes would probably have been intimidating to anyone else. I just smiled politely back at them while Sister Joan sat down beside me.

She then proceeded to interrogate me on the subject of the Hollow Women, hitting me with question after question, drawing out everything I knew. She didn't challenge or correct anything I said. I got the impression she was checking what I had discovered against what she already knew. The other nuns remained silent throughout, never taking their eyes off me.

More and more, the great open hall made me feel uneasy. It was all very clean, nothing out of place, but it was just so... characterless. The nuns had been here for twenty years and more, but they'd made no impression on their surroundings. No religious paintings or texts on the walls, not even a single crucifix. This had to be a really austere order.

In the name of self-defense, I interrupted Sister Joan's questions to ask a few of my own, including the lack of religious items on show. Sister Joan smiled tightly.

"Our order does not believe in idolatry or the need for religious paraphernalia. Our belief is pure without distractions. Let the world go its own way and we shall go ours."

"I've told you everything I know," I said. "Now it's your turn. What can you tell me about the Hollow Women? And why are you so interested? I thought the Hollow Women couldn't abide religious people and vice versa."

"It's all about faith," said Sister Joan. "So lacking in modern times. The legend of the Hollow Women is old... They have existed alongside civilisation under many names. Before this town was a town, there were Hollow Women preying on the men. Before there were people, there were Hollow Women. They learned to look like people, the better to prey on them. Perhaps these days they have learned to look like something else. It's hard to be sure of anything where the Hollow Women are concerned. They are very secretive. They've had to be to survive so long. The church has tried to stamp them out many times."

"Which church?" I said.

"All of them, Mister Grant! Perhaps because only those of true faith can see through the illusions that hide the Hollow Women from the eyes of the world. It is a war, Mister Grant. Make no mistake. There can be no forgiveness for things that prey on men."

"You've clearly amassed a great deal of information during your researches," I said carefully. "Would it be possible for me to take a look at what you've discovered?"

Sister Joan was already shaking her head, even before I finished speaking. "No, Mister Grant, it will not be possible."

"May I ask why not? My story wouldn't have to quote you or mention the Sisters in any way if that's what's worrying you."

"Information is ammunition, Mister Grant. And as I said, there is a war on. We guard what we know most jealously for when it might be needed."

"You seem convinced these Hollow Women of legend still exist," I said. "Do you see them as supernatural creatures? Like vampires or ghosts?"

"Those are dead things, Mister Grant. The Hollow Women are as real, as natural, as you. Every species has its predator."

"But you do believe they still exist, here in the town?"

"Oh yes, Mister Grant, we know they do. Hiding in plain sight. Only emerging to prey on the weak and then disappearing again. Any woman could be a Hollow Woman. That's the point. And be warned, Mister Grant. If you go looking for them, you can be sure they will come looking for you."

I looked up and down the table to see if the other nuns were taking this as seriously, and everywhere I looked, cold eyes and cold faces stared implacably back at me. There's nothing scarier than a faith backed up with utter certainty. They believed. Sister Joan stood up and indicated it was time for me to leave. And I couldn't get out of there fast enough.

§

The door closed firmly behind me. I heard the lock turn and bolts slamming into place as Sister Joan sealed Barrow Farm off from the intruding world again. I breathed in deeply and shook my head to clear it. Sometimes intense beliefs can be... catching. I had to remind myself I only got into this story to prove the mythical Hollow Women had a real world source in the Hollows women. The Holy Sisters of Saint Baphomet had been locked up together for too long. Stewing in their own conspiracy theories and the need for someone who needed punishing. I suppose, if you believe in devils and possessions and miracles,

it's not too big a leap of faith to believe in women who can only be seen from the front.

I shuddered suddenly despite myself. When faith turns inwards, it becomes unhealthy. I did not believe in anything supernatural. I'd spent enough years writing and researching the weird shit to know it was all just bullshit and wish fulfilment. Whatever the Holy Sisters knew, or thought they knew, I didn't need to know it. They were just a dead end. I needed to put them behind me and press on with my research into historical records. The church archives had been a good start, but where next? The vicar had mentioned a local historical society...

I turned my back on Barrow Farm and strode determinedly away, not looking back once.

§

I reached for my phone to call Emma and bring her up to date only to realise she hadn't given me her number. So the editor couldn't blame me if her precious new reporter wasn't a big contributor to what was, after all, my story.

I walked back into the middle of town and headed straight for my favourite watering hole: the Dandy Lion for a quick drink and a think. It's always been my experience that the two go well together as long as you don't overdo either of them. The Dandy is a cosy and comfortable drinking establishment with traditional fixtures and fittings and absolutely no piped music. I can usually find someone worth talking and drinking with. But I really wasn't expecting that when I walked through the doors, the first person I found waiting for me was Emma Tee.

She was sat by a table right by the door with a drink in front of her that she'd barely touched. She smiled winningly at me. I looked briefly past her to where a group of old friends were sitting round a table farther in, but I had promised the editor I would work with Emma. And Sam Walsh was perfectly capable of spiking my story out of hand if I didn't. So I got myself a pint of good cheer from the bar and sat down opposite Emma. She gave me her best happy smile, backed up by bright shining eyes... and it was hard to stay mad at her.

"How did you get on with the Holy Sisters?" said Emma, smiling perhaps just a little mischievously.

"Don't ask," I said. "I'm sorry about just going off and leaving you to cope with the mad old cat lady."

"Oh no, I should apologise to you!" Emma said immediately. "For not following the story. You were completely right. The story must come first. I just didn't want to meet the nuns. Nuns are creepy. Even more than old churches. So you didn't get anything useful from them?"

"Not a thing," I said. "Except that they seem convinced the Hollow Women of legend are still a real and present danger."

"Let them think what they like," Emma said firmly. "Our story will prove the Hollow Women are just an urban legend, mistranslated and misunderstood down the years. That's what reporting is supposed to be about, isn't it? Shining a light into dark places and uncovering the truth."

"Yes," I said. "That is what it's supposed to be about."

We sat and talked, and drank our drinks, and talked some more. She was very easy to talk to. And somewhat to my surprise, I found we were getting on really well. She had an endless interest in all things journalistic and was fascinated by my tales of researching weird stuff for strange magazines. And it helped a lot that she thought my jokes were funny. All my cynicism and world-weariness seemed to just evaporate in the face of her youthful enthusiasm. I'd forgotten how it felt to get properly excited about a story. But then it had been a long time since I had a story worth getting excited about.

Emma was quite open about why she wanted to become a journalist. She'd left her home, and her family, to make her own way in the world. I got the impression this had been very much against her family's wishes. That they were very strict, very traditional, and apparently believed they had a right and a duty to map out her life for her. And Emma wasn't having any of it. She wanted to be a journalist so she could tell the truth about things, things that mattered. Because her family had tried so hard to hide the truth about the world from her because it conflicted with what they believed. Emma wanted to know everything there was to know about the world. So she could tell everyone else. My heart went out to her. Looking at Emma was a lot like looking at my younger self.

"My parents never wanted me to be a writer," I said. "No money in it, that was what they said. Get a proper job with prospects. So I sort of drifted sideways into journalism. I did quite well for a while."

"What happened?" said Emma. "I know something happened. Ms Walsh said... some things when she told me I'd be working with you. What went wrong, Jason?"

"I did," I said. "I had my chance, and I blew it because I couldn't stand the hard discipline of real journalism. I decided it was more important to tell a good story than sticking to the facts. So if facts got in the way, I just changed or suppressed them to make the story more sensational. I wrote some really great

stories—they just weren't entirely true. On a modern daily tabloid, that wouldn't have been a problem. That would have been business as usual. But here, in the local paper of record..."

"Ms. Walsh fired you."

"Hell yes. More in sorrow than anger, I like to think. But it was definitely 'Go and never darken my doors again.' It's taken me years to get this opportunity. And years to understand that she was right. People need to be able to believe what they're told is the truth."

"Even when a little white lie can be so much more comforting?"

"Perhaps especially then. You can't base decisions that matter on someone telling you what you want to hear. No other local paper would touch me after word got out as to why I was fired, and without a good local history, the dailies didn't want to know. And that's how I ended up hacking it out and phoning it in for any rag that would have me." I smiled, briefly. "It does feel good to be working on a real story at last."

"I did get some more information out of Alicia Tiley after you left," said Emma. "After a little encouragement and open pleading..."

"You didn't actually drink that tea, did you?"

She winced. "Please. Don't remind me. And one of her cats pissed on my shoes. Anyway, Alicia remembered a part of the legend of the Hollow Women that was new to me. Apparently they only emerge, only reveal themselves as their true selves, at night. And only when the fog rises to blur reality... and hide them from prying eyes. That's when they go forth to prey on unattached young men. And strike down their enemies, anyone who might be getting too close to the truth about them."

"You mean they kill people?"

"Oh yes," said Emma. "They kill people."

"You're right," I said. "That is a new twist. Makes sense, I suppose. The women from the Hollows were probably professional women, plying their trade away from the light of day. And because what they were doing was illegal, they or their protectors would kill anyone who threatened their livelihood, or their territory. The Holy Sisters said the Hollow Women would come after me if I went after them."

"They actually said that to you?"

"Yes. Very sternly."

Emma looked at me for a long moment. "Do you really think you might be in danger, Jason?"

"From a supernatural myth?" I said, grinning despite myself. "Hardly. You mustn't take any of this too seriously, Emma. It's just an old moral fable that's out-lived its significance. Don't let the material spook you."

She forced a smile. "As long as you don't go hanging around the Hollow Estates at dawn."

"Don't worry," I said. "I never get up that early. Another drink?"

"Don't mind if I do," said Emma.

§

Time passed in a pleasant fashion. When Emma and I finally left the Dandy Lion, leaning on each other in a companionable sort of way and giggling a bit, it was well into the evening. A fog was slowly forming on the air, a pearly grey haze, swallowing up the distance and spreading milky halos around the street lights. It seemed to thicken slowly even as I looked at it. There was no one else about, not even any traffic passing. It was like staring off the edge of the world. Everything seemed vague and uncertain. As though if I went walking off into the fog, the places I expected wouldn't be there anymore.

It was all very quiet, the fog soaking up sound. I put an arm around Emma, protectively, and looked about me. Suddenly feeling a hell of a lot more sober. The foggy evening seemed the perfect setting for some old legend to come walking back into the world. I glared into the curling mists. I was damned if I'd let my own story get to me. I looked at Emma, and she was staring into the fog with wide, worried eyes. She turned suddenly to look at me, and she seemed genuinely scared.

"Don't worry," I said. "We're a long way from dawn."

She didn't smile. Not even a little bit. "You don't understand," she said.

"Come on," I said. "I think you've had a few too many. I'll walk you home. You've nothing to worry about as long as I'm with you. And tomorrow, when the fog's all gone, you'll see how silly you were. It's just a story!"

"It's a long way to where I live," said Emma. She looked at me. "Where's your place, James? Is it near?"

"Yes," I said. "Just a few streets away."

"Can I stay with you tonight?" said Emma, her wide eyes fixed on mine. "That's what I want, James. I want to stay with you, tonight. Can I?"

And I said yes.

§

I took her back to my place. Nothing special, just a reasonably comfortable flat above a newsagent's. It wasn't until I unlocked my door and ushered her in that I realised how much of a mess I'd let the place get into. I was a man who lived alone and let things lie

where they fell. I made a token effort to clear some of it up, while Emma looked around her, not commenting.

She was nervous. I could tell. I stopped what I was doing and went to her.

"You haven't done this before, have you?" I said.

"No," she said.

"It's been a while for me. Emma... you don't have to do anything you don't want to."

"I want to do this, Jason."

"There's a spare bed. I just need to sort out some sheets for it..."

"I want you, Jason."

I put my arms around her. And she put her arms around me. Our faces were so close now; I could feel her breath on my mouth.

"You're so much younger than me," I said. "And so beautiful. You deserve better than me..."

"Hush, Jason. You deserve me. I'm here for you."

She hugged me tightly, pressing the side of her face against my shoulder. The smell from her hair filled my head. She held me as tightly as she could, as though afraid someone might drag her away.

"Hey," I said. "It's all right. Really. Everything's going to be all right, Emma."

"Yes," she said. "It is." She looked up at me, and smiled. "Take me to bed, Jason. Take me to bed and love me so we can forget everything except us. That's what I want."

And that's what I did.

§

Sometime later, I lay on my back in bed, the sweat drying on my bare skin, stretched out and relaxed, feeling more at peace with myself than I had in a long time. Emma was sat up beside me, her back against the headboard, staring out across the room. I couldn't read the expression on her face. She suddenly swung her legs over the side of the bed, and padded silently across the bedroom, entirely naked, to stand before the window. She opened the curtains just a little, and looked out.

Nice arse, I thought.

"What is it?" I said.

"I thought I heard something." She didn't look back at me.

"Come back to bed," I said. "It's nothing. Just the night. There are always noises, at night."

"Yes," she said. "There's always something happening in the night."

I glanced at my alarm clock, on the bedside table. "Getting on for ten o'clock. The night's barely started. Come back to bed, Emma."

"In a minute."

She was still staring out through the crack in the curtains at the street below. I rolled over onto my side, thinking vaguely about getting out of bed to join her and that was when I saw her back reflected in the wardrobe mirror. She had no back. Seen from behind, in the mirror's reflection, there was just a hollowed out shell. A concave depth, all ridges and whorls. As though something had reached in and scooped out everything that made her human. It was like looking into the husk of a dead insect or the hollow trunk of a diseased tree with all the insides eaten away.

I cried out. I couldn't help myself. And she spun round to look at me. She saw the truth in my face and I saw the truth in hers.

She looked at my wardrobe mirror and then back at me. For a moment she seemed to shrink in on herself, and then she drew herself up again and faced me squarely. She seemed entirely human. As long as I looked at her from the front. But I couldn't forget what I had seen. And what I had just done with something that only pretended to be human. She started towards me. I sat up sharply and put my back against the headboard. She stopped at the foot of the bed.

"I'm sorry, Jason," she said. "I'm so sorry. I was so happy I let my concentration slip, just for a moment. I never meant for you to know."

"You're real," I said. "They're real. The Hollow Women. The ones who prey on men."

"Yes, Jason."

She reached out a hand to me, and I flinched back. She looked at me sadly and let her hand drop again.

"I could have loved you, Jason. Don't you know that?"

"How long...?"

"All my life. Hollow Women are born, not made. Just like you. I had no choice in the matter. That's why I left home. Left my family and my own kind because I didn't want to be like them. I wanted to be what I wanted to be." She smiled, briefly. "The name they gave me, that I never thought to change, should have been a clue. Emma Tee. Empty. I tried so hard, Jason! Trying to live as a human, among humans. I do care for you in my way."

"You can't stay here," I said.

She looked at the curtained window behind her, and then back at me. She seemed scared.

"Please, Jason. Don't make me go. Don't throw me out. It's night, and there's a fog, and I'm so scared about what might happen..."

"Scared of what?" I said. "Why were you so determined to spend the night here with me?"

"Because they're out there. Looking for me. I know it. You've been asking too many questions, Jason. Getting too close to the truth. Despite everything I could do to distract you."

"What is the truth, Emma? Really?"

"If I tell you everything, will you let me stay?"

"Tell me everything," I said. "Tell me all about the Hollow Women."

She turned her back on me and got dressed. It looked like a perfectly ordinary human back now. I got dressed too. And then we sat down on chairs a respectful distance apart, facing each other. And she told me what I needed to know in a calm, emotionless voice.

"I saw something moving, down in the street," she said. "Something in the fog. A human shape that didn't move like anything human. In the fog, in the night, the only time when Hollow Women appear as themselves."

"How do they... pass, normally?" I said. "How can they, how can you walk among us, and not be seen for what you are?"

"A glamour. A broadcast telepathic illusion. It can be undermined, seen through, if someone has more faith in their religion than they do in the illusions of the world. That's why I was so nervous at the church, earlier. The vicar kept getting glimpses of me out of the corners of his eyes. That's why he was so jumpy. Only his refusal to believe what he was seeing with his own eyes protected me."

"Where are you from?" I said. "I mean, you said you left your home and your family. A family of Hollow Women. Where are they?"

"You don't need to know, Jason. It's safer for you if you don't know."

"I need to know! This isn't my story anymore. It's my life!"

"They'll kill you to keep their secret safe."

"It was the old woman, wasn't it?" I said. "Alicia Tiley. She was a Hollow Woman!"

"No, you fool," said Emma. "She was just an old woman. She didn't know anything. I already knew everything. All the Hollow Women, all that are left, live together in one place now because they're not human and when they're alone, they don't have to act human. You've already met them, Jason. At Barrow Farm. The Holy Sisters. Hole-y. Get it? What better disguise..."

"Where do you come from originally?" I said. My throat was tight. It was getting hard to breathe. "I mean, if you're not human, what are you? Mutations? Aliens? Supernatural? What?"

"I don't know," said Emma. "If the sisters ever knew, they forgot long ago. We're just predators. That's all you need to know."

"How is it that you're so... human?"

"Television," Emma said simply. "I'm the first generation of Hollow Women to be exposed to television. It really is a window on the world. A better world, a better way of living. And I wanted it." She glanced back at the window. "They'll know I've talked. They'll come for me. And for you. I was only allowed to stay away as long as I kept my head down. Didn't get noticed. I was doing so well. And then you came to Ms. Walsh with your idea for a story. I was the one who convinced her to go for it with me attached. So I could watch over you, steer you away from the truth. Towards a nice, safe historical interpretation that would help hide us. You can't defend yourself from something you don't believe in. But you wanted this so much and I..."

"You need to leave town," I said. I got to my feet. "Come on. You need to get away. Start over, somewhere else. I'll see you safely away, and then later, I can come and join you. With both of us gone maybe the sisters won't feel so threatened."

"You'd come with me?" said Emma, getting to her feet. She looked at me wonderingly. "You'd do that, for me? After... everything?"

"Of course," I said. "I care for you in my way."

I put out my hands to her, and she grasped them tightly, like a drowning woman.

"It's the human thing to do, Emma. I'm sorry I freaked out at first. It's just... I never had one of my stories turn on me before."

"I'm sorry too," said Emma. She didn't say for what, though I didn't realise that till later.

"We can't go by car," I said. "They'll be expecting that. Looking for that. No—I'll take you to the railway station. It's not far. There's still time to catch the last train out of here and you'll be safe among the other passengers. Just... keep going, keep changing trains until you're far away. You can hide yourself properly in a big city. They'll never find you."

"Will you come and find me if I call for you?" said Emma.

"Do you want me to?"

"Yes. More than everything."

"Good. Because that's what I want too."

We held each other for a long moment. In the end, she pushed me away.

"I have to go, Jason. It's not safe here. For either of us."

Outside in the street, the fog had come down hard. Thick, grey walls surrounded us on every side, cutting us off from the rest of the world. There was no one about. Not even a single passing car. As though everyone somehow knew it wasn't safe to be out and about this night. Emma held tightly to my arm, staring frantically about her.

"I've never seen a fog this thick," I said.

"I have," said Emma. "It's them. They're here."

"It's all right!" I said roughly. "I'll get you to the station."

I set out confidently enough, but in the fog, all the streets looked the same, and without landmarks to guide me, I soon lost my way and all sense of direction. I kept going anyway, striding out, Emma clattering along beside me, still hanging tight to my arm. And then, one by one, they appeared. Just dark shadows at first, appearing and disappearing in the mists around me like sharks circling silently in murky waters. Bursting out of the mists in front of me just long enough to turn me aside, guiding me, herding me, closing in from all sides. I kept going, even broke into a run, but it did no good. They were everywhere. Moving faster than I could because they didn't have human limitations. They never made a sound, just appearing and disappearing, until finally they all came out of the fog at once, forming a great circle around me and Emma. The Holy Sisters. The Hollow Women.

The black and white of their disguising robes stood out starkly against the grey mists. They stood very still, inhumanly still, watching me with their cold, empty faces. Sister Joan loomed up suddenly before me. I struck out at her, but she was gone before the blow arrived, vanished back into the mists. She reappeared while I was still off balance, and her fist came flying at me impossibly fast. She hit me once, clubbing me down with sudden, vicious strength. I hit the ground hard, driven to my knees by the force of the blow, all the strength knocked out of me. I cried out in shock and pain. When I looked up, she was standing over me, studying me with cold predator's eyes.

Dark shapes rushed in from every side, and just like that they were all over me. Lashing out with large, hard fists driven by more than human strength. Blood flew from my battered face. I tried to defend myself, but I couldn't even touch them. I ended up curled in a ball on the ground, hurting all over. And suddenly, they stopped. I slowly uncurled and looked up. Sister Joan was standing over me, her face entirely unmoved, unconcerned. She wasn't even breathing hard.

"Forget your story," she said. "Forget her. Forget any of this ever happened. And we will let you live as a cautionary example."

"All right," I said shakily, blood spilling from my mouth. "All right..."

"He lies," said another voice, from one of the Hollow Women looking on. Others took it up. *He lies, he lies...*

"You can't forget us because you won't forget her," said Sister Joan. "Such a pity... Say your prayers, Jason Grant. Your story has come to an end."

"No!"

I turned my head, slowly, painfully, and there was Emma. Standing beside me, her hands clenched into fists, glaring defiantly at Sister Joan.

"If you kill him, I'll never forgive you! Never!"

"You forget yourself, child," said Sister Joan. "You forget what you are. When he is gone..."

"No. I won't let you kill him."

Sister Joan considered her thoughtfully. "How will you stop us?"

"By giving you what you want. If you'll let him live, I'll come home again. I promise. I'll come back to you, and I'll never try to leave again. That's what you want, isn't it?"

"Come home?" said Sister Joan. "No more arguments, no more running away?"

"Yes," said Emma. She didn't look at me. "That's what I want."

It was the bravest thing I ever saw. A Hollow Woman, demonstrating her humanity. Giving up her life for mine.

Sister Joan looked at me, and then at Emma. "Did you...?"

"Yes," Emma said steadily. "I slept with him. And made a child with him."

I looked at her speechlessly. I had no doubt she was telling the truth. That she knew. It was, after all, what Hollow Women did.

"Then come home, child," said Sister Joan. "Your place is waiting for you."

Emma walked away from me, into the ranks of the waiting Hollow Women. And together, they turned sideways and disappeared, back into the fog. Only Sister Joan remained.

"I could still tell the world all about you," I said.

"But you won't," said Sister Joan. "Not if you want Emma to stay safe. Silence and obscurity are the price of your survival, and hers." She smiled, very briefly. "And anyway, who would believe you? A hack writer of so many wild stories? No one believes in the things you write. The world only likes its legends in stories these days. We have what we came for. Nothing else matters."

She walked away and left me. I caught a last brief glimpse of Emma standing alone in the mists. She looked at me and didn't smile or wave good-bye. She took one last look at me and then walked away forever. As she turned away, I saw her back was empty. Just a hollow shell.

And I was left alone, in the fog, and the night. Alone, with my hollowed out heart.

⚘⚘⚘

WHAT THE HELL EVER HAPPENED TO…?

An Interview with Gary Raisor

By Robert Morrish

Gary Raisor possesses one of the more apt last names that you're going to find for a horror writer, and on works such as the novel *Less Than Human*, his pen has proven just as sharp and cutting as his namesake instrument. Raisor got his start in the 1980s writing short fiction for revered magazines *The Horror Show* and *Night Cry*, and then edited a star-studded anthology, *Obsessions*, which was published in 1991 by Dark Harvest. When Raisor's debut novel, the aforementioned *Less Than Human*, was published in 1992 in both paperback (under Berkeys Book's Diamond imprint) and hardcover (by the Overlook Connection Press), it appeared that his career was on the verge of really taking off. But then…oh hell, why don't I just let him tell you? Take it away, Gary…

Okay, where to start? At the beginning I guess. A long, long time ago, I was bounced out of a covered wagon. As a baby, I woke up in the backwoods of Kentucky, where fortunately I was adopted by wolves. Why they took me in has always been a puzzle to me. But there I was, running around the hills buck naked and howling at the moon. Which happens in these parts more than you might think. It was a good life, running with the pack, although a mite rough when those winter snows came. As I grew older I noticed I didn't look the same as the other wolves, I was much hairier, so I left the pack and made my way to civilization, searching for others of my kind. There, in a clearing, in a small clapboard house, I was taken in by a kindly old couple. And so, with some strategic shaving and a rolled-up newspaper, I was instructed in the rudiments of civilized behavior. I made it through paper training, and suddenly life was sweet indeed; indoor plumbing and food that didn't try to kill me back.

Then school started.

I actually went to a one-room schoolhouse for a bit. Learned to read there, reluctantly. Ms. Carter, my third grade teacher, a small tough woman, thin as a mother-in-law's smile and rumored to have killed a man in her younger years, kept me from recess until I learned to make sense of those strange squiggly things on the pages. I finally did. And Brother, that opened up a whole new world for me. My first attempt at reading a book was something called *White Fang*, but I had trouble getting through it, because I kept getting all teary eyed every time I'd see a picture of dear old mom and dad getting shot.

My kindly human pseudo-mom saw my distress. She parked her morning jug of 'shine long enough to give me a copy of H.G. Wells' *The Island of Dr. Moreau*. More animals. Tortured animals this time. Still, at age ten, I was hooked by the dark side. I read everything I could get my hands on, as determined to evolve into a human being, as determined as Moreau's creatures were in "the house of pain," or those people I saw on that new-fangled invention that had begun cropping up everywhere. It was called a TV. Twelve inches of black & white magic with mono sound. Love at first sight. TV and books, horror and science fiction, they were my lifeline to the outside world in those early years. I couldn't get enough of the stuff. I spent some pretty idyllic times in a small town going to school, reading comic books and everything in the library while soaking up *Trek, TZ, Thriller, Outer Limits* on TV.

On reading, I branched out as I got older.

Mark Twain, O'Henry, Heinlein, Shirley Jackson, Shakespeare, Robert Louis Stevenson, Bradbury, Edgar Rice Burroughs, Arthur C. Clarke, Poe. When I wasn't playing sports in high school. Baseball, basketball, football. I was kind of a jock and a nerd, a fairly weird combo.

One day, I looked up from my book and noticed strange creatures roaming the halls of my school. No, it wasn't ma and pa wolf come down from the hills to take me home. I'm talking about girls. The feminine gender. The fairer sex. Now it took a keen eye in my hometown to spot the difference between a male and female. The females tended to be smaller and usually smelled better. But you couldn't always count on that. All I know for sure, there was a severe shortage of these exotic beings in my school. Competition was, as they say, stiff. To get a date for the prom, even with the homely girls, you had to put your bid in by the sixth grade, or you were going solo. That was risky business, my friends. You couldn't be sure how these things were going to turn out. A downy cheek at twelve could turn into a Sasquatch beard on a Vulcan head by seventeen. So I skipped prom. And not entirely by choice. You can put Bigfoot in a dress but that doesn't make her prom queen. Well, that's how I recollect it, anyway.

After high school, I put in a couple semesters of college, but I was growing tired of small-town life. Make that a girlfriend-less, car-less, and penniless life. I had to do something, bust a move, even if it was wrong. Had a buddy who talked about Chicago. Seems he worked there in the summer. Had himself a sweet ride, a '59 Corvette convertible he'd bought with the money he made in the Windy City. He talked it up. I ate it up. So at the age of nineteen, I packed up my meager possessions, burned my Marvel comics, including *Spiderman #1*, straightened up my room that used to be a screened-in porch, grabbed a crate of Nair (for the hair, remember?) and me and my buddy headed for "the big city." No sooner did we get there, my buddy gets drafted by Uncle Sam and shipped off to 'Nam. That's what we called Vietnam in those days. I was on my own. Two years would come and go before I would see him again.

What followed wasn't pretty. A lot of shitty jobs (sludge-pump cleaner being my favorite) and near-starvation. But yours truly persevered. I didn't want to go home with my tail tucked between my legs. (Another wolf analogy, sorry.) I stuck it out, worked the crappy jobs, went to college at night. I procured a better job and worked my way into the IT business,

bought myself a sweet ride, a '69 Chevelle. Oh, and I found a mate. A candidate for Miss Teen America, I might add. Cute with a rich daddy, too. Had him one of them cement ponds in the backyard. Ah, the fond memories. I can still recall my future father-in-law's words to my future wife as we stood there in the church with thousands of people and the priest looking on. He said to her, "Are you sure you wanna do this? You can do a lot better than this guy." But the future Mrs. Raisor and I plunged on ahead and tied the knot.

We set up house, but the blue-green hills of Kentucky were beckoning to me. Or maybe it was one too many trips to see the wolves at the Brookfield Zoo. You can't take the wolf out of a wolf-boy, so I returned home after eight years in the frosty north with the even frostier in-laws. With a wife in tow. Bought a house, had a kid, worked the IT job, you know, all the usual stuff people do. Hated it, felt like I was dying slowly.

I soldiered on. Then when I was in my mid-thirties, my dad died. He wasn't that old, either. It was what you'd term a wake-up call. Gonna be serious here for a moment. I decided if I wanted to be a writer, I'd best get to it. My dad was a talker, a spinner of tales, or yarns, as we call them here. Carrying on the tradition, I wrote a couple of short-short stories and sent them to my two favorite magazines at the time, *The Horror Show* and *Night Cry*. To my shock and amazement, I sold to both, and became a regular in both. The late David Silva and the late Alan Rodgers were two of my favorite editors ever. (That Robert Morrish guy who used to work for *Cemetery Dance* is okay in my book, too.)

While writing for these two magazines, I began meeting some cool people, Joe Lansdale in particular. We became good friends. I mentioned an idea I had for an anthology called *Obsessions*. Joe said go for it. I did. A lot of begging, a little blackmail, and a few hundred phone calls later, I put that book together for Paul Mikol at Dark Harvest. We did it the old-fashioned way, like they did back in the Gutenberg days. Snail mail, too. It was fun and it was horrible, all at the same time. Some writers were super nice, some didn't take kindly to being asked for changes. Let's just say in a few cases unkind words were uttered in ye olde editor's ear. But I persevered. Nancy Holder's story in the anthology won the Bram Stoker that year. To add insult to injury, I lost money on the book. Had to go into my own pocket to pay all the writers. I'm taking the best twelve stories from the book and re-issuing them in digital book format over at Crossroad Press. Think I'll call it something catchy like *The Best of Obsessions*.

So anyway, I got *Obsessions* done and it was a best seller for Dark Harvest. No paperback, though. After that, I said to myself, "Self, you need to do something big now. Something that'll take your writing to the next level." I talked to Joe Lansdale, told him I had an idea; that I wanted to write a novel. Joe said go for it. Offered some suggestions. He even hooked me up with his agent. She sold *Less Than Human* to Berkley Books based on a couple chapters and an outline. I wrote the book and it was published. Craptackularly, I might add. None of the promises they made were kept. Still, the book sold out its print run (rare for a first novel) and made the short list for the Bram Stoker awards, and it was picked up by the Overlook Connection and published as one of the nicest hardbacks you'll ever hold.

So time for novel number two. The moment of truth. That Raisor empire wasn't going to build itself. I did the outline and sent it to the agent lady. The silence was deafening. There was a slight problem that neither Joe nor I quite realized at the time. Agent lady was having a nervous breakdown. As if she'd gone completely off the rails. She told me Berkley didn't like my book idea. Then, later, told me she hadn't liked the idea and hadn't shown the idea to Berkley at all. I wasn't too happy about that, as you can imagine, and told her so. I was polite. Her reply was to drop me as a client. Then she died shortly after that. Heart attack. After going to her sister's funeral, who had also died of a heart attack. Make no mistake, life is stranger than fiction. Always.

Over the years, I found a few more agents, all of them bad. Or maybe not bad, just more likely interested in their bigger clients. Can't blame them for that. Long story short, couldn't get anything going. So without an agent or a place to publish, nothing much was happening in the ol' writing career, nothing major anyway. I attempted to work with Overlook Connection Press on a series of novellas *(Robert notes: one book in the series,* Graven Images, *was published, in 2001)*, but money issues killed that project. Throw in a divorce and some heavy drinking, and suddenly I didn't give two shits about writing anymore. I sort of quit. That didn't work out for me. Got bored. Started writing movie scripts. Did a couple of them. But I missed prose writing and time heals the wounds. Life isn't perfect. Things still fall in the crapper occasionally. Friends and family get sick. Some of them die. Life goes on until it doesn't. Nothing profound about that sentiment, just a fact. I try to deal with it better than I used to. I don't drink so much these days and have written a new sixty-page novella to lead off the new edition of *Sinister Purposes (Robert notes: a title originally published by Cemetery Dance Publications in 2006)*. I've retooled the entire book for Crossroad Press, including the novellas from the failed Overlook Connection Press project.

More good news: Davis Wilson at CROSSROAD has also commissioned an audio book for *Less Than Human* to go with the digital version. I'm getting interest on the movie scripts. Got a couple short movies playing over at *Chilling Tales for Dark Nights* — thanks to Peter Podgursky, Donna Thorland, Greg Bartlett, and Marvin Suarez. I got illustrated prose for graphic novel *Empty Places* at Crossroad Press thanks to an amazing artist, Jeff Austin. Oh, and last but not least, I have a wonderful, supportive girlfriend. Things are starting to look up.

Do I still read horror? Why yes I do, but only the older writers for the most part. King, Straub, Dan Simmons, Ramsey Campbell, F. Paul Wilson, Barker, Neil Gaiman, Joe Lansdale. When they write horror, that is, which isn't so much anymore.

And lastly, if you ever run across a pack of wolves carrying around a ragged paperback of *Less Than Human*, pretending they can read it, tell 'em I'm doing fine.

☘☘☘

HELLNOTES

THE HORROR
REVIEW

HORROR, SCIENCE FICTION
& FANTASY REVIEWS

FICTION, MOVIES, AND ART
DEDICATED TO THE HORROR GENRE

JOURNALSTONE
YOUR LINK TO ARTISTIC TALENT

**Queen of the Dead: Zombie
Ascension II
Vincenzo Bilof
Severed Press
$12.75 PB
ISBN 978-1925047202**

To be honest I didn't find this an easy book to get into with regard the characters. I don't mind having anti-heroes as the main protagonists, but there are anti-heroes and anti-heroes, and for the most part I didn't really care for many of the people in this novel, most of whom seem to be sociopaths to one degree or another, with little or no concern about the welfare of anyone other than themselves – or, if they have, for very few, usually one. There are a few exceptions, but they are a minority. Perhaps that would be a requirement to survive in such a world, though. It probably is.

That said, the graphic horror of the situation in which they are trapped, a global apocalypse of zombies ripping apart the fabric of society and the bodies of their victims, is vividly described – sometimes, it should be added, with maybe a tad too much concern for literary turns of phrase, which only serve to remind you that you are reading a book. Even so, the descriptions are vivid, the characters quickly and memorably drawn, and the speed with which events unfold truly breathtaking.

This is the second volume in a trilogy. Not having read the first, I was at a disadvantage to start with, though I was soon able to catch up with what was going on. That says a lot for the writer. Not only did I quickly catch up with things, but in a way that avoided long pieces of exposition. At no point did the pace slacken.

Despite almost a glut of books, movies and TV series over recent years zombies are still popular. If everyone could strike the originality of Vincenzo Bilof in his depiction of what would happen in such a catastrophe, there is no doubt in my mind that there is still a lot of life in the trope yet. It may not be a pleasant ride, but Bilof has

certainly provided us with one hell of an exciting one in this book.

-Reviewed by David A. Riley

**Deeply Twisted
Chantal Noordeloos
TMH Publishing
$9.95 PB, $2.99 Kindle
ISBN 978-9491864049**

In *Deeply Twisted*, Dutch author Chantal Noordeloos presents readers with a world where hidden—and not so hidden—fears come to the surface. It is a darkly elegant, and often extremely violent, world reminiscent of that of myth, fairy tale, and legend. In these twenty stories, some of them short enough to be considered "short shorts," others more developed with separate sections, readers encounter various types of evil, often disguised by surface beauty or innocence. These stories are indeed twisted both in subject matter and in plot. Although several of these stories have been published elsewhere, Noordeloos weaves them together with the new material in a way that produces a collection that is cohesive while still keeping the integrity of the individual stories. A few of the stories connect, serving as prequels or just providing more information, but they are not organized chronologically, so one of the joys of this book is that the reader is encouraged to reread even before finishing the collection. Even those stories that are not directly related may include variations on a theme which can make the reader stop for comparison or reflection. To get the full impact of these connections, the reader should read the stories in order rather than randomly sampling. After a first read, playing with the order of the stories might be fun!

In this exploration of evil and fear, Noordeloos is at times reminiscent of Nathaniel Hawthorne—which may seem like an odd comparison. However, like Hawthorne, Noordeloos knows that evil can lurk in any human heart and that appearances are deceiving. If anything, these stories show the darkness that is beneath the pretty, the innocent, and the saintly. And in several of the stories, those who appear to be monstrous are actually the ones holding evil in check. Also, like Hawthorne, at least two of Noordeloos' stories often seem to be fables where those who commit evil for greed have to suffer the consequences, and here those consequences are supernatural and very scary.

Many of the settings of these stories are ordinary but are imbued with the extraordinary or the nightmarish. For example, in "When the Bell Tolls," a very ordinary town suddenly has a very extraordinary clock. In "The Dispensation of Jack Harrington," there seems to be an ordinary convention with normal convention activities; however, these conventioneers are far from ordinary. "Dinner Date" seems to be an ordinary dinner party with ordinary friends in an ordinary town, but in this case evil lies beneath the surface of these ordinary people and only absolute evil can sort them out. In "Soulman," a story that could take place on the streets of any American city, a mysterious stranger, who shares characteristics with a popular Norse deity, walks among the homeless. Other settings are more specific. Two stories, "The Widow" and "Deeply Twisted" are set in the Netherlands. However, this setting is more a place of dark fairy tale than the modern country. The village of these stories is a place of evil, where a darkness or curse necessitates the death of many of the village's children.

Noordeloos has commented on her webpage that she is scared of just about everything. In this collection, readers are presented with a wide variety of horrors: zombies, serial killers, witches (or supposed witches), evil children, cannibals, grave robbers, evil storms, and various demons and monsters. She taps into the childhood fear of something truly scary being under the bed. Even gold turns out to be a catastrophic horror. The ultimate terror in this collection is Lovecraftian, and Noordeloos does a fine job of making it universal and final.

In the midst of scaring her readers in multiple ways, Noordeloos also explores relationships, especially those between parents and children, between siblings, among friends or even between captor and captive.

Readers who are looking for a thrilling ride, who like their blood and gore handled with a delicate touch, and who enjoy a deeply twisted plot will not be disappointed in this collection. They may come away with no desire to be a grave robber, may have expectations that a god or a devil might just walk among us, and may look more closely at their children, searching for the hint of something evil within.

-Reviewed by Leah Larson

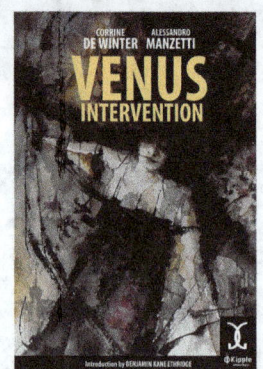

Venus Intervention
by Corrine De Winter & Alessandro Manzetti
Kipple Officina Libraria,
$2.49 Kindle
ASIN: B00LYUOH3G

The opening to *VersiGuasti 1: Venus Intervention* describes the work as "a gothic and disturbing poems collection, an exciting journey into the nightmare that will leave you breathless." This description, while accurate, does not truly capture the horrific beauty poets De Winter and Manzetti have laid before us.

In his introduction, author Benjamin Kane Ethridge discusses the "gradient shadows in between" darkness and light. The poems in *Venus Intervention* dance and weave along the borderland between those two realms. "Part I: Morning" is a collection from Corrine De Winter. Her work is haunting and emotional. "Do I make you write ethereal music" evokes images of phantoms, operas, and deadly passions. In "Terminal," she writes, "Even my wild horses are tethered by cold reason." It is this vivid imagery that brings each poem to life like a point of light in a black room. "Part II: Evening" by Alessandro Manzetti serves as a contrast to De Winter. His brutal edge cuts like a knife. "The city is destroyed" he declares in "The Rope." "Dark guts are uncoiled" and "the smell of death is too keen." It is in the contrast of styles where we glimpse the borderland. Both poets plunge into the psyche, exposing the menace and hope that make us human. De Winter says, "you are beautiful in a certain light," and Manzetti tells us we are merely "herds of souls" in a world of chaos. Dark, mysterious, and threatening at times, *VersiGuasti 1: Venus Intervention* does not disappoint.

-Reviewed by Alex Scully

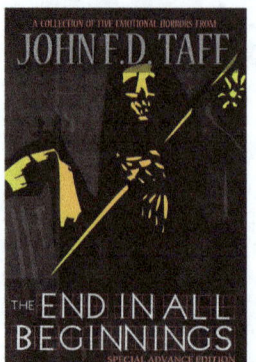

The End in All Beginnings
John F.D. Taff
Grey Matters Press
$15.99 PB; $6.99 Kindle
ISBN 978-1940658285

As the old saying goes, there are only two certainties in life – death and taxes. Although a compilation of tax-themed stories would be quite horrific, author John F.D. Taff chose to create his solo collection, *The End in All Beginnings*, about death and the human condition.

The anthology begins with *What Becomes God*, a tragedy about a young boy and the sacrifice he makes in an attempt to save his ailing friend. Childhood innocence is the driving force here, allowing the reader to empathize with the protagonist and the choices he makes, no matter how disturbing they may be. The story does take a few pages to get going and starts with a more sullen tone, but once the horror hits, it hits hard and doesn't let go.

The second novella is *Object Permanence*, a story that centers on a select few who have the ability to manipulate time and those around them, ultimately cheating death for themselves while subjecting others to the consequences. The story shifts effortlessly from first person to third person point-of-view, showcasing Taff's abilities as a writer and conjurer of compelling ideas.

Love in the Time of Zombies, the third in the collection, gives the reader a rest from the serious tones of the first two novellas and brings out a comedic air to lighten the mood. The title gives away the plot as the zombie apocalypse has swept the Earth and, amid the chaos, our hero finds himself falling for a girl he once knew. Thing is, the girl is now a part of the undead. While that may not appeal to the average person, it doesn't stop our hero and his undeniable affections.

The highlight of the collection is the fourth story, *The Long, Long Breakdown*. It's a post-apocalyptic tale that examines a father's love and overbearing protectiveness for his daughter in a world ravaged by rising waters. *The Long, Long Breakdown* touches upon horror in a different way than the other stories do, taking a realistic approach to death and loss. The characters face threats of change, of venturing out into the unknown, but ultimately prove that life can flourish even in a constant state of fear.

The final novella, *Visitation*, pushes past horror and delves into the world of science fiction. A galaxy-wide lottery is held where the lucky winners receive a two weeks' stay on Visitation, a haunted planet that is said to attract the souls of the deceased. Once there, the lotto winners are divided off into their own lake-side cabin where they wait for a sign from their loved ones. One man ventures to the planet to reconnect with his wife, but as he catches fleeting glimpses of her, he starts to believe something sinister is afoot. Taff's take on the afterlife raises a great question of morality: if we had the chance to see our dearly departed one last time, would we take it?

Visitation is a fitting finale for our journey through death, a journey that starts as children in *What Becomes God*, takes us into adulthood with *Object Permanence*, then into the role of a parent in *The Long, Long Breakdown* and ends with the afterlife, placing a sci-fi spin on a good, old fashioned ghost story. Taff acknowledges the coming-of-age motif in his author's notes section at the end of the book; a section that proves to be quite informative, offering insight to the origins and influences of each story.

Taff has penned an entertaining bag of tricks. *The End in All Beginnings* focuses more on the human element of death. He

examines the human condition, how our emotions influence our decisions when faced with life-changing choices, and how our choices may not always work in our favor. From making sacrifices to save the ones we love, to having the ability to postpone the inevitable, Taff reminds us that although death is inevitable, meeting the reaper face-to-face may not always mean the end.

-Reviewed by Jess Landry

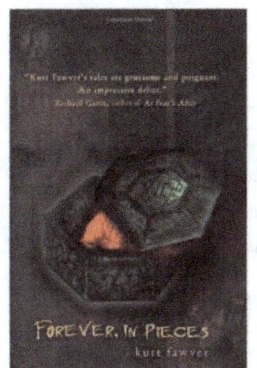

Forever, in Pieces
Kurt Fawver
Villipede Publications
$14.99 PB, $0.99 eBook
ISBN 978-0615903965

Forever, in Pieces. It's got a nice ring to it, doesn't it? It seems at first glance to be a bold choice for a short story collection. After all, forever is arguably the most difficult concept to depict. Probably a wise move to take it piece by piece. The title has more than one meaning, of course, given a little bit of grammatical finessing. Whatever the case, Kurt Fawver proves to be up to the task of writing stories that both live up to the title and scare their readers into submission. What you'll find here is a different kind of fear than you might expect.

The stories showcased in *FiP* aren't particularly gory (though gore has its time to shine), nor are they deeply character-driven (though the characters are relatable enough in an everyman sort of way). In an unusual take on the zombie genre, "The Waves from Afar", the dead simply stand motionless on the beach, staring at the tides. No explanation is given, and it's absolutely chilling in its subtlety. Another story turns ritual on its head and sees Santa Claus as judge, jury, and executioner, and it's not at all flippant. This is the case with most of the stories. Even the most frivolous-seeming subjects are approached with a disturbing angle and a straight-faced respect. To compound this, these stories seethe with a fatalistic bleakness that might just eat away at you if you read them back to back in a lengthy stretch. As Fawver says himself in the introduction, it's all "… banality and ineffectuality in conflict with chaos and deepest darkness."

The brand of horror that Fawver brings to the table might be described as cosmic, but it reaches that ineffable peak by scaling things way down to the microcosmic level. The dire situations befalling ordinary people in nondescript places, seemingly by chance, are ubiquitous to the point where it seems that all roads naturally lead to nothing. All that's out of our control seems rooted in something far deeper than the mortal mind can imagine. There's no distinct mythos framing this viewpoint, but the further you get into the collection, the more pronounced it becomes. The final story, "Rub-A-Dub-Dub", best encapsulates this, its central plot device being a hierarchical nesting doll of death upon death, end upon end.

Considering this is the note the collection goes out on, it's fair to say that these stories are far away from the bright and shiny side of our beloved genre. Instead of rooting for characters who are treading the line between life and death, it's just as likely you'll be rooting for the damned line to snap so these poor souls won't have to struggle any longer. You know things aren't going to end well anyway. The real draw here is the morbid genius between the lines, and the antiquated prose style that lulls you into the darkest of mires. *Forever, in Pieces* strips away all the excess of standard horror fare and delivers something that will both give you nightmares and make you feel like you're living in one. It's emotionally draining stuff, to be sure, but it's very much worth reading.

-Reviewed by Josh Black

Dark Work
Keith Minnion
SST Publications
$35.95 HB
ISBN 978-1909640153

Back in the early 1990s, I discovered a fantastic magazine called *Cemetery Dance*. I was ready to broaden my horror reading horizons after spending my high school years reading mostly King and Koontz. And they were excellent of course, especially at that time, but I wanted more. Finding *CD* was perfect for encountering new horror writers.

One thing I absolutely loved that didn't happen in mainstream novels – illustrations. I hadn't really seen much horror art at the time, so I was blown away by the artistic talent in those pages. One artist's name I kept noticing, and became a big fan of – Keith Minnion. According to the index on his website, Keith's first piece of artwork for the magazine was in fall 1992. I looked back through my collection of *CD* magazines, and unfortunately I don't have that issue. However, I do have many issues after that with his work. It would be impossible to pick a favorite, but looking through them, his talent consistently shines through.

In addition to Cemetery Dance, Keith has illustrated many other magazines and books. Quite a few are sitting on my bookshelves. One unforgettable night, while I was attending a horror writers' convention in Rhode Island, I was sitting at a table outside under the stars, when the man sitting next to me introduced himself. It was Keith, of course, and I was thrilled. He is one of the nicest people I have ever met, and a lot of fun to hang out with.

Recently, SST Publications published a retrospective

of Keith's art called *Dark Work*. And while it doesn't include everything he's done (no way it could), it's a great representation of his amazing talent. Some of his *CD* work is here, and I recognized many of my favorites. There are also book illustrations, and even some unpublished works.

Dark Work is the perfection addition to any horror lover's book shelf. And if you aren't familiar with Keith Minnion's art, there would be no better way to discover this fantastic artist.

-Reviewed by Sheri White

SNAFU: An Anthology of Military Horror
Edited by Geoff Brown and Amanda J. Spedding
Cohesion Press
$18.95 PB; $4.99 Kindle
ISBN 978-0992558109

"Military horror."

The phrase seems almost as tiredly redundant as the time-worn joke about "military intelligence" is oxymoronic. After all, by its nature, the military is expected to deal with horrific things. That is a given.

But when the already difficult and dangerous job of soldiering meets…well, *other* things, the term "military horror" takes on entirely new meanings.

SNAFU collects seventeen thrillers, tales in which otherwise deadly military operations ramp up even further with the addition of the outré, the macabre, the unexpected, and whole ranges of things bloody and gruesome. To increase the interest, settings range from 48,000 BC to 50,000AD; from nineteenth-century India to the twenty-first-century Pacific Northwest; from the coast of Japan during World War II to the scene of battle in the Civil War; from San Francisco in the 1960s to Berlin in the…well, you get the idea.

The anthology includes original work from major names in military horror, including Jonathan Maberry, Weston Ochse, Greig Beck James A Moore, Joseph Nassise, and Eric S Brown, as well as many others.

Solid, every one of them.

If I have any objections to the stories, it would be that several just aren't long enough. They read like chapters; they engage me with fascinating characters—both villains and heroes—follow exciting adventures, then concluded by intimating deeper problems, more dangerous situations… and I want to read more! Seems like a healthy objection to well-imagined tales.

Not one of the stories failed to attract and hold my

interest. Not one of them failed to suggest new ways of looking and old monsters, and old ways of looking at new ones. It's been a while since I've encountered a collection whose authors responded to the theme with such wholesale enthusiasm or one that so neatly defined and redefined its title: *SNAFU*.

Strongly recommended.

-Reviewed by Michael R. Collings

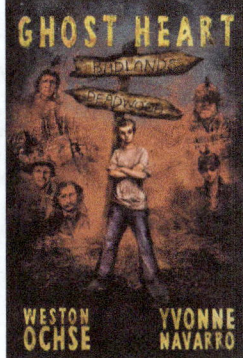

Ghost Heart
by Weston Ochse and Yvonne Navarro
Dark Regions Press;
$14.95 US

Matt Cady is having a rough time: His parents are headed for a divorce, and his best friend, Regina Running Deer, is planning to run away from her own broken home to join her shady cousin and his motorcycle gang on the road. When Regina finally makes her move, Matt gets the brilliant idea to run away with her, hoping that his disappearance, and subsequent miraculous return, will bring his parents closer together and save their marriage.

Aside from Regina, Matt has a couple of unusual traveling companions: Jacket and Raisin, a pair of spirit guardians, who have been watching over Matt and Regina, respectively, for years. Regina has outgrown her guardian Raisin, but he still follows her, unseen and unheard, hoping to break through to her and get her off of the path her life is taking. When Matt and Regina finally hook up with Regina's shifty cousin Ali Baba, things take a turn for the worse, and Matt is left alone with Jacket, and soon finds himself confronted with an enigmatic witch, vampire kitties, a ravenous phantom, and the ghosts of Wild Bill Hickok and Calamity Jane.

GHOST HEART is a quick, light read…it holds the reader's attention, and the tender relationship between Matt and Jacket is enough to cover up the novel's narrative flaws, but this is ultimately a slight little book, that will likely be forgotten soon after turning the last page.

— Dan Reilly

Fear City
by F. Paul Wilson
Tor
$25.99 US

When a good childhood friend moves away, one doesn't want to admit you will likely never see him or her again, never create new good times, or experience wild new adventures. Sometimes, the chance is given to relish those last moments, tough as they are, laughing as that choked up feeling reminds that the end is near and soon memories will be all that remain. Yet too often, that friend leaves for good, a face pressed against a car window fading into the distance.

Such is the case here in the third "Early Years Trilogy" novel (is read?). Pages turn much too quickly toward the shattering end as the reader attempts to slow down time.

F Paul Wilson may have given his fans the last new look at Repairman Jack yet at least they know the score.

The first two books of the trilogy, COLD CITY and DARK CITY set up Repairman Jack's immersion into New York City when he was just….Jack. As engrossing as the Young Repairman Jack series but much darker, the reader follows Jack along a path that explains the iconic character seen in THE TOMB, LEGACIES, and NIGHTWORLD. The relationships with Abe and Julio further deepen as Jack finds most people he encounters cannot be trusted.

Kristen (Cristin), his girlfriend from the first two books, has dumped him yet wishes to make up, then disappears. A group of terrorists plot the destruction of two signature structures in Manhattan and aim to cripple the States with the gesture. Dane Bertel has returned to enlist Jack's help, although his motives remain as shadowy as the man himself. Finally, a grisly murder (of a high priced call girl), the "Ditmas Dahlia," has made headlines +and has Jack on a mission to find the killer of a someone that most consider a "no one." The reach of the Septimus Order is ever present and begins to unfurl its true mission that will continue through the "Secret History Of The World."

As usual, while the plot is tight and has more twists than usual, the writing +is succinct and powerful, it's the characters who make a F. Paul Wilson novel. Readers can almost see the darkening of Jack's psyche as he clings tight to who he wishes to be. The bonds he has created tighten and the friendships deepen, keeping him from being truly alone in his off the grid life in the big city. Abe shines throughout, leaving this reviewer hoping to see the man again, hopefully with his own story? Nobody is safe in this series, which makes certain events that much more wrenching. Each wonderfully drawn character lives and speaks his or her story, even the villains, who are never one-dimensional.

One the final page is turned, just about every fan will be wishing for more, but knowing the tale has been told and the city will continue to mold Repairman Jack into +the man who Wilson's fans have grown to love over the years. Hopefully, he will reemerge one day when ready to spin a new yarn. Until then, readers will have to reread the entire series during the period of withdrawal.

Jack might be gone but readers will keep a close eye on neighborhood street, hoping to hear that old friend coming back home to visit once more.

— Dave Simms

Dario Argento
L. Andrew Cooper

Dario Argento Contemporary Film Directors Series
By L. Andrew Cooper
University of Illinois Press
December 2012;
$22 Trade Paperback

This book on Dario Argento has been out for a bit now but I think has gotten unjustly overlooked (I was only recently made aware of it myself as well) - at least in the horror world. So I thought I would give it a much-deserved review and push. Andrew Cooper is an assistant professor of film and digital media at the University of Louisville and actually taught a course on Dario Argento at Georgia Tech (which led to the book in this focus) back in 2010. So anybody who pushes the Italian master in the education circles is okay in my mind. The fact that the book itself is quite well written and interesting makes it even easier.

The book breaks down into four sections following Cooper's Acknowledgements and Introduction: Against Criticism: Opera and The Stendhal Syndrome; Against Interpretation: The First Five Gialli; Against Narrative: The Three Mothers Trilogy and Phenomena; and Against Conventions: From Trauma to Giallo. Each section has an overview and examination of each film and links them within a thematic area. Two rare previously only French language interviews with Argento are translated and run at the end of the four sections, followed by credits list for each movie. This caps it off nicely.

Although there aren't necessarily any new or startling revelations about Argento and his film work per say, the book is a nice critical look at his work with some photos sprinkled throughout the book. The two interviews are a nice bonus as well and help to increase its value. Cooper also includes synopses of two lesser known Argento works, the Television production Door Into Darkness and the historical feature Five Days In Milan, that are often overlooked by most critics and fans.

Overall and excellent study on the Italian Hitchcock himself and a book I would recommend picking up, whether you are a casual fan of Dario Argento or a super fan.

— Reviewed by James R. Beach

BOOK REVIEW:
SAVAGING THE DARK
Christopher Conlon
Evil Jester Press, 2014
$11.95 Trade Paperback

Let's get the 800-pound gorilla off the table. "Savaging the Dark" tells the story of a woman approaching middle-age, Mona Straw, and how she falls in love with, and has an affair with, eleven-year old Connor Blue. I've heard from several big, tough horror readers who said they were stopped early in the book due to this, one even going so far as calling the story child pornography. It is not, and here's why.

The purpose of pornography is to titillate and excite. "Savaging the Dark" is not that story. We begin the tale near its end, as Mona licks Connor's filthy feet. This seems over the top. Absurd. It crosses all sorts of lines. But, I urge you to read past, and to get to the end, because the set-up and reveal later on make so much sense, and illustrate how something we only see a small part of may seem a certain way, but in truth . . . in someone's else's truth . . . is far from it.

Mona Straw is a decent looking, nearly average woman. Even her name reflects that: Straw. She's content with a fulfilling job as a grade school teacher. She's got a loyal husband, and a beautiful young daughter. As life happens, her once buoyant, passionate lover has aged into a safe, dependable husband. His days as a sexy activist have long passed, and their lovemaking has settled into tired, uninspired familiarity. She sees him as nearly dead. Mona is anything but.

She desires love and passion. She wants to live again, deep down, not just exist. She's not ready to just give up and cruise through the rest of her life. Enter Connor Blue. Of course, she initially only sees him as an intriguing young man. He's a loner, and happy to be so. He's not affected or stigmatized, but enjoys his solitary time. Like Mona. Strikingly, he has a passion for both reading books and watching classic films, both of which Mona loves. So they begin a friendship. Mona, being a mother and a teacher, makes Connor a pet project, recommending books and films for them to discuss at their after school meetings.

She discovers Connor has an abusive father. Of course, as in real life, it's more subtle than dramatic, inconsistent, and not life-threatening. Just enough to tweak both of them. Taking him under her wing, Mona soon projects the emptiness of her life—very adult feelings—onto Connor, using him as a stand-in. Her intrigue quickly turns into a small crush, which she dismisses as motherly, but grows steadily, just as her marriage grows apart just enough for Connor to take hold.

What follows are a series of perfectly timed events that bring them both initial joy. Mona unlocks a part of Connor at just the right moment in his life where his sexuality has blossomed, and she schools him. She goes through a tremendous amount of emotional turmoil—guilt, terror, lust—but can't help herself. The same with Connor.

Until . . .

That's where "Savaging the Dark" takes its turn into no-going-back. What follows are a few things I believed might happen, but many I did not.

This is a meditation on love. Falling in love is expertly composed. Readers of Mr. Conlon's other works will recognize echoes from his previous books and collections, as so much of his work has explored the intricacies of love gone wrong—of passion grown to obsession—of relationships that should not have been, but are. "Lullaby for the Rain Girl" comes immediately to mind, as it, too, has its fingers on a deep, secret guilt that infuses the story from the start, as does "Savaging the Dark".

Conlon's work has always brought you right inside the mind of living, feeling people. In "Savaging the Dark", you feel for Mona Straw. You understand every bit of it. She knows it's wrong, but is helpless. Who hasn't fallen in love with precisely the wrong person for them? Who hasn't gotten into a relationship, knowing full-well it would end in pain and heartbreak?

One of the things art does best is to dive into uncomfortable, confrontational places. Art can examine scary things, dark thoughts, wrong feelings . . . and places them where they can be understood, discussed, and brought to light in a safe zone . . . a place that isn't real. It's an important facet of art, and one of its true gifts to us.

How could someone fall in love with a child? Are they sick? Are they insane? Just perverts? Lost souls? "Savaging the Dark" explores those questions, and does so with an honesty that is not easy to read. And it shouldn't be easy. This is a book that is hard on a reader. It makes you question yourself. It makes you wonder what you'd do in a similar situation. Personally, I thought back to when I was Connor's age, and if a Sharon Stone or a Grace Kelly had come on to me, do you think I wouldn't go for it? Do you think I'd be scarred

by it? Tough questions.

Here's the thing: if Connor were just a bit older, he'd both not be as intrigued, and he'd be less likely to be in the situations he was in. He'd likely have already had sexual experiences, and Mona Straw would be a non-issue. He'd be able to push beck mentally a lot more, too. So he had to be slightly younger. Again, all these things converge to make the events unfold.

"Savaging the Dark" is not an easy book. For me? I'm glad I took the step, and made it through to the end. It was well-worth it. I feel as though I have just that bit more understanding of what would make something like this happen. To be blunt: readers who will read Jack Ketchum, Edward Lee, Brian Keene, and Richard Laymon will find far worse confronting them there. Being familiar with Conlon's other work, where a theme of inappropriate and/or doomed relationships are a big part of their stories, "Savaging the Dark" feels like a further, darker exploration. Check out "Midnight on Mourn Street", "A Matrix of Angels" and "Lullaby for the Rain Girl", and you'll find definite parallels.

A truly fascinating read, and beautifully written. The prose feels both economical, and lyrical. I never felt the story became exploitive or judgmental, instead, giving an even-handed, intriguing glimpse into the tragic love story of these unforgettable characters.

— John Palisano

✳ ✳ ✳

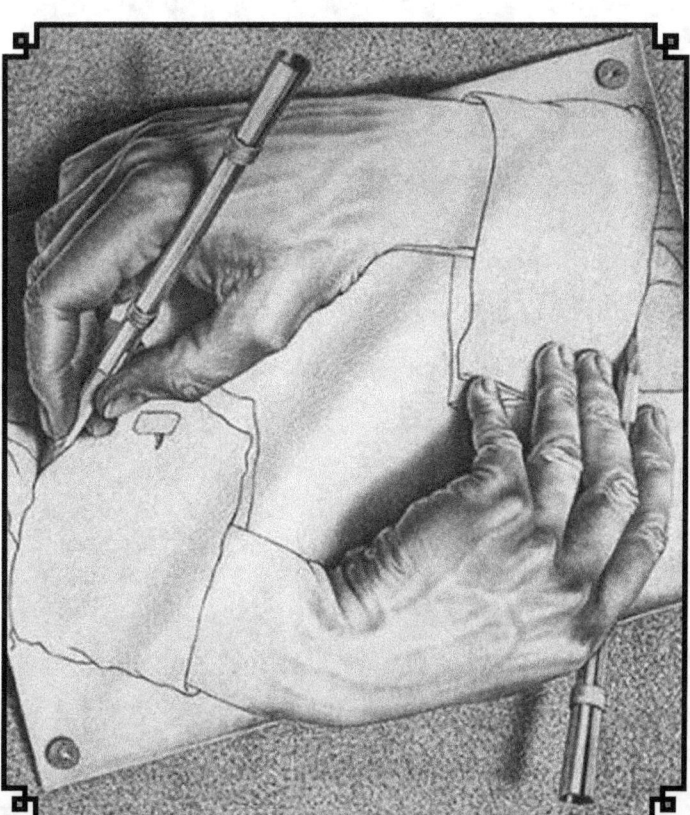

UNSETTLE... EDIFY... INVOLVE...

DISCOVERIES

SUBSCRIBE and never miss another issue of...

www.darkdiscoveries.com

FEATURES:

Weird Fiction & Film, Extreme Horror, Comics & Pulps, New Blood, Dark SciFi, Twilight Zone, H.P. Lovecraft, Horror in Rock, Forgotten Horror & SF TV...

INTERVIEWS:

Ray Bradbury, Bruce Campbell, Christopher Lee, Joe R. Lansdale, William F. Nolan, EC Comics Al Feldstein, Brian Keene, Jack Ketchum, David Cronenberg...

FICTION:

Richard Matheson, Ray Bradbury, Thomas Ligotti, Richard Laymon, John Shirley, William F. Nolan, Ramsey Campbell, Joe R. Lansdale, Lisa Morton, Edward Lee...

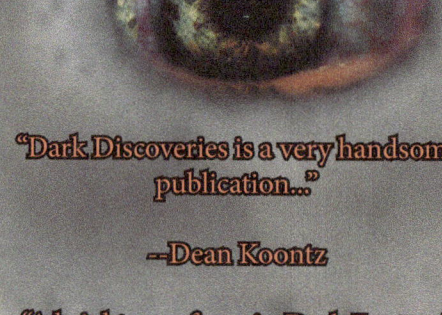

"Dark Discoveries is a very handsome publication..."

--Dean Koontz

"A bright new force in Dark Fantasy."

--William F. Nolan

"Dark Discoveries is a high quality mag... and it keeps getting better..."

--Horror Fiction Review

PRINT SUBSCRIPTIONS

4 issues (1 year): US ($37.95) Canada ($46.95) Overseas ($69.95)

8 issues (2 years): US ($74.95) Canada ($92.95) Overseas ($139.95)

(*Shipping is included on print subs)

ADVERTISERS!

Inquire via E-mail for rates!

Please Note: Future content subject to change without notice. All rights reserved.

DIGITAL SUBSCRIPTIONS

4 issues (1 year): $19.95
8 issues (2 years): $39.95
Payment accepted via PayPal: christophercpayne@journalstone.com
Also by Check/M.O. (Payable to)

JournalStone Publications
439 Gateway Dr., #83, Pacifica, CA 94044

JOURNALSTONE
YOUR LINK TO ARTISTIC TALENT